ALSO BY LEE GRUENFELD

IRREPARABLE HARM

Published by
WARNER BOOKS

ATTENTION: SCHOOLS AND CORPORATIONS

WARNER books are available at quantity discounts with bulk pur-
chase for educational, business, or sales promotional use. For
information, please write to: SPECIAL SALES DEPARTMENT,
WARNER BOOKS, 1271 AVENUE OF THE AMERICAS, NEW
YORK, N.Y. 10020

ARE THERE WARNER BOOKS
YOU WANT BUT CANNOT FIND IN YOUR LOCAL STORES?

You can get any WARNER BOOKS title in print. Simply send title
and retail price, plus 95¢ per order and 95¢ per copy to cover mail-
ing and handling costs for each book desired. New York State and
California residents add applicable sales tax. Enclose check or
money order only, no cash please, to: WARNER BOOKS, P.O.
BOX 690, NEW YORK, N.Y. 10019

LEE GRUENFELD

ALL FALL DOWN

WARNER BOOKS

A Time Warner Company

Grateful acknowledgment is given for permission to quote from "High Flighn" by John Gillespie McGee. Used by permission of the Ferguson Publishing Company.

MYSTERIOUS PRESS EDITION

Cover design and illustration by Tony Greco

Warner Books, Inc.
1271 Avenue of the Americas
New York, NY 10020

W A Time Warner Company

Printed in the United States of America

Originally published in hardcover by Warner Books.
First Printed in Paperback: May, 1995

10 9 8 7 6 5 4 3 2 1

To the memory of U. S. Navy fighter pilot Lieutenant Gary Bede Simkins, killed in action in the South China Sea, flying his A-7 Corsair off the deck of the USS Coral Sea on April 3, 1973.

The brother-in-law I never knew....

This is a work of fiction.

In several instances, technical details have been deliberately obscured.

The events described in this book cannot happen.

Information continues to trickle in concerning the spectacular midair collision that lit up the morning skies over the Los Angeles basin. The explosion, heard as far as Point Dume to the west and San Bernardino to the east, prompted thousands of phone calls to area authorities, who were initially at a loss to explain the cause.

Crews currently fishing pieces of wreckage out of Legg Lake in Pomona have been noticeably closemouthed about the incident, but the Los Angeles Times *reports a confidential source as saying that one of the aircraft has been positively identified as a World War II-vintage fighter plane.*

This has led to speculation that drug running was involved, since this particular type of airplane, a propeller-driven P-51 Mustang, carrying one pilot and no passengers, is much favored by smugglers due to its high speed and extreme agility.

Local pilots observing recovery operations have told WorldWide that, based on the wreckage they have seen, the second aircraft is a modern, single-engine plane that could carry three passengers in addition to the pilot.

The presence of F-15 jet fighters from nearby Norton Air Force Base fueled the rumor that a pursuit had been under way, and that the second plane was very likely an innocent victim of the intended interception.

FAA and NTSB representatives on the scene have refused to comment. The FBI is also apparently involved but has also declined to comment....

Prologue

CHAPTER 1

May 10, 0800 hours

Something didn't feel right.

Not an uncommon occurrence among pilots. Like doctors, professional flyers are among the worst hypochondriacs, not about themselves (quite the opposite—they never get sick, or at least never admit it), but about their planes.

Mathematically this is not an irrational paranoia. Airplanes are among the most complex pieces of equipment in everyday use and consist of dozens of systems, each of which comprises multiple subunits, which are in turn made up of hundreds of individual components, each containing hundreds or thousands of parts.

The probability of failure in any one component or assembly is small but finite. The probability of a failure occurring *somewhere* in the plane is the product of all the individual probabilities taken together. Seen this way, what would be incredible is not that something goes wrong, but that at any particular point in time everything is working correctly. Mathematics being the harsh taskmaster that it is, the fact is that rarely, if ever, is everything working perfectly. The challenge, then, is not to spend a great deal of time worrying about whether anything has gone wrong, but to determine whether whatever it is that *is* wrong is important.

And, as Captain "Red" Reddersen knew only too well, all those probabilities got a cosmic boost whenever it was nighttime, or stormy, or you were running low on fuel, or simply trying to perform a complex instrument landing while plowing through an overcast layer so thick it felt like it was grabbing the wings and slowing down the plane.

Like this one was doing now.

So Reddersen didn't say anything to his first officer, yet. Even with twenty thousand hours of flying in his logbooks, almost all of them in the captain's seat, he still didn't say anything. It wasn't so much that he was afraid of looking like a green airman, or that Vince Badaluca would think that the veteran was losing his nerve. It was just that he didn't know exactly what it *was* that didn't feel right. No spurious vibrations, no inconsistent readings from the instruments, nothing subtly transmitted from the steering column that might have signaled something to his experienced and sensitive hands. Just . . . ? A feeling, that's all. And after this many years, Red was smart enough not always to trust his feelings. He had learned to trust his instruments.

All this played through his mind only at the bottom of his priority queue. The rest of his attention was focused on the approach.

There used to be a piece of paper clipped to the yoke in front of the pilot. The "plate" contained everything needed to execute an approach to landing relying solely on instruments, without any outside visual cues. Fly this heading until you get such and such a signal from a ground-based navigation station, then turn to this heading until you pick up the next fix, then turn again and start losing altitude. If the airport had the right equipment, you'd soon pick up one signal that told you whether you were over or under the standard descent profile for your present position and another to tell you if you were too far to the left or right of the runway. They were combined in a single readout. "Fly the needles" down and pretty soon you would break out of the bottom of the clouds and there before you? A miracle, the runway in the distance, beckoning like mother's bosom. And you'd be at exactly the right altitude and heading, and every time, no matter how often you'd done it, you would smile. Because even a monkey could fly an airplane up off the ground, but flying an instrument approach was on another astral level entirely.

No reliance on plates alone anymore, though, at least not in sophisticated aircraft. Now the entire procedure was programmed into an on-board computer that flashed it all on a screen and painted a little airplane over it to tell you where you were at every point in the approach. It also told you how many minutes and seconds remained until the next fix and how sharply to turn, and provided gentle chiding if you flew outside of its preprogrammed envelope. You could even couple the autopilot to the navigation unit and let the plane do everything, including land. But most pilots preferred to hand fly the approach, as though this anachronistic minirevolt against advanced technology could preserve some of the allure and mystique that drew them into this profession in the first place. Unlike some doctors who worried about cash flow more than patient care, or lawyers more concerned with partnership than justice, or administrative bureaucrats who cherished the application of rules more than the provision of services, most pilots, at least the older ones, loved to fly. The thought of being ground-bound kept an extraordinary number of them from seeking corporate advancement, much to the consternation of wives or husbands or lovers. And flying, *really* flying, was a lot different from sitting back and keeping tabs on a computer display in case a transistor somewhere decided at an inopportune moment to melt down and take a circuit board and possibly the whole airplane with it.

Red was flying by hand now, and his unease started marching up the queue to the point where he decided quite unconsciously to devote a small corner of his attention to locating its source. All he knew at this point, or sensed, was that he wouldn't have noticed anything at all if he were not flying by hand. So absorbed was he that he failed to notice Badaluca struggling with himself over whether to chance a comment. Finally he did.

"Cap'n? Something doesn't feel right here."

There. Vince had broken the ice, made the first move. Being the enlightened soul that Red was, he wasn't about to make his young copilot regret venturing forth at the risk of ridicule. No, he would reward the professionalism by immediately reinforcing the bold and timely comment with a supportive reply.

"Izzatso," he grunted without taking his eyes off his instruments. He let it go at that, trying hard to uncover the source of his own discomfort and well aware of Vince's heightening trepidation following such a sarcastic, noncommittal response.

Vince paused, too. He was hoping for at least a grudging confirmation from Red, or even a probing question or two, which he couldn't answer anyway but at least it would get the conversation going, but now he had no idea what the captain was thinking, and he became acutely aware of the cockpit voice recorder buried somewhere in the airplane, its reels of tape turning inexorably and only the microphone above the instrument console making itself known in the cockpit, and how the hell was *this* going to sound, he with his fresh new right-seat wings and now afraid of things that go bump in the clouds—

"I'm a little uneasy myself." Red figured Vince had had enough teasing. "But I'm not sure why."

"What're you showing for airspeed?"

Red glanced at the airspeed indicator. "One eighty on the nose. You?"

"The same."

"Why'd you ask?"

Vince shrugged and looked at the magnetic compass, then at his gyrocompass, which read two degrees farther south, as it was supposed to do at this longitude and with all the radios turned on.

"I dunno. Seems like we've been on this leg an awful long time." He depressed a small red switch on the yoke that activated the boom microphone hanging from the side of his headset. "Alpha Air two three five at forty-five hundred feet, inbound for Bellingham one six." He was broadcasting to nobody in particular on 122.8 megahertz, standard procedure for this airport when the control tower wasn't operating.

That was it. Red had flown this one hundreds of times. At this airspeed they should have held this leg for about a minute and a half before turning right toward runway 16 at Bellingham, Washington. But who bothered to time legs anymore? You held the leg until the navigation unit needles centered and then you turned right and it wasn't important how long it took. Except that this one felt like it had already been at least two minutes. And Bellingham International, its antennas torn down by the same storm that had left this overcast in its wake, was temporarily uncontrolled, meaning that there was nobody in the tower, nobody coordinating traffic, and nobody watching on radar except Vancouver approach control, which had already cleared them for the approach and probably wasn't paying close attention anymore since they weren't showing any other aircraft in the vicinity. The pilots were on their own, trusting the instruments.

"Must be one helluva southerly wind," Red said. The biggest, heaviest aircraft in the world still flew relative to the air around it. If you were doing 200 knots against a 30-knot headwind, your speed over the ground was 170, period, whether you were a Concorde or a Cessna.

"Maybe. But it's pretty smooth for a wind that strong. And the overcast probably wouldn't be here if the wind was."

"Well, we've got a three-thousand-foot ceiling, which is a lot higher than anything sticking up from the ground in these parts."

"Waypoint's coming in," Vince said with some relief. The needle on the display was starting to center, meaning they would soon be over the last fix.

"You got the plane. Turn a few seconds late." If there was a strong wind off the nose, delaying the turn slightly would allow it to blow the plane back onto the track instead of off it. "I'll give you altitude."

"Got it." Like a bowler hefting the ball before rolling it, Vince took the yoke, waggled the wings just a touch and pressured the rudder pedals to get a feel for the plane before initiating larger movements. With the needle halfway to centerline, he turned the yoke and held it until the turn-and-bank indicator told him he'd reached a standard rate of turn, then he returned the yoke to its center position. This would keep the wings at the correct bank and ensure a ninety-degree turn in exactly thirty seconds. If he were precise enough, and he usually was, he would roll out with the localizer needle dead center, telling him that he was perfectly aligned with the runway.

Red kept his eyes moving among the altimeter, the airspeed indicator and the ILS needles. "Thirty-five hundred feet," he called out to assist Vince. They would break out under the overcast in less than a minute at their present rate of descent, and they'd both pretty much forgotten their earlier anxiety in anticipation of exiting the scud into clear air. Besides, the instruments were behaving perfectly, both redundant systems in complete agreement.

A few more seconds and the clouds began to thin visibly. Red looked downward out the side window. "Can't believe it. They actually got the weather right this time." He looked back at the altimeter. "Coming up on ... three thousand." The sudden clarity was startling, like waking up from a dream, and both pilots looked out the forward window to make the remainder of their approach visually.

"What the fuck ... !" yelled Vince, oblivious of the cockpit voice recorder.

Red stared openmouthed before reacting. He tore his eyes away from the scene before him to look at his instruments. The ILS needles were still hovering close to centered, with no red flags to indicate a loss of signal or an instrument failure. He looked back up.

Before them, but still comfortably below their altitude, was the hill bordering the western side of the town of Bellingham; the calm waters of the bay were to their right, and no airport was in sight. Vince instinctively pulled the nose up, leveling the plane. Continuing to follow the glideslope needles was clearly going to take them right down onto the campus of Western Washington University.

Red quickly looked out all the windows to check for any traffic. "Start a half-standard turn to the right and hold this altitude," he commanded, then keyed his own mike. "This is Alpha Air two three five, three miles east of Bellingham at three thousand feet level, commencing right turn to two seven zero degrees. Any aircraft in the vicinity, please acknowledge." All planes in the airport traffic area were supposed to be tuned to the same frequency, standard operating procedure for uncontrolled airports.

As the plane neared the new heading, Vince began leveling the wings. He was sweating and visibly shaken. "I don't get it. What the hell happened?"

Red shook his head. "You stay on this frequency. I'm gonna talk to Vancouver." He switched frequencies and keyed the mike. "Vancouver Approach, Alpha two three five, over."

The response was immediate. "Alpha two three five, Vancouver Approach, go ahead." Before Red could answer, he heard: "Alpha two three five, you are well east of course."

"Vancouver, got a little problem. Just aborted our approach into Bellingham. We broke out off course, presently proceeding two seven zero degrees at three thousand feet, airspeed one five zero knots, present position"—he released the mike key and looked past Vince out the right window—"approximately two miles east of runway sixteen. Going to VFR, Alpha two three five, over." No longer trusting the instruments, he was going to fly under visual rather than instrument rules.

"Roger, Alpha two three five, IFR is canceled, proceed VFR your own discretion. Say problem if you can."

Red and Vince exchanged glances. "All instrument readings completely normal. We have no bloody idea. Alpha two three five."

"Copy that. We have one aircraft inbound, eight miles north. We're still talking to him and will inform him of your situation. Stand by one. Lear one-niner-kilo, Vancouver Approach."

"Lear one-niner-kilo, roger," answered the business jet. Red listened as the approach controller told the Lear jet its flight plan was being amended to reduce its airspeed and let the 727 perform the landing. He also told them of what had occurred.

"Roger, Center, understood," said the Lear pilot. "We're gonna go ahead and shoot the ILS. All readings normal so far."

So were ours, you idiot! Red thought. He was reluctant to break contact with approach control. "Vancouver, Alpha two three five, permission to stay on this frequency." Red wanted to listen to the Lear's radio conversations while Vince talked to any other traffic in the vicinity.

"Roger, two three five, stay with me 'til you're down. And call us when you've docked."

Shit! The words every pilot dreads: *"Call us after you've landed."*

"Okay, Vince, we're visual. I'll take it. You'd better talk to the passengers."

"It's all yours." Vince took his hands off the yoke and took a few deep breaths, working the fingers that had had a death grip on the wheel without his realizing it. He switched the radio to public address and tried to calm his voice, using the slightly southern, drawling style frequent flyers everywhere had come to associate with pilot confidence and experience.

"Hello again, ladies and gentlemen, this is First Officer Badaluca. Those of you familiar with this route may have noticed that we flew farther south of the airport than we usually do. This was in response to a request from the Whidbey Island Naval Air Station to make way for a squadron of F-14 fighters passing this way." He looked at Red, who widened his eyes and then looked heavenward, as if for forgiveness from the Great Pilot. "So we're gonna take it around here just a little bit, give you the scenic tour and have you on the ground in about three minutes. It's been our pleasure . . ." and so on and so forth.

Red looked down at the instrument panel. "Whaddya say we fly the ILS again? Pick it up below the clouds and stay visual."

"Good idea. But we couldn't *both* have been seeing things."

Red turned the plane to the base leg, alternately watching the needles and the runway out his right window.

"I don't believe this," said Vince. The localizer was beginning to center as they approached the imaginary extended centerline of the runway. Red turned the plane to final and intercepted the glideslope perfectly. Both needles barely wavered as he brought the 727 to the ground, then they flipped to the off position as he greased the wheels onto the runway and kicked in the thrust reversers to minimize their rollout on the short Bellingham runway.

"Perfect, all the way down," said Vince. "They're never gonna believe us."

Red stayed silent. Vince was right, of course. There would have to be an investigation, one in which some code other than British common law applied: the pilots were always guilty unless proven otherwise.

They stayed in the cockpit and watched the Lear come in, listening to its conversation with Vancouver. "Lear one-niner-kilo, on final. We have the runway in sight." Vince gritted his teeth and prayed. "All readings normal," radioed the Lear. *Damn!*

Red patted Vince's arm as he pushed back and rose out of his seat. "Don't worry about it. We've still got the black boxes."

Vince was not appeased. He grabbed Red's arm and stopped his exit. "Yeah. But what if *those* fucked up, too?"

Book 1

Your true pilot cares nothing about anything on earth but the river, and his pride in his occupation surpasses the pride of kings.

—Mark Twain
    Life on the Mississippi (1883), ch. 7

CHAPTER 2

May 10, 0900 EST

"Y'know," Jack Webster said to nobody in particular and his wife at the same time, "I'm sure as hell not one to bemoan the good old days, but there is some shit, up with which I will not put." He threw the report angrily across the den.

Betty Webster smiled indulgently. "Not to bemoan the good old days, of course."

Jack slapped the worn leather sidearms of the overstuffed chair and stood up. "That's it. No more paper bullshit. I took a day off and I'm taking the day off."

"Bravo! It's only nine o'clock. You've got the whole day ahead of you."

"Woman," he commanded, sweeping his arm imperiously, "fetch me my paper, pour me some coffee, and disappear from my sight."

"Nuts to you, fly-boy," she answered, but went to comply with items one and two, relieved that he was putting aside the tedious homework.

"What's the most sinful thing you think we can do today?" he yelled into the kitchen.

"You mean minor sin or mortal?" she called back.

15

"I'm talking the eighth circle of hell here. No holding back."

The harsh sound of the coffee grinder came back at him, continued for a few seconds and stopped. Betty appeared in the doorway, hands hidden behind her, flashing him a conspiratorial grin. "Let's go to an afternoon movie."

"My God, woman, you are an evil one," he said with respect. "Done!" She brought the paper out from behind her and handed it to him, already opened to the entertainment section, and went back to finish making the coffee. Jack picked up the discarded budget report, smoothed the pages and put it back into his briefcase before heading into the kitchen.

He might have noticed, while her back was to him, what a good-looking woman she still was. Just a few inches short of his own six feet, perfect fighter-pilot height, not slim in the sense of skinny but with little excess fat to betray her years, nicely dressed even at home alone with him and no company. He might have noticed, but he didn't, some deep recess of his mind having consigned her long ago to the category of standard, proper military wife. He loved her, of course, in the regimented way of their life, likely would have been lost without her, but his appreciation, such as it was, was far from the surface, something akin to the appreciation a rich kid has for a cashmere sweater that he was brought up to simply assume he deserved and ought to have, and so he had one. He loved her; he just didn't think about it all that often, and why should he? They rarely fought—never, in fact—they enjoyed each other's company, they shared things as long as they didn't involve his job or his friends or his worldviews or his problems or any of the other things he best handled on his own. There was that one time, sure, and for a few weeks he appreciated her more than even his own life, but that was a while ago, and he had come through it okay, and so now it was back to normal.

In short it was a perfect, government-issue union.

Jack sat down as Betty poured him a cup of coffee and was just sliding his legs under the table when the phone rang.

"Let's not answer it," Betty said quickly.

Jack stayed silent and pretended not to hear the phone. Betty started counting the rings only after it became clear that it should have stopped ringing already. Jack rose resignedly and walked back to the living room, reached into his case and pulled out his beeper. The sound was turned off, but the red light was blinking rapidly: two flashes, pause, three flashes. Highest priority.

He walked back to the kitchen and, without saying a word, held up the beeper for Betty to see, then picked up the phone. "Webster," he said with all the gruffness he could muster, and started to sit down again.

"Hiya, Jack. Amy Goldberg."

He stopped halfway down onto the chair and stayed that way, motionless.

"Jack? You there?"

"What is it?" Betty asked him.

He turned his head toward her slowly and sat down when he found himself suspended above the seat. "It's Amy Goldberg."

Betty stopped pouring her own cup. "Jack . . ."

He cut her off and motioned for her to bring him the television remote control. "Hello, Amy." His voice transmitted everything he felt about hearing from her.

"Yeah," said Amy, "I know. You want me to skip the bullshit apologies?"

"No," said Webster, "give 'em to me." It might have been a social call, which would have been all right, except that his beeper was blinking red, and this wasn't a coincidence. Betty handed him the remote, and he turned on the television, changing the channel to CNN.

"Very funny. I do hate to do this to you, boss, but we think you'd better get in here pronto."

"I'm not your boss anymore. And who is *we?* Where is *here?* And I don't see anything on the news."

"'We' is me. And you won't see anything because there isn't anything. Yet."

Amy Goldberg was a senior investigator of the National Transportation Safety Board, an innocuous-enough-sounding name for the agency charged with investigating the nation's air disasters. One of the only truly apolitical bodies in the federal government, the NTSB reported directly to Congress and had only the best and brightest on staff, people who could examine an otherwise undistinguished lump of charred metal and tell you if the engine was running at the time of the crash, or on fire, or tearing apart explosively. People who could synthesize a million pieces of incongruous and often contradictory physical evidence, blend this in with unreliable eyewitness accounts, toss in a dash of the creative engineering of natural laws and tell you, for example, that the aft lavatory on a Boeing 727 leaked toilet fluid through a crack in a spar joint, dripped it out onto the skin of the fuselage, where it froze in the icy upper atmosphere and turned into "blue ice," eventually breaking off in the slipstream and flying backward toward the tail, where it was ingested into the engine intake, lodged in the turbines and caused the spinning rotors to seize, whereupon the engine was torn from its mount and tumbled down seven miles, finally landing in Las Cruces, New Mexico. Or who could patch together a total wreck and discover that a bomb had gone off in the luggage compartment, which the plane might otherwise have survived had the sudden loss of pressure not collapsed the floor underneath the passenger cabin, compromising the overall structural integrity of the craft so that it fell out of the sky. All this, where others saw only smoldering, twisted metal scattered in the wreckage, human and machine, where others couldn't even tell if it had been one airplane or two.

And those best and brightest, who reserved their highest respect only for those whose abilities surpassed their own, revered Jack Webster. Not as the smartest, which he wasn't, or as the most experienced, or friendliest, but for an uncanny, almost preternatural ability to put the most disparate evidentiary elements together into a cohesive and rational scenario. Especially if there was a malicious perpetrator involved, and especially if that perpetrator was on the loose and needed to be caught.

Only problem was, Jack wasn't with the NTSB anymore.

"Whaddya mean, 'yet'?" Now Amy had his full attention.

"Come on in, and I'll explain it to you."

"Forget it."

"Jack . . ."

"I said forget it. Call Pressman. I don't even want to hear about it."

"We spoke to the director. He wants you here."

The director? Jack tightened his grip on the receiver. "You spoke to the director? Yourself?"

"No. Pressman did. I asked him to."

"You realize," said Jack, even as he rose to hang up the phone, "that this is a potentially career-limiting move for you, don't you? Not only do you seem to have gotten your agencies mixed up, but it's my day off. . . ."

"Tell you what, boss—"

"And stop calling me that—"

"—you think I'm overreacting on this one, the steaks are on me. For the next ten years."

Jack grunted, hung up and looked at Betty. Her eyes were on the television, which was still displaying only a relatively bland stew of the usual slow news day drivel. "I don't get it. No crashes. And why you?"

"She didn't say what it was, but Amy's no Chicken Little. Sky must be falling somewhere."

She turned and reached for his plastic car mug, forty-nine cents from 7-Eleven with a free refill, and filled it with hot coffee. "Well, show a little defiance and don't wear a suit, at least."

"Hold that coffee. I'm not going anywhere."

He picked the receiver back up and dialed a number, drumming his fingers on the table as he waited. "Angie? Jack Webster. Gimme George, and yes, it's important." He fumed for a few more seconds, and then the director of the FBI came on the line.

"Now, Jack, don't go getting your—"

"Dammit, George, we had an agreement!"

Betty stepped toward the table and put her hands on her husband's shoulders, imagining the other end of the conversation but hearing only Jack's answering grunts and the acquiescence gradually creeping into his voice.

"Okay," he said at last, "but only to listen. All right. Bye."

He put the receiver down softly, in subconscious deference to the status of the person on the other end. He looked up at Betty, who had already stepped back to the coffeepot and resumed filling the plastic car mug.

He stood up and headed for the hall closet to retrieve his jacket.

"And I won't shave, either, dammit."

1115 hours

The nondescript offices at 490 L'Enfant Plaza East, SW, were singularly unprepossessing, for several good reasons.

First, only the grandly unimportant bureaus went in for stately fittings, often in direct proportion to the lack of self-esteem among their staffs. Pretense was a dead giveaway of uselessness.

The NTSB was not given to such introspective musings. The headquarters office itself, unpretentiously occupying two floors above a downtown hotel, was the least important site of all of those where its members did their business.

Second, there was the issue of security. Whenever an air disaster occurred, serious concern was not squandered on human victims and their families—they just received a canned-in-advance tidal wave of apologies and unsolicited assurances that it was somebody else's fault other than the apologizer's. Real concern was reserved for those who would be targeted for liability. Notable among these were the aircraft manufacturers, each of which had an entire department devoted to ensuring that their silver bird emerged from the debacle not only blameless, but (and those who think the best talent works in the design division are very much mistaken) praised for how much worse it would have been had some competitor's inferior contraption not held together as long as theirs did, or not given as much advance warning, or, if the crash were not totally catastrophic, not contributed to the preservation of several of the souls on board. This was a matter not of self-esteem, but of the preservation of profit margins, of vulnerability not so much to lawsuits (else what's an insurance company for?), but to the whims and caprices of the flying public, the travelers who are savvy enough, or fancy themselves so, to say to their travel agents, "Don't book me on a DC-10!" for the six months following the destruction of American Airlines flight 191 out of O'Hare on May 25,

1979, even though the safest plane to fly in after an accident is always the same model that just crashed, owing to the standard overreaction of doubled or even tripled maintenance schedules.

The Airline Pilots Association, union representative of most commercial flyers, was similarly diligent in its insistence, usually even before learning any facts, that the accident was clearly and demonstrably the fault of any involved parties who were not the pilots. While this might seem hopelessly transparent and self-serving, which it was, it was also a response to the automatic assumption by everybody else that it was the pilots' fault.

This is not irrational. Such a conclusion was satisfying because of the narrow confines of assigned culpability. There were no other nested levels of responsibility once you got down to the pilots, unless you wanted to go after their supervisors for driving them to drink, or their spouses for nagging them into mental distraction, or maybe their parents for failing to teach them responsibility. No, pilots were terrific scapegoats; perfect, in fact, because even if there were other causes, every one of them short of a UFO abduction should have been noticed, properly identified and dealt with by the pilots. Once you pinned it all on them everyone else could go home and rest easy.

And then there were the ground maintenance workers who repaired the plane, the people who fueled it, the National Oceanic and Atmospheric Administration that provided the weather reports, the controllers who routed the craft, the weight-and-balance manager who distributed the passengers and baggage, the person who drove the tractor that pushed the plane into position before the engines started, the refurbisher that overhauled the engines and even the seat maker, who should have known that the fabric covering the cushions emitted cyanide gas when heated to eight hundred degrees centigrade. It was to the frustration of all of these, each of whom had everything to gain and nothing to lose from every scrap of information that could wend its way through the doors, that the NTSB offices sacrificed nothing in the way of security in favor of cosmetic embellishment. This concern was even further underscored when Congress decided that no

NTSB report could be used in a court of law, and NTSB investigators could not be compelled to testify. All of their results, however, were made available to the public, and the board had its own code of *omertà* to prevent premature and out-of-context leaks.

The last, and least obvious, reason for the office's blandness was simply that, in the main, there was no urgent business that needed transacting, and thus no need for lavish reception areas to coddle VIPs, no gauntlet of secretaries barring access, because there was very little to access: the board had no power to regulate and no power to enforce, only to investigate and recommend. It was like an air bag, lying passively, billowing into action only when needed. The metaphor suffered considerably in the temporal perspective, though: unlike the air bag, by the time the NTSB sprang into action, it was too late. And that was something that had always galled Jack Webster and continued to do so as he rode up from the parking garage in a small elevator at the rear of the building.

Board staffers consoled themselves with the thought that their primary function was not so much to affix blame in pursuit of punishment (pretty useless pursuit, that, it almost always being the pilots' fault and they almost always being dead), but to teach lessons that would prevent similar occurrences in the future. This methodology was unique in that it required a tragedy in the first place in order not to have another like it in the future. *Once*, Jack thought, *just once I would like to have prevented a disaster before it occurred.*

He was not unconscious of the stares that followed him as he walked. Some came from people who remembered him; to others, Jack was a signal that something was up.

Purposeful, deliberate, self-confident even to the point of a slight swagger, Jack was someone who was used to giving orders and being obeyed. To anyone schooled in the art of Washington-specific observation, he was ex-military all the way, a common background among board investigators. Were they able to see beneath his shirt, they would have noted the kind of flat but creased and eddied belly common on older men who now kept themselves fit but had at times put on and lost weight. The thinning crewcut-plus-a-bit haircut topped an angular face graying at the temples, a jaw that could vary in an instant from hard-set to smiling, and the crow's-feet that bespoke a lifetime of either staring at the brightly lit outdoors or whooping it up with close friends. In the case of an ex-naval commanding officer, it was usually both.

What gave him away today was his angry look. Nobody who toiled for years in government circles and reached any level of responsibility could help but own a permanently pissed-off countenance. Yep, for sure, whoever that was pumping through the corridors was a former military type whose wishes were not being attended to at this time.

He was unused to the surroundings, having left the NTSB just at the time it was moving from its old quarters at 800 Independence Avenue. He walked briskly past the actual boardroom and reflected on the clever use of the word *board*. Well, they didn't want to call it an "agency," something one tended, by reflex, to suspect was concerned primarily with the perpetuation of its own existence, ninety-five percent of its budget consisting of fixed costs having nothing to do with the mission at hand. A "committee" was even worse—a dozen political appointees who could barely work the coffee machine, maybe peppered lightly with two or three people who actually knew what they were doing but who quickly disappeared into the astronomical singularity of procedure, protocol and deference—a part-time job and a nuisance for everybody on it.

But a board, that was good, because that term connoted an agglomeration of relevant skills and talents rather than a sitting group of bureaucrats. A board came together when needed, did what it was created to do and then got the hell out of the way without spending more public funds than it needed to, which in the case of the NTSB came to $35 million a year. All five board members were appointed by the president and confirmed by the Senate, and even though politics was involved, the party of the president in power getting the majority of members, it was generally the case that four of the members had aviation backgrounds, and at least three actually knew what they were doing, the positions being full-time, not honorary.

He strode past the boardroom and into Conference Room B, a familiar locale optimized for function rather than looks, containing blackboards, flip charts, 35mm projectors, tape recorders, secure telephone and fax lines, model airplanes and all the other paraphernalia that were the tools of the trade. Amy Goldberg sat at the head of the rectangular conference table and started to get up so Jack could assume his traditional place, but he waved her back, took a middle seat on a long side, glanced around at the other assembled staffers, spread his hands and said, "So?"

Amy looked down and shook her head. "Look, you don't mind, let's skip all this chitchat and get right down to business, okay?"

"No coffee, no business," Jack shot back, and looked around. Lower-level functionary #1 picked up a phone, punched an intercom button and ordered refills for the empty pots. Jack noticed that there was little activity in the room. Normally, by this point, a conference room assigned to a particular investigation would be buzzing like an options pit on the last Friday of the quarter. Instead there seemed to have been only conversation and some idle note taking, and there was none of the flushed and self-conscious excitement that usually accompanied the opening of an investigation into a crash. That inability to hide excitement when the game, however tragic, was afoot was one of Jack's primary recruiting criteria in hiring these people. And now they looked tense, nervous and—*what was it?*—yes, that's it: scared.

He looked back toward Amy. "What've we—*you*—got?"

She reached for a Federal Express envelope on the table and held it up. "We've got this. You can read it for yourself a little later, but let me give you the essentials." She referred to a yellow legal pad where she had made some notes. "It arrived about eight-thirty this morning. It's a letter, looks like it came off a laser printer—"

She glanced knowingly at Jack. Used to be that typewritten notes were like fingerprints. You could always find a teensy little flaw somewhere, maybe an L that tilted a half degree to one side, or a W with one line slightly thicker than the other, something. And when you found a typewriter with matching characteristics, you usually had the owner dead to rights.

But not with laser printers hooked to personal computers.

As long as the perpetrator didn't touch the paper with bare hands and as long as he managed to spell most of the words correctly (not a difficult trick with the spell checkers built into their damned word processors), it might as well have been written in snow with an icicle.

"It starts with an account of an incident," Amy continued. "It says a 727 crew inbound for Bellingham, Washington, was making an instrument approach in the clouds, had the needles dead centered all the way to breakout and found themselves three miles off course, descending on a collision course with an institution of higher learning."

"And when did this incident supposedly occur?" asked Jack.

"About three hours ago."

Jack raised his eyebrows. "Oh?"

"Which of course is the day *after* this letter was sent." Amy could tell that Jack already knew what was coming and all he needed were the details. They wouldn't have called him in if it had been a crank letter. "So Tim"—lower-level functionary #2—"was manning the station here and he decided he better go through the motions."

"I called the Vancouver radar room," said the thoroughly intimidated staffer, "because Bellingham control tower is down, and the supervisor, uh, expressed incredulity at the call." Tim paused, recalling the man's exact words "How the flaming fuck did you guys find out about it so goddamned fast?" and decided efficiency of information transfer required no elaboration.

"And it happened?" asked Jack, phrasing it more as a question than he'd intended it to sound, but his amazement had gotten the better of him.

"Oh, no," said Amy, and then she paused before continuing in a tone of sardonic amusement. "The letter was off by four hundred feet on the lateral track." A virtually insignificant amount of error.

Jack, not normally at a loss for words, was so now. Amy let it sink in and then went on to underscore the significance. "Like this guy was the pilot and wrote the letter ten minutes after it happened. But it was written yesterday."

"Which means," said Jack, finding his voice, "he could do it again."

Amy held up a photostat of the envelope's contents. "And, in fact, so he says. At will, whenever he wants. The original's already on its way to the lab, along with our prints for elimination."

"What's the guess so far?"

"It could have come from the instruments on the ground," said another staffer, after observing that Webster the reputed hard-ass had refrained from abusing Tim, "but the equipment shed alarm hasn't been tripped, according to the airport manager, and he found no immediate evidence of tampering. There's a full check under way right now."

Amy consulted her own notes. "And it gets weirder. Another plane inbound, a corporate Lear, shot the same approach without incident, needles centered all the way to the ground with nary a flicker. Four minutes after the 727." She was supposed to be their expert in psychology, complete with a Ph.D., but for reasons of her own she preferred to downplay that expertise. She'd taken courses in aeronautical engineering and also had air-traffic controller training, and she tried whenever circumstances permitted to emphasize those skills. Besides, Webster liked his people cross-trained. Or had when he was the boss. Amy's biggest shortcoming was that she had never actually been to a crash site, there being little need for her talents until later in an investigation.

Jack considered the perplexing data. "Could have been jamming from the side, with portable gear. Highly directional, let's say, and pointed toward the 727."

Amy had already considered this, and she turned to a flip chart on which she had sketched out the configuration. "Maybe. But remember, they followed the instrument landing system in from eleven miles out. And they were in the clouds. So the guy would have to have been aiming for them in the blind, and from a very large distance."

"Why so far? Oh, I see. . . ."

She was nodding. "If he was too close to the inbound path, he couldn't stop the signal from getting past the 727 to the Lear. The closer he is, the more of a straight line he forms with both planes. He'd have to be far away and get the 727 from the side in order to keep the beam only on them.

"And that's why we don't think that's how he did it," she concluded. "Because from that distance, he'd have a lot of trouble keeping the beam trained on the plane without seeing it. And the power requirement to run the rig and overwhelm the ground station would have been huge."

Jack considered this analysis. "The main thing we have to keep in mind is, however he did it, he didn't consider success a risk. That letter sent in advance proves he thought it was a sure thing. So anything we come up with that might just as easily have failed, is probably wrong. What about the plane itself?" he asked, not waiting for anybody's concurrence on his thinking.

Tim, emboldened now, said, "Alpha Airlines maintenance guys have taken it off the line and are going over it now. They also yanked both nav units—"

"And that's another thing," Amy interrupted. "Both navs had identical readings."

"So he would have to have gotten to them both," the other staffer added excitedly, "which would be mighty difficult. And he would have to know exactly which aircraft was scheduled for that particular flight on that particular day."

Tim finished it off. "To make it even harder, remember that they flew the last few miles of their visual with the navs still on. The needles read correctly the second time."

Jack shook his head in bewilderment. "Seems almost impossible. I agree with you, tampering with the nav units is out of the question. Beaming a jammer from the ground seems almost as unlikely."

"But less so," said Amy, "and I think our time would be better spent figuring out how he did that than anything else we've got right now. At least while the nav units are being checked."

"What about the pilots?" Jack asked her.

"Being interviewed by FAA people in Seattle. But it would be too transparent a scam, so I wouldn't look for much hope there."

Jack sat quietly and thought for a few minutes, but he felt like the mathematician who proved bumblebees can't fly: what the guy did was impossible, and yet there it was. "So what's he want?" he asked finally.

Amy turned back to her notes. "Not much. But I'm a whole lot less worried about giving it to him than I am about what he can do when he's got that and then wants more, or just decides to get back at his mother for not giving him a lollipop when he was two."

She looked up at him. "I know you already figured this out, Jack, but it sounds like this guy could bring the entire system to its knees if he wanted to."

Jack drummed his fingers on the tabletop. "He could bring down a lot more than the system. Suppose the cloud cover at Bellingham was only at five hundred feet and he put them two miles farther south?"

He searched his memory but knew of nothing that came close to this in all of his experience. The implications were staggering to begin with and then multiplied logarithmically. The larger airports were less of a problem. They had radar and monitored planes inbound on the ILS landing system. They could communicate by voice and warn aircraft off if there was a problem. *If* they noticed it in time. *If* they weren't too busy.

But there were literally thousands of uncontrolled airports into which planes flew every day, the pilots totally and completely dependent on the instruments when flying in weather so thick they couldn't even see their own wingtips.

The 727 pilots were smart and alert, having sensed a problem even without formal indications. But it was a calm day, little traffic, an uncrowded airport. In a larger metropolis, with controllers giving them new instructions every two minutes, it was all a crew could do to bring the bird down without chewing off their fingernails in the process. An extra minute or two before turning to their final approach course would never be noticed, especially if the controller had ordered speed changes, and at 180 knots that could knock them seven miles off course.

"How long we got to comply with whatever he's demanding?" Jack asked at last.

"A week," said Amy. "But that's not a lot of time. The payoff is complicated—"

"You won't believe that part of it either," Tim added.

"—and we've got no way to communicate with him until it's all set up."

"Okay." Jack stood up and began pacing. "This thing's bigger than just us. It's not about picking up pieces after the fact, we've got an extortionist on our hands." He stopped and looked at Amy. "You're most senior on this crew. Call the secretary—"

"Secretary?" Amy interrupted. "What secretary?"

"DOT," Jack replied.

"Transportation? I don't get it. We have investigatory primacy here—oh."

Jack nodded. "Ain't been no accident, lady. Not even clear the board belongs in this one." *The FBI, however, clearly does.* Jack grimaced inwardly as the first intimation hit him that he might not be able to squirm his way out of this one.

"Anyway," he continued, "call the secretary personally, emergency basis on my authority, give her the five-minute version and ask her to designate a senior official, one of her direct reports if possible. Tell her we're probably going to need him full-time for an indefinite period."

"What authority?" asked Amy.

"Say again?"

"You said, on your authority. You're just an FBI puke now." The gathered *apparatchiks* blanched at her easy familiarity with Jack. "No authority."

Jack stopped his back-and-forth walk and looked at her. "Fine. Call Pressman in."

"Can't do that."

"Why? Where is he?"

"The new chairman didn't get much chance to celebrate his new post. The Norway deal? Probable sabotage? Only way Oslo would invite us in, he takes personal charge."

"Tough." Jack reached for his jacket and headed for the door. "I'm outta here. Get another board member." NTSB rules called for every investigation to be headed by a board member, at least nominally. He or she would be the one to communicate with the press and coordinate findings and recommendations.

"Jack!" said Amy sharply.

He stopped and turned. "What?"

"What'd the director say?"

He gave her a confused and innocent look that didn't fool her.

"Tell me you didn't call him after we hung up," she said.

"He said I only had to listen."

"Fine. I'll invoke Pressman's authority. Don't need a board member 'cuz there's no accident, remember? Should I tell the secretary we want Ferguson?"

"Suggest, don't tell. And call the FAA and get an assistant administrator."

"Not the director?"

"No, you want someone who can roll up sleeves. Get both of them in here as soon as possible, with staff assistants, but no later than two P.M. today. Stay on top of Bellingham and tell them to get us as much as they can by that time. Call them now and tell them to break at one-thirty with whatever they have and brief you. While you're at it, fax an authorization to pull the black boxes. The pilots are probably sweating bullets, so let's see if the readings back up their story." *Unless somebody got to those, too.*

As Jack spoke, Amy pointed or nodded to various of her staff and indicated who was to handle what. After they left the room and she was alone with her former colleague, she said, "So what are you going to do?"

"I'm not kidding around, Goldberg, I don't want any part of this."

She sensed the hesitation in his voice and the telltale modulation that signaled his intrigue, but she chose not to press it: confronting him with his own interest might compel his ego to walk away. Besides, she knew his reasons, and as much as she would have wanted to work with him again, she was also a friend, and friends were supposed to understand. So she didn't even tell *herself* that, hell or high water, she'd con him into this one somehow. Instead she threw up her hands in mock surrender. "Understand completely. Not an issue. But you'll help me 'til Pressman gets back?"

"Just 'til then."

Yeah. Like Popeye would spit out some half-eaten spinach.

He turned at the door. "Gonna go put on a suit."

"Good idea. Better shave, too."

CHAPTER 3

Bo Kincaid squinted hard in the bright sunlight. It was
difficult to tell whether that was a minute scratch on the
gleaming aluminum surface or just an odd reflection from
a barely perceptible wrinkle in the otherwise smooth skin. He
bent in closer to block the sun and ran his hand over the surface.

His wife respected the basic passion but claimed no understanding of its more fanatical aspects. "Tell me something, old
man: You swipe at every stray gnat with the bad luck to touch
the damned thing. Then you take off and it gets smacked with
dust, grass, rocks, birds and I don't know what-all, not ten
minutes after you cleaned it all up. So what's the point?"

Bo would slowly turn his dark, black face to look at her through
clear eyes—he was still too proud to wear glasses. "You take a
shower ten minutes before we hit the hay, knowin' I'm sure 'nuff
gonna mess *you* up, don'cha? So what the hell's the difference?"

"The difference is, me looking nice for you, that's the difference."

He would turn back to his paper, or his coffee, or his maintenance manual. "Ain't no difference far as I can see."

Lenore had to admit, though, that the plane was a true work
of art. If there had been only one still in existence instead of
nearly two hundred, the P-51 fighter would be in a museum,
too valuable to risk in flight. One of the most popular dogfighters

in history, the Mustang survived, in "civilianized" form, through the dogged efforts of obsessed pilots and collectors to whom its disappearance would represent a calamity as great as the extinction of a living species.

Bo's was a D model, the last incarnation of the series before the jets of the Korean War obviated the necessity for a piston-driven powerhouse that could hit well over four hundred miles per hour in level flight. Built originally as a dive-bomber, by the winter of 1942 it had been fitted with the twelve-cylinder Rolls-Royce Merlin engine, whose 2,640 horsepower could sling the sleek plane up through eight miles of sky, where it was still fully operational. When its range was doubled to 1,700 miles, a new escort was born as well. The Mustang could accompany bombers all the way from Italy to the heart of the Reich and was also able to get farther away from the bombers to engage the enemy, rather than be forced into close-in fighting.

While its reputation as a supremely agile ace maker was formidable, its popularity among pilots had much to do with this new range, one of its lesser-known virtues. To the combat flyer this translated into some relief from his second most popular worry (after being shot down): Do I have enough fuel left to make it back home, or am I going to ditch in enemy territory? Sometimes this advantage turned against the pilots, as the more complacent forgot about the tanks entirely, overstayed their range and were ignominiously swept earthward. "Three things that do you no good," his friend Jud Greaves used to say. "Runway behind you, altitude above you and fuel back in the truck."

The new Mustang went into combat service in 1943 and did more to seal the fate of the Luftwaffe than any other Allied plane in the war.

And Bo had one all to himself, almost, so pristine and shiny that it looked as good as, probably even better than, it had the day it was delivered from the North American Aviation factory over forty-five years ago. Flew as good, too, and it didn't have all that snarly-toothed nose art, just the markings of the Ninety-ninth Fighter Group, the "Red Tail Angels," in 1943 becoming the first all-black unit to go overseas. Some of the offers he had received from air show performers, private collectors and aviation museums were almost unbelievable (good thing Lenore didn't know about them), but he and his partners declined them all.

Running his hand over the forward fuselage just below the half-dozen exhaust nozzles, Bo was so absorbed that he barely noticed the shadow wavering in front of the bushes near the rear of the hangar. Only the sudden glint from the buckle of a baseball cap set backward on the kid's head caught his attention. He stopped moving his hand but didn't turn his head, only shifted his eyes slightly for a better view.

The shadow moved forward tentatively, and at the very periphery of his vision Bo watched the far edge of it hook up to a pair of legs, skinny and brown, the feet stepping lightly to avoid any sound. Bo resumed wiping the plane, but slower now, and idly; his eyes still strained to see without moving his head.

As the shape moved into his vision, he could see that it was a young black boy, maybe thirteen, high-top basketball sneakers ("felony flyers," the cops called them), baggy shorts three sizes too big, a plain white T-shirt and the cap. The kid's eyes were locked on to Bo, alert for any overt signs of recognition. His right arm hung straight down, the hand held back, but only slightly, as though hiding something without wanting to make that fact obvious.

As the boy inched forward, keeping his body turned slightly in preparation for a fast bolt away in the event of trouble, Bo focused in on that hand, his eyes straining to see what it held. The kid turned his foot ever so slightly to avoid stepping on a rock, and Bo caught a quick glimpse.

Mudball.

Now he noticed the boy's face, surly and devious. Combined with the turned hat, this was the face of a troublemaker, hardcore. Bo briefly contemplated protecting the plane with his own body, for a fraction of a second unmindful of the considerable disparity in square footage. The boy moved closer.

Bo could no longer pretend he didn't see him. He rose and straightened slowly, looking directly into his eyes now, challenging him. The kid was only fifteen or so feet away, still coming forward. Bo could rush him, but there was little doubt that the boy's nimbleness would carry him away safely. The hand with the mudball boldly presented itself, hefting the dripping concoction with brazen contempt. Bo held his ground, trying to communicate with his eyes the deadly consequences of the boy's pending action.

He stopped. They stared at each other for a brief and final second, and then the boy attacked, raising the mudball high in the air and heading straight for the polished leading edge of the starboard wing.

Bo leaped and met the kid before he made it to the wing. He wrapped his big arm in front of the boy's chest, put his free hand at the base of his back and swept him up into the air, letting go at the top of the arc so the kid hung free for an instant. The youth screamed, and Bo caught him in a bear hug from behind and wrestled him to the ground. They both grunted as they hit the ground, and soon Bo was on top of him, the kid yelling at the top of his lungs, Bo digging his fingers into the thin ribs beneath the T-shirt.

Choking and sputtering, the boy yelled for Bo to stop, then the choking turned to gagging laughter, and after a few more well-placed jabs, Bo relented and rolled away. The kid doubled up and rubbed his ribs and belly, then got to his knees and leaped at Bo, throwing his arms around the bigger man and kissing both sides of his face. "It's jus' a dumb ol' plane, you dumb ol' man!"

Bo hugged the boy back and held him for a few seconds, feeling the small bones and the young skin taut against them, feeling the kid's heartbeat against his chest and his breathing on his neck. "That so, huh?" He held Lamarr out at arm's length and looked at him. "Guess that means you don't wanna sit in it, then."

Lamarr whooped and danced away, jumping onto the low wing and reaching for the base of the bubble canopy. "Hey, take your shoes off, y'damned fool kid!" Bo yelled. Lamarr did so and tossed them toward Bo before clambering up over the cockpit wall and disappearing inside. Bo watched the ailerons and elevator go up and down as Lamarr played with the stick, then watched the rudder waggle back and forth as his feet found the pedals.

He walked toward the plane and slowly pulled himself up onto the wing. He looked down into the cockpit and saw Lamarr, delirious, with the earphones clamped comically onto his too small head, talking professionally on the dead radio, requesting clearance and warning of bogies, three o'clock low. Bo ran his fingers along the metal railing that supported the canopy. He wondered how many pilots had scrabbled at the latching mechanism and slid the top back in a frenzied effort to bail out of a wounded and plunging Mustang.

Sensing his uncle looming above him, Lamarr took off the headset and looked up. "How you feelin' today, Uncle Bo?"

There was more behind the question than an offhand inquiry about his health. "Not bad, not bad." Bo looked at the hangar, the grass field, the sky. "Some days better'n others, y'know?"

Lamarr nodded knowingly, looking at nothing in particular and idly fingering the webbing of the seat belt. Bo looked down at him and rapped his knuckles on the top of Lamarr's head. The boy turned his face up to look at Bo, who waited a few seconds and then said, "So y'wanna go flyin', or what?"

Lamarr pumped his arms in the air and snapped off the four-point seat belt in preparation for giving up the single-seat fighter for the two-seat Cessna in the hangar. He stood up on the seat just in time to see Bo jump off the wing and started laughing.

"The hell's so damned funny?" Bo asked crossly, but Lamarr was giggling helplessly and didn't answer. Bo turned away, muttering, and Lamarr continued laughing at the two, small, muddy handprints on the back of his flightsuit.

September 26, 1956

If you have no idea where to go or what to do, California is about the best place to go to do it.

Contrary to the prevailing sentiment in every other state of the Union, Californians do not suffer from an inferiority complex. What group mentality does exist regarding the question of the Golden State's place in the Western Hemispheric scheme of things exists only in the minds of media people on slow news days. The average Californian spends a surpassingly minuscule amount of time worrying about what everyone thinks about the state, not really much caring about its bohemian reputation, or the amount of cargo passing through the port of Long Beach, or the aggregate asset base of its banks, or the number of astrologers per square mile, or the per-picture salaries of Hollywood stars, or how much cocaine is consumed at a typical Beverly Hills party.

The Californian cares little about what outsiders think of

any of these things and is affected by them only when meeting those outsiders who jump to a grotesquely rich set of preconceived notions about what a single individual from California must be like in light of everything they've read in magazines of dubious editorial integrity.

That things are looser on the West Coast is inarguable, the general tolerance level for differentness being about as high as anywhere on earth. That such tolerance frequently approaches self-destructive proportions is also inarguable; the keepers of the flame of enlightenment often fail to distinguish between the right to hold an opinion and the value of that opinion, affording undue credence to the latter in misguided deference to the former.

This sociological laissez-faire, coupled with weather to make the angels weep, traditionally draws the dreamer, the culturally disenfranchised, a goodly sprinkling of outright lunatics who misread nonrejection as acceptance (and who are occasionally correct in that perception), and a fair number of people who would be considered criminals in other venues but are pitied in California, where, as the millennium draws to a close, things have generally evolved such that it could be easily demonstrated that nothing was ever anybody's own fault. The complete shifting of responsibility from the individual to dysfunctional parents, dismal schools, incompetent doctors, bloated government, cosmic rays, cigarettes, toxic waste, computers, UFOs, God, oversugared packaged snack pastries, video display terminals, ergonomically incorrect keyboards, volcanic dust, overhead power lines, disembodied voices, Jupiter rising, PMS and attention deficit disorder reached its apotheosis in the acquittal of a small-town city official charged with accepting a bribe that a prominent local businessman was convicted of giving him. The smart money guessed that the official really needed the cash because of medical bills sustained as a result of whipping himself as part of his participation in an obscure southern Pakistani religious cult, while the businessman unfortunately suffered from no politically cherished diseases, had a wife who didn't work, had not one but two country club memberships and was making too much money as it was and should have been ashamed of himself;

this was as good an opportunity as any to help him understand this.

It was into the blossoming precursor of this environment that Bo Kincaid wandered in 1956, the same year that America's first Vietnamese puppet, Ngo Dinh Diem, refused to hold the popular elections called for by the Geneva peace conference, leading to a series of events that would eventually impinge on Bo's carefully ordered and quiet life.

Bo's had been a miserable existence since mustering out of the Army Air Corps in 1945; a series of odd jobs was about the only thing available to a black in the American South during the Jim Crow days. Bo was sorry that he had left the flying army. At least there, his life had some structure, some purpose. It also had some meaning, there being a greater good behind the act of hurling oneself into harm's way in pursuit of a worthy cause.

What it also had, although Bo hadn't realized it at the time, was an opportunity to expiate the guilt that continued to plague him. The guilt concerning his best friend, Judson Greaves. He wouldn't have been able to do so entirely, but couldn't he have maybe taken Judson's place? Couldn't he have carried on the good fight, protected his buddies, saved a few lives and made Jud's death mean something?

Sure, if he'd stayed in, he could have done all those things, done some good, maybe made the pain of his friend's death diminish over time instead of hanging poised over his waking consciousness like a heavy, soggy thing. Maybe, just maybe, he could even have . . . died.

That was really it, wasn't it? Maybe I could have died in combat, been a hero. Now: that *was a way to walk out of this thing whole!*

Bo shook his head hard to clear his brain. *Got to stop this shit, dammit! Now is not the time!*

He squinted into the sun and ran his eye down the row of buildings adjoining the Santa Paula airport runway until he spotted the sign: "Cutter's Aviation." There was a fair-size ramp area, two large, corrugated metal hangars and a tiny, white-painted office building.

Sitting on the ramp was a varied assortment of light planes, the standard Pipers and Cessnas, along with a Stearman, a

Waco, and a couple of exotic-looking things he couldn't place. He wasn't able to see inside the hangar from his vantage point.

He took a deep breath and walked toward the office building. As he passed by the open hangar door, he could see several planes in various stages of disassembly, some all the way down to the airframe beneath the missing skin. Props, motors, wheels, tubes, rolls of fabric and dozens of packing crates and storage boxes lay strewn about, like pathology samples of autopsied bodies.

He opened the office door and stepped in. The paneled walls were covered with posters of classic aircraft, both military and civilian. Some had been hanging for so long that they had faded past recognizability. An ashtray made out of a blown piston and littered with butts graced a chipped and peeling Formica-topped table. An assortment of flying magazines, the newest eight months old, was scattered over the table and the vinyl couch against one wall. A coffeepot simmered on a burner in the corner.

A glass-topped counter separated the front reception area from the back office. Bo tapped the bell sitting on it and waited.

Joe Cutter appeared through the doorless doorway. Of average height, he wore greasy blue overalls and two-day stubble, out of which poked a cigar stub that might last have been lit at Christmas. He wore a New York Yankees baseball cap and had a grease spot on his forehead where his hand had brushed it while pushing the bill up. His eyes were permanently narrowed from endless hours squinting into the sun. He was slightly underweight, his face lean, tough but not unkind. He eyed Bo.

"Yeah, what?"

"I'm Kincaid."

Cutter took a moment to remember, because this wasn't what he was expecting. "Oh, yeah, you the pilot?"

Bo nodded. *Okay, let's hear it. I'm a Negro, and yes, I can fly planes. I learned in the service where, yeah, they had Negro pilots, but they didn't let us mix with the white boys. Uh-huh, I was honorably discharged, eight confirmed kills, a bunch more probables, and no, I won't steal any parts.*

Cutter came around the counter and put out his hand. "Joe Cutter. So what do you fly?"

Bo took the offered hand. "Most anything's got props." He

pointed out the window with his chin. "All o' that stuff, 'cept I never tried a Waco." He pronounced it "Whack-o," which indicated to Cutter that he knew his planes.

"Just like a Stearman, couple different knobs and switches. Learn in the service?"

"Yessir. Three thirty-second."

Cutter perked up at this. "P-51s?"

Bo nodded. "Hunnerd 'n' forty-three missions."

"No foolin'?" Cutter turned and poured two cups of coffee, handed one to Bo without asking if he took cream or sugar and led the way out the door and over to the Stearman. "So what do you see?"

Bo wasn't sure he understood, but he saw that Cutter was looking at the silvery plane as he asked the question, so he followed suit.

Bo ran his hand along the fuselage, feeling the skin beneath his fingers. "Coupla wrinkles. Musta done some time in turbulence, or more'n likely overstressed it doing loops 'n' stuff."

He pointed to streaks of oil fanning back from the engine cowling. "Blowing charcoal here." He ran a fingertip through the black patch and noticed that underneath a fresh top layer was a more stubborn and older stain. "Been going on a long time." He rubbed his fingers and brought them to his nose. "Old and gritty. Way overdue for a change."

He looked up at Cutter. "First glance, I'd say a sloppy pilot, careless, doesn't seem to care much about the plane. What's it doing here?"

Cutter considered him for a moment. "Owner rented it out to a flying club. Didn't occur to him they wouldn't take better care of it. Rental time dropped because the engine started acting up. Guy almost fainted, he went out and saw the thing." He put his hand on the wooden Hamilton-Standard prop, idly checking for leading edge chips and gouges out of force of habit, really just an excuse to touch the plane. "Wants us to fix it up before he figures out what to do with it. Would you replace that wrinkled skin?"

"Wouldn't bother. It's not structural. What's the job?"

Cutter nodded slightly in approval. "Lot of these planes get used by student pilots. FAA's got a rule, plane's gotta be flown by a licensed pilot after any major repair. We do that for the owners. Also ferry 'em around, pick up and deliver, that sort of thing. And odd jobs here and there."

"What happened to the last guy?" Bo wasn't sure he wanted to hear the answer.

"Bum ticker. Feds grounded him. And I'm too old for this shit."

No, you're not. You just scared yourself once too often. "What about those?" Bo pointed to the planes he couldn't recognize.

"Well, that's up to you. Some of 'em are homebuilts, some restorations. Another FAA rule. Gotta get test-flown a lot before a private ticket can fly 'em. Pays good money, but some of these guys, they have more dough than sense, it comes to building planes. You got a commercial ticket?"

"Sure. You check 'em out first?"

"Yeah. But you can't check everything. Like I said, it's up to you. Not required. So, what do you say?"

Bo had unconsciously wandered down the fuselage. He touched the upper surface of the biplane's bottom wing. Most people were mystified as to why anyone in his right mind would use flimsy pieces of fabric to cover a wing when lightweight aluminum was available. They didn't realize that cloth was far superior to metal in its ability to withstand stresses that deformed the wing shape to an alarming degree during high-stress maneuvers. Metal buckled and weakened and occasionally bent irretrievably out of shape. Fabric was forgiving. It gave just enough and held fast just enough, as long as you didn't tear it with an errant screwdriver or wait too long for the sun's ultraviolet rays to degrade it before replacing it. Bo thought he heard a breath of wind whistle through the tightly strung guy wires that zigzagged between the upper and lower wings. He thought he saw the wings flex slightly, as though the pilot had hauled back the stick after a steep dive to put the plane into a tight loop. And he felt the engine vibration pulsing through the stays like electricity in a wire. He smelled engine oil and gasoline; the sun streaming through the rarefied upper atmosphere warmed his face in spite of the wind blast from the open cockpit.

The pay would not be very attractive, he could tell from the Stearman that the work was risky, there would be a lot of weekends, a lot of demeaning tasks to be done, a lot of arrogant and nasty airplane owners on his case all the time . . .

"Sounds okay to me."

June 15, 1957

Bo stopped short of the runway and pivoted the Aeronca around on one braked wheel, pointing it into the wind. With both feet planted firmly on the toe brakes, he ran the engine up to 1,800 RPM. It seemed that he had to push the throttle in farther than normal, but he flew so many different aircraft that it was hard to keep track of what was appropriate for each one. Besides, he was testing this one out following a throttle rebuild, so some change in the usual feel was to be expected.

When the engine had settled into a smooth *thrumm*, he reached for the key and switched it to magneto one, noting the RPMs drop to 1,600. He went back to both mags and then switched to the second, getting about the same drop again. Returning to both mags brought the revs back to 1,800. Everything was in order, and he proceeded down the remainder of the checklist.

Scanning carefully for planes, he positioned himself on the runway. It always made him a little nervous to fly without a radio, but it was not an FAA requirement to have one, and pilots who had spent years scraping together enough money to buy an old beater very often left out the radio to save money (they *said* it was to save weight).

He pushed the throttle all the way in, revving up to full power, although again it seemed to fall a little short of where it should be. Releasing the brakes, he applied pressure to the right pedal to compensate for the stream of air hitting the left side of the vertical tail fin and the elevator. As the single prop sent a twisting stream of air back along the fuselage, it swirled around the plane in a clockwise direction, coming up from below on the left side. When the plane picked up speed, a little bit of right rudder kept the nose pointed straight ahead during the takeoff roll.

The eighty-five-horsepower engine seemed to strain to accelerate the plane. Within a few hundred feet, there was enough air flowing over the wings to allow Bo to push the stick forward, the opposite of what one might expect, but it tilted the plane forward and allowed the tail wheel to come off the ground, leveling the wings and stopping the plane from trying to fly before there was enough lift to get it off the ground. He put in a little more right rudder because the spinning prop, acting like a powerful gyroscopic disk, tried to twist sideways when pushed out of the angle from which it had started.

Constantly checking the airspeed indicator, Bo waited until it hit fifty-five knots, which took a lot longer than it should have, and gently pulled back on the stick. Rather than try to yank it into the air, he let the plane fly itself off the runway at its own pace. He climbed using the airspeed indicator only, pegged at sixty knots. If it dropped lower than that, he eased off on the stick, lowering the nose slightly and trading angle of climb for speed. If it crept higher, he pulled back, climbing faster and reducing speed. In this way he rose at the maximum vertical rate for this particular aircraft. He also knew that this same speed, in the event of an engine failure, would guarantee him the longest glide possible to make it to a safe landing spot.

It was not a fun day to fly, overcast and dreary. This was typical June weather for the coast, but the marine layer rarely crept this far inland. When it did the hills to the south pushed it up a thousand feet or so, making pattern work feasible but limiting distance flying to instrument-rated pilots, a relative rarity at Santa Paula airport in 1957.

All indications from the plane seemed nominal to Bo, if somewhat sluggish. He extended the pattern a little, then turned crosswind to come back to the field. On the downwind leg, he could see Joe Cutter standing near the hangar, probably looking up at the Aeronca. Bo's eyes were sharp but not enough to gauge the angle of a man's face that far away.

As he came abeam of the end of the runway, Bo turned on the carburetor heat. That was standard operating procedure for the Aeronca, and even though it robbed the engine of a small amount of power, it was included to make certain that no ice intruded into the engine during the critical landing phase. Made sense, except that in deference to the FAA's compulsive insistence on procedure, no dispensation was allowed for flying in climes such as those at Santa Paula, where there was more chance of the pilot's having a heart attack from the exertion of pulling the carb heat knob than there was of finding ice in the intake pipes.

He pulled the throttle knob back to bring the engine RPMs down to 1,400, but nothing happened, so he pulled it out a little more. Still nothing.

He tapped his finger on the glass face of the tachometer. Sticking needles were a very common occurrence, but it was a reflex gesture only. He hadn't heard or felt the engine speed drop, so he knew there was really nothing wrong with the gauge. He pulled the throttle out all the way to the stops.

The engine kept spinning at 2,000 RPM. He pushed the throttle all the way back in and then out again. There was no change at all in the engine speed. He was in level flight, traveling at 120 knots, about twice the speed for a safe landing approach. And if he dropped the nose to descend, his speed would increase dramatically.

Flight training is 90 percent about dealing with emergencies. Fire in the cabin, landing gear that won't come down (academic in the fixed-gear Aeronca), ice in the carburetor, sudden loss of visibility, radios out (again, academic for this flight). Here was a new one, though. Who would have thought to include a section on what to do when the engine won't throttle back?

It would seem that Bo had a lot of time to figure out what to do. After all, he was airborne, the engine was humming smoothly, all instrument readings were within acceptable parameters. However, he knew well that one problem was usually an indicator of several more waiting to happen. He figured that the throttle linkage had come apart, leaving the engine setting where it was when it broke. It was quite likely that engine vibration would gradually ease the carburetor pins back in, since there was nothing to hold them in place, and he might lose power altogether.

Bo quickly did some mental calculations, integrating his present speed, distance from the runway, the two turns he would

have to make to line up, and the performance characteristics of
the Aeronca, which he kept on a plastic "V-speed" card in his
shirt pocket (he had one of these for every plane he flew).
Checking carefully for other traffic, he spotted a twin-engine
Beech in the distance, approaching for a straight-in landing,
contrary to procedure. The Beech should have entered the pattern first, but straight-ins were not uncommon and were generally tolerated if the pilot was respectful of other traffic.

With no radio to communicate with the twin, Bo extended
his downwind leg well past his comfort zone, twisting his head
backward periodically to keep an eye on the Beech, ending up
three miles beyond the end of the runway by the time he saw it
about to land. Staying high, he made two right-angle turns to
line himself up with the runway. He kept his altitude as insurance in case the engine quit, knowing that he would have to
struggle on his way down not to overshoot the runway later.
Besides, starting down would have shot both his revs and airspeed up even higher. Fiddling with the throttle some more, he
soon gave that up as useless and concentrated on how he would
bring the plane down. There was only one way.

About a mile before the beginning of the runway, Bo
reached for the key and turned off the ignition, an eerie quiet
suddenly assaulting him. There was no stranger feeling for a
pilot than to be up in the air without engine noise. He was
committed to the landing now, feeling the drag that grabbed
at the Aeronca without the tractor pull of a powered prop. He
realized that the blades still turning in the wind were themselves now a great source of drag. Taking a deep breath, he
pulled back on the stick, raising the nose and dropping the
airspeed dangerously low. He could feel the airframe start to
shudder as the Aeronca approached a stall, too little air flowing
over the wings to sustain controlled flight. He held on, watching the propeller get slower and slower, feeling the plane start
to go out of control.

Just when it seemed that the powerless bird was about to
breathe a death rattle, heel over onto its side and tumble
earthward, the propeller came to a complete stop. Now the
silence was nearly total, only the white-noise *whoosh* of wind
discernible. Bo quickly shoved the stick forward, getting the
nose pointed downward until his speed picked up enough for

the wings to get a solid bite out of the air and return some
control feel to the stick. He was now about 1,500 feet from
the runway.

And way too high. The little plane had no flaps to reduce
speed and steepen the glide angle. Bo pulled back the stick
as much as he dared and, when he had slowed the plane down,
pushed it forward and to the left and at the same time pressed
the right rudder pedal to the floor. The controls completely
crossed, the Aeronca crabbed its way down to the runway.
The right rudder fought against the left aileron to keep the
plane steady, and all of that extra control drag allowed a
greatly steepened angle of descent.

Seeing that he would make the end of runway, Bo eased
back on the cross control, buying back a little speed. Now
that a safe landing was assured, he remembered the last time
he'd brought in an aircraft dead stick and figured he had a
little showing off coming. Touching down gently, he stayed
off the brakes, letting the plane run, until he approached the
Cutter Aviation ramp. Joe Cutter watched as Bo put in a touch
of left brake, swerving the plane slightly until it was off the
runway and heading for the ramp. It slowed some more as
Bo steered it with differential braking, bringing it to a stop
in the exact spot where it had been sitting when he'd first
climbed into it. Using the forward motion he had left, he hit
the right brake hard, swinging the plane around until it faced
in the direction from which it had just come.

Bo undid his seat belt, opened the flimsy door and hopped
out as Cutter came running up to the plane, his cigar so
chomped up that flakes of tobacco leaf trailed behind him.
"Now what in the hell was that all—"

"Throttle busted," Bo said casually, turning the handle to
secure the door back in place.

Cutter stared at him a moment before flipping open the
engine cowling for a look inside. He reached in and soon
brought out a length of brass tubing with screw fittings at
either end. He held it up for Bo to see before turning in the
direction of the hangar. "Speiser!"

A sloppy-looking mechanic with heavily-lidded, sullen eyes
appeared in the doorway, wiping his greasy hands on a rag.
"Yeah?"

"C'mere a second."

Speiser shuffled slowly toward the Aeronca. Cutter held up the brass assembly. "Came loose in the air."

Speiser took it and turned it over once or twice, then shrugged. "Sorry."

"The retaining pin wasn't put back. It might'a killed this pilot."

Speiser looked up at Bo and then back at the linkage. He shrugged again. "Said I'm sorry." Walking back to the plane, he started to pull a screwdriver out of his pocket when Cutter walked up behind him and snatched the assembly out of his hand.

"Not good enough, Speiser. Other boys, they're tired of covering for your shitty work all the time."

The mechanic turned slightly so Bo couldn't see his face and said out of the side of his mouth, just loud enough for Bo to hear, "Jesus, Cutter, it's jus' a damned nigger, what you gettin' so excited about?"

Cutter nodded. "Yeah, well, I guess you're right."

Speiser smiled conspiratorially and reached for the throttle linkage, but Cutter moved his hand away. "But that's a damned fine plane you might'a ruined, too."

As Bo smiled, Cutter turned back to Speiser. "Pack up your stuff and get the hell out of here. Allerton!"

A heavily muscled black maintenance man came out of the hangar. "Yeah, Joe?"

"Al, make sure this fuckhead don't steal nothin' on his way out."

Allerton looked at Speiser. "Ahh, he won't steal nothin' "—a wide grin came over his face—"will ya now, son?"

With a backward glare at Bo, Speiser marched off toward the hangar, giving Allerton a wide and respectful berth.

Cutter turned back to Bo. "How'd you get it down?"

"Cut the ignition, I knew I had the runway made."

Cutter pulled a screwdriver out of his shirt pocket and walked over to the plane, shaking his head. "Dumb."

"Oh, yeah? How would you'da done it?"

Bent over the cowling, Cutter said matter-of-factly, "Woulda pulled back on the choke, slowed it down that way.

Use it just like a throttle. Wouldn'ta had to chance shutting it down."

Bo stared at Cutter's back with respect, annoyed with himself for failing to have seen the obvious. "That so?"

"Yep."

"Well, I'll remember that next time one o' your boys shits up the throttle."

"Yeah, well, you do that. Can't have you bustin' up the customers' toys." He stood up and stretched his back. "Back up you go, fella." Walking away, he called back over his shoulder, "I fixed it so's it'll break the same way again. Give you a chance to do it right this time."

"Very funny," Bo yelled back, smiling but looking under the cowling just the same before reentering the plane.

It was a good situation—perfect, in fact. He got to fly and even got paid for it. Cutter treated him with decency and respect, even though the same was not true for some of the other employees. His job was considered cushy, and some of the younger men with licenses thought it should have gone to them. But none had Bo's experience, nor could they match his innate feel for planes and flying. The observations he was able to make were of invaluable assistance to the mechanics, and many of the aircraft owners had come to insist that Bo personally fly their planes after repairs.

The testing of homebuilts and restored classics was a little more harrowing. At least with conventional craft there was a history of many actual hours in the air, so you knew flight was at least possible. Some of the exotics had never been off the ground before, and the number of things that could go wrong was mind-boggling. Bo came to understand that the real estate speculators and investment bankers who thought the idea of building their own planes was romantic were often not as attentive to detail as they should have been and didn't like asking for help when they needed it. Crossing control wires was not an uncommon occurrence, but that was an easy one to check on the ground. That the plane was balanced properly or that its stall characteristics were manageable were a good deal harder to predict.

But he needed the money, so he went up, relying on Cutter and his people to inspect as much as they could. He came to establish a rule of never going up in anything that he couldn't bail out of and never staying with any out-of-control aircraft below three thousand feet, his own threshold for a safe parachute ride down. So far he'd ditched three, landed countless others with dead engines, although not always on the runway, and only slugged an owner once, a surgeon who had told him that the plane already had eight flying hours in another state. The landing gear on this plane had failed to come down because the extension mechanism was missing, a vital part that made it an impossibility that the plane could have ever left the ground before.

That part of his job didn't last long, because he found a safer, albeit less-well-paying substitute. His initial odd jobs at Cutter had consisted of the usual menial tasks: cleaning up grease spills, putting away tools, hoisting engine blocks. But as he hung around the professional restorers more and more, he picked up some skills by watching and helping and gradually was entrusted with an increasing number of more satisfying jobs. He began learning how to carefully strip away old paint and varnish, file away rusted and corroded control surfaces and mix up the fabric doping chemicals. After a while he assisted in restringing guy wires on biplanes and soon graduated to making replacement parts from scratch when originals were no longer available. This meant learning about metal and wood lathes and training in how to use a wide variety of unusual tools and techniques.

What intrigued Bo the most was the creative challenge. It was exceedingly rare for the restorers to work on the same aircraft type more than once. Just when they were completely up to speed on every nuance involved in rebuilding a crashed Spitfire with major structural damage, that job would be finished and they'd start on a Stuka dive-bomber whose primary problem was extensive corrosion after being recovered from a marsh. It was never the same thing twice, and the most important skill was the ability to improvise. As Bo soon learned, the best preparation for improvising something new was a thorough grounding in that which was already known. He learned about materials, structures, basic stress analysis, engine operation and fuel systems. He learned how to conduct research and eventually discovered the UCLA library, a ninety-minute drive away, where he spent time looking at photographs and structural diagrams, even reading narrative accounts, trying to uncover clues when the available details were few.

He gradually came to make contacts in aviation societies all over the country and even a few overseas, discovering that the fraternity of airmen, and airwomen, placed more stock in expertise and the pure love of planes and flying than it did in matters of color, gender or formal education.

Best of all, he got to fly the planes.

Piloting other people's rickety crates had lost its allure, but sometimes his own hands had helped with the work, the bulk of which was done by those among the Cutter staff Bo had come to trust. His best days came when the museum-quality restoration was wheeled out into the sun (they always waited for a sunny day, no matter how eager everyone became) and posed this way and that for photographs (first things first, since who could tell if it would survive its first flight?). Then Bo would climb into the cockpit.

He made up a V-speed card for every plane, based on his research or, failing that, on the estimates of an aerodynamic engineer Joe Cutter occasionally brought in as a consultant. By the time he strapped himself in, he had thoroughly memorized every procedure required by the original manufacturer for that make and model, even though a written checklist accompanied him on every flight.

After some low- and then high-speed taxi tests, he'd head out to the end of the runway. A small crowd would usually have gathered by then. He'd point the plane into the wind, gun the throttle and ride the bird into the sky where it belonged, the only place both he and the plane felt truly comfortable. After a standard series of tests, he'd do one or two low passes over the field, giving the crowd a chance to gawk and the photographers an opportunity for some dramatic flying shots.

Then back down, after only thirty minutes or so, for a thorough check of how well everything was hanging together. Were the strut wires still taut? Were the engine mounts still bolted on tight? Any signs of metal fatigue or overstress or fabric separation or leaking oil?

Those were Bo's very best days. Those were days he didn't think about Judson Greaves.

CHAPTER 4

1330 EST

"What kind of contingencies have we got on the equipment, in case of outside tampering?" asked James Buchanan Davison, deputy undersecretary of the Department of Transportation.

Robert L. Ferguson, assistant director of the Federal Aviation Agency, cleared his throat and looked from left to right before answering. "Well, we don't have any. That'd be very expensive, and our budget appropriations haven't really allowed—"

"I'm sorry?" Davison's flunky, Arnold Waznowski, saw an opening and went for it. "Did you say there aren't any? Any at all?"

"Not exactly any, or I mean, not exactly none, no. There are innumerable security measures that are a matter of standard procedure."

"Such as?"

"Uh, redundancy. Yes, backups upon backups, alternatives in case something goes wrong with one thing, well, you can cross-check on, uh, other things as you proceed along."

"Other things? Like what, f 'rinstance?"

Jack Webster sat quietly and thought about his heart. His

mitral valve had a slight defect, and a tiny amount of blood managed to sneak its way back from the ventricle into the atrium with every beat. It didn't show up on his EKG, which was required for a first-class medical certificate for pilots over thirty-five. Jack hadn't needed a first-class certificate, since he flew only for pleasure, but he was proud of it and proud of his clean EKG, incontrovertible evidence of a healthy heart, or so he thought. Until a sharp-eared flight surgeon picked up the little anomaly by auscultation and ordered an echocardiogram. As was his right, Jack had gone to a private cardiologist, at his own expense, and done the whole routine. The doctor was impressed that his little problem had gotten spotted at all, given its mildness, but it was certainly there.

"So what's it mean, Doc?" Jack asked. "What do I do?"

"Not a damned thing. Or better stated, do everything exactly as you normally would. There's essentially no risk, so there're no restrictions on your activity. Millions of people have mild mitral regurgitation and the vast majority of it goes undetected and none of it makes a difference."

Except to the FAA. Which is how Jack came to the attention of the NTSB. He engaged an attorney and fought tenaciously to reverse the policy, arguing with cold logic and hard facts, never exhibiting strident or unseemly behavior, just nailing every counterargument with a wealth of statistical data and expert testimony.

His prodigious research and bravura personal performance won a number of admirers within the board staff, not a great surprise considering their traditional adversarial relationship with the FAA, and they recommended him to the chairman. The outcome was as expected, but the major irony was that he no longer had time to fly. During the protracted battle, he had simply let his license run out of currency. He hadn't bothered to get it back after he later quit the NTSB.

He tried to bring his mind back and listen.

"Well, let's say the VORs go out, the really precise navigational aids, maybe for preventive maintenance, for example. You see, we don't wait for them to fail, we do preventive maintenance, and this is our policy, because it ensures that the overall system is always operational in—"

"Okay. The VORs are out. So now what?"

"There are the NDBs, that's a good example. Nondirectional beacons, very inexpensive—"

"Also not too accurate"—now Ferguson's flunky, Louis Melnick, got a turn up at bat—"but that's what you get because the devices themselves are inexpensive, and in light of our very tight budgets—"

Actually, it wasn't really his heart Jack was thinking about, it was sailboat racing. While his heart problem had him grounded, he took up the sport for something to do that combined skill and motion and speed. It was easy being part of the crew, since the helmsman did all the brainwork, but the really interesting part was the start, and this was what Jack couldn't help but recall as the meeting got under way. He mentally propped open his eyelids to sustain the illusion of interest but thought about the most interesting part of racing sails, the start.

The start was an imaginary line between two powerboats sitting about five hundred yards apart in open water. Reasonable, except that sailboats have the disadvantage of being completely and utterly uncontrollable when not under sail. So there is no way to bring all the boats to the line and hold them there until the gun goes off.

Instead the boats sail around behind the line, and the skipper's job is to be as close to the line as possible, pointed in the right direction, with the boat moving through the water as fast as possible at the exact moment the starting gun is fired.

This is a fiendishly difficult objective and the most important one in the race. Among relatively well-matched boats, overcoming a bad start is almost impossible. There are lots of tricks, both clean and questionable, that can be brought to bear to gain advantage, but sailing is ostensibly a gentleman's sport, although anyone even noddingly acquainted with it knows better. Jack looked at Jim Davison and contemplated his almost pathological desire to succeed, and then he looked at Bob Ferguson, who shared this trait and, like Davison, coupled it with the requirement to maintain at least the outward appearance of civility.

"Not accurate, you say? How not accurate?"

Jack looked at them both while they and their designated

seconds lobbed grenades back and forth across the table in Conference Room G, and his mind went back to how each boat tried to sail an eccentric circle that looked like a lopsided oblong. When facing directly toward the starting line, sails would go slack, the boats held in a barely controlled drift in the hope that the gun would soon be heard, and they could tighten the sails up and shoot off with no more turns.

As they drew closer and closer to the line, things got tense with the fear that there would be no gun on this circuit. If they got too close, the tightest, fastest turn possible was attempted in a desperate effort to get the vessel far enough back to come about once more and start the slow trip forward yet again. If you got caught facing backward when the shot finally came, you might as well hold course and head back for the dock. It was quite common for someone on the crew to fixate on the starting boat with a pair of binoculars, trying to ascertain if the arms bearer was loading a shell, hefting the gun to his shoulders or just milling about waiting for instructions to get ready.

And about the only sound that could be heard, other than the gentle ruffling of sails, was the frequent shout of "Foul!" accompanying the unfurling of foul pennants as the sportsmen accused each other of crimes most vicious, such as failing to head up when being overtaken to starboard, or stealing another's wind more brilliantly than that other was able to do to you, or deeds equally heinous that made cheering for the first boat over the finish line an exercise in futility, since no boat could be declared winner until all the accusations of rule infractions had been equitably contested.

"You wouldn't want to shoot an instrument approach with NDBs, although that can certainly be done and is in fact authorized with very high minimums, but you can use them for cross-checking, kind of an extra little teensy bit of assurance on a tough approach, and in some cases—"

"So what you're saying, in really bad conditions, in a tight environment, say, with mountains on both sides and a narrow passage, these—whadja call 'em, NDBs?—these NDBs couldn't really be relied upon—"

"That depends, it all depends—"

"On?"

"On a lot of things, it just depends, that's all. . . ."

The start was a ballet of advance, retreat, manipulation, stealth, wiles and covert subversion, all carefully orchestrated beneath the traditional umbrella of fellowship and the camaraderie of similarly engaged mariners.

Like the meeting commencing in Conference Room G.

Jack let it go on for a little while, so everybody could get on the record early in defense of themselves and their respective agencies. At this point, that record was not even remotely important with respect to the ultimate outcome. It was there for only one purpose, to demonstrate to their various superiors that they stoutly defended the home turf and set a tone that would make it more difficult for anyone else to hurl accusations without substantial evidence. Since everybody was doing the same thing, the net effect was zero, but that was higher than it would have been if everybody else was doing it and you weren't. And since nobody was acknowledging that they were doing it at all, there was no way for anybody to suggest waiving the process.

Jack grinned inwardly and wondered if any of his colleagues had also noticed that none of the invitees was complaining about the fact that the FBI seemed to be heading the investigation, and doing so out of NTSB headquarters, and without an NTSB board member present. It made no sense from either a procedural or protocol perspective, but nobody raised an objection. The reason was obvious: they didn't yet know how it was going to turn out. If things looked truly terrible, they'd let it go and effectively avoid the blame. If things looked good, they'd look for an opportunity to wrest control into their own agencies.

Jack listened for a few minutes longer and then started to get annoyed. *Good Lord,* he thought, *you fuckers don't even know what the problem is yet, and you're at each other's throats already.* "Bob, Jim, it might be helpful if we step you through the whole situation. It gets a little complicated, so we probably don't want to jump the gun on any solutions just yet."

Ferguson and Davison hadn't been discussing any solutions, but Jack managed to quiet them without giving the appearance that they had been bickering. Their respective points made, they calmed down and let Jack continue.

"We need to proceed on three tracks. First of all, find out how the guy did it, so we can figure a way to prevent it and eliminate him as a threat.

"Second, we need to catch him and do it without jarring him into doing anything dangerous until we've solved step one."

Ferguson was a technician by nature, good but not great, and sought to recapture part of the credibility he might have lost at the meeting's opening. "What I see, the only two possibilities, he screwed around with the plane itself or jammed it from the ground, right?"

Amy Goldberg looked at Jack, whose standing policy was to let his staffers do most of the talking, even if they weren't really his staffers anymore, and she got the nod from him. "That's exactly right, Director." *Well done, Goldberg.* "Just what we thought, but there are a couple of problems with both scenarios, and we're getting more information to go on."

"Problems like what?" asked Davison, not to be outdone by his FAA counterpart. When in doubt, ask an open-ended question.

Amy spread out some notes and picked up a pencil, tapping the point on the yellow sheets. "It's possible, if you're very smart and have the right equipment, to beam signals to the plane that would overwhelm the real signals and fool it. But that would have affected another plane that was following a few miles behind. That plane had no problems."

"You're a shrink, aren't you?" Ferguson was insulted that a low-level staffer would do the talking, and a woman at that. And why wasn't NTSB chairman Pressman here?

"Yes?" she answered, the upward inflection at the end clearly indicating the irrelevance of that question. She did not bother to correct the inaccuracy of the insult, "shrink" normally being reserved as an epithet in place of "psychiatrist" rather than "psychologist."

Ferguson turned back to Jack. "Webster, you did carrier duty in the Philippines. You guys fooled around with highly directional radio beacons, didn't you?"

Stay cool, Amy. The only real test is when you're losing.

"Yessir, we did. The idea was, confine the signal to our own planes coming back to the ship and keep them away from enemy aircraft."

Ferguson glanced at Amy in triumph, then announced to everyone gathered, "Well, there it is, then. The guy shot a narrow beam at the 727, monkeyed with its tracking. So what's the big deal?"

"The big deal," said Amy, her voice level and professional, "is that it didn't work on the carriers and it wouldn't have worked on the 727 either. The only way to isolate the plane is to hit it from the side, otherwise there's no way to stop the signal from continuing on past *your* plane to *their* plane. And that couldn't have been done in this case."

Ferguson sought to recover quickly. "Ah, I see, I see."

No, you don't, you asshole, Amy thought. *You can't possibly see it until I've given you the rest.*

Jack could tell that Ferguson burned with a dozen questions, all of them probably quite reasonable, that he was afraid to ask for fear of further embarrassment. Amy wasn't making a friend here, but that's why it was so nice to work for an independent agency. As it had been for him at one time.

Davison was not up on the technical details but tried to think of some other alternatives. "Is it even remotely possible, I don't know, maybe the pilots were in collusion with the guy? Or there *was* no guy?"

Amy cleared her throat, as though to clear away the last interchange, and leaned forward. "Actually, it's the best technical possibility we've got, since it's the only one fits all the facts. And it would make a second demonstration a piece of cake for the perpetrator if there were other pilots involved as well."

"But . . . ?"

"But, it's highly doubtful. It's so transparent it's unworkable. Besides, it's too easy to check."

"How?"

"The black boxes," said Ferguson, who had been following the exchange closely.

Jack looked at him with surprise. *Hey, two points for you, Bob.*

"Exactly," Amy agreed, looking at Ferguson and nodding.

She turned back to Davison. "It's real simple. We yank the black boxes, check the record of instrument readings. That way we know for sure, were the pilots being square."

"They were," added Jack without hesitation. "You can make book on it. We'll check anyway, to be thorough, but that's a fruitless branch of inquiry to waste time on now."

Amy leaned back in her chair. "The ground instruments checked out perfectly, no signs of tampering on the equipment sheds. The nav units are on their way to Autonav, the manufacturer, even as we speak."

"Maybe somebody who was authorized tinkered with the ground units?" offered Davison.

Amy shook her head. "Doubtful. We've still got one plane had no problem, remember?"

"Okay, yeah. Now what about fooling with the 727 itself?" Davison caught himself immediately. "Nope. He'd have to have known at least a day in advance which plane was making that run, so he could get the letter off."

"And," added Ferguson, "he would need complete access so he could have gotten to it at will, whenever he wanted to."

"Oh. Yeah." Davison furrowed his brow. "This *is* complicated."

Sometimes, thought Jack, *sometimes the* apparatchiks *forget themselves and behave like professionals.*

There was quiet for only a few moments. "What's the third thing?"

"Sorry?" Jack looked over at Ferguson.

"You said we need to proceed on three tracks. What's the third?"

Jack shifted uncomfortably on his seat. That was something he never did, and it caught the attention of both Ferguson and Davison as well as their respective aides. "The third is, we arrange to meet his demands." He squinted and turned his head as the barrage came.

"Never!" shouted Davison, his louder voice ensuring temporal primacy on the written record. "We do not submit to extortion. We—"

"We do not deal with terrorists!" Ferguson yelled, successfully elevating the adversary from a lone troublemaker up to an international operative of the first rank.

"The United States will not be held hostage—"

"Nobody is going to put a gun to our heads—"

Jack looked over at Amy and rolled his eyes skyward as the hubbub continued for several more minutes, then he put his chin in his hands and rolled his head face forward, scanning the table with his eyes. His lack of responsiveness had an ameliorating effect on the noise level. "Are all you fucking loudmouths through now? Are you ready to shut your traps and listen?"

He didn't say that at all. He just *wanted* to, but remembering Amy, he said instead, "I agree with you all. Submitting to the demands of an extortionist is not our policy and never will be. But sometimes the best strategy is, pretend to go along, lull him into a false sense of success." *And it'll buy me some respite from you guys before I tell you we're gonna have to pay up for real if we're nowhere by this time next week.*

"Well, I don't like it, don't like it one damned bit," said Davison, "but let's hear it. What's he want?"

Amy sniffled and scratched her cheek. "He wants five million dollars."

For the first time that day, the FAA and DOT officials were speechless, until Davison's assistant managed to say, "Excuse me?"

"Five million dollars?" Ferguson echoed mindlessly. "And what else?"

"Nothing else."

"I don't get it," said Davison, genuinely perplexed. "He's got the power to take out the entire system, all he wants is pocket change?"

Jack nodded in affirmation. "Scary, isn't it? Wait'll you hear how he wants it paid."

"That's the best opportunity for getting a guy like this, isn't it?" asked Ferguson. "The payoff, I mean."

Amy pulled a yellow sheet free and set it in front of her. "It sure is. That's always the dicey part, and this one's complicated. You all know what FundsNet is, right?"

"Sure," said Waznowski. "They run the ATMs, the cash machines. I've got one of their cards."

"Right. Our guy wants us to stick the five million in a bank that's hooked into FundsNet. Then he's gonna go anywhere he wants, start pulling it out a little at a time."

"Hold it a second," said Melnick. "Didn't some guy try that once? New York, I think, a kidnapping ransom. It didn't work, as I recall."

"You've got a good memory. Exactly so. Except that was a lot of years ago, when ATMs were still a novelty. Each bank had its own, and there were few enough, you could stake them out with enough people. FundsNet has over a hundred thousand of these things, scattered all over North America. And they're open twenty-four hours a day, seven days a week."

Davison whistled softly. "But he can't bounce all over the place. He's got to hit small geographic areas and work them before moving on. He moves into a location, can we mobilize fast enough?"

"Possibly," said Jack. "We should be able to easily track where he hits, and then we might be able to contact local authorities through the Bureau and scramble 'em rapidly."

"And another thing," added Ferguson's toady, not to be outdone by his counterpart across the table. "Those machines can't give out more than five hundred bucks at a time. Christ, the guy'd have to visit, what, a thousand machines. That's gonna be some drawn-out party."

"It's actually ten thousand visits. Only problem is, our guy's no dummy. He's thought of all of this, and a lot of other things besides. It's all in the instructions," said Amy.

"We're set up to talk to the FundsNet people," said Jack, "and we've got investigations going on a number of fronts. We've got two questions for this bunch, though. First, do we involve the airlines at this point?"

Davison answered without hesitation. "That's a no-brainer, Webster. We bring 'em in right away."

Ferguson nodded—reluctantly, it seemed. "To do otherwise would be irresponsible. We've got to bring them in on it."

A predictable response, given that it spread the responsibility across a larger number of shoulders. Jack had no objection: he'd rather deal with businesspeople than government bureaucrats anyway. "Second question: Do we alert the flying public?"

Lots of head scratching and shifting of positions, accompanied by throat clearings and fingers tapping on the tabletop. They were all thinking the same thing: the general media's handling of aviation matters was hopelessly inept and often dangerously misleading. Jack's thoughts went directly to the news anchor's favorite trick every time a small, private plane collided with a big, commercial one: at the end of the sound bite, the camera would zoom in to a tight close-up as the "reporter," wearing a mask of knowing concern and feigning some inside knowledge of dark secrets, solemnly intoned, *"The light plane"*—dramatic pause—*"was not on a flight plan,"* and waited for the fade to a commercial while a million viewers nodded knowingly and clucked their tongues at the awful irresponsibility of the pilot who failed to file a plan and thus caused this terrible tragedy. What Jack knew, what every pilot knew, but the viewing public generally didn't, was that a flight plan, which is not an FAA requirement for a visual flight, didn't have anything whatsoever to do with the safe conduct of a flight, and, in fact, for short hops over populated areas such plans were unnecessary nuisances that only clogged the system.

"Look, let's be honest with ourselves," Ferguson said eventually. "We don't tell the public and there's an incident, we get drawn and quartered. People still remember Lockerbie. If we *do* tell them and there's a nationwide panic? Same result."

Davison nodded at the analysis as Jack asked, "So what's the recommendation?"

The deputy undersecretary looked at the assistant director and then at Jack. "We do what we always do when the net political risk is equal either way."

"And what's that?"

"The right thing. We keep it quiet while there is no overt threat on the table. As of this moment, the guy is in control, and he's telling us we've got a week. The airline execs think different, let 'em tell their passengers. That's their call."

Jack shrugged. "That's good by me. Bob?"

"Agreed."

"Okay, then, here's how we proceed." He knew that the two things everybody needed most at this point were a confident, commanding leader and a definite plan. He felt himself getting sucked in deeper and deeper and sensed there was no graceful way to stop it. "Amy, send somebody to Washington to oversee the examination of the 727. And make sure he doesn't muscle in on the locals unless they do something really dumb. Slightly dumb is okay, long as they don't damage evidence."

"We're gonna have to bring the black boxes back here, though."

"They'll know that. Make sure they're on their way before your guy leaves. Jim, can your people round up the airline execs?"

Davison thought for a minute. "We'll hint there's some great new legislative initiative brewing." He smiled and rubbed his hands. "Maybe reregulation."

"Don't do that!" Jack exclaimed after the laughter had died down. "Their hearts would never survive the trip, and we want 'em here alive!"

"Let's only get a few of 'em in here, though," Davison said soberly. "The three or four biggest, let 'em represent the rest, otherwise we'll never get anything done."

"How about just one?" Amy said.

Buchanan looked up in surprise. "Just one?"

"You bring in a bunch," she said when she had everybody's attention, "you declare an official problem warranting a gathering of the brass. Everybody who's *not* invited will scream like hell in retrospect. Bring in one, you're managing it like a local problem."

"Cavanaugh," said Davison, catching her drift. "Alpha Airlines."

"Cavanaugh," Amy confirmed. "It was his plane, he comes in to handle it, nobody gets to complain."

She let the consenting nods get recorded, grateful to Jack for old lessons in helping bureaucrats cover themselves, then looked sideways at her old boss. "Lemme guess. I go to FundsNet, tell them to start gearing up for the payout. And I don't get to tell them why."

"You got it. And take an FBI field guy with you, shake 'em up a little."

Everyone in the room prayed that this contingency plan would never be implemented. Jack was certain it would be.

"We're back here tomorrow morning at oh nine hundred

with Cavanaugh." Jack eyed everyone around the table. "Any questions?"

"Are you kidding?" Ferguson said sarcastically as he stood up.

"I've got a real one," said Davison, making no move to rise. "Who are you here, Jack?"

"Not sure, Jim." Jack nodded his acknowledgment that he understood what Davison was getting at and that it was a reasonable question. "NTSB usually has primacy, but there's been no accident, so it's unclear. The FBI has a letter of agreement with the board so they can call them—I mean, us—call us into any case, so I got a feeling Pressman and the director are gonna just make this an interagency operation. Probably with the FAA consulting on it."

Nice guess, thought Amy, who already knew the chairman was going to do exactly that and was even now working on the FBI director to lend the NTSB a certain ex-investigator, with or without that ex-investigator's consent.

CHAPTER 5

Watching Lamarr's expression, Bo tried to remember the timeless lines. He could never quite be sure what they were exactly, but he hesitated to look up the poem for fear that the real words were not as good as he liked to remember them. *When* he could remember them.

Lamarr was a good kid. Better than good. But, as with any youth in close proximity to a place like Los Angeles, the pounding waves of his environment could easily overwhelm the pilings of his upbringing. It had happened to better kids. As much as he loved the boy, Bo also knew that losing him to the seamier elements of city life would mean losing himself as well. Lamarr was one of the few reasons Bo bothered to stay alive anymore, knowing that there was still a chance to be of use, to shape a life. To maybe make up for—

"Look!" Lamarr yelled. "Two o'clock!"

Bo could hardly hear him over the roar of the four-cylinder Lycoming engine but saw him point out the front windscreen. He squinted and followed Lamarr's arm with his eyes. There, about two miles to the northeast, a pair of hang gliders balanced motionless in the sky, their fluorescent Rogallo wings gleaming like absurd parrots against the cobalt blue.

Bo looked down at his altimeter. "Those boys are up high. Wanna go play?"

Lamarr looked at him and nodded eagerly. Bo checked out all three windows, as did Lamarr, then gently banked the Cessna 150 trainer first to the left, then to the right, as they looked again. Completing the clearing turn, Bo came left and headed for the gliders. Lamarr strained his head upward to see over the front console.

When they were about a thousand feet away, Bo eased the wheel over and began a long, sweeping turn behind the gliders. When he was sure they had him spotted, he throttled down to the lowest-possible setting short of a stall and crept up slowly, coming up behind them and about five hundred feet to their right. One of them, with a shimmering purple wing, dipped his nose suddenly and dropped, then pulled back up and down again. Bo pushed the wheel forward in response and porpoised the Cessna. Both gliders began leaning into a turn and inched themselves closer to the plane. Bo checked his altitude and heading and held the plane dead steady, letting the gliders choose their relative positions.

"Must be one hell of a thermal, them able to keep up with us like that," he yelled to Lamarr.

Casting an expert eye down and to the right, Lamarr examined the clouds hugging the mountains and hills near the Santa Paula airport. "I think it's ridge lift, Uncle Bo. Lookit those lenticulars and how fast those guys are moving without rising."

By now the two gliders were on either side of the Cessna about two hundred feet off each wing. The pilot on the right raised one gloved hand and waved, and Lamarr waved both hands back in answer. "He sees me!"

Bo looked out his own window and touched a finger to his cap. The glider pilot on his side did the same. For several minutes the three aircraft flew in formation, the gliders squeezing every bit of forward speed they could without descending, Bo straining with the effort of minimum controllable airspeed.

Lamarr was enchanted with the gliders, flimsy-looking contraptions of tubular aluminum, Dacron and some thin wire, whistling almost silently through the vast skies, completely free of whatever lunacy was taking place on the ground.

Bo had taken him to the Grand Canyon once, and they had walked together along the stone parapets of the Kaibob Trail.

Rounding a bend in the narrow pathway, they happened upon a group of several dozen tourists who were standing, silent and motionless, very close to a precipice that dropped straight down to the canyon floor. Bo and Lamarr edged closer to see what could be holding their attention so firmly.

Peering over the edge, they saw a large black hawk, roughly a hundred feet down. It had found a thermal and was circling slowly, its wings perfectly still. With each completion of a circuit, the hawk gained another twenty feet or so of altitude.

After about five minutes the hawk had risen high over the heads of the crowd and not once betrayed any motion of wings or head that anyone could spot. As they craned their necks upward, they could see that the great black bird had run out of rising thermal. Suddenly, with no obvious preparation, it tucked its wings well back along its body, stuck its head out forward and plunged straight down toward the canyon floor at an extraordinary rate of speed.

Lamarr caught his breath and let out an involuntary yelp, certain that the bird had gone crazy from the heat and would hurtle to a horrible death thousands of feet below them. But as the seemingly doomed creature dropped almost out of sight, it abruptly opened its wings straight out, its feathers ruffling wildly in the powerful slipstream. As soon as it caught enough air, the hawk turned several tight circles until its forward and downward speeds both slowed. Before too long, it had resumed its earlier lazy climb upward and, when it was high overhead, once again executed the death dive to repeat the cycle.

Lamarr and Bo watched this display for nearly half an hour, too mesmerized to speak and afraid of disturbing the bird's rhythm if they did. Finally the hawk's upward speed began to diminish in the fading thermal's dwindling force. It flapped its wings several times to break free of the column of air, headed out toward the middle of the canyon and was gone.

The crowd of tourists let out a collective breath and gradually drifted away without speaking. Lamarr blinked once or twice and looked up at Bo. "Why'd he do that, Uncle? What was he doing?"

Bo knew exactly what the bird was doing, and there was nothing romantic or poetic about his answer to Lamarr. "He was just flying. And don't ever let anybody try to tell you different, kid. That bird was just having a good time." Bo believed it with all his heart, as did everybody who had watched the performance.

Bo looked at his watch and was surprised at the time that had passed. He turned the wheel to the left, then to the right and back again several times, waggling the wings. The two gliders did the same, then dove away. When Bo was certain they were clear, he turned the plane southward and pushed in the throttle. Lamarr continued looking out the window to catch a last glimpse of the purple glider as it disappeared into the haze.

"You ready?" Bo yelled. Lamarr turned quickly around and nodded, yanking the bill of his baseball cap until it faced backward on his head, wiping his hands on his pants.

Bo did another clearing turn as Lamarr's hands wrapped themselves around his own control wheel and the tips of his toes found the rudder pedals. "Okay, you got it!" Bo yelled again, and let go of the controls, slapping Lamarr's left hand off the wheel at the same time. Lamarr smiled sheepishly at the rebuke but sobered quickly and flew the plane one-handed with the unwavering seriousness Bo had taught him. He confidently trimmed the elevator, tuned the throttle and twiddled dials with his free left hand, touching and adjusting everything that he was familiar with. ("Fly the damned thing, kid, don't just sit in it: you don't fool with the instruments all the time, you'll never notice when one of them goes on the fritz.") He kept his head on the move constantly, alternately scanning the panel and looking around for traffic.

When Bo had ascertained that Lamarr was settled in, he patted his shoulder, yelled, "You're on your own, kid," and reached down and pulled the lever on the floor, sliding his seat full back to a more comfortable position. "Stay on heading zero three zero at this altitude and come left to zero six zero at the Burbank two eight zero radial."

Lamarr nodded and reached for the radio, changing to the Burbank frequency. With a professional attention to detail even commercial pilots usually ignored, he turned up the volume momentarily to make sure he had the right navigation station tuned in before trying to track the beam. "Burbank

VOR," came the tape-recorded voice, and he turned the volume back down.

It would be a good half hour before they hit the Burbank 280 radial. "Tell me again, Uncle Bo."

"Tell you what?"

"You *know* what. Tell me again how you joined up."

"Can't believe you want to hear that silly story again."

Lamarr turned to shoot him a lip-pursing look of exasperation, and Bo waggled his finger toward the front windscreen until he turned back and resumed his scan. He looked at Lamarr, all skinny arms and stringy legs and unworried innocence, and then he told him.

1944

Beauregard Kincaid had practiced the look in front of a mirror for weeks. His small room was overflowing with movie magazines, pictures with the right look torn out and pinned to the walls. James Stewart in *Destry Rides Again*, John Wayne in *Stagecoach*. Anyone who showed exactly the right amount of confidence, just this side of arrogance, but calm, like they had nothing to prove. Like it would never occur to them to be questioned.

"Eighteen, sir," he said, perhaps for the ten thousandth time. "Born September fifth, nineteen twenty-six." Or, just in case: "September fifth, nineteen twenty-six, sir," without stating his age. Depended on how they asked it.

Not just men. This was no time to give in to stereotypical prejudices. Marlene Dietrich in *The Blue Angel*. Katharine Hepburn in *Woman of the Year*. *Don't even* think *about asking me*. He even had his younger brother shoot three rolls of eight-millimeter movie film using a borrowed camera and badly out-of-date film he'd picked up cheap.

The recruiter had never even looked up, never glanced at Bo's slightly faked papers. It was 1944, and induction officers had stopped caring long ago about the finer points of armed forces recruitment criteria. Especially for colored boys. And most especially for colored boys who scored well on aptitude tests.

Bo stood motionless for a second. All that work, all that practice, and this guy wasn't even going to look at him? For a very small fraction of a second Bo was tempted to force a challenge until reason recaptured him just as the recruiter was starting to wonder what the problem was. But the gangly sixteen-year-old had moved off and was quickly forgotten.

The U.S. Army Air Corps had started admitting blacks—reluctantly—in 1941. Like all other black servicemen, they were kept separated from everybody else throughout the entire war. By the time Bo Kincaid made it into the program, the Army Air Forces Flying Training Program was in full swing at Tuskegee, Alabama.

Doubt was the predominant sentiment regarding the ability of black men to fly airplanes in combat conditions. The withering racism of white instructors in the deep South that led to wholesale and indiscriminate washing out of otherwise qualified black airmen didn't help matters much, but in a twisted Darwinian process it did ensure that only the strongest and fittest survived.

The first to earn pilot's wings was Lieutenant Colonel Benjamin O. Davis, Jr, the first black graduate of West Point in this century and a fiercely determined and strong-willed officer. Davis went on to lead the Ninety-ninth Squadron, one of four comprising the Red Tail Angels, an escort unit assigned to the Fifteenth Air Force.

The Ninety-ninth became the first all-black squadron sent overseas, to Fodjouna in North Africa the year before Bo signed up. Their accomplishments came swiftly, although recognition did not. While the Fifteenth's white bomber crews rapidly came to depend on the Red Tails, word of their heroism and skills was slow in settling in important command quarters. By the end of the war they would have damaged or destroyed over four hundred enemy aircraft without losing a single bomber they escorted over Europe.

The 99th was eventually incorporated into the 332nd Group, and Bo considered the record being compiled by his future compatriots as he awaited his turn in the air. Lieutenant Colonel Davis had accompanied three of his most highly rated officers back to the States to check out the latest graduating class. The best would join the 332nd in the Mediterranean.

The final exam was not a multiple choice questionnaire administered in a classroom. It was combat flying, simulated, but realistic in every aspect other than the use of live ammunition.

Bo ran his hand over the side of his P-51D Mustang, the latest and most advanced model, feeling for telltale wrinkles that might indicate overstress. He didn't know it yet, but it wouldn't have surprised him that the Mustang would come to be regarded as the best piston-powered fighter ever built. Commissioned by the RAF, North American Aviation had produced a working prototype 117 days after the go-ahead. Don Blakeslee, leader of the RAF's Fourth Fighter Group, had begged Major General William Kepner for a few planes for his own squadron. After being refused, he told his boss that he would have the planes in combat within twenty-four hours of delivery. He got his request and sent some of his pilots into the air with as little as forty minutes of flying time in preparation. "You can learn to fly them," he was fond of telling his amazed men, "on the way to the target." It was nearly true.

Bo looked up into the late summer Michigan sky to watch the thirty-seventh dogfight test of the day. His friend Judson Greaves was flying "Junkyard Dog," a C model Mustang, in pursuit of the instructor's B model. The B screamed over the field first, followed about a half mile behind by the C, too far for a good shot from the fifty-millimeter cannons. Greaves was closing in slowly, and as the instructor turned sharply to the left, he followed. Suddenly the B went nose up halfway through the turn, then yawed left with hard rudder, passing over the pursuing fighter trying to keep up.

As Greaves kicked in rudder to point his nose toward his prey, he rapidly lost speed and lift in the awkward position. The instructor's plane stopped its skyward climb, rolled onto its back and nosed earthward, heading straight for Greaves, who managed to right his plane and gain control, only to find the B behind and over him, drilling in for an easy hit. "Rat-a-tat-tat," came the instructor's voice over the field speakers.

Bo looked down, heartbroken. Judson had washed out, and now, even if Bo made it, he'd be heading out without his best friend. "Damn," he muttered to himself.

" 'S'matter, Kincaid?" ask Major Ed Hartley, standing close by.

Bo looked up at the sky where the planes had been but were now gone. "Jud got his tail waxed. He's a good flyer and he flunked."

Hartley laughed. "No, he didn't. He passed. And pretty good, too."

"Sir?"

"That's Davis himself in the B. Never seen him beat yet. But Greaves did real good. He's in for sure."

Davis. No wonder.

"Kincaid!" His name blasted out of the field speakers. "Into the air south-southeast and wait until called."

His training had gone smoothly. Bo was that rarity, a natural pilot, who instinctively felt the physics of airflow and understood in his belly what the effects of a particular control movement would be. He didn't so much sit in the airplane as strap it onto his back, and while most pilots felt a twinge of nervousness in presuming to guide several tons of metal high into the air, Bo truly relaxed only when he felt the huge Merlin engine throb to angry life, the stick grow stiff and heavy in his hands as the wings bit into the air, and the shaking through the rudder pedals suddenly go slack as the wheels left the rough ground.

He was only a few steps away when he wheeled around on impulse and said, "Major!"

Hartley turned to look at him. Bo hesitated only slightly and said, "I want to fight Davis."

Hartley considered him for a moment. Nobody *wanted* to fight Davis. Bo turned and walked away without waiting for an answer.

Within twenty minutes Bo was in the air a few miles from the field, trying to get his timing down. Like a basketball player taking shots before the game, he executed a series of loops, rolls and dives, pulling high G's until he felt his reflexes settle into their comfortable and familiar rhythms. While standard operating procedure called for a full load of fuel, Bo had talked line operations into leaving his tanks seven-eighths empty. The weight advantage would help, unless the instructor stretched out his flight, in which case he would run dry. He also checked the fittings on his parachute one more time. He was going to pull out all the stops on this one and needed to know that bailing out was a real option if it came to that. Even long after the war, when he would own his own P-51, he would never fly it without a 'chute. By that time it would become an FAA regulation for aerobatic flight anyway.

"Kincaid!" The crackle in his headset broke into his thoughts. "Form up over west end of runway with aggressor, heading zero six five until in formation."

Bo took a breath and hiked the plane hard over to head for the field. He took a long, straight approach path in until the B appeared off his left wing. The nose art said "By Request" in black letters on a yellow background.

It was Davis.

They flew in parallel until the command came over their radios. "Break!"

And Davis disappeared.

Bo yanked the stick to the right until his plane was completely on its side, then pulled back hard, initiating a five-G turn that sent him streaking away perpendicular to the runway but less than a hundred feet above it. He needed to buy time to figure out where Davis had gone. It could only have been to the left or up. Or both, the way he had done to Jud.

He straightened out and came left, parallel to his original track but a mile away. He looked out his side window and spotted Davis, three hundred feet up at the five o'clock position. That was bad. With his height advantage, Davis could quickly dive on him and move in for a kill.

Bo pulled back on the stick, pointing his nose nearly straight up, trading speed for altitude. The Mustang climbed rapidly, but its speed diminished quickly as well. Even with the Merlin spinning at full power, the P-51's thrust-to-weight ratio was much less than one. It could not sustain a vertical climb.

But it got him to three thousand feet, and he pulled the plane onto its back, giving him a wide-field view through the top of the canopy. He could only hold that position for a few seconds before the fuel drained back from the pump and into the wing tanks, but it was enough for him to spot Davis in a controlled climb toward him and no more than a thousand feet away.

He nosed over into a vertical dive, then turned the plane until his canopy was facing the B. When he had built up sufficient speed, he pulled the stick into his lap and held his breath against the enormous G forces as his plane leveled out and headed straight for Davis's position at over three hundred miles per hour.

The last thing Davis expected was for Bo to come straight at him, but it was a good move. Bo was moving too fast relative to Davis's position for a clean shot, and the B was forced to snap right and give way in the hope of trying to give pursuit on a return pass. By that time, though, Bo had executed a sharp one eighty, and Davis suddenly found himself with a snarling Mustang on his tail and closing.

Bo knew that some left and right jinking moves were coming, but he also knew that their previous maneuvering had put them two thousand feet above the deck. That meant that Davis was free to dive if he wanted, which would eliminate most of Bo's advantage.

His fast closing speed reminded him that his plane was lighter and therefore faster. Before Davis could make up his mind to dive, Bo suddenly hauled back on the stick and sent his plane rocketing skyward once again, away from the aggressor.

Davis jinked left and right, looking backward to see where Bo was, but there was only empty sky. He flipped the plane over on its back and looked down. Nothing. "Where the hell is this guy?" he yelled without thinking, and it boomed out across the airfield, where it was heard by everybody watching the strange fight.

High above Davis, Bo flipped his own plane over, fixed the other Mustang in his sight and began a screaming dive earthward at a forty-five-degree angle and still upside down. Davis kept the B mostly straight and level, jinking randomly, trying to find Bo.

On the ground, Hartley stood with the just landed Judson Greaves and watched in puzzlement. "That dive's gonna put him too far in front of Davis," he ventured, and the truth of his observation was apparent to everybody.

Still the D plunged downward, still upside down and still headed for a point well ahead of the B. Then they saw Bo, with no control hesitation, suddenly pull the Mustang back and *hold* it back until its nose went down and then came up the other side, so that it was right-side up and heading straight for Davis at an astonishing rate of speed. "Twelve o'clock high and dropping!" came his voice over the speakers for the first time, a brash warning that indicated his confidence in the coming kill.

By the time Davis looked up and out of his windscreen, he had time only to see the D looming large in his field of vision and to hear, "Rat-a-tat-tat, you're dead!" coming through his headset. It was a clean, unambiguous kill, from the front. Bo turned his plane at the last possible moment and sent it skyward once again.

On the ground, the black airmen went wild with delight. Hartley could only shake his head in disbelief. They watched as the beaten B set up for its approach to landing and craned their necks to see Bo high overhead.

Bo felt a shudder as the Merlin coughed and sputtered. A quick glance at the gauges confirmed that all his fuel was gone. As the great, four-bladed prop came to a halt, he set up a spiraling descent over the west end of the field, timing his turns so he would be at about eight hundred feet and half a mile away on the final turn.

"Now that's plain showing off," said Hartley. "Dead-sticking it in."

Finding himself too high on the final turn, Bo dropped his landing gear early to increase drag and lined up for the runway, the usual roar absent as the powerless bird whistled in, touched down and rolled off onto the grass. Bo cranked back the canopy, leaped nimbly onto the wing and down to the ground, then walked slowly toward the small but jubilant crowd. Behind him, Davis was just setting down, and Bo paused to wait for him.

Davis pulled his plane in next to Bo's, got out and then stepped onto the wing of the D that had just waxed him and poked his head into the cockpit. He flipped the master electrical switch up and checked both fuel gauges, then pushed the switch back down.

He jumped to the ground and headed for Bo, who was now surrounded by his smiling and congratulatory friends. They quieted as Davis approached. His face looked stern and not at all amused.

"Son," he bellowed, "you tryin' t'make a monkey outta me?"

Bo stood stiffly at attention and thought for only a second, remembering how Davis had been "silenced" for his entire four-year stay at West Point for no other reason than his race, how he didn't even have a roommate and how he had his own pew in church because none of the other cadets would sit with him, and yet he'd managed to graduate with the top 10 percent of his class. Bo considered all of this and then took his chance. "Yes, sir!" he yelled. "Wasn't that the point, sir?"

Davis gave him one last, murderous look and tilted back his head, laughing at the sky, then stepped forward and held out his hand. Bo took it amid applause and back slapping, the most unabashed admiration coming from Judson Greaves.

That December, Bo and his crewmates celebrated Christmas in Ramitelli, Italy, proud members of Davis's Fighting 332nd.

They flew without speaking for a while, Lamarr occasionally banking the slow-flying trainer to the left and right to watch for overtaking traffic. As they flew into the San Fernando Valley, Lamarr announced, "Burbank two eight zero radial, turning left to zero six zero." He looked back at Bo. "You did mean right when you said left before, din'tcha?"

"Just testing."

"Yeah, baloney."

As Lamarr executed a perfectly timed standard rate turn, Bo reached for his headset and put it on, adjusting the thin boom microphone until it was an inch from the side of his mouth. He tuned in L.A. Approach, waited until there was a break and called in, announcing his tail number and his intentions. "Requesting VFR flight following through the TCA southbound for Catalina." The TCA was a large chunk of restricted airspace over Los Angeles International Airport. No entry was permitted to aircraft flying VFR, visual flight rules, without explicit permission from the controllers, who were normally busy enough with commercial instrument flights.

In the L.A. terminal radar approach control room, TRACON

supervisor Jerry Bradley sat at the hand-off position next to Anthony Carelli, listening in and observing as the newly certified controller handled the "Zuma" sector. The hand-off position was normally used to allow another controller to relieve some of the burden and distraction from the person handling a busy sector. It was equipped with an exact duplicate of all the controls and switches at the main workstation and lacked only a radar screen, which was shared with the sector controller. Carelli had at least two more years to go to become an FPL, a full-performance-level controller. After Zuma, he'd train on Coast sector, then Downey, and so forth down the line until he was capable of handling any of L.A.'s ten radar positions or even two or more simultaneously when traffic was light.

Bradley smiled on hearing Bo's call and reached for a cigarette that wasn't there, the entire TRACON having gone smoke-free the year before, much to the consternation of several of the veteran staff. He keyed his mike by depressing the long footbar on the floor, cutting into Carelli's frequency. After acknowledging the request and Bo's tail number, he said, "Standby one," and then said to Carelli, "Handle it alone?"

"Sure," said Carelli. There were only four inbounds in his sector, all under instrument flight rules, and several VFR flights that had declined to establish radio contact. That was their right, as long as they stayed above the TCA boundaries.

Bradley turned back and rekeyed the mike, calling up the Cessna. "Frequency change approved to sideband monitor one-niner. Over."

"Roger," Bo answered, leaning forward and flipping off the built-in com unit. He reached into his flight bag and pulled out a small portable radio, then plugged the connecting cord into a receptacle in the console. He tripped the power switch, turned on the cockpit speaker and waited.

Back in the radar room, Bradley lifted his coffee cup out of the special holder at the base of the work surface: the rules forbade setting it down anywhere else, for fear of spilling anything into the delicate innards of the workstation. As he stood, Carelli gave him a sideways look. "What's with this 'sideband one-niner' shit all the time, anyway?"

"Need-to-know basis only, son," Bradley answered in lowered tones. "Keep a sharp eye."

He walked the length of the eerily dark room, which was illuminated almost entirely by the glow from the switches, dials and keyboards at the radar positions. The light in the room was so dim that everything a controller might need to see had to have its own light source, usually tiny lamps shining beneath color-coded, translucent control surfaces. The bank of workstations was a wild profusion of red, green, yellow and blue Christmas lights surrounding each of the large radar screens that served as the focus of each station, the circular sweep of the green lines on their faces providing the only discernible motion.

Bradley went into the equipment and supplies room and closed the door behind him. On the table was a radio unit about the size of a small television set, powered up and waiting as it always was. It was an old tube model, and the stress on its components of heating up and cooling down was much worse than simply leaving it on all the time so it could stay at a constant operating temperature. Bradley lit a cigarette, blew the smoke toward an air vent and picked up the microphone.

"Hey, Bo, what's shakin', man?"

"Hey, Omar, whaddya know?"

"Same ol', same ol', you know how it goes." Bradley settled onto the worn leather chair and put his feet up on the table. "Goddamned feds cut another three of my staff this week. How'm I supposed to keep you maniacs from slamming into each other, tell me, I wanna know?"

"Never needed you featherbedders in the first place. Don't come cryin' t'me."

"Yeah, right. That brat kid got the stick again?"

Lamarr smiled as Bradley's voice came over the cockpit speaker. "Tell him to stick it in his ear, Uncle Bo."

"Tell him yourself." Bo leaned forward until his boom microphone was close enough to Lamarr's face.

"Stick it in your ear, Omar!" Lamarr yelled.

"Nice, Kincaid. Nice how you're teaching the kid to crack wise. And while he's flying yet."

"Yeah, well, you take care, Omar."

"You take care, Bo."

They broke off, and Bo disconnected the portable, restowing it in his flight bag. The best skill he'd picked up at Cutter Aviation, and the one he seemed to have the most aptitude for, was electronics. He'd built the little portable himself, completely from scratch, and reconstructed Bradley's ancient table model out of spare parts. "One eighty and home, kid," he said into Lamarr's ear, declining to finish the rest of the story this time. It was too nice a day to bring up the bad part. The boy knew it and didn't press.

Lamarr nodded and banked the plane steeply, pulling back slightly on the wheel to compensate for the reduced lift. Man and child wafted across the limitless sea of air, buoyed as much by their faith in each other as by the immutable laws of physics and the thin metal cocoon that enclosed them.

"You really need to go out of town, Uncle Bo?"

" 'Fraid I do."

"Get some spare parts?"

"Yep. Spare parts."

" 'Lectronics, I bet, huh? Radio stuff?"

Bo nodded, then pointed at the panel until the young pilot turned his head back to his instruments and remembered to fly the plane. He looked out at the achingly beautiful blue sky and back at Lamarr, idly placed two fingertips lightly on the side window, and then he remembered the lines that spoke for every pilot who couldn't find his own words:

Oh, I have slipped the surly bonds of Earth . . .
Put out my hand, and touched the face of God.

CHAPTER 6

May 11, 0900 EST

L etitia May Hubbard looked like anything other than what she was.

A black woman on the back slope of middle age, of below average height, possessed of a physiognomy of little apparent grace that had been a lifelong stranger to athletic activity of most any sort, she was correctly characterizable as a frump and dressed accordingly. Today she sported an undistinguished cotton dress, of a light fabric covered in a profusion of gaily colored flowers of no known phylum, topped with a turbanlike affair of similarly undifferentiated flora. Set against wire-rimmed bifocals and the costume jewelry earrings she'd picked up for $3.95 while waiting to retrieve her 1978 Pinto at the car wash, the overall sartorial presentation was quite consistent in its depiction of a Louisiana kindergarten teacher or a Baptist preacher's doting wife or a librarian.

Abelard Fedder, senior senator from Tennessee and head of the Senate Select Committee on Aviation Policy, rose from his seat and pointed a bony finger across the table. "I tell you here and now, *here and now*, nobody"—his well-modulated voice rose five decibels and half an octave to lend weight to the repetition—"*nobody* holds this country hostage, and I don't give a good tinker's damn what kind of button he's got his dad-blamed finger on!"

The impact of his eruption was palpably intimidating, and nobody was willing to break the embarrassed silence he had brought about.

Almost nobody.

"Oh, hush the hell up, Abelard," scolded Letitia May Hubbard, secretary of the U.S. Department of Transportation, waving a dismissive hand in the air. "My word, man, people hold us hostage all the damned time, so what's all the fussin' an' fumin' about?"

Amy Goldberg's face was bright red from the effort to keep from laughing. She was about to lose the struggle and turned away to cough into her hand. The other officials and the airline executive had more practice in the control of their emotional behavior, but they sympathized completely with Amy's predicament in light of Hubbard's black version of Senator Sam Ervin's "jes' a po' country lawyer" act, an act that fooled few who knew either of them well.

Fedder was doubly skewered, once by the rapier public put-down and again by the refutation of his stated premise. "What—what in God's name—?" he spluttered helplessly. "Not true, Madame Secretary! Why, how can you insinuate such a thing?"

"Oh, please." The feisty matron shifted her dowdy bulk and leaned into her point. "They do it all the damned time. Every time an American is kidnapped, every time some two-bit celebrity gets a new cause up his butt and starts mouthing off to the newspapers, every time some special-interest group parades a bunch of 'victims' around—Lord A'mighty, Senator, three weeks ago you threatened to sink Willy Blanchfort's environmental protection bill, he didn't vote for another air force base in your state, you don't call that a gun to our heads?" She paused and sat back, tapping the file on the table in front of her. "At least this sumbitch's being up front about it."

Most of the people in the room were aware of Hubbard's reputation, but few had seen her in action. One who hadn't was G. Preston Stanley, assistant deputy director of the FBI, who looked at the moment as if his skin couldn't possibly contain the stretch around his widened eyes.

Many insiders considered Hubbard one of the most powerful people in Washington, not because of her law degree from Harvard, or the extraordinary story of her rise from bayou obscurity, or the competence and common sense she brought to bear on her job, but because she possessed two characteristics that nobody else of similar stature in the entire governmental infrastructure possessed. First, she didn't need the job. Second, she didn't give a damn if she lost it.

Not that she wasn't interested or didn't feel it was important. It was simply that nothing was so important that it warranted taking crap from posturing politicians, aspiring aides and self-aggrandizing special-interest groups. And so she didn't.

Prior to the meeting, in small groups of one or two as they showed up, the participants were briefed on the basics of the current crisis, or at least what the basics were yesterday when it all began. To the original group meeting in Conference Room G were now added Hubbard, Stanley and Sam Cavanaugh, chief executive officer of one of the largest airlines in the country.

Senator Fedder stared at Secretary Hubbard openmouthed, too flabbergasted to resume his diatribe. Never one to belabor a point, Hubbard turned her attention back to the table at large. "What do y'all say we let these good people finish what they have to tell us before we go try and save the Union from pernicious damnation." It was an order, not a request. She acknowledged the murmured "Yes, ma'ams" and "Certainly, Madame Secretarys" and nodded at Jack Webster.

"Thank you, ma'am. We've got one of our field people on the line from Washington State, and I'm going to put him on the speaker so he can brief you, and then we can let him off to continue his work. We sent him out to participate in the examination of the affected airliner."

Jack pushed a button on the small panel in front of him and was met with an answering squeal. He turned down the volume and moved the microphone pad away from the speaker. "Victor, you with us?"

"Yeah—uh, yes," came the tinny voice. Even over the speakerphone, the awed hesitancy came across clearly.

"Go ahead. You already know who's here. Just start right in."

"I'll make this short unless there are any questions." A ruffling of papers could be heard over the speaker. "We found no evidence of any tampering with the plane. Both navigational units were pulled out and sent to the manufacturer, which is fortunately nearby in Redmond. I'm there now, and standard diagnostics have come up completely empty. The black boxes should have gotten to you yesterday, Mr. Webster."

"We got 'em. Jess Willett ran a quick prelim just to see. It looks like what the pilots said they saw was really on their screens. Both navigation units with identical readings. Both wrong."

There was a pause at the other end. "And there's nothing so far on the ground stations, which have had complete operational checks, top to bottom. So what we discussed last night is all I can think of."

Jack looked around the room. "Any questions?"

The FBI field agent leaned over the table. "Uh, Vic—" He looked over at Jack. "What's his last name?"

Jack shrugged and looked at Amy, whose eyebrows began to rise in ignorance, when Secretary Hubbard waved in annoyance at Stanley's concern with formality.

Stanley caught the impatience and continued. "Vic, this is Preston Stanley of the Bureau. Have there been any more incidents on that approach?"

"No, sir. The radar controllers suspended all approaches except in visual conditions, but instrument readings have been nominal, so they resumed full instrument authority this morning."

Stanley chewed his lip as he thought. "I might suggest that both those nav units be kept out of any airplanes for the time being."

"Affirmative." Vic subconsciously lapsed into militaryese while addressing the agent. "Soon as the 727 inspection is complete, it'll get replacement units, and we'll hang on to these."

"Anything else?" asked Jack.

Heads shook around the table. Jack turned back to the

microphone. "Thanks, Vic. Well done and stay close to it. You get anything at all, call in immediately." He tapped off the speakerphone.

Jack pursed his lips and stared down at the table before speaking. This was not a group of people that dealt well with great quantities of the unknown. Regardless of the situation, they, like most people in positions of authority, needed a constant influx of intelligence, scraps of information, uninterrupted streams of input, to feel that progress was being made. The quality and reliability of that information was almost beside the point: as long as they were surrounded by the steady buzz of data, they were in control, because as long as the stuff came pouring in, there was always a chance that the next scrap could be the key piece.

In the absence of same, a discomfort took hold, at first just the familiarly queasy feeling of being lost at sea, like a bad dream in which everyone knew what was going on except you. Later, that feeling could develop into a nameless dread, the bureaucratic nightmare that your carefully constructed empire was only so much straw, about to come apart under the withering glare of public scrutiny and the blistering heat of attack from other, equally insecure bureaucrats who seized any opportunity to bask in your suffering as a deflection of their own. (The Germans called rejoicing over another's misery *Schadenfreude*, and there was no English equivalent, although the concept was as familiar to D.C. bureaucrats as breathing.) The canniest underlings kept their bosses bombarded with data, however trivial, in a headlong attempt to hold their fear in check.

Those in positions of responsibility, like Jack, struggled to formulate hypotheses and develop action plans, knowing that should they inadvertently allow a vacuum of ideas to evolve, elected and appointed officials would fill it with self-serving, and thus inevitably counterproductive, notions of their own. This was to be avoided at all costs.

And Jack could sense the dread starting to develop as the brilliance of their adversary began to contrast with their own shortcomings.

"Our best thinking so far, and the only possibility we've

come up with other than the pilots lying or going crazy, is that somehow the guy got to the software charts."

FAA assistant director Bob Ferguson caught it immediately. "The plates? You mean he altered the database?"

Amy jumped in, hoping it would annoy Ferguson. "That's what it looks like." For the benefit of Stanley and the other non-aviation-oriented around the table, she explained. "To fly an approach on instruments, you need a chart that shows the navigational aids that you use to fix your position. Most pilots use the printed form, clipped to the steering yoke so it's right there in front of you."

She inclined her chin toward Sam Cavanaugh of Alpha Airlines, who had thus far stayed silent. "On sophisticated aircraft, like a lot of commercial jets, the 'plate' isn't on paper but is downloaded into an on-board computer and displayed on a screen mounted in the console. All the frequencies, distances and timings are provided on the database, so the computer essentially tells you where you are, when to turn, when to descend and so forth.

"It seems our guy may have gotten to the database at the manufacturer of the nav units and fiddled with the numbers."

"But that would affect every plane in the country using that unit," Ferguson protested. "Whose did you say it was? Autonav's?" To Amy's answering nod he added. "Hell, they got over seventy percent market share. Why isn't everyone blowing the Bellingham approach?"

"Maybe the Lear had another brand?" ventured his aide, Louis Melnick.

Amy saw no need to cream him. "That's a good thought, so we checked. They've got Autonav, too."

"Then I don't get it. If you're right, how come only one of them went off track?"

Ferguson snapped his fingers. "The Lear! Maybe our guy was in the Lear!"

Amy shook her head. "Another good idea, but the Lear was bound for Vancouver and diverted at the last minute because of weather. We checked with the controller who handled the flight, and it turns out he himself suggested Bellingham. The pilot originally had Seattle as an alternate in his flight plan."

Jack leaned forward and folded his hands in front of him. "We think maybe the software was altered to respond to a signal from the ground. And before you ask, no, we don't know how that signal got to the 727 and not the Lear. That's the one mystery has us completely stumped." His choice of words was deliberate, as though they had only one mystery.

Hubbard listened carefully to the conversation around the table before asking her own question. "Ms. Goldberg, how often are these units reloaded? Things change, don't they? The stuff must get outdated."

"You're getting to the good news, ma'am. It doesn't matter how much of what's in there changes, the entire database is downloaded into every plane every month, no matter what."

"Hold it a second," said DOT deputy undersecretary Jim Davison. "If that's the case, why did he wait until May ten to pull his stunt? Why not do it right after the data was loaded?"

"Ah!" Amy said excitedly. "That's one of the things that lends credence to our current theory." She turned to include the rest of the people gathered around the table. "He had to wait until the weather turned bad in the Bellingham vicinity. It had been nothing but clear skies since May first. He needed a full-scale front to move in, not just some scattered clouds, to make sure that the reduced visibility would be there the morning after he sent the letter. The 727 incident took place on May ten." She rooted around in the papers in front of her and came up with a faxed weather map. "That was just two days after a mass of cold Canadian air drifted south to mingle with warm, moist air in Puget Sound. And since there had been plenty of rotten weather all throughout April that he didn't take advantage of, we figure the 'mole' software got in during the last update, which was the beginning of May, and the guy waited until the first opportunity, which was the tenth."

The secretary was nodding her head in impatient agreement. "Yeah, I get that. But you said the Autonav people couldn't find anything wrong with the data."

"That's true." Amy didn't understand where this was going and was concerned that she hadn't explained things in lay terms very well.

"Well, I'm betting the 'good news,' way you put it, is that next month everybody gets a whole new load o' these electronic plates, and the mole is gone." Amy nodded an acknowledgment at Hubbard's grasp of the technology and wasn't fooled by her down-home act. "But your people can't find out what's wrong with the stuff they got now, what makes you think it's gonna be any different next month?"

There were some audible grunts and sighs of dismay around the room as Hubbard's point was made. Amy milked the moment for a second or two before replying. "Right now, all of the information is sitting in a giant database at Autonav's facility. Changes come in, the database is changed accordingly. So, you're correct, any mole software sitting in it now would probably not be flushed out.

"But—" She leaned back in her chair and tapped two fingers on the table several times. "We're going to have Autonav erase the database entirely and reinput every bit of information from scratch. That will absolutely guarantee a virgin copy in the next download."

"How long will that take?" asked Stanley.

Jack consulted his notes of Vic's private phoned-in report from Autonav's Redmond plant that had preceded his speak-erphone briefing. "The entire month. The task of reinputting everything is gigantic. In fact"—he turned to Secretary Hub-bard and then to Ferguson—"you're going to have to put a complete freeze on changes to all navigational aids, proce-dures and airways. No way Autonav can keep up with those and re-create the database at the same time."

Ferguson nodded. "Except for emergency situations, we can do that. What you're saying, this guy can't hurt us after the next download."

"No," said Hubbard. "What they're saying is he can't hurt us if their theory is correct." She didn't wait for confirmation of this. "And you still don't know how they hit the 727 without getting the Lear." Jack and Amy both nodded.

Deputy Undersecretary Davison spoke up. "Maybe he indi-vidually coded each download set. Then he could beam up the code and only the plane with the right key would get hit?"

"Thought of that," said Amy. "Problem is, he'd have no way to know which plane got which set. The downloads are distributed on plug-in cards. They're all identical, so the operations people just grab a bunch and start plugging them in."

There was little more to be said about the method. Senator Fedder, feeling it safe to step back into the water, ventured a question on a new tack. "We know anything at all about this—this terrorist, this Captain Marvel?"

Jack took an immediate dislike to the moniker. His limited FBI experience had taught him that applying cute labels to vicious and amoral sociopaths had a subtle but discernible effect on the perceptions of not only the public, but the pursuers. It tended to dull the sharp edge of hatred and fear that was so necessary in maintaining motivation among the law enforcement personnel assigned the task of investigation and apprehension.

On the other hand, he had been staying alert for a way to reengage Fedder. Things were going to be difficult enough without having an insulted and ridiculed U.S. senator trying to score points in retribution. So he repeated it, "Captain Marvel!" and laughed, looking around the room, which permitted others to laugh as well, along with Fedder instead of at him.

Fedder smiled. He hadn't meant to start anything, but he was quick to capitalize on the opportunity Jack had thrown him to reassimilate himself into the mainstream of the group dynamic that had almost ostracized him. And now Jack had at least one high-level favor sitting in his kip.

Jack addressed Fedder directly. "We know one thing damned important. It pretty much has to be an Autonav employee, and one who was there during the last month and had access to the database."

"Nope," said Letitia May Hubbard from somewhere out of left field.

"Ma'am?" prompted Jack.

"Coulda been years ago."

Jack exchanged a cautionary look with Amy.

"If I get the secretary's drift," ventured Samuel Cavanaugh, president and chief executive officer of Alpha ("the First Word in Air Travel") Airlines, "what she's saying, the mole could have been planted in the database anytime after the last time it was completely entered from scratch. The guy just decided to trigger it now."

Jack reeled inwardly with sudden understanding. He could see from Amy's face that she was thinking the same. "My hat's off to you, Madame Secretary. That one shot by us."

"No matter. But we should probably find out when that was, eh?"

"Indeed." Jack considered the implications. "Sure widens the scope of our search."

"Like you said, Captain Marvel ain't no dummy." Hubbard considered Jack's crestfallen look. "C'mon now, don't you be fadin' on us, Mr. Webster. What're we lookin' for, anyhow?"

Jack cleared his throat and his mind and looked back up. "Disgruntled employees, people fired or laid off, those with not only the technical skills but the access to pull this off. We've got people who are going to go over the old database bit by bit so we know how it was done, and that might give us some clues."

"I'm troubled by this five-million-dollar demand," said Cavanaugh, ever the practical businessman. "This can't be about money, or Captain Marvel knows a lot about nav systems and damned little about the real world."

"What are you thinking?" asked Stanley.

He shrugged. "I'm not sure. Either there's another motivation somewhere, or he's not pushing it because he's got other plans for after this wad of money is paid off."

"He's got a lot of work to do just to get this wad in fourteen days," said Amy.

Cavanaugh nodded thoughtfully. "I know. But something doesn't ring right here. Goldberg, you used to do psy-ops: any possibility we've got a mad serviceman here, somebody used to work on navy or air force navigation systems?"

Now how the hell did he know that about me? "I don't think so. We've got experience with military types who crack up, go for revenge, but almost all of it has been directed at military targets."

Fedder was fidgeting and leaned his elbows on the table. "Well, I'm sure these NTSB folks know what they're doin', and I assume"—he cast a glance at Stanley and Jack and then at Amy—"that interagency cooperation will be at a high level

on this thing. . . ." He waited for answering nods from the
three of them. In fact, the two FBI men had barely met each
other and hadn't even had time to discuss the matter yet. "So
I also assume that the investigation is well in hand and you
don't need all o' these people settin' around tellin' you how
t'do your jobs, am I right?" Fedder had one advantage over
Hubbard in his situation: the Department of Transportation
had no influence whatsoever over the activities of the NTSB,
which reported directly to Congress.

"Reasoned input is always welcome, Senator," said Jack,
casting a sidelong glance at Hubbard.

"Fine, fine. But now I wanna know, what're we going to
do about Captain Marvel's demands in the meantime."

Sam Cavanaugh spoke without hesitation. "We're going to
pay, Senator."

"The hell we are, Mr. Cavanaugh."

"There isn't any choice." Cavanaugh now knew why he
was here. As an executive he appreciated the strategy. "Look,
none of us here likes being pushed around, but we're all savvy
enough to know when somebody else is holding all the cards.
We don't know a damned thing about Captain Marvel—no
offense, Webster—"

Jack held up a "none taken" hand.

"—except that he can probably bring down a plane full of
people anytime the weather's right. We've got to play along
until we've got something hard to deal with. And the money's
got to come from us. More specifically, from me."

"Why Alpha?" Davison asked innocently. "You weren't
threatened specifically. He just used one of your planes as a
demo."

Cavanaugh didn't rebuke the undersecretary for his failure
to grasp the implications. "Because I'm the only one can keep
it quiet without it seeming like a cover-up."

"And your pilots?" asked Hubbard. "Are you going to tell
them?"

"Not unless you want the public to know, Madame Secretary. There are thousands of pilots we'd have to tell, and that
secret'll last about an hour, if we're lucky."

"Let's at least give 'em the sunspot story," suggested Ferguson. Sunspots were to meteorologists what viruses were to

doctors: a technical-sounding catch-all filler for when you hadn't the foggiest notion of what was really going on. "We can tell 'em to be extra alert for anomalies and to report them in. That way we at least have some flying professionals on the lookout for us."

"I agree," said Jack, fully aware that it was useless but would at least be on the record as a good faith attempt to contain the situation.

"Are we concluded?" asked Hubbard, meaning, *"We are concluded."*

"I think so," said Jack. "Preston, could you stick around for a couple of minutes?" The FBI veteran nodded.

Hubbard put the wraps on the formal portion of the meeting. "Ms. Goldberg, the NTSB have any problem workin' with the FBI on this one, lettin' Mr. Webster here keep his hand on the tiller? I'll cede whatever rights the FAA has to this team and handle oversight personally."

"Sounds reasonable," Amy replied without hesitation, ignoring the withering looks not only from Jack, for his personal reasons, but from the FAA people for the loss of turf. Having the FBI in charge was a good idea, since their resources were deeper and more geared to this kind of work. The NTSB frequently called the Bureau in anyway when criminal activity was suspected, just as they called in customs, the DEA, border patrol and anybody else with relevant skills and jurisdiction. And keeping the central operation at NTSB headquarters would make logistics more convenient, owing to the established connections with all facets of the aviation community. But she wouldn't have agreed to any of it if Jack Webster weren't the man in charge.

Seeing that protest was useless, Jack decided on the spot he might as well appear to jump in and do it right. "Absolutely. We'll set up a command post here and clear all information through it."

Hubbard nodded in approval. "I've got a cabinet meeting tomorrow morning. I'm going to take the president aside and brief him. If we need him to mobilize something big, I don't want it to be a surprise." She pushed back her chair and stood up. "Whatever you need, Webster . . ." she finished, and left with the others.

Jack, Amy and Preston Stanley watched them all head out. When they were gone, Jack turned to face Stanley.

"We might have some overlapping authority here, Preston."

Stanley held up one hand, palm facing Jack. "It's yours. This stuff is out of my league. You honcho from here, let me handle the fieldwork."

"Fair enough. What we want is a core of, let's say, five agents and access to the field. Only thing I can't guarantee, they get busy immediately. We need something more to track."

Stanley nodded. "Two of my locals are pilots, one with a commercial ticket. We'll start with them. And your access is me. I'll brief the director before the end of today."

He stood to leave and paused at the door. "Hey, Webster: You know we tried to recruit Goldberg here two years ago? Said she didn't like guns!" He snorted and walked out the door.

Jack turned toward Amy. "That so?"

She turned up one corner of her mouth and shrugged. "You woulda got stuck with my sorry ass either way, boss." The FBI had wanted her for her expertise in psychological warfare and related skills—psy-ops—and that's why she'd turned them down. She wondered if Stanley had let that slip to Cavanaugh or if the executive had found it out on his own. She also wondered if he knew why she'd left, then decided that wasn't possible. It was a purely personal matter, no great trauma, no special, dramatic event.

"Horseshit. Don't let the cooperation act fool you. Soon as Pressman gets back, I'm gone."

He sounded even less convinced than before.

CHAPTER 7

Amy Goldberg was acutely aware of how she looked as she entered the FundsNet operations building. About five-eight, she was not tall enough to be considered imposing, but she surpassed petite by a comfortable margin. Keeping fit had always been a priority, albeit a dreaded one. Exercise bored her nearly to tears, but her schedule had never allowed her to participate in more stimulating competitive sports that required adherence to a timetable.

She had tried running for a while and, as nearly everybody in that activity did eventually, had overdone it, graduating to ever-longer distances, straining joints and ligaments past the point of reasonable benefit and losing weight no matter how much she ate. When a co-worker had discreetly suggested counseling for *anorexia nervosa*, she'd considered the enormous quantities of food she had been eating while running seventy miles a week and decided to switch sports. She'd hesitantly entered a local, short-distance triathlon and begun light training in bicycling and swimming in addition to a greatly reduced running program. She soon found that the rotating combination of the three activities, together with a basic weight-training routine, provided some relief from tedium. After a year, the change in the shape of her body was so gratifying that she stuck with it, despite the difficulties of keeping it up in Washington, a city with a winter season. And dressing her new shape was getting to be fun, too.

These thoughts ran through her mind at this moment, but not out of vanity, of which she possessed very little. In fact, she didn't remember giving this much thought to her appearance in a very long while. She just couldn't help it, because she'd just met Florence Hartzig, and all of the preceding had occurred to her in a flash between the time she saw the face and accepted the outstretched hand.

Florence Hartzig was—*There's a word for this*, Amy thought—hard to describe. She was about Amy's height, maybe even a touch taller, although the overall effect of her appearance was to make her seem much shorter. Her body had clearly emerged from the days since her birth unscathed by any superfluous physical activity of any sort, and her hair was obviously on the backside of whatever multiday rotational schedule she maintained for washing it.

Her clothes betrayed care in their choosing only insofar as they did nothing to detract from the dominating effect of her body shape. *What the hell is that word*? A loose-fitting, silklike pullover top barely disguised the shapelessness of the breasts underneath, and her sagging behind was perfectly complemented by the sagging pants. Amy didn't see but instead sensed sensible shoes down there somewhere, was not at all surprised by the dark-framed glasses and, if forced to make a positive statement about something, could look favorably upon rather nice-looking skin, probably a fortuitous result of genetics rather than conscious attention.

By the time she spotted a bulky calculator in a vinyl pouch hanging from a belt, she thought she knew pretty much everything she needed to know about Florence Hartzig. She was— *A nerd! That's it, that's the word!* Had there been a Band-Aid wrapped around the bridge of Florence's glasses, Amy could not have contained herself. She took the offered hand, which was firm in its grip, and looked directly into her eyes. She was surprised at their brightness and at the laugh lines that seemed out of place on the face of someone who she had automatically assumed was not a happy person. She also noticed a wedding band.

"It's nice to meet you," the face was saying. "They didn't tell me there were such pretty women in that bastion of male superiority over there."

"What—?" Amy was momentarily nonplussed by Florence's openness and candor. She blushed. "Oh. Yes, there are. No, no, I mean, thank you, that's—very nice. You, uh—" *Dammit, get a grip here!*

Florence smiled and took Amy by the arm. "Let's get you a pass and head for my office." She had Amy sign in at the reception desk and show her NTSB identity card, which had been precleared before her arrival. The security guard handed her a laminated card that read "FundsNet Operations—Visitor" in bright red letters, with a clip attached at one end. Amy hung it off her jacket lapel, and they were buzzed through the heavy, windowless door.

Florence's office was large and airy, with a conference table big enough for six and an enviable view out a broad bay window. Amy already knew that Florence was something of an anomaly in the otherwise staid and stuffy financial concern. Essentially, she was the dreaded "key man," the one kind of employee the book said you were never supposed to allow to exist. Florence was the only person alive who completely understood the insanely complicated, labyrinthine intricacies of the computer systems that constituted the company's only truly valuable asset. While nobody liked the idea of being so wholly dependent on one person, the essential truth was that FundsNet could not exist without her. It used to be that computers sat in the back room to provide support for the primary business of an enterprise. Today, and especially in financial institutions, it was frequently the case that the computer system itself *was* the service.

It had taken ten months of negotiation with Lloyd's of London to craft an insurance policy on her, not simply on her life, but for "involuntary and irreversible cessation of services." She also owned a surprisingly large number of shares, with a program of graduated vesting of more shares that would make it extremely costly for her to leave. It was a sign of corporate management's

complete misunderstanding of what motivated her, which had
little to do with money.

Something about the abbreviated background check Amy
did on Florence led her to disregard Jack's order to take along
an agent. Florence was a lone eagle, intensely self-motivated
and absent any easily exploitable desire to please superiors.
Amy sensed that any thinly veiled attempt at intimidation
would backfire badly. She looked around at the workspace,
overflowing with printouts, technical manuals, books unre-
lated to her job, two personal computers, credit card statements
and many other personal effects. It was clear Florence spent
a good deal of time here. "Nice digs. All you need is a cot
and a refrigerator and you'd never have to leave."

Florence opened a bottom cabinet and pointed inside.
"Already got the 'fridge. And *Mr*. Hartzig cuts me a lot of
slack, but sleeping away from home isn't part of it. Want
something cold?"

"Sure. Any plain water?"

"No problem." She pulled out a bottle of designer mineral
water and opened a glass door at eye level, drawing out two
crystal tumblers. She brought the bottle and the glasses to the
table and sat down. "So. What's with all the mystery?"

Amy poured some water and took a sip, looking at Florence
over the top of the glass, trying to determine how much to
tell her. Florence's clear blue eyes looked back at her calmly.
Amy set the glass down and withdrew a printed sheet from
her briefcase. "First, I have to ask you to sign this. It's a
confidentiality agreement."

Florence took the paper and began to read. After a minute
Amy said, "No big deal, just a standard agreement not to
discuss this matter."

Florence nodded while she read. "I'm sure, but I've never
seen it before. And it doesn't make sense."

"What?"

"It says I can't talk about anything you tell me. But what
if something you tell me I already know? Or is already in the
public domain?"

"I, uh, I'm not sure on that one."

"And what if some governmental or judicial body calls on
me to testify, or asks me to submit evidence or an affidavit?

Do I violate this agreement if I comply? What if I'm the subject of a lawsuit and proving my innocence depends on revealing this information?" She stated it simply, without malice or sarcasm.

Amy was flustered. She'd always found it so much easier dealing with psychopathic maniacs than with calmly intelligent cynics. "I don't know. It's never come up before."

Florence shrugged her shoulders and tapped her fingers on the piece of paper. "You leave it with me, I'll amend it and then sign it."

"But I don't know if I can do that. Look, it's just a standard agreement, everybody signs it."

Florence rested the side of her head on two fingers, elbow on the table. "Y'know, I had a friend once, former CIA guy. He signed an agreement like this without thinking about it. Then he wrote a book about some of his experiences, and the CIA took him all the way to the Supreme Court. Now the poor bastard can't even write out a shopping list without giving the Agency the right to approve it."

Amy didn't like being one-upped. "Well, it's real simple, then. I can't tell you anything about what's going on."

"Gee, that's too bad. I did *so* want to know. That's why I begged you to come here."

Amy stared hard at Florence, saw the laugh starting to form around her lips and then laughed herself. "You kinda got me there."

Florence poured herself some water. "Believe me, I'm not a hard-ass, and I'll help you if I can. But I won't sign a piece of paper just because it's put in front of me. And anything you tell me about what the words *really* mean but that you won't write down? Far as I'm concerned, you never said it."

Amy considered Florence for a second, then took the sheet of paper and put it back into her attaché case. "We've got a problem, and I only want to tell you what you need to know for you to help, and no more. And you shouldn't ask me anything unless you need to."

Florence nodded and settled back on her chair as Amy went on. "We need to pay five million dollars to someone using FundsNet ATMs. Your management has already approved it."

Florence raised her eyebrows.

"Someone else is guaranteeing the funds. All we need from you is the access. The guy we need to pay gave us specific instructions on how to set it up. This"—Amy pulled another sheet from her case—"is a retyped transcript of the original instructions." She handed the sheet to Florence and gave her some time to read it, which she did in silence.

When Amy saw that she had finished and was going over it again, she said, "We figure the guy must be intimately familiar with how these things work." It was one of their stronger leads, and she wanted to gauge Florence's reaction.

The computer whiz tugged at her lip and shook her head without looking up. "Nah, not really. You could come up with this knowing only what you read in *Business Week*. It's clever conceptually, but not sophisticated technically."

"You mean for you or normal people?" *Shit!* "I mean people not as computer literate as you."

Florence looked up. "The guy probably has a good technical background, but I'd be surprised if his ability to concoct this little scheme provides you with any useful clues about him." To Amy's disappointed look she added, "But its execution might be used to trip him up." She waved the sheet in the air. "Did you get all of this?"

"The gist, I think."

Florence got up and walked to the whiteboard, using a paper towel to erase the existing scribbles. She took up a black felt tip marker and drew some simple diagrams. "An ATM has a little computer inside of it. When you swipe your card through the reader, that computer runs the display, asks for your personal identification number—the PIN—and what you want to do: deposit, inquire, withdraw, whatever.

"Suppose you want to withdraw some cash. The built-in computer doesn't know the status of your account. Remember, there are thousands and thousands of these things scattered all over the continent, serving millions of users who have accounts in several thousand banks. You couldn't fit all that information in a little computer and then duplicate it in a hundred thousand others, and you certainly couldn't keep all of them updated with millions of new transactions."

Amy nodded. "I understand. So?"

Florence turned back to the board. "So the little computer

makes a telephone call. There are regular phone lines running into each ATM. It calls up our central computer, which is located in Kansas City."

"Why there? Why not here, at headquarters?"

"Because Kansas is close to the center of the United States, which keeps the lines nice and short. And the taxes are lower and labor is cheaper. That's why a lot of the airline reservation systems are there as well."

"Okay, so the ATM makes a phone call . . ."

"Right. Our machines know who all the subscribers are, and what their PINs are. When the call comes in here, our machine makes a call to the bank where the user has his account, checks for funds availability and then tells the bank's computer to debit the account for the amount being withdrawn. Then it shoots a message back to the ATM that allows it to give out the money. Understand so far?"

"Does that explain why it seems to take so long? I always thought computers were lightning fast and never knew why it sometimes seems to take forever."

"The computer could start counting out money a fraction of a second after you enter the information. It's the phone call that takes time, and if the lines are slow, or there is a misconnect and a retry, you could be there for several minutes."

"So now I *am* confused. Our guy wants the money to come pouring out immediately. How do you get around the phone call problem?"

Florence came back to the table and sat down. "That's where he does get a bit clever. It seems he got himself an ATM card, probably stolen or discarded or something like that. He gives us the card number and a PIN." She looked back at the transcript. "We're supposed to reprogram the little computer in the ATM. That's easy, we can do it from here and load the new program down to every ATM in a couple of days."

"And what's this new program supposed to do?"

"As soon as it detects that particular card and that particular PIN, it immediately spits out a hundred twenty-dollar bills, without waiting to make a phone call to the central computer. And if your guy hits the OK button, another hundred bills.

And so on until he presses CANCEL, gets his card out and walks away."

Amy marveled at the simplicity of it. "How long will it take?"

Florence looked toward the ceiling. "About twenty seconds." She looked back down with a sly smile. "I hate to tell you this, but it's a pretty slick idea."

"I can see that. Can we figure out where he is while it's going on?"

"Oh, sure, that's easy. We'll count out the cash, but there's nothing that stops us from having the ATM make a phone call in here and pop the location up on a monitor. We do it all the time—" She stopped abruptly.

Amy didn't understand why at first. Then she did and reached into her bag, pulling out a special identity card and handing it to Florence. "I'm three-Alpha cleared. I already know you are, too."

Florence took the card and examined it closely. She lowered her voice and leaned toward Amy. "It's how an intelligence agent can bring himself in without blowing his cover. He uses a normal-looking ATM card, which rings an alarm in our central operations. We inform the correct agency, they contact local law enforcement, and the agent gets arrested, for speeding or something like that, and he's safely off the streets. He comes in, and it looks completely normal."

She sat back up. "But your extortionist can be long gone by the time all of that takes place."

"Who said he was an extortionist?"

Florence lowered her head and looked at Amy sarcastically over the tops of her glasses. Amy said, "Guess you figured he wasn't Santa Claus. We're hoping he stays within a geographic vicinity long enough for us to scramble local law enforcement on him, or at least try to get an ID. Speaking of which, what about cameras? Aren't the cash machines covered?"

Florence shifted on her chair and looked uncomfortable. "Kind of a sore spot topic with us. A few of them are, in high-crime districts, but mostly, no. It's terribly expensive, maybe a couple hundred million to do it everywhere, and it's not very effective anyway. The bad guys aren't stupid: they just wait until the customers make the withdrawal and walk a few steps away, then conk them over the head."

Amy nodded. "Will you help us?"

"Sure. Why not? Sounds like fun. Only we're going to have to involve one more person to do the actual programming."

"Who's that? Can't you do it personally?"

Florence shook her head. "Nope. It's pretty specialized and time-consuming, and I turned that part over to others a long time ago. We need Mel Tobin, but he's not cleared for anything. You'll have to take care of that on your end."

"How long will it take?"

"Oh, figure a day to do the coding and five to get it out to all the machines."

"We haven't got that long!" She caught herself and got under control in a hurry. "What about just the United States?"

Florence considered for a moment. "Four days altogether."

Amy slumped back. "That's about all we've got, but that doesn't include vetting Tobin before he starts. Shit."

Florence stood up. "That part's up to you people. I'm telling you that technically it can't be done faster. Each download is an individual phone call, and we can only do so many simultaneously."

Amy rose as well and retrieved her case and purse. "I can't authorize that myself. I'll try to call you before the end of the day."

"Tell me something: How much did you say was authorized?"

"Five million dollars."

"Doesn't sound like such a big deal. How bad if we don't make it?"

Amy looked at her levelly. "A lot worse than that amount makes it sound."

"Yeah. Well, I guess if it was about some pictures of a congressman naked, you NTSB guys wouldn't be in it, would you?"

"Jack? Amy."

"How did it go?"

"Good. It can be done, but it needs another body at FundsNet and there's no time to clear him."

"Do it anyway. We'll vet him while he's working."

She nodded even though Jack couldn't see it over the phone. "That's what I figured. Where else are we?"

"Stanley has a team at Autonav going over personnel records, and he's also got somebody trying to figure out where the ATM card came from. What's Hartzig like?"

Amy smiled. "She looks like a chemical engineering major from CalTech. Only smarter. But I like her, and she wants to be helpful. And oh, yeah: I couldn't get her to sign the confidentiality agreement."

Jack laughed. "Sign it? The VP she works for bet me lunch she'd make you *eat* it."

"Thanks a lot."

"He also said that if Hartzig can't be trusted, we might as well pack up the operation and go home."

Amy paused and leaned against the pay phone door. She was hoping for some reassurance from Jack. "Now what?"

"Simple. We put your end in place and wait for Captain Marvel to start collecting."

CHAPTER 8

May 17, 0900 EST

Bureaucracy has a bad name in Western society, and deservedly so. It didn't have to be that way, but like many efforts of the human species, the fault lay primarily in the execution, not in the idea.

In a society consisting entirely of several dozen people, matters of societal mechanics such as obtaining a driver's license, hooking up a telephone line, registering to vote or cashing a check are of little logistical consequence and could be handled via direct dealing with one or two citizens, ignoring for the moment the likely absence of the aforementioned services in such a small human colony.

When that society increases to several million people, or several hundred million, the provision of essential services is no longer the province of individual negotiation and barter. Such a system would be disastrously unworkable and hopelessly frustrating, in which each citizen's ability to achieve success in carrying out even the most mundane activities would be purely a function of happenstance or bargaining ability.

The bureaucracy, in the most technical sense of that term, is a theoretically ideal system by which the minimum number of people can cater to the needs of the overall populace. Sigmund Freud taught that some measure of insanity is the inevitable fee that mankind pays for living in a larger society rather than alone. Bureaucracy is another of those fees. Only in this way can a few hundred thousand people deliver mail to 250 million others, even if it makes them a little crazy in the process.

The problem arises when bureaucrats at all levels start to forget who is there because of whom, when the beast alters its physiology for the comfort of the bacteria within, at the expense of those who would be serviced, when the smooth flow of forms becomes more important than the service being provided and when the citizenry is viewed as a hostile invader without whom the beast would be so much better off.

Few people are more acutely aware of this situation than those in government service, and of those, few are more aware of it than those in the federal government, where in one typical year less than three hundred of several million government workers were fired for incompetence, a rate vastly less than the number who ceased working because they had died.

Which makes it all the more remarkable how quickly the bureaucratic organism could react in an emergency when under the command of public servants with the authority to commandeer whatever resources are required to address the crisis.

Jack Webster examined the command post that had been established in a spare conference room at NTSB headquarters in L'Enfant Plaza. It had been seven days since a lone madman had somehow managed to knock a commercial airliner off course in the Pacific Northwest and only five since the high-level meetings that had triggered the crisis mechanisms of not one but several entrenched bureaucracies. Those mechanisms were stunningly simple when contrasted with the normal functioning of the participating organizations: someone at or near the very top said, "Do it," and it got done. On whose authority, at whose expense and with what kind of paper trail all got figured out later. Sometimes the payment was by check, sometimes it was by favor. More often than not it came in the form of a minor legislative or regulatory concession that passed unnoticed in the *Congressional Record* but was worth many times the cost of the emergency cooperation to the beneficiary. But it was always paid somehow, despite vehement protestations of altruistic intent at the outset.

The command post had eight new phone lines, three of which were specially conditioned for high-speed telecommunications, any one of which would normally have taken a month to install, assuming the local carrier didn't lose the order two or three times in the interim. One of the telecom lines was a dedicated private link between the command post and FundsNet operations. It ran directly into a communications processor attached to a display terminal. The terminal was normal in appearance except for a small speaker mounted on its side.

Another telecom line was connected to a personal computer on whose hard disk was a complete directory of every local law enforcement organization in the United States. Controlling the directory was a software program that would allow someone at the keyboard to enter the name of a town, city, county or any other form of political subdivision and instantly see the names of the top five people in command, their office and home phone numbers, size and resources of the force and any other pertinent data about their capabilities that could fit on a single screen. At the click of a mouse button, any one, two or three of those numbers could be dialed simultaneously, each corresponding to one of the three standard telephones sitting on a table nearby. The computer came courtesy of the FBI's Local Law Enforcement Liaison Division via G. Preston Stanley, who had decided personally to oversee the Bureau's field operations with respect to Captain Marvel. The hard disk would self-destruct if the computer was tilted more than three degrees in any direction or if any attempt was made to remove its back or the special base it sat on, which was bolted to the worktable, which was also supplied by the FBI. They didn't care about the phone numbers. That was public knowledge anyway. They cared about the comments on capabilities, which had been gathered over the years by agents in the field and were extremely useful but often not very complimentary.

The NTSB's own private paging dispatcher also sat in the command post. It piggy-backed off commercial systems but had an automatic priority-demand feature that overrode whatever else was going on. In addition to all NTSB field staff, every FBI agent assigned to the case was carrying a small gray paging unit.

Jack was trying hard to concentrate as Florence Hartzig explained. It was difficult not only because the technical information was all new to him, but because she was, too, and Jack had a special knack for spotting talent. Especially the kind complemented by smooth self-assurance and an immunity to intimidation based on rank or position. And this lady knew her stuff.

"This terminal is an exact duplicate of the ones we use in special ops. Anytime your target swipes his card on any machine anywhere in the system, it'll show up here but not in our office."

"How can we be sure it won't?" asked Stanley.

"Because we programmed it that way. I did it myself."

"But how can we be absolutely certain that nobody else will see it?" he persisted.

"Mr. Stanley." Florence sighed and tried to explain. "In the history of modern computing, nobody has ever figured out a way to guarantee that a piece of programming is foolproof. Everybody's trying, and a lot of very smart people are working on it, but believe me when I tell you it will never, ever happen."

"So how can we be sure?"

That's what I'm trying to tell you! "You can't."

Stanley shook his head. "Not good enough. That's unacceptable."

Amy Goldberg, sitting off to one side, saw it coming and resisted the temptation to cackle. Jack also perked up and settled in for the fun.

Florence nodded her head. "Fine," she said, folding her arms across her chest.

Stanley stared at her for a moment, then looked over at Webster, then at Amy, then back to Florence.

"Word of this gets out, we could easily start a nationwide panic."

Florence only stared back.

"I know you haven't been filled in on all the details—"

Still no reaction.

"—but believe me, the consequences could be dire."

Zip.

"Preston—" Jack stood and scratched his head. "We're going to have to play with what we've been dealt here. We're not facing a lot of options."

"Look," Florence said, pushing off from her leaning position and seeing no need to let Stanley twist slowly in the wind. "I know somebody is trying to extort five million dollars. I know you got the phone company in here to install special lines in less time than it normally takes them to even answer their own phones. You got my management to authorize an outside alarm link for the first time in the company's history, and I'm sitting at NTSB headquarters." She unfolded her arms and leaned back with her hands on the tabletop behind her. "So I figure somebody somewhere is threatening to do something about the friendly skies and you all believe he can do it." She paused to gauge their reactions. "How'm I doing so far?"

"Completely wrong," said Jack. With a glance toward Stanley, he added, "But do continue."

Florence sneered benignly and turned back toward the display terminal. "As soon as the guy swipes his card, the new software we've sent down to all our cash machines will detect it and immediately place a phone call to this terminal"—she tapped it with one hand—"using the dedicated line. An alarm will sound through this speaker to alert whoever is manning the post.

"The screen will show you the exact location of the terminal, right down to the street address and the name of the building, if that's relevant. It'll also tell you exactly what's going on, as it happens: what buttons he's pressing, how much money is being dispensed, and when he hits CANCEL and withdraws his card."

"One thing," said Amy. "If he *swipes* the card, doesn't that mean he gets it back right away?"

Florence shook her head. "It's just a leftover expression. In our machines, we swallow it and give it back at the end."

"So we could keep it if we wanted to," Jack observed.

"Sure," said Amy. "If we want to piss him off. And what would we do with it? I gotta believe he's gonna use gloves."

There were no further comments or questions. Amy looked

at her watch. "Couple hours 'til noon. I'm betting he hits pretty close to the deadline."

Stanley nodded. "He's gotta be going crazy in anticipation."

"Let's have an early lunch and be back here by eleven-thirty," said Jack.

"I assume I'm dismissed?" said Florence.

Jack stood up and reached for his jacket. He seemed reluctant to let her go. "You're welcome to join us," he said. Amy turned in surprise, knowing that Hartzig's presence at lunch would cast an awkward pall on their ability to talk freely.

"Sorry. I'm late for a very critical meeting of the marketing department. Doubt they could carry on without me."

Jack smiled at the self-deprecating sarcasm. "You know about the desk, right?"

She nodded. "Central coordination, my location twenty-four hours a day, twice-a-day check-in . . . I got it."

She picked up her briefcase and started for the door. Jack caught her by the arm and gently held her back. "We don't have a lot of time for the niceties, but I want you to know you did good. Real good."

She inclined her head slightly. "Then let me ask you one question, okay?"

"Okay. But no promises on the answer."

She straightened her head and looked at him directly. "Is it safe to fly? Not just me, but my husband? Anybody?"

Jack looked at her levelly and answered without hesitation. "Absolutely. Don't even give it a second thought."

"Would you tell me otherwise?"

"For someone whose profession is based on logic, you can't be serious with a question like that."

Florence laughed at his response, the only possible answer to the unanswerable question she'd posed.

"Trust me," Jack said soberly, mustering all the sincerity he could.

He had no choice.

Jack had done some sprinting in his high school and Annap-olis years. Not bad at the fifty, much better at the hundred, where he had some time to unwind from what was usually a sloppy start.

His coach had trouble figuring out why someone with his reflexes kept alternating between false starts and slow starts. "Don't anticipate the gun too much," he'd say. "Sometimes the starter'll be right on the money after the count, other times the sonofabitch'll be a half second late, just to screw you up. Wait until you hear it, then go."

It wasn't until years later that it occurred to Jack why his starts were so bad. "Anticipation anxiety," it was called, a fairly common consequence among people who tended to focus too intensely. His mind was so tightly clamped around the gun that he would hallucinate, thinking he heard the shot, or the trigger start to pull the hammer back, or the echo long after the gun had gone off. He sometimes panicked, thinking he wouldn't recognize the sound at all, might confuse it with something else. He would get so lost in the tension that it took him a moment to figure out what the hell had happened when it did fire.

Years later he discovered the secret of dealing with the problem, which was not to think about it at all, simply take his mind away and trust his reflexes to call him back at the right time. By the time he had that down, he was too old to compete and had moved on to other pursuits anyway.

Now, after all those years, here it was again. He was grinding his teeth unmercifully, staring at the speaker until it started drifting in and out of his vision, forcing him to blink and look away for a moment, then look back again. He had told himself a hundred times in the last ten minutes that looking at it was useless, since its appearance was unlikely to change when it went off. He watched Amy quietly read a magazine, envious of her ability to relax under the circumstances, not realizing that her bladder was getting ready to explode but she wasn't about to get up and go take care of it.

"Maybe we should test the speaker," Jack ventured. All he really wanted was a preview of how it would sound so it wouldn't scare the hell out of him when it went off. "What if it's set so low we don't hear it?"

"That's sure possible, Jack." Amy looked up from the magazine. "But I doubt very much you'd miss the readout on the screen, given the holes you've been boring into it."

"Oh, yeah." *Wise-ass dame.* "What if the screen is—"

His suggestion was cut off as the speaker came to life, emitting a high-low series of alternating pitch changes that, while not overly loud, were guaranteed to call attention to themselves.

In her haste to get to the terminal, Amy knocked over her chair, giving Jack a small moment of quickly forgotten satisfaction. The alarm had gone off as soon as the phone line sensed a call coming in. Now they waited, huddled in front of the screen, as the connection was made and the first data arrived.

The screen that had been blank except for a blinking cursor in the upper left-hand corner came to life, and they watched as the transmitted characters lit up the display:

```
5/17, 1205 EST
Terminal MW4039
Grand Rapids, MN
540 East 22nd Street
First County Bank
WD—$2000
```

"Grand Rapids!" yelled Amy, who immediately started entering the information on the FBI's PC.

"Hold it a second," said Jack. "Look." He pointed to the third line on the screen. "That's Minnesota, not Michigan."

"Got it." She made the correction, and almost immediately the screen filled with information. "Chief of police is Lawrence O'Herlihy. Time zone's one hour earlier than ours. I'm dialing now."

The modem in the computer had a speaker, and they could hear the dial tone and then the tones as the computer sounded the number into the phone line. Amy indicated the first phone with her finger. "Go ahead and pick it up. I can listen over the modem."

Jack reached for the receiver and held it to his ear. After two rings it was picked up and answered by a female voice, sounding appropriately bored and jaded, as though professionally incapable of surprise. "Police station. Officer Balwitz."

"Officer, this is Jack Webster of the FBI in Washington,

D.C. We have an emergency, and I need to speak with Chief O'Herlihy without delay."

"Stand by," answered Balwitz. They heard the phone click as she put them on hold.

"Woulda scared me," said Amy.

"He's hit it again!" said Jack, pointing to the screen, which had changed with the addition of a new line.

```
5/17, 1206 EST
Terminal MW4039
Grand Rapids, MN
540 East 22nd Street
First County Bank
WD—$2000
WD—$2000
```

"Ring his home on another phone," ordered Jack.

"But she's already gone to—"

"So what?"

Good point. She moved the cursor to the home phone number and clicked the mouse key.

As line two started ringing, line one came back on. "O'Herlihy," said the gruff voice.

"Chief, this is Jack Webster of the FBI and the NTSB. We've got an emergency and we need your help. We want you to—"

"The NT-what?"

Jack hadn't counted on this. He had rehearsed the rest of the basic story until he could get it all out in under a minute. "We're the federal agency that investigates air disasters, and we—"

"Air disasters? We got us a crash?"

"He hit it again!" Amy called, monitoring the display while Jack handled the phone.

Dammit! "No, Chief, there's no crash. Now please listen to me carefully. Someone is stealing money from ATMs— cash machines—in your city, and it is desperately important that we catch him, do you follow me?"

O'Herlihy's voice had grown deferential, in case this was for real. "Yessir, I hear you."

"He's at the cash machine at First County Bank on East 22nd Street, but he's probably gonna move on to another one real soon."

"Already has," said Amy.

The last line of the screen read **END**

"Okay, Chief, he's moved on. Can you pull some plainclothes into the vicinity and get them close to as many ATMs as you can cover? You only have to worry about the ones without cameras."

"You bet," came the answer. "We'll scramble the whole force."

"How many's that?" Jack mouthed silently to Amy, who held up seven fingers in response. *Great.*

"What're we lookin' for?" asked O'Herlihy.

Good question. "We don't know what he looks like. But the instant he sticks his card in the machine, money starts coming out, and it keeps up for about twenty seconds. If he's covering the machine with his body, listen for a fluttering sound that lasts a long time. He may hit a single button and start it up again. And he'll have something to put it in, or shove it into his pockets."

"Not much to go on," answered the policeman. "And none of the machines around here have cameras, so that's not much of a help."

"It's all we got," answered Jack. "And it's damned important. Remember to keep squad cars well clear, and no sirens."

"Gee, thanks for telling me that, Webster."

"Sorry. I'll stay on the line while you get started. I can tell you what machine he's on soon as he hits. And one other thing . . ."

"Yeah?"

"It's much more important to make sure you don't spook him than it is to catch him. Unless you're a hundred percent dead certain of a clean collar, don't do *anything.* Got that?"

"I got it. Stand by."

Amy watched the screen anxiously, but there was no new message. "Six grand," she muttered. "Just"—she snapped her fingers—"like that."

Three minutes passed, and then O'Herlihy came back on.

"We're moving into position, Webster. Some of the boys keep their civvies in lockers at the station. I've had the clerks run the clothes out to the cars. Should get us about five people on the streets in a couple, three minutes."

"That's good thinking, Chief, real good. Can you stay with me and relay instructions?"

"Yessir."

After another minute the speaker sounded again and a new message flashed on the screen. Jack motioned for the monitor to be turned toward him. He watched the screen, then spoke into the phone.

"Okay, Chief, here comes another one"—he stretched out his voice on the last syllable, waiting for the address to appear—"658 Twenty-seventh Street, a Kmart."

Jack heard the chief bark instructions, probably through the dispatch console, then come back on the line. "That's a few blocks from the first one. He could be walking or driving. Two cars on the way."

"He's gone!" yelled Amy. "Only took two grand and split, just like that!"

Jack clenched his teeth tightly. "Stand down, Chief. He's outta there already."

"You want my men to question the customers still in line?"

"No! For all we know the guy lives in Grand Rapids and is testing us out. Besides, we'll have IDs on everybody who used the machine before and after and can always go back and check."

"Gonna get stale in their minds, Webster."

Jack knew how true that was. "Stay with me, O'Herlihy."

"I'm here. Should have the entire force downtown by now. By the way, that Kmart has three machines side by side. Bank's got four."

"Sounds like a lot for a little town."

"Doesn't seem like a lot on payday, you best believe. People crawlin' all over the place. Looks like L.A. sometimes, not like when I was a kid."

Amy, listening over the speakerphone, looked up at Jack, who put his hand over the mouthpiece of the phone and said, "Marvel is not a stupid guy."

"That's for damned sure," Amy agreed. "He's picked out crowded spots in broad daylight."

"But we can use that," said Jack, uncovering the mouthpiece. "Chief, you know where all the machines are, don't you?"

"Sure. We watch 'em at night, make sure nobody harasses the customers. Panhandlers like to work 'em, too, and times bein' what they are . . ."

"Good. Try to get your men to the ones where there's likely to be a lot of people around: shopping areas, banks, like that."

"Town this size, that's where all of 'em are anyway."

Of course. Close to ten minutes had passed since the last hit. It was possible that Captain Marvel had packed up and moved on. Jack started to say something when the alarm went off once again.

"Another one, Chief, stand by."

Jack watched the screen as the letters appeared once again. "Okay, 1513 Highway Fifty-five," he said into the phone. "Hemisfair Shopping Center."

"Whoa!" O'Herlihy responded. "That's a good ten miles out of town, we'll never make it!"

"Well, what have you got out there?"

"You kiddin'? I told you: every last man's in the middle of town!"

Jack watched as the first $2,000 registered on the monitor, then the second about a half minute later, then yet a third. He slammed a fist down on the worktable. "That sonofabitch!"

Another line on the screen registered the fourth payout. "I don't believe this," Amy said quietly. A fifth line appeared, and only then did "END" flash up to end the transaction.

She shook her head slowly and then looked up from the screen, and said with an admiring tone her voice, "He pulled every available cop into the center of town, then yanked ten G's out in the boonies."

Jack got control of his anger before talking to O'Herlihy. "He's finished out there, Chief. And I'm betting he's through with Grand Rapids. How many ways out of town are there?"

"By highway, four. By the back roads?" He paused. "Too many to count."

Jack took a deep breath. "Let's stay connected just to make

sure, but there's no need to keep your people concentrated downtown." He listened as O'Herlihy barked out orders and then came back on the line.

"You wanna tell me what this is all about?"

"I can't, Chief. But you did about as well as any of us here could have expected. I've got a big long speech about how important it is to national security to keep this absolutely secret. You want to hear it?"

O'Herlihy chuckled. "Spare me, Webster. I'll give the troops some bullshit cover. None of them know I got the NT-whatever on the line anyway."

"We appreciate that."

"Just gotta ask you one thing, though, and I want a straight answer, okay?"

"Okay."

O'Herlihy cleared his throat and lowered his voice. "Is it safe to fly? Just askin' for my family."

Jack answered without hesitation. "Absolutely."

0202 EST

Jack thought about an old golfing trick one of his buddies from the CIA had told him once. Chet McNally had been attached to the Behavioral Sciences Section, an interesting name for the department since it was the same name the FBI used for its division that concerned itself with serial killers and the like. In the CIA's case, the section dealt not with the analysis of pathological behavior, but with inducing and controlling it. The section was also known as psy-ops.

Chet's idea, which he swore to Jack he had actually tried, was to make a wager with a better golfer on gross scores, giving up your handicap adjustment. "Now, you might well be wondering how you recover that advantage, right? Okay, here's the catch: You tell the guy you're allowed to scream at him twice while he's shooting, at the two times of your choice, without warning."

Jack eyed Chet dubiously. Sure, yelling at somebody in the middle of a shot would probably screw him up, might even cost him a stroke, but that's only two strokes for two yells, and how could that make up for a five- or ten-handicap difference?

Chet smiled sardonically. "What you do, you yell in his ear on his very first drive and then never do it again."

Jack relaxed his eyebrows and raised his chin. "Aahhh . . ."

"Exactly! It's like the Chinese water torture! The poor slob spends the rest of the game in mortal dread of when that next scream is coming. By the back nine you could plug a toaster into him, he's so wired. By the time you're done, he'll be lucky not to putt his own toes."

Jack watched Amy, now stripped of her former pretensions of relaxed alertness. She'd had a staff assistant get a sweatsuit out of her locker earlier in the day and bring it to the command post, where she changed unabashedly to avoid leaving the room for even a few minutes. She was on the floor doing stomach crunches, push-ups and other random exercises she thought might squeeze some of the overwhelming tension out of her body. After she had broken down and scrounged a cigarette ("Don't you fucking say it, boss," she'd snarled as the first exhalation curled into the air), Jack had ordered a switch to decaf all around.

After the hits in Grand Rapids, there had been one each in the tiny communities of Coleraine and Bovey. They'd held their breath on the former, because there was only $1,400 in Coleraine's ATM, the sleepy town not likely to have needed much more than that on a normal day. A message to that effect had automatically come up on the screen, and they'd hoped that Captain Marvel was smart enough to realize that it wasn't a trick. After that, all activity had ceased, and that was an hour and a half ago. Now, their collective anxiety was approaching overload.

They had speculated about what was going on. Maybe he'd had a car accident, maybe got pulled over for speeding. Jack opined that he was simply moving on to fresh ground, not willing to risk concentration in a single area, and after a while the conversation died down. They could only surmise so much from such little data, and the water torture had resumed.

Amy tried to continue her exercising, but the tones from the speaker caught her in midsquat and she reflexively tried to shoot up faster than her spent thighs would allow, causing a moment of awkwardness that made her stumble.

She shot for the screen, then remembered her assigned position and sat in front of the FBI computer instead as Jack took up his stance in front of the FundsNet monitor.

"Here it comes!" said Jack for her benefit as the first letters appeared.

```
5/17, 0204 EST
Terminal MW3342
Detroit Lakes, MN
501 13th Street
Becker County Savings & Loan
WD—$2000
```

"Detroit Lakes!" Jack shouted at her. "Go!"

She typed in the information. "That's the county seat. They've got police right in the city, Captain Waldo McCluskey. Dialing now." The dial tone and punched numbers sounded from inside the PC. She pointed to one of the phones. "Line one."

Jack picked it up. Amy continued to stare at the screen, her head tilted at a funny angle, her brow creased in confusion.

"Captain McCluskey, please. This is an emergency."

Amy turned from the monitor, lost in thought, and walked over to the detailed map of the United States nearly filling one wall. Numbered red pins had been inserted at the sites of the first ATM hits. Her eye traveled west and slightly south of Grand Rapids until she found Detroit Lakes.

"Captain McCluskey, this is Jack Webster of the FBI." He had revised his patter to see if he couldn't speed the process up. "We need your help and we need it fast. . . ."

Amy picked up a felt pen from the holder running the length of the bottom of the map and held it up until it connected the two cities, marking the distance with her thumbnail. She was barely aware of the conversation taking place behind her.

Jack was looking at the monitor and saw another $2,000 withdrawal register. "He's at an ATM at Becker County Savings and Loan right now, but likely to move on within a few minutes. Here's what I need you to do. . . ."

Amy moved the marker to the distance scale on the map
legend in the lower right-hand corner and held it with the end
of the barrel at "0." She read the distance where her thumbnail
hit the scale, staring at it for a while and then moving back
up to check her measurement.

She went over to where the printed log was sitting and
checked the time on the Bovey hit, the last one before things
went quiet. Then she looked at the time on the monitor and
compared it, checking finally against her own watch. She did
a rough mental calculation. "Jack . . ."

He was giving final instructions to the Detroit Lakes captain
and waved her away in annoyance. She went to the table
where her briefcase was lying, retrieved a calculator, punched
several buttons and then went back to the wall map. "Jack!"

"Okay, scramble your people and stay with me." He put
his hand over the mouthpiece and looked at Amy. "Dammit,
what?"

"There's something wrong here." She glanced stupidly from
the map to her calculator, as though not knowing what to
make of it.

"What?" Jack turned halfway around and tried to watch
her and the screen at the same time. "What is it?"

Amy turned back to the map and touched a finger to it.
"It's a hundred and twenty miles, Bovey to Grand Rapids."

"Yeah, so? Come on!"

Amy looked back at her calculator and shook her head,
unsure of herself. "He couldn't have made it there that fast."

Jack forgot about the phone and walked to the map as Amy
continued. "He hit Bovey at twelve thirty-five, right? At two
oh-four he's in Detroit Lakes." Her voice grew more confident
as she explained. "How did he go one hundred twenty miles
in an hour and twenty-nine minutes?"

"How fast would that make it?"

Amy held up the calculator. "Over eighty miles an hour."

"Okay, so?"

"On an interstate or something that's not out of the question.
But look—" She turned back to the map. "Nothing but country
road connecting these two towns. One hundred twenty miles
is as the crow flies. So not only is the distance longer than
that, but there's just no way anybody's going to do eighty on

those roads, and that's an *average* of eighty. Realistically, there would have to be spots he was doing over a hundred." She paused to catch her breath and watched as confusion crept into Jack's face.

He stared at the map, looking back and forth between the two cities. "But I don't get it. Unless—"

Amy looked at him and nodded as Jack, a faraway look in his eyes, got it. "There's two of them."

As the shock of this realization set in, Jack suddenly remembered the phone, but Amy snatched it out of his hand. "Captain!" she yelled into the mouthpiece. "Captain, you on the line?"

No answer could be heard through the modem speaker. "He's got us on hold," said Amy. "Shit! Call the station back on line two, and hurry."

Jack gave her a bewildered look even as he complied with her instructions. "The hell are you doing? Why don't we call Grand Rapids back, get them to start spreading out?"

"We've gotta call off Detroit Lakes, that's why. Right away!" The sound of the second line ringing came into the room.

"I don't—"

"There's two of them, working in tandem. The hits were staggered purposely. That means—"

"They're on," Jack said, pointing to the indicator on the screen, acting in befuddled obedience.

Amy snatched up the second receiver. "This is Amy Goldberg, NTSB. I'm holding on the other line. Get me McCluskey, immediately!"

The desk sergeant started to protest. "But he's—"

"I said now, dammit! This is an emergency! Move!" She hung up the first phone and turned back to Jack. "I think— Hello, McCluskey? I'm with Webster, so listen to me carefully: Stand your men down. No, no, that's— Listen to me!" she shouted. "Stand down! Operation's over, ended. Call your people off. We don't want this guy touched. Okay, I'll hold." She turned back to Jack. "Calm this guy down and get rid of him."

Jack finished handling the miffed police captain and hung up the phone. He walked back to the map and stared at it for a moment, going under the assumption that Amy hadn't lost her mind, trying to ferret out the source of her strange behavior. It wasn't long before he saw it.

"They're a team. Watching out for each other. The other guy doesn't start until the first one's in the clear. Either one of them gets snatched and misses calling in, the other knows. He leaves town and——"

"Starts crashing airplanes." Amy let out a long breath and leaned against the wall. She considered how many other men she knew would have trusted her enough to have reacted as Jack had.

"But I don't get it," he continued, unaware of her appreciation. "What's the point of a setup like that, they don't tell us? We could've nabbed the first guy in Grand Rapids and blown the whole thing. What the hell's the point if they *don't fucking tell us!*"

"Because——" Amy turned back to the map and bobbed her head in reluctant admiration—"because he's very, very smart."

" 'He'?" said Jack. "Don't you mean 'they'?"

She shook her head. *There's too much precision here, too much patience.* "There's only one leader," she said without explaining her reasons. "I just know it. And this was his clever little way of telling us he knows we're monitoring him real-time. Communicating without having to talk to us."

Jack sat heavily on the tabletop. The monitor beeped again as another machine was hit in Detroit Lakes. "Y'know what's even scarier?"

"I can't imagine," said Amy.

"Who's to say there's only two?"

CHAPTER 9

A s the day wore on, the FBI man and the NTSB investigator found themselves beginning to nurse a hatred
for Captain Marvel, or Marvels, or whatever in hell
they were. It was starting to appear as though two parallel
tracks were being worked.

"Marvel West" had moved on from Detroit Lakes in a
southward direction, making stops in Fergus Falls and Morris.
"Marvel East" had so far been to Brainerd, Little Falls and
St. Cloud. If this pattern kept up, Jack figured, it was very
likely that there were only two of them, most likely the brains
and an assistant.

During the day, various visitors with the proper clearances
had stopped in. Preston Stanley brought sandwiches and spent
the better part of an hour talking strategy, in addition to
bringing them up to date on the results of the FBI's investigation of Autonav personnel, which had so far shown precious
little progress except to uncover more possibilities than they
had managed to eliminate.

Stanley was not yet dismayed. By its very nature, fieldwork
was destined to be 99 percent useless, since the universe of
possible avenues of inquiry was astronomically larger than
the number that would provide useful results, and yet all
had to be checked. Thus, the power of statistical probability

underwrote the investigator's suspicion that, most of the time, he was on the wrong path.

Stanley also reported on the results of visits to the ATM sites where Marvel had withdrawn cash. Hundreds of prints had been taken, and Stanley had obtained permission to "cartoon" them all, meaning they would be checked against the entire FBI fingerprint file rather than just against known suspects, the more usual procedure. It was a long process, even for computers, and the first several dozen thus far checked against the local bank's records of regular users had revealed no anomalies.

His agents had even gone so far as to obtain withdrawal records for the few minutes either side of their prey's appearance, tracking down and interviewing everybody who had used the ATMs and might have seen Captain Marvel. The problem was not that this produced no suspects, but that it produced too many, with detailed descriptions of some thirty extremely suspicious characters, all of whom turned out to be other people who had used the machine legitimately during the time in question and who described suspicious characters of their own.

Jack was out of his league on the criminal aspect and admitted it readily. When he was with the NTSB, the FBI had always been his agency of choice to bring in when sabotage or other forms of lawlessness were involved. His specialty was figuring out why planes crashed and only parenthetically related to criminal behavior, and then only insofar as his conclusions supported the proposition that someone could be held responsible for a deliberate act leading to a disaster. In cases where a bomber or other miscreant was still on the loose, his insights into likely methods were of immeasurable assistance in subsequent investigation, but this case was new to him. There had been no crash, none of the physical evidence he was so familiar with. Here there was only potential, and they knew, or thought they knew, what the method was in advance.

So he welcomed Stanley's willingness to discuss the aspects of the case he was less familiar with. The FBI veteran was turning out to be a good deal less territorial than Jack would have suspected.

"If there're two, then what we need to do is make a positive ID on one and start tailing him as discreetly as possible, although that's not easy out in the rural areas where he's operating."

"Yeah." Jack nodded while munching a ham and Swiss on rye. "Then, we get a positive make on the other, we grab 'em both."

"Right. Only . . ."

Amy set down her diet cola. "Only we don't know if there are only two."

"Or three," added Jack. "Suppose the real Captain Marvel is sitting in a cozy living room somewhere, orchestrating a pair of flunkies who do the legwork?"

Stanley shook his head. "Possible, but not likely. That kind of money in free and easy reach, he'd have to be some trusting soul to sit it out remotely while the other guys pulled all the dough out and stuffed it into their coats."

"What if they were family?" Amy ventured. "Or part of some other strong affinity group where they would trust each other implicitly?"

"Like what?"

"I don't know." She took a bite out of her chicken salad on whole wheat, the least offensive in the batch that Stanley had brought in. Mouth stuffed, she said, "Maybe Jehovah's Witnesses."

Amid the laughter, Jack said, "Why not? It's just like going door to door, isn't it?"

"The concept's not bad," Stanley observed, "although the problem is you couldn't get anybody as straight as Jehovah's Witnesses to throw in with you, and anybody less straight than that is a great risk. Even family, believe me. I could tell you stories. . . ."

Amy had quieted while Stanley spoke, and she stared absently at the tabletop, unmindful of the cessation of conversation.

"What?" asked Jack.

"What what?" she said.

"Where are you?"

Embarrassed, she straightened up. "There's something really wrong with this—" she began.

"No shit," Stanley interjected. "The whole—"

Jack held up a hand and motioned for Amy to continue.

"Guy like this? Recruiting and trusting cronies?" She shook her head. "Doesn't wash. Doesn't fit."

"What if he's not a self-starter?" Stanley offered. "What if he himself was recruited, maybe by a foreign organization?"

"Terrorist thing? What for?"

Stanley looked perplexed. "Whaddya mean, what for? You know, your basic, uh, y'know, what terrorists do—I mean—"

"Doesn't work. This is a sophisticated operation, well planned, a long time in the making."

Jack picked up the thread. "Why go through all that trouble for a crummy couple million? Guys like that, they'd know this was worth giant bucks."

Amy nodded her agreement. "And if it was for sensation, why not trash the planes? This guy is keeping things quiet."

"Okay," said Stanley, "not an outside organization. So?"

"So"—Amy sat down and leaned back in her chair, looking up at the ceiling—"everything points to a loner, and he isn't alone."

She continued to look upward and ponder the problem, then became aware that Jack and Stanley weren't talking. Amy's conundrum had stalled the conversation, since it intimated that they were heading down a dead end. She was suddenly concerned that her idle musings carried with them more authority and certainty than she had intended, and she sought to get things moving again until she had more time to think or more data to think about.

She ripped open a bag of potato chips and put her feet up on the conference table. "Let's get back to a possible collar." She pointed a chip at Stanley. "Assume there's no way to ascertain for sure whether there are more than two, or whether Captain Marvel is somewhere else. How long do we let this go on without doing anything, because we're afraid?"

Stanley was only too willing to pick up on the earlier theme. "First of all, we're not doing nothing. We're banging away at personnel records, we're trying to get visual IDs in the small towns—"

"Wait, you know what I mean. We get the IDs, we know

who the field guys are . . ." She put her feet back on the floor and leaned forward. "Do we take them or not?"

Stanley pursed his lips, then stood and walked to the wall map, arms folded across his chest. "There's no way to predict where they're going to hit. Other than moving south in zigzag lines, we can't see a pattern. Some towns they've hit one machine and moved on, some towns they've skipped completely."

Amy knew Stanley wasn't answering the question, but she also knew he hadn't forgotten it, either, so she let the agent continue without interruption.

"We've contacted local law in five communities to no avail; we keep that up, some smart people are gonna start asking a lot of embarrassing questions, and we need the press to get hold of it like I need another asshole."

The speaker bleeped again. Amy walked over to it halfheartedly, read the screen and dutifully logged it in. "Owatonna," she said. "South again."

Stanley turned away from the map and sat back down, facing the others. Amy came back to the table as well.

Jack took a sip of coffee and stared at the cup, then looked at Stanley. "So unless we get anything hard says there're more than these two, we try to take 'em, right?"

Stanley looked at Jack and nodded slowly. "But not that fast. I'm willing to bet the fieldwork turns something up." That wasn't quite accurate: what he was really hoping for was a tip, the kind of anonymous phone call to a local FBI office that cracked more cases than he would care to admit.

"Another thing," said Amy. "Time runs out at the end of the month when the databases are reloaded. Does anybody think maybe we let this bastard get away with a little bit of dough and disappear, rather than risk a bad collar, have him start knocking planes out of the sky?"

She had voiced what all of them had thought but none had been willing to say out loud. Stanley was the first to respond. "First of all, there's no reason to assume he can crash any airplanes." All eyes turned to him. "I mean, we think he's going to try, we just warn all the pilots, authorize only visual approaches, stuff like that." He looked around. "Right?"

They hardly knew where to respond. Jack gave it a try.

"You're technically right. We could prevent planes from crashing. Nobody needs to lose their lives. But you got any idea at all how completely crippled the entire air traffic system would be? And it's not empty planes ferrying air. It's businesspeople, the U.S. mail, private overnight delivery services, donated organs, medicine, politicians, emergency transport, military flights—"

Amy continued crunching potato chips. "Even a quick analysis would show you that the economic impact would run into the billions even if we're only down for a few days. And then how fast do you think the public would climb back aboard when we tell them the danger is over but, oh, by the way, we're not sure what it was in the first place?"

Stanley stared, slack-jawed. "Oh," he finally said, quietly.

Jack stood up and stretched his back as Stanley strolled over to the monitor. "When was that last hit?" Jack asked him.

He glanced at the log in front of him. "Six forty-five. Took four grand. Why?"

"I'm betting it's the last for today."

Amy nodded. "I agree. It's nearly six in the Midwest. He's been operating in broad daylight, high traffic areas, nobody pays attention. He won't want to risk an evening when things are quiet and people tend to notice more, especially in a small town."

"We're gonna need a volunteer for night shift," Jack said.

"Why?"

Jack looked at Amy. "Whaddya mean, why? Somebody's gotta stay and monitor the situation. What if we're wrong and he hits again?"

"What about it? We're dead in the water, Jack. There aren't any action steps." She knew this would grate at him, but there was no denying it.

Stanley looked down, mildly embarrassed at not having any strong leads to follow through on. "Lady's right, Webster. Might as well get some rack time and hope my people give us something soon."

The thought of leaving the command post was untenable to Jack. "Okay, I'll stick around for another hour, try and straighten things out. You all get outta here."

"Straighten out what?" Stanley started to say. "There's nothing—"

But Amy grabbed his arm and led him toward the door, knowing full well that her former boss was going to get Betty to send some things over and then he was going to spend the night. "See you bright and early, sports fans."

Jack was right. There were no further withdrawals that night.

Captain Marvel struck next at 0830 EST, or 7:30 in Oakes, North Dakota, where Farmers Finance Company maintained two ATMs to service the cash needs of farmers throughout Dickey County. It was the first indication that he might not have thought of exactly everything.

It had seemed thus far that he was being careful not to arouse attention or create any sort of notoriety, a curious facet of his operation that seemed to Jack not consonant with the likely personality type. The team was in agreement that money could not be the primary motivation, given the paucity of the financial demand in light of how much he could command if he wanted to. Yet the whole situation was pretty much under control as far as public knowledge was concerned.

It was also the case that Captain Marvel was a brilliant adversary, with no recognizable mistakes as far as they could tell. He had obviously played out the scenarios many times, likely even entertaining devil's advocate challenges, perhaps from the same accomplice or accomplices now collecting money all over the American Midwest. Jack guessed that a monumental ego was at work, and that the solicited challenges were dispatched with haughty arrogance, even those that were valid and probably incorporated into the plan without acknowledgment or thanks to the original contributor. (Jack wished Amy were less reluctant to revitalize the unique skills she'd abandoned in an earlier professional life. They could use a specialized psychologist on the team, but he had vetoed the idea of bringing in another person in favor of containing knowledge to the least number of people.)

But yanking that much money out of the FarmFinCo cash machine was not a smart move.

Those particular machines stood in mute testimony to the

devastation bearing down on the small American farmer. The combination of economic downturns, inadequate or acidic rainfall and the rampant consolidation of small spreads into corporate megafarms had all but turned a once proud breed of people into the only endangered species not protected by the U.S. government. While federal lawmakers agonized over the imminent demise of the snail darter and the spotted owl, farmers across the heartland who had mortgaged their souls during the easy money times to keep from losing land that had been theirs for generations were giving away acreage, sometimes entire farms, to pay off those loans. The luckiest ones found themselves nearly destitute but at least debt-free. Others went to work for scandalously low wages driving combines for the syndicates. A few were constitutionally incapable of accepting the reality that theirs was a place from which no return was possible. Once in a not-so-great while, some would turn weathered faces to one more sunset, run their fingers through the crumbling soil and point shotguns at their hearts.

In every such portrait of sorrow there was always a symbol, some poignantly focused signpost that epitomized the heart of whatever point there was to be made. For the farmers of Dickey County, it was the cash machines at FarmFinCo.

The company had made loans during the 1970s and early 1980s, and there was no denying the benefits that accrued from that seeming largesse. Farmers made long overdue investments in mechanized equipment, new barns, fencing and breeding stock. Money was plentiful, and even the most naturally pessimistic agriculturalists never entertained the notion that paying back the loans would be anything but routine.

Loan documents containing long pages of covenants and restrictions were rarely read. "Standard," intoned the bank officers. "Same no matter where you go." As though this piece of information constituted a rationale for ignoring provisions that could spell ruin for the unsuspecting landowners.

While checks for many thousands of dollars were the primary vehicle by which the loan proceeds were disbursed, the ATMs hanging off the side of the FarmFinCo building's brick exterior seemed like mother's breasts, especially to the chil-

dren of the farms. It was a Saturday morning treat to go into
town with Daddy, slide his plastic card into the slot, press a
few buttons and, miracle! watch cash—not food stamps or
checks or coupons or chits for feed, but actual greenbacks—
come flitting down the chute. The sudden availability of a
pocketful of cash had a magical effect, something small merchants knew quite well. It was almost impossible to fold a
wad of new twenties into your pocket without the overwhelming desire to spend some. That was why newsstands, shoe-
shines, candy stores, ice-cream parlors, coffee shops and every
other kind of impulse-oriented, high-volume, low-price vending establishment fought like hell to locate next to an automated teller. The combination of the foot traffic and ready
cash was worth every penny of the premium rent that building
owners quickly learned to charge for such prime locations.

So the FarmFinCo ATMs reflected the heady whirlwind of
easy money and good times. And now they mirrored the
catastrophic aftermath.

Lines of suddenly prosperous farmers were replaced by
shabbily dressed wraiths with averted eyes who approached
the machines with apprehension. Never good at keeping
detailed records of personal assets in the first place, they held
their breath as the machine whirred and clicked. Somewhere
in its bowels, in the wires and cables and well-oiled gears,
sat a Christ-like electronic entity, arm upraised while seraphim
and cherubim danced in the murky interior of the steel-encased
tomb. "Please Wait" burned across the green screen, and they
waited, twenty seconds in a Purgatory more real than Dante's.

They didn't bring the children anymore, not willing to risk
the ignominy that either outcome would bring. If the silicon
Christ checked the heavenly ledger and the supplicant was
found wanting, the Cyclopean display would indicate it in
artfully ambiguous but unmistakable verse: "Sorry. We are
unable to complete that transaction at this time. Please contact
your . . ." and so on.

Or if the hosts were smiling that day, the triumph was still
small. What Captain Marvel may not have realized, the reason
that the children no longer accompanied their parents even
when the accounts were not drained dry, was that the vast
majority of withdrawals from the FarmFinCo ATMs were in

the amount of twenty dollars, the minimum allowed, or forty. That outlying farmers would often drive for half an hour to retrieve such an amount was not a surprise to anyone in Dickey County, especially since those local merchants who were still in business had grown unquestionably leery of cashing personal checks. That's why the machines had not been stocked to capacity in three years.

What *was* a surprise was that both ATMs would be completely depleted at the very beginning of a working day. It was also a surprise that the log printout awaiting morning workers in FarmFinCo's offices showed "Call FundsNet" instead of the transaction detail that would have explained what had happened.

Normally this would not have caused much of a stir. But branch manager Janet Kerr knew immediately that there was nothing normal about what the reaction would be in Dickey County. She examined the log.

Running her finger down the neat columns, she noted that prior to the branch's opening that morning, two customers who had tried to suckle at the company's dry nipple probably suspected that they had inadvertently depleted their accounts and walked away (sullen and dejected, she imagined).

Then somebody who knew better had camped on the doorstep and accosted one of her clerks as soon as she arrived to open the doors, demanding an explanation. When one wasn't forthcoming in the half second that the angry depositor had allowed, he accused the company of running out of money and deliberately failing to inform its customers, in a manner reminiscent of the crash of 1929.

The unfortunate clerk was ill equipped to do anything but apologize profusely and to do so in that irritating manner that communicated that she had no idea what in hell she was talking about, but wasn't her contrition explanation enough?

By that time, another worker arrived and closed both ATMs, which automatically displayed red signs to that effect next to the monitors. She also had the wits to hand-write a sign indicating that transmission lines were down and service would be restored as soon as possible. This seemed to placate the four people who had shown up during the interim, one of whom had driven thirty-five miles to use the machine.

In standard bureaucratic fashion, both clerks refused to open their own cash drawers before the nine o'clock official start of business. When queried as to the rationale underlying their inaction in light of the unavailability of the twenty-four-hour ATMs, both replied according to time-honored tradition: "We don't open until nine because that's when we open," thereby reasserting a policy whose roots related to the requirement to pay workers for their time and the need to limit working hours so as to limit the amount paid to workers, which was certainly reasonable but heroically irrelevant in the present circumstances, considering that the workers were already here and their time cards had already been punched.

This started a series of phone calls to FarmFinCo headquarters by irate customers, leading to awareness of the drained ATMs by executives who otherwise never would have heard of it and who naturally felt compelled to initiate inquiries at an equally high executive level within FundsNet, with whom they contracted to service the machines and who in turn contracted back with local firms. One of the latter coincidentally had encountered a similar situation at one of their Minnesota outlets the day before, which led to an embarrassing series of questions that threatened to precipitate exactly the kind of public disclosure the FBI and the Department of Transportation wanted desperately to avoid.

At Amy Goldberg's behest, Florence Hartzig came to the rescue, drafting a memo to the involved parties in Oakes, North Dakota, congratulating them for their successful participation in one of FundsNet's periodic security checks and the alacrity with which they had spotted a potential breach and reported it up through proper channels. Any suspicions that FarmFinCo employees might have had over what kind of genius it took to figure out that your cash machines were empty and make a phone call, or over how sophisticated a security test it could possibly be, were summarily allayed by the attachment to the memo of a crisp fifty-dollar bill in grateful appreciation for their efforts in helping to make FundsNet North America's safest and most efficient financial transaction network, and keep up the good work.

But it was close, nevertheless, and a patently stupid slip-up, and by midafternoon Washington time would make Jack and his people wonder if their complacency in assuming Captain Marvel was going to play his part in keeping this under wraps was premature.

The tandem duo had worked northward from Oakes through Lisbon and Mayville in the east, Bowman, Belfield and Beulah in the west. Jack's attempts at involving local law enforcement had been to no avail, and sometimes worse. In a moment of anger following the report of a potential bungle, Jack had exclaimed to Stanley, "Those boondock hick cops are gonna kill us, Preston! Where do they breed these jerks, can't even set up a simple tail!"

Stanley bummed a cigarette from Amy, who had bummed a couple from somebody else, and lit it, taking his time to let Jack calm himself. "I'm gonna let you in on a little Bureau secret, Webster." He inhaled, held it and blew the smoke up in the air. "Big-city cops are always giving the backwoods boys a lot of shit about blowing tails. They'll say they tracked somebody out of town and into the sticks and then the local boys blew it."

"Yeah, so?"

Stanley held the cigarette and contemplated the glowing tip. "Fact is, a city's about the only place you *can* tail somebody. Damned near impossible in a small town. Can't be done unless the perp's blind or a complete idiot."

"Y'know, I've always wondered about that," said Amy.

Stanley nodded. "It's one of the standard ways the city boys make the country boys feel inadequate." He looked up at Jack. "If we're lucky, we might get a visual on him, but you can forget about a tail unless you don't mind him knowing."

But in the ensuing days, they got nothing. Stanley's field investigators had finally tracked down the ATM card. After needlessly terrifying an elderly man, they satisfied themselves that he had simply thrown out his card, without cutting it up, in the normally correct belief that since it was expired, nobody could use it anyway, and he could safely avoid exercising his badly arthritic hands in the superfluous act of trying to mutilate it.

"Where does he live?" Amy asked.

"Southern California."

"Interesting." She touched a finger to her lips as she thought out loud. "The navigation units are made in the Pacific Northwest, the flunkies are banging around all over the Midwest, and our guy pinched a card in California. Pretty damned peripatetic creep we got here."

"Peripa-who?"

"Travels a lot. Very mobile." She turned back to Stanley. "What's it mean to your people?"

Stanley shrugged. "Best suggestion I've heard so far, it means nothing. It would have been worth a plane trip to get a card, just to throw us off. The nav software is handled not too far from where the 727 got waylaid, and the figuring is, the guy is familiar with the area because he used to work for Autonav, which is one of the reasons we believe your theory about a former employee."

"And the gallivanting all over the Midwest?"

"That has us beat," the agent admitted. "Can't see a reason, unless Captain Marvel really is sitting it out in the Northwest somewhere while his minions are doing the collecting."

"So maybe the minions are familiar with the Midwest and Marvel isn't?" Jack ventured.

"Maybe. Probably." He took another drag. "I have no fucking idea."

They had been at this for almost a week. Captain Marvel had collected nearly $600,000.

And the notion of Captain Marvel having "minions" was really starting to rankle Amy.

CHAPTER 10

May 31, 0900 EST

When they had first met in this boardroom, the air had rippled with the kind of electricity only a full-blown crisis could generate. Yes, certainly, a crazed maniac holding the entire U.S. air traffic system hostage was hardly cause for celebration, but there had been danger, there had been purpose. It was the kind of situation that brought out the best in people. It also brought out the worst. *But that wasn't the point*, Jack thought. *No, not the point at all. The point was . . . ?*

They had argued and fought over tactics, but only from such chaotic disagreement could truth and direction hope to emerge. Their vital energies had spit from their pores and flared around the room. Even while they openly contemplated the potential cataclysm that a misstep could bring, even as they bullied and argued their way through all possible scenarios, envisioning falling planes and burning bodies, even as they ruminated on the awful political and personal ramifications should their collective wisdom fail them, somewhere, deep inside, in the unspoken place, they felt . . .

Alive. *Yes, that was it*. This group of overachievers who, over the years, had inadvertently participated in the creation of organizational torpor so stagnant they refused to acknowledge its very existence, especially to themselves, some even presuming to believe that their own powerful personalities shaped the look and feel of it, mistaking numbing conformity for "corporate culture." These people, whose primary source of excitement and challenge came from the willowy opinions of the voters, or from the intricate maneuvering of predatory financiers who contributed nothing of substance but believed they provided the oil on which society ran, or from the irrational but inescapable vagaries of market reactions to groundless rumor, or from the caprice of overbearing, bureaucratic superiors.

Then, suddenly, in the NTSB conference room, the small wars were as nothing, only worth the mild embarrassment it took to conjure up how important they had once seemed. That day, they had been cast into the burning vat of reality, out of which no grand feat of public relations or fast shuffling could rescue them. How they behaved could cost lives. What they decided could bring economic chaos. They could topple entire agencies and whole administrations.

Now, nearly four weeks later, they were reconvened in the same room. The aura of aliveness that had surrounded the crowned heads and glowed its presence to Jack Webster had faded slowly and then retreated altogether.

During the span separating the two meetings, some citizen and his presumably tiny band of henchmen had run roughshod over not only their respective organizations, and the laws of the land, and notions of decency and moral propriety in general, but over their most basic sense of self. All of them felt innately that they were people of great power, as evidenced by the speed and willingness of large numbers of underlings and associates to do their bidding, from chauffeurs and lawyers to entire buildings full of middle managers.

To be brought to earth and confronted with their own truly puny places in the cosmic firmament by this ... this ... *infidel!* This was an insult not to be taken lightly. And they reacted to the insult in the grand style of nobles everywhere: they sought to shift blame elsewhere. Contrary to popular belief, this trait was motivated in the main by preservation not of position or status, but of self, of the very image that the noble sees in the greater mirror than the one of mere glass.

"Dammit, Webster, you said that if we cough up the dough, you'd nail the bastard!"

Sam Cavanaugh of Alpha Airlines had worked himself up into a red-faced fit of righteous indignation. "Now you're telling us he's been casually stepping up to teller machines all over God's country and we don't have squat on him?"

Jack repeated in his mind the mantra he'd given himself when he'd left home that morning. *I will not let them get to me. I will not* . . . "No, sir, I don't believe I said that. I don't think I—"

"The hell you didn't!"

Cavanaugh looked around the room for support, in that style long ago perfected by congressional inquisitors in the age of television, that indicated that Jack was the last person for whom his words were intended. "The hell you didn't! Else why would we have put up that kind of money?"

Jack gritted his teeth and hoped it didn't show. "Mr. Cavanaugh, I doubt very much I guaranteed to apprehend the perpetrator."

He knew how horribly annoying a polite reversion to standard terminology could be. The closest he had ever come to hitting a cop had been when an officious rookie had stopped him for a routine traffic matter. "What'd I do?" he'd asked the stern-faced and obviously self-impressed officer. "Would you please step out of the car and place your hands on the roof, sir," the cop answered. As he got out of the car, Jack had said again, "Sure, but what's going on?" and the cop said: "Would you please step out of the car and place your hands on the roof, sir." At which point Jack said, "I'm *getting* out of the fucking car, you idiot, you mind answering my question?" "Please place your hands on the roof, sir," and so forth.

He knew his answers would grate on Cavanaugh the same way, but he couldn't stop himself, knowing full well that, technically and in retrospect, he would be the one behaving properly and Cavanaugh would look like a bully, though in fact the reverse was probably more true. "I merely outlined a plan of action, the best one we had at the time, and you elected to pay the ransom—"

"Which I opposed!" threw in Senator Fedder.

"All right, look, everybody hush up here for a second."
Letitia May Hubbard held out her hands, palms down, in a
restraining gesture. "There's a bright side here we can't ignore,
distasteful as it may seem."

She turned to look in turn at Jack and Preston Stanley.
"Why we're here, today's the last day of the month, right?"

Stanley shot Jack a pained look. They had gone over their
strategy for this meeting many times in the last thirty-six
hours. "Yes, ma'am. By tomorrow morning every aircraft's
got an Autonav unit will have a brand-new database downloaded." He nodded toward Amy.

It would still be several years before Amy perfected the
ability to pay polite and deferential attention to such ravings
as Cavanaugh's while inwardly nodding off until the diatribe
was ended. She could do it easily with serial killers or terrorists
or other brands of sociopath, but she was still new enough in
this particular venue to be intimidated by the posturing rant-
ings of the high and mighty. She cleared her throat and tried
to shake herself into some semblance of cool professionalism.

"Every single navigation chart was reentered into the computer database from scratch. We had our own guy on the
premises." She consulted some notes in the manila folder in
front of her. "The corrupted database was removed physically
from the Autonav master computer—"

"Now how'd they do that?" asked Hubbard. "Everybody's
always telling me you can't hold those things in your hand"—
she mimed holding a box in the air—"it's some kinda ethereal
something or other that's there but not really there."

Amy looked up and smiled without condescension. "That's
true, but the database sits on a disk drive. Like the one in
your personal computer, only much larger." She pointed to
the invisible box Hubbard had created. "About the size of a
breadbox, actually."

At Hubbard's nod, she returned to her notes and continued.
"So they pulled the disk pack off the machine. We'll keep
studying the files, of course. Then they put a fresh pack on
the machine and built the new database there." She looked
up. "No possible way the new one can be contaminated.
None."

"Oh, hogwash," Cavanaugh shot back. "Hell, there's always a way. They just computerized my lawyer's whole office, I betcha ain't nothin' safe in there now."

"That's not true!"

All eyes turned to Florence Hartzig, present at the behest of Jack Webster, over the objections of Preston Stanley and Amy, who suspected that Jack's apparent intellectual infatuation with her might be clouding his judgment.

This was Florence's area of specialty, and the man or woman who could intimidate her hadn't been born yet. "The fact is, your lawyer probably used to have papers all over the place that nobody could keep good track of. Any secretary, any clerk or visiting lawyer walks off with a whole stack or a sheet at a time, nobody would have any idea."

She had Cavanaugh's attention now and pressed on. "You get all of it onto a computer, it's ten times easier to control. It's all in one place, there's technology to protect it, there's no way to just 'walk off with it' if you have the right procedures. Once it's electronic it can't get any more secure than that."

Cavanaugh had regained his composure by the time Florence had finished. He was rubbing his chin and listening carefully. He indicated with a waggle of his fingers that Amy was to continue.

"Anyway, the new database is completely clean. They finished two days ago and have been transferring it to the plug-in cartridges that go into the airplanes. Distribution has already begun and is on schedule. We're starting with category three aircraft, working down from there."

"Category three?" asked Fedder.

"Planes that can land themselves, Senator," said Hubbard. "Even in no visibility."

"So what happens now?" asked Undersecretary Davison.

Preston Stanley looked at Jack again, then at Amy Goldberg. "Well, it means the threat is over."

"What'd we pay out?" asked Cavanaugh.

"A little under two million," replied Amy.

Cavanaugh looked up in surprise, then smiled broadly. "Say, that's not too shabby, then! Three mill less than we ponied up."

"True," Amy affirmed.

"Well, then, what're you lookin' so gloomy for?"

Jack answered for her. "We have a request, Mr. Cavanaugh." He surveyed the faces around the room before speaking again. "We'd like you to keep paying for a while."

The commotion was instantaneous and sustained, rising to a crescendo of shouted questions, each voice trying its best to dominate and prevail. Jack let it go until it started to die under the realization that there would be no answers until order was restored.

Finally he said, "We want you to pay because we haven't caught the guy yet. Long as he's running around loose, he may still be a danger."

"What about those fancy speeches over here?" said Cavanaugh, pointing to Amy and Florence. "How the hell you square that, telling us we still got trouble?"

Jack shook his head. "I don't know. It doesn't feel right. We've got this genius of a maniac who probably planned this for years. I just don't believe he's gonna crawl back into his hole with only two million dollars for his trouble."

"He had to have seen this coming," ventured Amy. "He has to know we were going to figure it out. It must be in his plan somewhere."

"Maybe he never figured us getting the database reloaded that fast?" offered Bob Ferguson.

Davison jumped in as well. "Or he didn't realize how long it would take to get that kind of money out of ATMs."

"Maybe," said Jack. "Possibly. But we don't know. And we're about to cut him off. And that's gonna make him mad."

"Well, ain't that just too bad."

Cavanaugh rose from his seat and hitched up his pants. "My airline's got a lotta mad customers, mad agents, mad suppliers."

He turned and took a step toward the door. "I got scared every one of 'em was gonna start crashing my planes, I'd be handing out money all day long."

"This one's different," said Jack. "This one already demonstrated he can do it."

Cavanaugh waved a hand dismissively without turning back. "You clipped his wings. Far as I'm concerned, I'm out a few hundred G's and this clown's outta business." He put his hand on the doorknob. "Y'all take care."

"Hold it a second." Jack looked around the table, interpreting the silent acquiescence as a willingness to let Cavanaugh shoulder the entire responsibility for this decision. He was unwilling to saddle the executive with that burden but was less concerned with that than with the possibility that he might be able to embarrass them all into rethinking the options. "We let him walk?" he asked of nobody in particular.

"I don't know," said Fedder, turning his attention to Hubbard. "Madame Secretary? Let's not put the whole burden on the airline here. What about DOT money?" He turned his inquisitorial stare on Stanley. "Or Department of Justice? Isn't this what you guys do for a living?"

Stanley kept his voice level as he explained. "The Bureau never pays ransom."

"Great," said Cavanaugh with a sneer, "but you don't mind if we do. Nice policy! I can use that in a few places at Alpha."

Hubbard tried to rescue the embarrassed agent by throwing in her own department's position. "We could never swing it. You already know that."

She turned back toward the dejected team, assuming correctly that they would want to hear it straight. "Looks like your man walks, Webster."

Jack felt the edges of his control start to fray. This was not about budget allocations for new desks. He gripped the edge of the table. "This is wrong. Dead wrong. We've got a highly sophisticated maniac out there. We don't know his motivations, we don't know his pals." He shot a warning glance at Amy: *Now is not the time to air your problems with the multiple perpetrator theory.* "What if they don't like the payment shortfall? What happens they get pissed off and decide to do something a little less sophisticated?"

Hubbard looked at Amy. "You guys can continue to investigate, out of your general fund. No way anybody but Congress can stop you."

"But Madame Secretary—" Stanley began.

She held up a hand. "You, too, Mr. Stanley. But no more money for Captain Marvel from DOT or Alpha Airlines." Had Cavanaugh felt differently, the secretary could easily have pressured him into reconsidering; the last thing an air carrier needed was the Department of Transportation on its back. As it was, Hubbard and the CEO were already in agreement.

Most of the meeting participants were more interested in getting out of the room without having to face Webster and Stanley than they were in scoring any more points.

"I guess we're adjourned, then?" said Senator Fedder.

"It's not over," Jack said to no one in particular. "It can't be. This guy's not that stupid."

Or maybe he is? How the hell do I know? Jack deliberately refrained from pressing the ransom point any further. He had played his own political card. He was on the record as urging continuance of the payments, but he had stopped short of winning them over and risking the humiliation of being wrong. If Captain Marvel was dead in his tracks, nobody would remember much about his impassioned entreaty. If he somehow resurfaced, Jack was covered. The thought that he had fallen into the game filled him instantly with revulsion, but what the hell; he didn't make the rules, only had to survive by them like everybody else.

But what if he really was overly paranoid? What if Marvel really was out of action? *Jesus H., it was only another couple of million, what could it possibly mean to these guys?* "How about just the balance of the five million? It's not that much for Alpha Airlines, you already reserved it on your books. . . ."

Cavanaugh turned and eyed him levelly. "It's not the money, Webster. Believe me."

And it really wasn't, as Jack could see.

"It's the thought of being held hostage by some sonofabitch thinks he's smarter than us," Cavanaugh continued. He turned to Amy, Florence and Preston Stanley in turn, graciously including them in his heartfelt gratitude. "Or any of you. I think you beat him, and I'm grateful. And I hope you catch him. But you're not going to get any more leads out of him than you got already, and I don't want him getting any more of my company's money."

He nodded his appreciation and left. Hubbard and Fedder, following some mumbled accolades, did the same, and soon only the core team was left in the room.

"Have you made shut-down arrangements?" Jack asked Amy without looking at her.

She nodded. "Eight tomorrow morning Florence'll disable the programs in each ATM. They'll still be in there—there's not enough time to download new ones—but they'll no longer respond to our guy."

"What'll he see?" Stanley asked idly.

"The usual," said Florence. " 'Sorry, that card is not recognized,' or some such."

"Gonna piss him off," Stanley observed.

"Maybe," replied Jack. "But only because of how fast we unloaded his bogus databases. He has to have known we'd fix it sooner or later."

"You want to continue to track him until it's really over?" said Florence. "You can hang on to the monitor."

June 1, 0800 EST

Like the last bright burst of a dying star or the frantic squirming of a web-trapped fly, Captain Marvel's final attempts to withdraw ransom money from three ATMs in Stanton, Nebraska, were almost tragically pathetic.

The FundsNet remote monitor in the command post was still dutifully recording even rejected attempts. The first one showed a card swipe and the personal identification number entry, followed by a seven-second interval of inactivity. Jack could just picture the stunned look as the smug extortionist stared, disbelieving, at the standard screen message that really meant "You are back to being just another worthless citizen."

Then another swipe and PIN entry followed, then another, in quick succession. There were over twenty attempts at the one machine, totaling nearly two minutes, the longest he had ever stayed in one place since the odyssey had begun four weeks before.

Not six minutes later, the scene was repeated at an ATM only three blocks away, and he had stayed for nearly three minutes. By that time Jack had contacted the local police, explained the situation and authorized a collar if they could swing it, but they had missed by less than a minute.

Half an hour later, the same thing was repeated in Madison, and then in Columbus shortly after that. Then the monitor went quiet and stayed that way going on an hour now.

"The other one's going to give it a try somewhere else," offered Stanley, referring to the second collection team.

"Wanna bet?" said Amy, fixated on the dark screen.

Stanley turned to look at Amy, who continued to stare at the screen. Florence cocked her head inquiringly at Jack, who lifted his shoulders slightly as if to say, "Beats me."

After another half hour, they found themselves sitting around the small conference table, Amy with her legs up, head back on the edge of the chair, eyes closed. Stanley, hunched over, rested his chin on the backs of his arms, which were planted on the tabletop. Jack chewed on a pencil and stared at the trees through the half-closed blinds, while Florence took her turn at the monitor. Nobody had said a word for a long time until Jack started speaking softly.

"Remember *The Godfather?*" he asked.

Stanley grunted in response. Amy shifted position to indicate she was listening but made no other sound.

Jack continued to stare out the window, a faraway look in his eyes. "There was this scene. Clemenza's leaving his house with his driver and a mob lieutenant. His wife yells to him, don't forget the cannoli. You know, those little Italian pastries? Only they're going out to kill the driver, see, and they drive around near some reeds and they stop and Clemenza gets out to go take a leak."

They didn't know where he was going, but he had their attention. Florence swiveled her seat around to face him.

"While he's standing there, the lieutenant in the backseat puts a bullet in the driver's head. Clemenza never blinks, right? And as he walks back to the car the guy in back is getting out and he closes the door, only Clemenza says, 'Hey, get the cannoli!' and the guy opens the door, reaches in over the body and grabs the little pastry box."

By this time Stanley had turned his head toward Jack without lifting his chin from his arms. Amy had one eye cocked open and trained on Jack as well. Florence's expression could best be described as anticipatory skepticism.

"You know what I think?" Jack was saying distractedly but

with great seriousness. "I think maybe that's all any of us are doing . . . leaning over the body to get the cannoli."

Stanley stared at him for another few seconds, then tilted his head back the other way so he could see Amy, who was looking at him out of her one open eye. Then he turned back again.

"Jack . . . ?"

"Hmm?"

Stanley paused, but Jack didn't turn his way, and Stanley said, "What in the freaking hell are you talking about?"

Jack tried to keep a straight face, but the crinkles forming around his eyes gave him away, and he couldn't take Amy's penetrating stare for too much longer, and as the effort to keep from giggling inanely constricted his throat, he said, "I have no fucking idea!"

Florence yelped in surprise, Amy's laughter nearly knocked her off her chair, and soon they all had tears in their eyes as the overpowering paroxysms, fueled by weeks of nearly unbearable tension and frustration, rendered them weak and helpless, just as Jack had intended.

CHAPTER 11

March 24, 1945

I t wasn't a surprise to anyone who thought about it long enough that Benjamin Davis's Fighting 332nd had amassed one of the most enviable combat records of the war. While black consciousness, at least as it would be defined years later, was arguably still barely nascent in 1945, a smaller, more grass-roots kind of self-awareness had already begun to take hold. Unorganized, even unspoken, it manifested itself in spirited bursts of achievement across many and diverse fields whenever the opportunity arose.

While historical retrospection is always risky in asserting the presence of forces and conscious motivations that may never have really existed, it would be hard to argue that the black population did not take near-to-bursting pride in the accomplishments of its most visible members. But in order to overcome the distinctly American historical imperative that a Negro couldn't play baseball or do science or fly a plane, it was not enough simply to demonstrate that such was not the case, for it left open rebuttals as to the level of skill.

It needed a Carver to attain extraordinary heights of creative and technical innovation, a Robinson to shatter cultural stereotype and attain heroic stature in a game previously dominated by "real" Americans. In the military, it took the 332nd to put the lie forever to any notions regarding a colored man's ability to wrench engine and airframe through the thin blue gas and point his wing-mounted cannons up the tailpipe of the enemy, in this case Germans. White Germans. The Aryan super race that Davis's undereducated, genetically deficient, shiftless, lazy and untrainable men shot out of the sky with awe-inspiring regularity. It grated on the Führer's soul like salt in the wound Jesse Owens had opened at the 1936 Olympics.

So it wasn't a surprise that the airmen of the 332nd fought with the summed ferocity of repressed generations, that they regularly surprised the designers of their aircraft by discovering new limits in the flight envelopes that were never intended to be explored.

There were some puzzles presented by the new recruits, though. Some of the students had a great deal of trouble with spatial orientation, more specifically an inability to accurately judge distances. Judson Greaves in particular caused his instructor no small amount of exasperation during the approach to landing phase, where he demonstrated a frustrating inability to tell the difference between a thousand feet from the runway and five miles. At first his instructor attributed this to a generalized trouble with simple arithmetic, until he learned that Greaves had been halfway to his teaching credentials in secondary mathematics when he'd enlisted.

Other airmen exhibited the same problem, and it was only after weeks of head-scratching bewilderment that a sharp-eyed lieutenant noticed that all of the afflicted cadets were from big cities. All the country boys were excellent judges of distance, some of them uncannily so.

It was a problem that later would be well-known to volunteer pilots in the Northeast working with disadvantaged youths from the inner city. These kids had grown up in the very bowels of the concrete canyonland, some of them rarely venturing more than several blocks from home, and then only on the subway. The only sky they saw was when they looked straight up, and the longest distance they regularly experienced was as far as the side of the apartment building on the next block. They couldn't judge a mile because they had never actually *experienced* a mile.

Which is how Bo Kincaid met Judson Greaves. To solve the problem, flight instructors had created "farm and city" teams that spent an hour each day flying in the open countryside between measured landmarks at various altitudes. When the city boys had learned to gauge these fixed distances accurately, they moved on to another set of marks and started over. They kept it up for weeks until the city half of each team scored reasonable marks when presented with virgin targets.

Bo was impressed by the fierce concentration of his assignee. Jud Greaves, like Bo, was a natural flyer, the stick in his hands not so much a part of the plane as a part of himself. He was a moderately good ground school student, certainly not outstanding, dutifully taking notes on aerodynamics, systems and related topics. But once in the air, Jud knew instinctively what others had to struggle to learn.

Banking his P-51 at dangerously high angles of attack, he needed no instruments to fly at the very edge of a stall, his fingertips held lightly on the stick, in almost psychic communication with the minute tremors, ripples and vibrations that his brain instantly computed into a precise visual image of his craft's situation. To Jud, flying was the perfect antithesis of every negative experience of his childhood. It was the complete and total control of his immediate environment that was denied to the inner-city kid, it was the freedom to dance, unhindered and in all directions, in a limitless ocean with just the flick of a wrist, and it was the opportunity to be good at something difficult. Not just good. Great.

Jud had a secret that, had any of his commanding officers known of it, likely would have washed him out.

He flew barefoot. As soon as his canopy was closed and he was alone, he reached down, unlaced his flying boots, twisted and turned in the cramped cockpit until he had worked them off, then stuffed them in the space between the back of his seat and the long-range fuel tank behind him.

All that leather and fabric between his feet and the rudder pedals dampened his communion with the plane. He felt as though the last fraction of an inch of control, that small gap denying his total feel for what the air around the vertical fin was telling him, was too great a price to pay for complying with regulations. That he might be shot down over frozen wasteland and lose his feet to frostbite, or that they could be ripped to shreds during a frantic bailout, or even that a stray round could find his foot unprotected never occurred to him, or at least didn't bother him. Truth was, Judson Greaves didn't care much for combat. He just did it because that was the only way he would be allowed to fly, and flying was what he had been waiting for all his life without knowing it.

As they flew together in the bulky trainer, Bo found himself drawn to the quiet airman, not so much out of admiration for his ability, but because of the intense appreciation he seemed to have for simply being alive and allowed to fly. He reminded Bo of an otter he had seen once at a zoo.

He came upon it first as the slick-furred animal was out of the water, scrambling across the flat rock for a mackerel tossed in by the feeder. The ungainly waddling and flapping about was wildly comical, and Bo wondered how so uncoordinated a creature ever managed to survive in the wild.

Then the otter shuffled itself back into the pond and was transformed into something else entirely, a sleek bullet knifing through the water with such hydrodynamic perfection that it left no wake on the surface.

Thus it was with Jud, on the ground a shy and deferential kid barely out of adolescence, intelligent and wondering but hardly demonstrative, and in the air a supremely confident master of his art, whose aerial demonstrations of extraordinary skill held even his jaded instructors spellbound.

He and Bo became a team, and when the fighting started, others in the squadron found themselves semiconsciously gravitating toward them when the skies seemed dark with Messerschmitt fighters.

Jud was an aggressive enough dogfighter and proved effective in the 332nd's basic escort mission of protecting the bombers. But it was when one of his crewmates got into trouble that Judson Greaves truly exploded across the sky and claimed it all for himself.

Jud carried his sense of street loyalty into the skies over Europe, exacting terrible revenge that had nothing to do with winning a war, or even a battle, but only with the simple idea of taking care of his brothers. Men with years more experience, who found themselves surrounded by enemy aircraft, no friendlies in sight, tracers spitting all around their heads, would later recall how the heavenly host revealed itself to them in the form of Judson's P-51 Mustang screaming in from the eye of the sun, plunging downward and streaming ammunition into the fuel tanks of the pursuing Hun, flying undeterred through the exploding ruins of the smashed enemy aircraft in search of other godless heretics who would presume to attack his friends.

Back on the ground, he would shrink from the acutely embarrassing adulation until, over time, the rest of the squadron learned not to make too big a deal of it, the unwritten rule evolving until only a silent handshake or, at most, a beer sufficed as thanks, not so much that Jud wanted it, but that the rescued flyer needed to do it. As often as not, while the rest of the squadron sacked out in exhaustion or nursed their irritated nerves playing pinochle, Jud checked out a trainer and turned a few lazy circles in the sky, barrel rolling and looping his way into a relaxation of spirit that only flying could bring him.

Everyone knew that the Luftwaffe was aware of Judson Greaves. Rumor had it that the Führer himself had put a bounty on the *verdammenswert Schwarze* who not only took out German pilots, but embarrassed the Reich. This scared Jud, but only when he was on the ground, where he found himself subconsciously gravitating toward Bo, a much bigger man, as though the physical proximity might offer some measure of protection. Neither was truly aware of the depth of their friendship. They didn't talk about it, any more than two brothers would.

Sometimes, if it was warm enough, Bo would lie on his back, squinting into the sun, watching the *pliés* and *grands jetés* of Jud's aerial ballet. Other times, like now, flying from Ramitelli into the very heart of Germany on their most dangerous mission thus far, the bombing of Berlin itself, he would look out over his wing every few minutes to make sure that Jud's plane was in sight.

In these, the closing days of the war, relentless continuance of saturation bombing was considered crucial by the Allied Command. There was little doubt in many minds that Germany was heading toward surrender. The effort now was oriented toward making such a capitulation definitive, undermining whatever negotiating position the Reich thought it might have and rendering ineffective any last minute posturing Hitler might decide to undertake.

The Luftwaffe commanders were under similar orders, to increase the intensity of their resistance to presumptuous invasions by the prematurely celebratory Allies. Some of the heaviest fighting took place in the last months of the war, a situation temporarily boosting morale among the combatants, while mothers on both sides wept at this questionable expenditure of their sons' lives.

Thus did the 332nd find itself once more plying its trade, escorting the scarred and creaky B-17 bombers of the Fifteenth Air Force deep into the territory of an enemy made bold by the realization that, barring some miracle of diplomacy or military brilliance, their dreams of victory were like so many dissipating contrails.

Like his fellow airmen, Bo was getting nervous. They had already crossed the border and expected at least the obligatory flak lines and saturation air bursts. But there was nothing, no dirty black puffs, no tracer streaks, no telltale metallic glints from the countryside below.

After ten minutes of the strange solitude, Davis's voice came over the radio. "Open it up on the outside. Red Squad, you hug tight, go high and low." The Mustangs flying the outside of the formation would widen out to the left and right, spreading out the formation and offering a less concentrated target. The "Red Squad," closest to the bombers, would maintain tight formation, spreading out vertically rather than horizontally to increase both their surveillance and their ability to respond quickly to a threat.

As they continued unimpeded, anxiety mounted throughout the squadron. The Luftwaffe typically lacked nothing in aggression, attacking early in the game and priding itself on disallowing deep penetration, even if that meant sacrificing the tactical advantage of home port fighting. Now they were nowhere, and that meant something new and unexpected.

"Stand by! Stand by!" The call came from one of the

B-17s, unusual in that the big airplanes generally saved their chatter for the actual bombing run.

"We got tail gunner sighting, from the six, high, way high!" The voice was young, almost out of control with fright and excitement.

"Kincaid!" came Davis's voice over the headset. "Break one eighty and get us a visual!"

Bo dropped his plane down and sharply to the left, bringing the nose around until he was facing back and away from the formation. High, nearly into the sun, he saw what at first looked like a small dark cloud, but which he soon saw was a massive flight of Messerschmitt 262s and Focke-Wulf 190s. The cloud was spreading horizontally as the formation broke into a deadly swarm, high overhead, holding the advantage not only in altitude, but in the speed they would soon gain as they began to dive and let gravity do what their engines couldn't.

"Bogies confirmed, big crowd, at the six high, breaking for attack! Don't think they know they're spotted yet!"

"Outside, break right and left and climb!" Davis yelled. "Red, stay closed, maintain heading! How many, Kincaid?"

Bo squinted and tried to estimate. "I make it at least fifty, skipper!" He'd never seen an enemy formation that large, and he thought of the twenty-three escort fighters behind him and shuddered. The Hun had sucked them in and now threatened to overwhelm them.

"Okay, reverse heading and climb with us." Davis didn't want Bo's out-of-formation plane to alert the Germans to the fact that they'd been spotted. He was going to take part of the squadron to the highest altitude he could before the fight started.

As they climbed, wingmen periodically broke to look back at the enemy formation. Before long, the Germans had spread out and stabilized into three discernible groups, with the largest number of planes in the middle. Bo guessed that those were going after the bombers directly, the rest tasked with drawing off the protective escort. It also appeared that the group was closer now. Composed entirely of fighters, they were not constrained by slower bombers and could easily overtake the American formation.

By now the tail gunners in the B-17s had taken over surveillance, and the fighters concentrated on their climb. In order to gain altitude and at the same time not fall behind, they had revved up to full military power, a setting so hard on the engines that it could not be maintained for more than fifteen minutes, and that gulped fuel at the alarming rate of 182 gallons per hour. If the Germans didn't move in soon, they would have to initiate the fight themselves or risk fuel problems later on. The enemy was in home territory, and there was little doubt that their tanks were nearly full.

"Breaking right and left!" shouted Vinnie Damotta, tail gunner on flight leader Captain Lewis Westheim's *Will o' the Wisp*, as he watched the flanking planes suddenly split off. "Center group diving"—he kept watching for another few seconds—"dropping fast, holding steady!" Bo's guess was correct: they were reserved for the bombers. He and his comrades had turned on their weaponry when the enemy was first sighted. Now they all reached for their panels and switched the guns to the fully armed and ready position.

"Okay, Westheim, stay tight and give us a core to protect. Red, open it up a little." Davis was forming a battle plan, knowing it was only an opening position. He would try to divide the fight into several sections, knowing that as things developed, he would have to give his men free rein to use their own judgment within the overall context he would set. "Outside, stay with me, we're coming around!"

Davis halted his climb, leveling out and turning at the same time. They would engage the attackers behind the bomber formation and do as much damage as they could, then turn quickly and rejoin the main group, to continue the fight there. They were outnumbered and could not allow themselves to be drawn away, leaving the B-17s naked to the Germans, several of whom would be sure to get through.

The P-51s slowed and stayed at twenty-two thousand feet, watching the enemy formations accelerate into their dive. They were still several miles away but closing fast. Bo noticed, as did several of his crewmates, that the dive was sloppily executed, some of the planes slipping back or to the side as they failed to maintain speed or heading. "Stand by, stay

alert," came Davis's voice as the attackers neared. "Steady. . . .
Anticipate attack formation Pincer. . . ."

The bomber group was about four miles behind them now,
the Luftwaffe about three miles ahead. The attack dive was
proceeding without diversion, a center group aimed for the
bombers and two flanking packs to distract the Red Squad.
Bo realized what Davis had already figured out: the Germans
were unaware of the outside Mustang pack waiting high overhead. *Stupid idiots don't know we're here!*

Davis kept it to the brink until the black Luftwaffe planes
were almost directly below. "Get ready . . . ready . . . *Now!*"

The P-51s to the left and right snapped into hard-over rolls
to the inverted position, plunging into steep dives that would
pinch the group below them from both sides. Davis took his
wingmen straight down and slightly behind the enemy pack.
Forgotten for the moment were the outside German groups:
if everything went as planned, the Americans would rain
destruction down on the fighters pursuing the bombers before
the flanking groups could join the fight.

The carefully timed pincer formation thundered toward the
unsuspecting Germans at speeds nearing six hundred miles
per hour. Not a shot was fired as they closed in, waiting
until they were well within range. But without warning, the
Germans started breaking formation, and Davis realized that
the flankers had seen them coming even though the center
group couldn't and a warning had gone out over the radio.

At that point he opened fire with all six wing-mounted
Browning .50-calibers, and the rest of the P-51s did the same.

The first kill came almost immediately, several dozen slugs
ripping into the engine and right wing of an FW-190. The
crippled plane slewed out of control, fuel spilling out of the
wing, catching fire and exploding in a spectacular fireball.

As the German flankers struggled to close in, the Americans
poured fire into the heart of the center group, quickly taking
out three more in rapid succession. It was a turkey shoot, the
Germans scattering more in panic than in skilled maneuvering.
Amazingly, the resistance was minimal, the pilots seemingly
more intent on evasion than on returning fire. Bo was having
trouble grasping the meaning even as the Mustangs continued
to knock off the enemy planes one by one.

What the hell is going on here? he wondered. Even as that thought went through his mind, he stared in stupefied bewilderment as an impossible sight unfolded before him. The badly outclassed center group was forming up again, regrouping and heading for the bombers, in tight formation.

Two Mustangs from below the group were climbing rapidly, wing cannon firing continuously. They scored easy, direct hits on two of the planes, which instantly began trailing black smoke and dropped out of the formation. The rest of the group plowed onward relentlessly.

Bo swooped in from overhead, blasting apart a Messerschmitt canopy. The dead pilot fell onto his stick, pushing the plane hard over to the left, where it slammed into the side of another 'schmitt, damaging the wing and sending the plane into an uncontrollable tumble. He'd knocked out two enemy aircraft with a single burst.

And so it went for several more seconds, the Americans wreaking terrible devastation on this passive formation of suicidal lunatics, taking full advantage of the bizarre situation, not knowing what was going to happen when the flankers caught up.

What the 332nd didn't know, couldn't know until much later, was that they were fighting children who had barely completed a full course of flight training before being sent up in the skies.

As the war ground toward inevitable defeat for the Axis powers, Hitler's vast armament industry had churned out aircraft faster than it could turn out skilled pilots. When the shortage of aviators began reaching critical proportions, strategy turned into a numbers game, the theory being that if they could just get enough planes into the air, some would have to get through, some damage would be inflicted on the enemy and, while the losses would be inordinately high, they would be honorable and acceptable deaths.

The flankers were another story entirely. The ME-262 they flew was the first operational military jet aircraft. Reich Marshal Göring, acting under orders from Hitler to use it as a bomber in the misguided belief that an air offensive could still win the war, had nearly come to blows with Colonel Gunther Lutzow, who insisted on its deployment as a fighter.

Goring threatened to have Lutzow shot but was ordered by Hitler to accede following a near rebellion by Lutzow's pilots.

The task fell to Adolf Galland, who rounded up fifty veteran pilots, nearly all of whom had been in combat since the opening of the war, most of whom had been wounded at least once, many rousted directly out of the rest homes where they had been recuperating from battle fatigue. The very speed of the ME-262, 540 miles per hour in level flight, shocked the undertrained pilots, who continually blew past their targets before slowly adjusting to the new realities of jet-powered flight.

These were the two extremes that greeted the Fifteenth Air Force on its way to Berlin. When the center Luftwaffe group of beginners had begun scattering under the stinging fire of the P-51s, the order had gone out from the flanking lead to close ranks and remain in pursuit of the bombers. The lead made it clear: If you do not re-form and stay on heading, we will shoot you down ourselves.

So the baby pilots had formed up obediently to die like farm animals, each one hoping that the laws of probability would weigh in his favor and that he would be the one whose wings were still intact, whose engine was still turning, when the sheer numbers of the Luftwaffe squadron eventually prevailed over the better-motivated but badly outnumbered Americans.

But if the center group didn't fight back, what weakening effect would the turkey shoot have on the 332nd? Not surprisingly, the demoralized military commanders of the Third Reich believed that depleting the enemy's fuel and ammunition was an objective that merited the loss of undertrained pilots and expendable aircraft. And as soon as that center group performed its sacrificial role, the real battle would begin.

Because the pilots barreling in from the two flanks were not children, were not amateurs. They were battle-hardened veterans, the product of the harshest form of natural selection, which ensured that any pilot who survived this long in the air war did so not out of luck or divine intervention, but because of consummate skill, daring and ingenuity.

The flankers attacked with unhesitating and supremely self-confident command, with a ferocity that at first stunned Davis's flyers, who had been lulled into near complacency by the sheeplike ineptness of the center group. While the flankers had lost the altitude advantage, they still had numbers on their side and the unprecedented speed of the new Messerschmitt jet.

They had also perfected the art of double teaming, using one plane to engage and distract the enemy, trying not so much to get off a clean shot as to get the target in position for a solid hit by the second plane. This ran counter to the great traditions of one-on-one fighting established by the gentlemanly daredevils of the First World War, but the Germans had one advantage over the Americans when it came to philosophy: their dying Reich was fighting for its very existence and cared very little for the honorable trappings of the good fight. The realities of this war brooked little tolerance for tradition and honor, which were privileges available only to those who were winning.

The flankers were able to pull Davis's outside group immediately to full-scale battle and began inflicting heavy losses. Even while locked in his own dogfights, Davis continued to command the overall fight, deliberately keeping the theater away from the B-17s. Knowing the pitiable caliber of flyer in the advancing center group, he ordered the Red Squad to break and engage them, anticipating that they could decimate the baby brigade quickly, in enough time to return and keep the bombers safe. The only remaining question was whether the outside group could do well enough against the flankers to keep them away from the bombers before the Red Squad could re-form around them.

Bo had never seen the sky filled with this many planes. It seemed to him that a midair collision was almost as much of a threat as the Luftwaffe.

"Kincaid, your six!" Judson's voice bellowed at him through the headset. "Your six!"

Bo jerked his plane left and then back to the right, holding the turn as he watched tracers race past his port wing. The attacking FW-190 had fallen for the feint and fired past his plane. He pulled the nose up sharply and continued the turn, looking over his right shoulder to see the FW pull up with him, snapped over on its side, trying to tighten the radius of its turn so it could maneuver inside for a side shot. Bo was pulling over six G's, which meant the German had to be exceeding that, yet the black plane held steady under the crushing force and continued lining up for the shot.

Bo stomped his foot onto the right rudder pedal, which skewed the nose downward. While it didn't result in a great change in the plane's flight path, it was enough to displace it a little, and do so quickly, and he watched as another burst of rounds passed harmlessly overhead.

Now he was out of flying trim, his rudder and ailerons crosswise to each other, and for the half second it would take him to stabilize the plane, he was vulnerable. If the FW pilot recognized the condition, he had only to tap his stick forward to realign for a sure kill. In that moment of frozen time, Bo saw that the German was a good flyer. He was so close that Bo could almost see the upward flick of the elevator panel that would tap into the powerful slipstream rushing past it and twist the aircraft slightly upward, bringing the wing cannons into dead alignment with the P-51.

Bo did the only thing he could, which was to haul back hard on the stick, initiating a violent turn away from his attacker. He was risking a flat spin, but if the shot was late by even a fraction of a second, only his tail would be presented instead of the entire underside of his plane, and maybe, just maybe, the smaller target would result in a miss.

But even as he poured all his strength down his arms and into his hands, he knew it was too late, that even now the German's thumb was clamping down on the trigger and the gears and chains in his guns were spinning into action, feeding in rounds and cocking the hammers that snapped irrevocably toward the firing pins, and then the deadly black FW-190 disappeared, evaporating in a murky grayish cloud that spread out explosively from what a lifetime ago had been a completely intact, hellish marauder whose only purpose in this world was removing Bo Kincaid and his plane *from* it.

Bo blinked once, and then again, and as the turn that should have been too late finally started swinging his plane around, he couldn't see the spot anymore, and he wondered if maybe he was dead. Then he was able to look back over his left shoulder, and he saw that the cloud was clearing slightly, and parts were falling out of the air and heading for the ground. And where there should have been a triumphant German fighter turning victory rolls, there were only puffs of smoke and Judson Greaves's Mustang pulling up to avoid the debris it had just produced, this kill already forgotten as the avenging angel rocketed away to be useful elsewhere. Bo could have thought of many things at that moment, but the only thing he seemed to notice was the side of the disappearing Mustang's fuselage and how the one black fighter pilot with the most confirmed kills flew the only plane that had no little swastikas painted on the side to commemorate them because Judson Greaves, who was normally not one to take symbolic stands, nevertheless steadfastly refused to have them painted on his plane and wouldn't say why to anybody, except to Bo, who knew that Jud took little pleasure in ending the lives of fellow aviators who, but for the accidental circumstances of birth, might have danced the clouds at his side rather than taken up arms against him.

"Kincaid, you resting up or what?" The commander's voice rasped through his head and broke his reverie. "We're getting murdered over here!"

While the Americans were shooting down more planes than their enemy, the latter's numerical advantage was still deciding the battle. At this rate, the last fighters left flying would be German. As Bo rejoined the battle, Davis made a difficult decision and radioed the bomber commander. "Westheim, you're gonna have to drop your load on the nearest alternate and turn around!" Their only chance was to hold on long enough to get the bombers back over the border. Red Squad had already scattered what was left of the center group but could only join the rearward arena once the B-17s were safe. Until then, they were useless.

"Roger, we're there now, commencing run." Davis knew that accuracy was going to take a backseat to clearing out the bomb bays and getting the hell out of there, but he couldn't worry about that now. All around him, his embattled squadron was taking a pounding and couldn't keep this up without some relief from Red Squadron.

Bo sensed the entanglement devolving into a defensive strategy. The only aggression from the Americans was saved for shaking dual pursuers from other flyers' tails. The Germans were so intent on their teaming strategy that they occasionally forgot their own vulnerability, and the 332nd scored several kills by firing on one half of a pursuing team from above or behind.

Time was against the Americans now. The intense maneuvering had eaten away at their fuel supplies, and ammunition that had seemed so plentiful was now dangerously low. Several P-51s were already depleted of rounds, and they were relegated to harassing dives and chases that would have been futile if the Germans had realized that their guns were empty. They would realize it soon.

"Greaves, five o'clock low, headed your way!" Bo couldn't tell who made the call, but he swung his head around to see Judson's plane in the distance, several hundred feet higher than his own altitude and completely alone. Behind him, a half mile back and below, were two ME-262s, in formation and headed directly for Judson's Mustang. Bo pulled his own plane around and gave chase.

Responding to the warning, Judson turned left and began an evasive climb. Almost immediately, one of the Messerschmitts also jinked left. By now it was at Judson's altitude but kept climbing, cutting off the Mustang's escape route. Judson saw it and turned right, only to see the remaining 'schmitt perform the mirror-image maneuver.

Bo watched, the realization dawning that the two German fighters had deliberately cut Judson off from the rest of the pack. They were going to isolate him and cut him to pieces. Bo guessed that the two pilots were among the best flyers in the squadron. He was still more than two miles away and, despite his dwindling fuel supply, punched in military power to maximize his speed. He wasn't all that worried, had confidence in his friend, and only let his anxiety get the better of him when he spotted the third plane, an FW, the reason Judson hadn't engaged the two Messerschmitts.

Greaves knew he was in trouble. He pulled violently upward and to the left, trying for a looping circle back behind the Germans, but a spraying burst of fire from the portside ME-262 held him locked in place. He kept jinking left and right to evade any straight shots. He could have fought off two planes that were trying to kill him, but these pilots were smarter than that. They concentrated on holding him in check rather than trying for a kill, a difficult but effective technique that left it up to the quarry to make a mistake, or run out of fuel, or somehow, some other way, trigger his own demise. The third plane was the key, and this willingness to pull three aircraft out of the main battle was no accident. They were after Jud. They knew who he was.

They were going to kill the avenging angel.

So intent were they that they didn't notice Bo's plane until he had pulled in behind the lower pair and fired a long burst. The hot stream caught one of the Messerschmitts, and a thin black line began spreading backward from the wingtip, but not before the doomed plane got off its own shot. It caught Judson's P-51 in the vertical stabilizer, not enough to knock it down, but sufficient to compromise both its maneuverability and its structural integrity.

"I'm on your six!" yelled Bo over the radio. "One down, come left, hard!"

Without hesitating Judson heeled over and pulled the stick back, and Bo looked up to see the third plane give pursuit. The ME-262 in front of him had pulled hard to the right, and now all four planes were scattered. Bo went after the one down low and left the other to Judson.

But the Messerschmitt wasn't interested in Bo except as a nuisance to be avoided. The objective was still Greaves. It swooped low and then back up to join with the FW-190, and in another few seconds both planes were behind Judson's crippled Mustang and closing fast.

Bo found himself in front of Greaves and looked out to see the two German planes on his tail. They were still too far for a solid shot at him but were gaining rapidly. There was still some time. He pulled the nose up into a steep climb, waited for Judson and then the Germans to pass beneath him. He could tell that the damaged Mustang was slowing down at an alarming rate.

As soon as they passed, Bo rolled inverted and dove, pulling out right-side up and behind the Germans, who themselves had slowed, taking their time to line up and ensure the kill. Bo squeezed the stick-mounted trigger to the A position, turning on his gun camera to record Judson's plane wobbling as pieces of the stabilizer peeled away in the slipstream. They were down to only two hundred miles an hour. Bo skidded left behind the FW-190 and squeezed the trigger further until it hit the B position, spitting rounds into the air at two thousand miles per hour. He saw the telltale black smoke as he scored a hit and kept squeezing as he watched sections of the wings wrinkle and buckle under the onslaught. Then he decided to let go because the guns only had forty-four seconds of firing time, and managing the ammunition was almost as important as managing the fuel.

The badly wounded FW came apart in the air and caught fire, but Bo had no time to exult because his plane suddenly went quiet, the staccato percussion of his guns now only a receding memory, his finger still on the trigger. He pressed it again and again, but it was like a dead thing under his finger, and no matter how much he squeezed and prayed and squeezed again, there was no deity present or listening who was going to reload the weapons that had coughed up their last rounds.

Bo looked out the cockpit in horror as the Messerschmitt, unheedful of the demise of its comrade, crept inexorably forward behind Judson's P-51, taking its time, no longer afraid of Bo, sensing that if the pursuing aircraft had had the ability to shoot, it would have done so long ago.

Panic-stricken, Bo pulled the plane up higher and increased power, veering off to the side for a better view of the unfolding tableau. Judson's ability to maneuver his stricken plane was practically gone, and it was all he could do to stay straight and level. The 'schmitt seemed to be connected to it by some great towline, slowly but steadily reeling it in, closer and closer, preparing to fire the shots that couldn't possibly miss.

Bo was out of his mind with blinding rage and fear. He yanked his useless plane left and right, but there wasn't another American craft in sight that he could call in time, and the German was practically on top of Greaves now. Bo slammed the stick over until it banged into his left knee and when he was completely inverted pulled it into his lap, plunging into a dive heading point-blank for the German's windshield at ungodly speed, hoping to make the Hun break off.

But the pilot was no fool, and his wingtips betrayed not the slightest tremor as he crept up on Judson, ignoring the looming apparition that threatened to rain fire down on him. He called the bluff, betting that Bo's guns were dead, and Bo saw it as he broke at the last possible second and he caught a glimpse of the German's face, which didn't even grace him with the courtesy of a sideward glance as his eyes bored in on Judson's crumbling tailfin.

Bo was pounding the top of his panel, drowning in his helpless impotence as the German finally let off a single, short burst that tore the skin off the outboard tip of Judson's right wing and then stopped firing as pieces of metal fell away and a thin line of smoke appeared. Bo saw his friend scrabbling at the bright red canopy jettison handle, knowing the game was over and choosing to bail out over enemy territory rather than burn up in a flaming coffin.

But then the German fired a shot at the clear Plexiglas cover and shattered it, deforming the frame in the process and making it impossible to get rid of what remained. Bo stared, disbelieving. The Nazi bastard had Jud dead to rights, and he was only going to shoot away pieces at a time, torturing Greaves even though the destruction of his plane was a foregone conclusion.

He saw Judson's arm come through the crumbling Plexiglas, trying vainly to shove away enough of it to let him get out. At that point he gave up on the jettison handle and tried instead to winch it back with the crank, but nothing was happening and Bo saw him twisted sideways, both arms straining to turn the crank, but it wouldn't budge because something was jamming it, but there shouldn't have been anything there and it was then that Bo remembered Jud's boots and he knew for certain that they were crammed into the small space behind the seat back, fouling the mechanism and dooming the pilot to a hideous death.

Bo was screaming now, screaming at the Hun, screaming Judson's name over and over, the circuits in his brain snapping into flames at his inability to prevent the developing atrocity.

The wounded P-51, its very life essences of oil and gas draining into the thin atmosphere, lost its feeble struggle to stay aloft and began arcing downward, its path traced by the thickening black smoke trailing out of its wing and belly. Its killer followed it down, cockpit cameras no doubt recording the unnecessarily cruel victory, to be played over and over amid beer and song as his Luftwaffe comrades reveled in the demise of the black angel.

And Bo envisioned Judson Greaves in his plane, still alive, the gentle man-child who wanted nothing more out of life than to fly like a hawk and, if necessary, to die, but only in the sky, now watching his sweet life end, hurtling downward in a tangle of dead and twisted metal, strapped to the wounded machine like a hellish amusement park ride, seeing the hard and implacable ground rushing up to claim him and smash his smooth and regular features back into shapeless and burning protoplasm.

There was enough fuel left in the falling Mustang's wings to ignite a fireball on impact, and Bo saw the flash from on high, watched it flare brightly and just as quickly darken and congeal into black smoke, and in that quickly fading glow Bo felt a piece of himself burn and die, a portion of a place within him that he never knew existed until now, cauterized and sealed off along with the last embers of his youth, now gone forever.

He wasn't sure how he had gotten back to home base that day. Like several other of his squadron mates, he had lost track of his fuel reserves and found himself dangerously low as he crossed the border. By the time he was in view of the field, his engine quit altogether and he dead-sticked it in.

Men were standing by the side of the field, white bomber crews as well as black fighter pilots. They were looking at him as he climbed out of the cockpit, scanning the skies back toward the border. Bo knew what they were looking for.

"He's gone," he said as he walked past them without stopping. He didn't bother trying to explain, about how it was three on one and he ran out of ammunition, how he had stayed with Judson, trying to distract the attackers, how he had come to manhood in the last seconds of his friend's life. He didn't try to explain because he didn't care. He didn't notice that all the bombers had made it back safely, that some Mustangs hadn't. He didn't bother to find out if anybody blamed him.

He had enough of his wits left to know that the exact circumstances didn't matter as much as the indisputable fact that he was the last pilot flying with Greaves, that it had happened on his watch, and all the consoling back pats and sympathetic tongue clucking and quiet beers, all the praise for the kills he had scored, the awarding of the Distinguished Unit Citation to the group, none of that made any difference anymore. Judson Greaves was dead, and he was alive, and he had stood by while it happened.

It was the seminal experience of Bo Kincaid's life, a psychological grenade that no amount of logic or explanatory cajoling could possibly defuse, a knot of guilt so dense and unyielding that it would affect all his thoughts and emotions and behaviors as it hung there, silent and poisonous, for the rest of his life, absorbing all the psychic energy he could lavish on it, trying to whittle it down and make the pain go away.

Unable to shake the feelings of desolation and hopelessness, he applied for an early discharge, which was readily granted in light of his extraordinary record of accomplishment. His only wish was to sink back into the obscurity from which he had arisen, a simple matter owing to the lack of recognition the 332nd would have outside the small circle of the Fifteenth Air Force.

He got jobs, he did them reasonably well; he got married, he did that reasonably well. About the only thing he was really good at anymore was reliving the last moments of Judson Greaves's life over and over and torturing himself about what he might have done differently. Maybe managed his ammunition supply better, maybe hung closer to Judson as he'd sped away after destroying the Messerschmitt that had come within a breath of blasting Bo to shreds. Maybe at least doing something smarter than pushing Jud into a shallow diving maneuver that depended for its success on Bo's ability to shoot at the pursuers, an ability he might have known was unavailable to him had he been more alert.

But the image that haunted him the most, even more than when he delivered the news to the dead flyer's pregnant widow, was the German firing into Judson's Mustang, while he, his best friend, hovered nearly within touching distance and did nothing.

It never changed, just played over and over, a demonic loop of tape in a penny arcade machine. Over and over and over.

It was the part of the story he'd waited for Lamarr to get a little older to hear.

CHAPTER 12

June 6, 0340 CST

Truth to tell, Guy Schiffman wasn't actually all that nuts about flying.

Oh, he had been at one time, in the military, zipping around in hot little jets and the occasional experimental numbers. Not nuts, maybe, not really head-over-heels gonzo nuts like some of those flyboys who thought strapping on a set of wings brought you closer to God. Not like those overly romantic embarrassments.

But he'd liked it well enough, the technical challenge, the admiration and respect, the looser atmosphere than in some other branches of the service. He was good at it, if uninspired, and didn't really *mind* flying per se, but he had been able to walk away from it easily when his obligation was fulfilled and there was no reason to stay.

That workmanlike attitude suited him perfectly for his current job with Alpha Airlines, flying domestic cargo planes around in the middle of the night, when goods packed up for distribution during the day could be moved around for delivery the next morning. Flying cargo at night saved money, too: at the rate the leviathan MD-11s burned fuel, in-air delays due to daytime airport congestion ran into some serious money, not even including added flight pay for the pilots.

Where passenger-toting pilots occasionally tried to inject some of the romance of flight into their intercommed relationships with the paying fares, cargo haulers had no such pretensions. The modern jumbo jet was perfectly capable of taxiing to the runway, taking off, flying from one coast to the other or to any big city in between, landing and rolling up to the gate without a human pilot ever taking his hands out of his pockets and regardless of whether there was any visibility at all outside the cockpit. Jumbo jockeys knew well, although they didn't like to admit it, that the McDonnell-Douglas Company's *magnum opus* could set itself down on the runway much more smoothly and with much greater precision if the pilot simply kept his hands off the wheel and his feet off the pedals and just watched the lights and dials to make sure the automatic systems were behaving. But the airlines would just as soon the passengers didn't know that the vast majority of MD-11 landings were made in exactly that fashion, the number of pilots who defiantly flew by hand rapidly dwindling as the younger set moved in to fill the ranks. The old, joking nickname for the cockpit, "the front office," had fallen into common parlance in the industry, perhaps in reluctant but honest confirmation of the retreating importance of the silk-scarved, intrepid pilot in favor of the systems manager, now relegated to the position of superannuated hall monitor.

It took a good emergency now and again to remind the pale and self-absorbed computer weenies that the human element could never be eliminated entirely, that only the wetware of the brain could be relied upon to fill in for the hardware and software of the computer when situations arose that were never contemplated during simulations.

Such was the case on July 19, 1989, when United flight 232 lifted off from runway 35R at Denver and its tail engine and hydraulic systems failed, killing virtually all of its aerodynamic control surfaces. Where a computer flight control system would have requested whatever was available as last rites for machines, Captain Al Haines kept control by applying asymmetric power to each of the remaining two engines, banking the plane without ailerons and controlling the descent without elevators, eventually cartwheeling the stricken craft across the runway at Sioux City Gateway but saving half his passengers from what would have been a sure death and proving once again that no matter how well you planned, it was a cinch the cosmos would come up with something you hadn't considered.

Ironically, the cockpit voice recorder, which contained only thirty minutes of tape on a continuous loop, faithfully recorded the sounds of the plane crashing but shed no light on the genesis of the control problem, that having occurred more than thirty minutes prior to the landing. International aviation authorities had been in heated discussions in the face of power-fully argued recommendations to increase the capacity of the tape, as yet to no avail. The issue wasn't technical but purely economic: they knew it was a good idea but were reluctant to make the airlines spend the money.

Schiffman flew by hand only occasionally, to make sure he didn't get too rusty in case the MD-11 autopilot decided to get cantankerous someday, a possibility so statistically remote that it wasn't really taken seriously by the airlines, who would just as soon the pilots stayed off the controls altogether but who had to comply with FAA pilot currency and proficiency regulations.

Schiffman's job four nights a week was to fly an empty MD-11 from Los Angeles International to Mepham, Indiana, drink coffee while containers full of turbochargers, truck axles, turbine blades, and other precision machined parts were loaded onto his plane, and then fly the whole thing back to the coast for eventual shipment to Japan, thus doing his small bit to reverse the trade deficit.

When he had first taken training on the plane, he'd stared in wonder at the sheer size of the thing, disbelieving for a second that a single human, weight under two hundred pounds, was in sole command of this half-million-pound behemoth, that tiny movements of his hands and feet could make the monster do his bidding. He'd wondered as well what the Wright Brothers would think of the aircraft, whose wingspan was longer than the entire length of their first flight in 1903.

But any trace of Schiffman's wonder faded quickly after he got down to the business of electrical systems, hydraulics, emergency procedures and, oh yes, how to fly the thing, which was taught almost exclusively by simulator. There was nothing romantic about hauling cargo, although you couldn't tell that to some of these clowns at Alpha, guys who couldn't find jobs in the overloaded passenger-carrying ranks but for whom flying was such a hopeless addiction that they were willing to accept lower pay and spend their daylight hours sleeping before the night shift.

To Schiffman it was just a job, a way to keep current until something better came along. His personality was hardly the kind that the company wanted their passengers to experience anyway, being a far cry from the supremely self-confident, drawling grandfatherly types who cultivated fetching imitations of legendary test pilots anytime they got their hands around the public address microphones in their airplanes.

Most nights he was able to shepherd the jumbo through its paces without incident, feeding in the computerized waypoints and taking over by hand only for the actual landing, since Mepham had no instrument landing system for the plane's autopilot to lock on to and track in. Mepham also didn't have a control tower, so Schiffman or his copilot had to radio in the blind in case some reprobate Cessna decided to get in some landing practice and failed to notice an airborne ocean cruiser dropping into the airport pattern. Not bloody likely in this stormy mess, but rules were rules, according to the FAA, which mandated the blind calls.

Some nights he had a little excitement. You couldn't get anybody to admit it, of course, but it was common knowledge that the maintenance mechanics weren't quite as thorough on the birds they knew would only be carrying three people instead of three hundred. The plane was simpler, anyway, in all regards, starting with a fraction of the electrical systems and ending with a lighter, stronger structure because there were no windows in the back. If the designers had their way, every passenger plane would be windowless, too, with all the paying customers facing backward as they flew. This would greatly increase their chances of surviving an accident, if you could get anybody to ride in it.

So he'd had more than his fair share of engine outages, a surprisingly benign emergency considering that the overengineered monster could actually take off on just two and had been know to fly around in control with just one, albeit with no passengers or cargo and hardly any fuel.

Twice he'd had trouble getting the landing gear down, several times the main hydraulics had gone out, and once the number three outboard engine had caught fire. He'd handled them all according to the book, and the book had not let him down.

He was more comfortable with mechanical problems than he was with weather. He didn't like flying in turbulence, and he didn't like flying inside clouds, both of which he was doing now. Weather reporting out of Mepham was not specific but was only part of a general report from a wider region, so he couldn't even tell for sure whether the ceiling was high enough for a legal landing. He'd busted minimums before, of course, pilots did it all the time, but there was a limit.

He could tell that the buffeting was worse than usual because the flight engineer, "Buzz" Poleppe, wasn't playing solitaire on the console in front of him as he usually did, and his copilot, Andy Corrigan, was on his third cigarette since they had begun their descent thirty-five minutes ago.

Schiffman looked over the instruments. While the bouncing certainly wasn't comfortable, they'd had worse, and all the readings were well within specs. He looked at the normally gregarious Corrigan and realized that he'd hardly said a word in over ten minutes, an unprecedented streak. Corrigan was flying, as it was an odd day of the month and that's how the two of them had agreed to rotate. He was unusually serious. As he looked at the instruments, it seemed to Schiffman that it was less the usual constant scan and more a search for something.

"What?" asked Schiffman.

"What what?"

"Whatsa matter with you? You got the willies?" It could happen to anybody and usually did on occasion.

"Fuck you, 'willies,' you shitting me or what?"

Yep, you got 'em. "So what, then?"

"What *what?*" Corrigan repeated with an annoyed tone, still denying. It was time to take the plane by hand, the final instrument fix just a few seconds away. "I'm slowing it down a few knots."

"Suit yourself." Nothing wrong with that. They were on schedule anyway, and a little speed reduction would buy a few seconds here and there to be more careful.

Corrigan spread his fingers out over the three thrust levers and felt them creep backward slightly as he commanded the autothrottle to reduce power. They moved barely an eighth of an inch before locking into place in their new positions. He then threw a panel switch that engaged the autopilot in manual mode. While it wouldn't automatically fly the plane through approach, it would respond to the pilot's inputs and maneuver as commanded. Corrigan turned a dial on the center console, ordering six degrees of bank to the left, and the autopilot responded as best it could, trying to sort out jumbled readings from the instruments being battered around in the developing thunderstorm.

Schiffman looked out the left window. Although they were still completely socked in and blind, the clouds themselves were Chinese lanterns flaring into brief, glowing brilliance as enormous, unseen lightning bolts streaked by in the distance. He found a slight sheen of sweat on his upper lip as Corrigan leveled the wings, hopefully lined up with the narrow runway somewhere ahead and below the clouds.

Several minutes passed. He turned to his copilot. "You okay?"

Corrigan nodded without turning his head. "Feels like we were forever getting to the final approach fix."

Schiffman checked the needle on the radio beacon dial, still pointing at a local radio station tower somewhere off the left wing, just where it was supposed to be. He shrugged. "You chopped power. Gonna take longer."

He picked up the radio and broadcast into the void. "Alpha Cargo Thirty-nine Charlie, inbound on final for Mepham, seven miles out, twenty-one hundred feet and descending." He released the mike key, expecting no reply and getting none. There was no need to talk to Indianapolis approach: they'd been cleared for the landing a long time ago. "Should bust out in another three hundred or so."

Corrigan took a quick glance out the right window, shielding his face against the glass to block the glare from the instruments. "Gonna surprise the shit outta me if we do. What've we got for the alternate?"

Flight Engineer Poleppe, glad of something to do and without a window of his own, checked the dials and fuel gauges on his own panel. "No problem. Even got plenty for some holding, you think it'll clear. Want me to call Approach for weather?"

"Sure, what the hell."

The flight engineer dialed in the proper frequency and made the call. "Indianapolis Approach, Alpha Cargo Thirty-nine Charlie."

There was a two-second delay, then, "Thirty-nine Charlie, this is Indie Center, go ahead."

"Request weather update on vicinity Mepham, say again, vicinity Mepham."

Pete Burnham, the approach controller who took the call, had spent most of the last hour taking routine hand-offs from centers and other radar rooms as transcontinental flights passed overhead, above the weather. He was surprised that somebody thought a landing was feasible in the Mepham area, from which several flights had already diverted.

Burnham looked for the flight on his radar, but the screen, except for the ragged splotches that were signal returns from the storm, was empty.

"Alpha Cargo, Indie Center: Say altitude and squawk." The squawk code would help him locate the plane on his screen.

The slightly annoyed voice of First Officer Corrigan came back, "Squawking one two five niner, nineteen hundred feet and slow descent. Any word on that weather?"

Burnham turned to the remote monitor off to the side of the radar screen, the one hooked in to the national aviation weather reporting system. Then he thought, *Ah, what the hell, it's not too busy tonight*, and he picked up the telephone, figuring he'd do these guys a favor and phone the field directly. There was a business jet maintenance facility, and it wasn't unusual for them to put in all-nighters getting some bigshot's Learjet fixed up so he could use the company asset to take the family to the Bahamas.

The phone was answered on the third ring. "Yo!" Who was civil in the middle of the night?

"This Parker Aviation?"

"You got it."

"Pete Burnham, Indie TRACON. I got a jumbo on approach, probably getting bounced all to hell, and he's got old weather. What's it doing?" It wouldn't be official, of course, but it might help the pilots avoid surprises. It would also be helpful to know if any other planes had made it in recently.

"Yeah, sure, I know the guys. Hang on a minute and lemme go look. We been heads down on a job."

"Thanks, 'preciate it." Burnham heard the thunk as the receiver was dropped on a workbench, and then receding footsteps, rubber soles squeaking on the coated concrete floor. A door opened and closed.

He called the MD-11. "Alpha Cargo, stand by one. Getting a firsthand from the field."

All he got back was a burst of static too indistinct for him to make out any words.

On slow nights, the Indianapolis controllers could track bigger planes down the Mepham approach from the old and antiquated Dome 7 on nearby Mule Hill, but not with the precision they were used to. Burnham hunched his shoulder to hold the phone to his ear while he punched the radar dome onto his screen. The blip from the MD-11 appeared immediately, but it seemed to be out of position. No wonder he couldn't get a clear radio transmission.

"I say again, Alpha Cargo: This is Indie Approach. Acknowledge."

A shorter burst came back and then stopped abruptly. In the phone perched on his shoulder, a muffled boom sounded, like a big overhead door being closed in the cavernous hangar. He looked at his screen just as the radar image shivered and changed in the wake of the constantly circling green line, and he caught a glimpse of the MD-11 blip, but it disappeared right away, probably as the plane dipped below Dome 7's ability to track it. On the chance that the crew could still hear his transmissions, which were much more powerful than their on-board unit could put out in reply, he started to key his mike to tell them to be patient when he heard the receiver being picked up at the other end. The workman's voice, which had been taciturn before, was pitched higher now.

"Hey, Center, looks like shit outside. I can hardly see the runway from here, and there was just some god-awful hellacious lightning off to the east!"

"*No foolin'.*" *Probably a ground strike just a few hundred feet away.* "They probably figured it out for themselves by now." That low, the MD-11 crew had to have started their aborted landing procedure already. "Gonna divert, save some fuel instead of trying for it again. Thanks anyway, though."

He heard more excited voices and running feet over the phone. "Anytime," and the phone was dropped onto the cradle, no doubt so the worker could join in the excitement and investigate the damage from the lightning strike.

Burnham keyed the mike. "Alpha Cargo, Indie Approach. Sounds like Mepham's a mess, no ceiling and severe lightning reported." He knew better than to suggest what their next course of action should be, even if they could hear him. That was entirely their own decision.

Getting no response, he waited a few seconds, long enough for them to have risen into range. "Alpha Cargo, Indie Approach." He gave it another few seconds. "Alpha Cargo, you on freq?"

He punched his standard radar back on line, expecting to see a fresh return from the MD-11, which he assumed had broken off its attempt and was diverting to the alternate, but there were no blips other than the ragged temporary spots indicating lightning. "I say again, Alpha Cargo, do you copy?" *Don't tell me those lunatics tried to land!* "Alpha Cargo, Indianapolis Approach, do you copy?"

There would be no answer.

What remained of the MD-11 was scattered at the base of the only ridge of appreciable height in the area. The brilliant burst that had lit up the skies around Mepham was short-lived, as all the fuel left in the wings burned at once, the intense heat expanding the flames into a giant ball whose glow was visible for miles but generally mistaken for a lightning strike, just as the booming explosion was taken for thunder. That residents in a forty-square-mile area all thought the single strike was within a few hundred yards of each of their own homes only came to light over the next several hours, as they learned that the small orange sun that had blossomed briefly and died was really the death knell of a cargo plane that had flown into a limestone wall at over 230 miles per hour.

In earlier days, the first official indication of an air disaster was the muted beeping of Jack Webster's pager. But not today. And not because Jack was no longer with the NTSB.

Generally, search operations don't begin until at least four hours after a plane is reported missing. Most commonly, a light plane will forget to close its flight plan at its destination. The FAA's computer flashes a message on the screen, and if the pilot doesn't report in within thirty minutes, the attendants start making phone calls to the destination airport, usually locating the plane within several minutes and delivering a wrist slap to the pilot, who is so embarrassed that no further punishment is needed.

If the plane cannot be located at the destination airport, an alert notification is issued to surrounding facilities. Soon after that, planes in the vicinity are asked to keep an eye out for a downed aircraft, word is flashed to local law enforcement officials, and a central air force facility in Illinois begins coordinating Civil Air Patrol searches.

But the search for the Alpha Airlines cargo flight was initiated well before the four-hour standard. First, it was on an IFR flight plan; these are closed automatically by the pilot via the last control facility handling the flight or by phone call once they have landed. In this case, the plan was not closed because Indianapolis Center controller Pete Burnham expected to reacquire control as soon as the crew called off the approach to Mepham. It could not have gone for the alternate, which was Indianapolis, without reappearing on his radar screen.

Second, this wasn't a four-passenger Piper but a 250-ton airliner the size of an office building. It couldn't set down in a corn field or a parking lot or on the interstate. When its fuel ran out, which Alpha central operations calculated to have happened at 5:10 local time, it was either wrecked or about to be. That nobody was picking up the characteristic *whoop-*

whoop of an emergency locator transmitter didn't deter Burnham from starting the search right away. The ELT was a device in the plane that would have been triggered by the severe shock of a crash, but it didn't always work. Burnham didn't realize that, in this case, the impact had been so powerful that the ELT itself was destroyed.

So the emergency call was made in plenty of time, but the search itself was not so easy. An air patrol was out of the question, as visibility from above was effectively nil. And the heavily wooded area surrounding the region was impenetrable by car. The only near-term option was a foot patrol, and the first place they would be sent to look was near the last place Burnham had tracked them, which was along the published approach path into Mepham. Barely an hour after the emergency call, a sheriff's crew and a handful of volunteers had divided into three teams and walked the entire seven-mile stretch, spread out about half a mile wide. They found nothing.

So Jack Webster's pager had not sounded yet, even though FAA headquarters knew about the situation shortly after 6:00 A.M. Washington time, because there was no action to take at that point, there being no confirmed accident.

As dawn broke over Indiana, wheat farmer Dwayne Stebbins awoke and looked in the direction of that big bolt that had awakened his family in the middle of the night to see that the lightning had set one of his neighbor's fields to smoldering about two miles or so away. He thought of calling over but remembered that Joe Bilford and his family were away, checking out the schools in Cleveland where Joe had a job offer.

He sat down to breakfast, and when he was finished the black smoke hadn't changed much, so he offered to drive his son Davey to school, figuring he'd drop in on his neighbor's place and see what was up. Coming up the drive, he was stunned to see that there wasn't one but many dozens of fires scattered in a wide arc, just below the ridge that defined the western boundary of Bilford's farm. Furthermore, there was a dark, charred section on the hillside that wasn't there the last time he'd visited. He drove around back of the house and up the small rise on which the main barn sat. As he reached the top and pulled up alongside the barn for a better view of the field, he involuntarily slammed on the brakes, skidding the car to a stop in the soft mud. He got out and rubbed his eyes, staring in horrified disbelief at the sight in front of him.

Staggering backward, he ran for the house. After finding the door locked, he turned and punched his elbow through one of the small glass panes, reached in and turned the lock, pushing back the door and running for the phone on the wall. He reached Sheriff Dilman and started a chain of phone calls that eventually found its way to the NTSB.

By the time the phone rang in Jack's office, he was already ensconced with Amy Goldberg and Preston Stanley, who had driven over from the J. Edgar Hoover Building. On the desk in front of him was a photostat of a facsimile transmission. It had arrived about two hours ago, sent from a phone in a train station. There were none of the customary identifying characters at the top of the sheet, the sender having carefully wiped that information from his fax machine's programming. A check with the phone company showed the call came from a public phone booth, paid for with hard-cash quarters rather than a credit card, which meant the "fax machine" was probably just an add-on board in a battery-operated portable computer. It was completely untraceable.

The first shift office services staff had arrived and processed the fax without bothering to read it. When it found its way to Amy's desk, she had put in place a series of phone calls to the relevant authorities in and around Mepham. She already knew about the search in progress, having read it in the morning briefing compilation prepared by the night staff, but after reading the fax sheet several times, she was able to give instructions for redirecting the search teams. At about the same time she was getting ready to ring off, she was put on hold. After several minutes her Mepham contact came back on the line and told her about a phone call that had just come in from one Dwayne Stebbins, a local farmer.

Now Amy sat with Jack as her one-time boss and mentor but still current friend read and reread the piece of paper. Jack looked up after a while. "We're not going about this right."

Stanley started to reply. "Don't know how much more we can put on it. We're not gonna have a problem getting back all our resources, and—"

Jack waved him off. "No, not more field people, there's enough of those. I mean we need to figure this guy out. Get in his head, understand who he is, why he's doing this."

"We've got some good psychs in the Bureau. You've met a couple of 'em, I think."

Jack nodded. "Yeah, I did. And they're real good." He turned to Amy. "But not as good as you."

"That was a long time ago."

"I think we should bring in some pros, Jack," Stanley persisted. "No offense, Amy, but you've been out of the field for a while, you're not current—"

On what? Amy thought. *The bends and turns a tortured mind could take on the way to acts of unspeakable and senseless destruction? What do you suppose the latest thinking is on that, Agent Stanley?*

But Jack would not be dissuaded. At the worst times he trusted his best people, and they rarely let him down.

He walked over to the desk and picked up the fax, rereading it for perhaps the twentieth time.

> June 6, 0400 hours.
>
> Alpha Airlines cargo flight inbound from LAX to Mepham.
>
> Impact on ridge 2.5 miles north of courseline VOR approach Echo.
>
> Are we ready to resume business?

It had arrived in the fax room at 0530 Washington time that morning, only thirty minutes after the flight disappeared from Pete Burnham's radar screen and more than two hours before Dwayne Stebbins discovered the wreckage.

Book 2

I hope to see my Pilot face to face
When I have crossed the bar.

—Alfred, Lord Tennyson
  "Crossing the Bar" (1889), st. 4

CHAPTER 13

June 7, 0912 EST

Jack gestured wordlessly for Amy to stop the car. They were still nearly half a mile away, so there wasn't much to see. As the car slowed, Amy turned slightly to look at him, but he gave no clue to why they were stopping.

She was full of dread and excited at the same time. She'd never been to a "smokin' hole" before, even though her professional career revolved around things like this. Jack thought a little field experience would be good for her, get her to understand what all those numbers and data points were really all about.

This was an easy one to start out on, too, at least from the stomach's perspective. A minimum of gore, being a cargo flight, nice clean scatter zone devoid of dense civilization and the complicating elements of telephone and power lines, buildings, cars and the occasional innocent bystander who was doing nothing more offensive than breathing or walking or eating or making love when the air above suddenly condensed into shards of metal set afire by a wanton deity. One was subconsciously prepared for many things in modern life. An automobile accident, a hurricane, an errant elevator, but *never* aluminum and kerosene and bodies precipitating out of an empty sky, like some phantom quantum particle suddenly sprung full blown from the nothingness of the previous moment.

None of that today. Today was nice and clean. Three bodies, at least theoretically, yet to be verified by the forensic paleontologists when they pieced the samples together, theorizing in their labs about the missing pieces as though they constituted some ancient reptilian fossil.

Only three families to contact. Jack thought fleetingly of the small details that made a passenger crash so poignant. Not the tabloid stuff: teddy bears, wrapped presents that had somehow stayed intact, clutched Bibles. None of that.

Jack thought about the parking lots at the airports, a hundred cars out there that were never going to be picked up because their owners were not coming back, windshields full of parking tickets until somebody started to figure out what was going on. Luggage sent to the wrong destination turning up after a week or two, the bag maybe late, but at least it made it. Empty seats on connecting flights, automatically entered into the computerized reservation system as no-shows, maybe even tweaking the airline's secret yield management algorithm into upping the overbook ratio for that flight for the next few weeks. Same for car and hotel reservations, the latter resulting in charges to credit cards that had guaranteed late arrival. Representatives from the company that places insurance policy vending kiosks at the airport opening up the machines and looking at the forms, the only time they ever did, generally throwing the contents right into the trash once a week and looking at them only if . . .

He was standing outside the car now, shaking the thoughts from his head and looking into the distance at the Bilford farm. A dark splotch was visible on the ridge just above the field. He turned to view the entire approach path, seeing a radio tower as the only other thing besides the ridge line itself standing over thirty feet above the ground. *One obstruction in the whole area and these guys hit it.* He leaned his head down into the car.

"Gimme the sectional, eh?"

Amy reached into her attaché and pulled out the map specially designed for pilots. It showed all navigational aids as well as prominent landmarks that could be seen from the air: roads, power lines, railroad tracks, rivers, lakes, easily identified buildings and airports. It was updated every six months, and use of an outdated sectional was contrary to the FARs, the Federal Aviation Regulations, that ruled the actions of every licensed pilot in the country.

Jack smoothed the map on the hood of the rented car, then turned it so that its orientation aligned with the direction he was facing. He marked with his thumbnail where the likely approach path of the plane had been. It was parallel to the correct path to the airport, just three miles off to the side. He saw the symbols for the precision VOR navigation device on the airport itself and the less accurate radio beacon off to the south. The combination of these two instruments should have provided the MD-11 with extremely accurate position fixes on its way in.

He took one more wide-perspective look, then folded the sectional and got back into the car.

"Okay, let's move on."

He knew that Amy was anxious to get on with it, not because she was so keen to see what lay ahead, but just to get past whatever her opening emotions would be. She wouldn't have a problem as long as he left her alone for the first few minutes. He didn't want her to come to it pre-numbed or so overloaded with tasks and responsibilities that she failed to grasp the enormity of what had occurred. It was important that it sink in, affect her. When next she sat in the safe office on L'Enfant Plaza contemplating some other calamity, he wanted her mind periodically to drift to Joe Bilford's field so that she could revisit the devastation, smell once again the odor of burning rubber and fabric, feel the power of an impact that could reduce a glimmering, flying city to so many pieces of ugly, mangled metal. He wanted her to feel it for good and proper reasons, but most of all because he himself could not for so many years, and now it was mercifully over for him— soon, anyway—but not for her, and it was pretty damned certain his successor wasn't going to take the time.

Amy was no stranger to death and mayhem and had seen things Jack would as soon not even hear about. But as any doctor or homicide detective or ambulance driver could tell you, getting used to the occasional corpse was no preparation for the shock of seeing the kind of mass destruction that transmuted a graceful airplane into a smoldering wreck.

"Locals are all set up." Amy pointed to flashing lights and a line of private cars in the road ahead. "Hope they aren't touching anything." She felt no contempt for their fascination with the dramatic destruction. She would have felt and reacted the same way if she weren't privileged to be an official part of the spectacle, with reserved front-row seats, a special pass to sweep her past the unwashed. The NTSB regional office would have gotten there as fast as they could to stake down the area and establish security, but there was no way they could arrive before local law did.

She leaned forward and put her arms on the back of the front seat. "I made it pretty clear on the phone. The chief of police asked me, shouldn't he check for survivors." She had responded by asking him what was the biggest piece of anything left that he could see and based on his answer did he think that anything human could have survived, and that had pretty much quieted him down because she had sounded so competent and authoritative and all she really was was scared and making herself feel better by making him feel stupid. Now she felt awful about it, seeing before her what he had seen.

Jack grunted. He looked at the ridge again and knew what had happened, how it had happened, and that there wouldn't even be enough left to match with dental records. NTSB headquarters had scrambled the special "go team" the instant the report had come in, and Jack was secretly hoping the investigator in charge would be—

"I think that's Sivara," said Amy, recognizing him from his personnel file photograph. "How'd he get here before us?"

A dark-complected man of about forty-five squinted at the car and then waved in recognition. He wore a royal blue windbreaker with NTSB in large yellow letters stenciled across the back over a jumpsuit of the same color. His name was printed on a piece of red fabric mounted at an angle over the slanted top of the breast pocket, above the board's official patch. A baseball-style billed cap also carried the logo. It was the same uniform worn by half a dozen others scattered across the field, who looked up in the direction of his wave. Sivara walked up to the car as it slowed.

"Hey, boss. Thought we finally got ridda you." Sivara opened the passenger door and offered a hand, pulling Jack out and shaking at the same time. They both smiled to show they were glad to see each other, which was genuine, but the smiles didn't reach their eyes. Sivara looked at Jack for a moment and then turned and swept the field.

"Only time I ever get to see you is when a shitstorm swirls up. Like old times, huh?"

"Yeah. Old times. You the two-IC?"

Sivara nodded. As IIC, the investigator in charge, he was in complete command of the situation, reporting only to a board member. "It's a weird one, Jack."

If you only knew. "Why's that?"

Before he could answer, the left rear door slammed and Amy got out.

"Gene, you know this lady?"

She walked around the car, trying to meet Sivara's eyes but unable to keep her own off the field. She was aware of the small crowd of people being kept at bay by the local police and how they stared at the car and the three of them, as though they were either something important or somehow carried new information.

"Dr. Goldberg, sure," answered Sivara, extending his hand to her. "Haven't had the pleasure of working with her yet, though."

Amy knew a good deal more about Sivara than he suspected. He had figured large in Jack's recounting to her of the incident on the *Constellation* that led to his leaving the navy. She also recalled that since that time, Sivara and Webster as NTSB colleagues had done time in the field together, when Jack was the senior IIC and Sivara was a group chairman specializing in pilot performance. Each member of the go team was a group chairman with a deep specialization, like the people she could see walking among the wreckage. She also remembered that Sivara had refused any of a number of desk assignments over the years.

"This business, we don't get a lot of good-looking ladies. Wish we coulda got together under more pleasant conditions."

She might have been offended under other circumstances, but Sivara's disingenuous smile and guileless manner carried no disrespect, and she decided to give him the benefit of the doubt.

"Well, it's a changing world, Mr. Sivara."

He brought his left hand to their still clasped handshake, dropping his right and taking hold of hers like two lovers walking. He ignored her confused expression and led her forward several steps toward the field. His smile was gone by now, and only sadness and resignation remained as his eyes surveyed the landscape. He gestured toward it with the left hand that still held Amy's own hand, making her arm rise and point where he indicated.

"You think so, Doc? You think it's changing?"

She turned her eyes full on the carnage for the first time and drank it in. Where moments before she had been embarrassed by his presumption in taking her hand, she now found herself squeezing back, taking comfort in the strength she found there, not because he was any stronger than she was, but because he had seen it before, seen it much, much worse than this, and held the advantage of familiarity and the practiced ability to hide his reactions better than she.

Amy didn't know how long she stared. Sivara was patient and stood steadily by. Jack had crept up silently, lost in his own thoughts, watching as the rising sun glinted off a thousand shards of aluminum.

From a distance, and straight on, the black splotch on the face of the ridge wall had looked like a simple burn mark. From here, off to the side, it was easy to see the tremendous hole that had been gouged out of the soft limestone by the force of the impact. From their vantage point they could see that the wreckage had shot outward in a fan shape from the impact point on the ridge. Smoke still curled upward from smoldering ruins, but no open flames were apparent.

There was a crude symmetry to the pattern radiating outward from ground zero. What remained of one of the MD-11's massive engines was visible, still attached to a section of wing, inside the leftmost arc of the fan. The other could be seen in the distance in the right arc, sticking up slightly out of the soft soil. There was no immediate sign of the center engine. Investigators dressed in blue jumpsuits could be seen walking methodically in a ladder pattern. It was a first cursory walkabout, a look for the obvious before the more thorough going-over later.

Amy relaxed her grip. As she did so, Sivara let her hand go.

"Thanks," she whispered, and shivered. Sivara nodded slightly.

"Where're we set up?" Jack asked quietly.

"Bilford's kitchen. Chief of police got him on the phone, told him a neighbor broke in to use the phone anyway. Said to make ourselves at home." He led the way past the police cordon. "Got some coffee goin'."

"Let's get some and take it outside. I want a fast briefing. You got any county law in here to keep the field clean?"

"Not a chance. They don't have anybody to spare."

"Shit. Could make your life tough."

"Maybe. Haven't had any time to deal with the local police yet, either. Want to handle it for me?"

Jack looked up at the clearing sky. "What's the chief's name?"

As they neared the farmhouse, Jack veered off and approached the police chief of the small town. "You Johanssen?"

The uniformed policeman nodded tentatively. "Yessir. Chief of police."

A pack of cigarettes poked out of his uniform. Jack reached inside the man's jacket without asking, as though they had known each other since birth, and pulled them out, shaking out two and taking one for himself. The policeman fumbled for a lighter and lit them both.

"I'm Jack Webster. FBI." He didn't think it critical to let Johanssen know that not all older FBI agents were veterans at the job. "You did real good keeping all these folks back," he said, leaning his head back and exhaling a stream of gray smoke into the air.

"Uh, thanks. Doin' our best." The chief started to relax within the aura of a shared smoke that Jack had created. "People around here, they ain't used to seein' this sort of thing, y'know?"

Jack looked into his face. "People aren't used to seeing this sort of thing anywhere, Chief."

"Well, I guess you're right about that. Damn . . ." His eyes swept the field for what must have been the hundredth time that morning. "Damn . . ."

Jack saw him start to get glassy-eyed. "Chief, we need you to keep up this work you started. It's important, you understand?"

The policeman forced his eyes back toward Jack. He took another drag, a deep one.

"It's important, because we have to know why this happened. Maybe the instruments went funny, maybe the pilots went funny—" He paused. "Maybe it was sabotage." The policeman's eyes started to grow wide, and Jack went on. "We just don't know. But we have to find out, you understand that?"

The chief nodded, relieved that somebody in authority, somebody in control, somebody who exuded confidence and competence, was there to tell him what to do.

"We need your help. Now, my people, I mean the NTSB investigators, they're not cops, they don't understand how to maintain control. And what's vital is, nobody's allowed onto the site, because if they were, see, they might destroy evidence without meaning to, so we can't allow that to happen."

"Sure, I get you."

Jack nodded. "I know you do. We're counting on you to help us out because you're the only one who can keep this site clean. Now, your men—" He looked around and spotted six or seven uniforms. "Can we count on them to do the job?"

Johanssen straightened his shoulders slightly. "Absolutely. Picked every one of them m'self. They're good boys."

Jack dropped the cigarette into the mud and ground it out under his heel. "Okay, then." He held out his hand. "I'm not gonna send in for any county help. You tell me you can do it, I believe you."

The chief took his hand and shook it. "Don't worry, Mr. Webster. Nobody's gonna trample that field, you can bet on it."

Amy came toward them, holding a cup of coffee for herself

and one for Jack, who took the cup and handed it to Johanssen. "Get your men coffee'd up, Chief. Gonna be a long day."

Johanssen turned to marshal his troops as the NTSB team headed for the field.

Amy flipped open the cover on a small reel-to-reel tape recorder about the size of a cigar box and pressed record and play at the same time. The reels turned unusually slowly, the objective being capacity and not sound fidelity. She unclipped a small microphone from the carry strap and held it in her hand. "NTSB Internal, June seven"—she glanced at her watch—"ten hundred hours. Sivara, Goldberg and FBI agent Jonathan Webster. Site is Mepham, Indiana. MD-11 cargo flight." Sivara gestured for the mike and she handed it over, walking close to him so as not to stretch the cord.

Sivara slid the switch to off and said to Webster, "Just ours, okay?" He didn't need Jack's permission, but old habits were hard to break.

"Okay." The tape would not be transcribed, at least not in any official capacity, and not logged in. That would allow Sivara and his people to make preliminary comments freely, without fear of contradictions being disclosed later when the hard data came in and everybody and their brother started scrambling to cover themselves.

He slid the switch back up. "Personal log of investigators, internal use only." He handed the mike back to Amy.

Jack stopped and looked up at the ridge, waiting for Amy to catch up. He pointed as he talked.

"See the markings on the wall? A big center impact, two nearly symmetrical lateral striations on either side?"

"Straight in," said Amy. "Wings level, or nearly."

"Right," said Sivara. "No attempt to turn, pull up . . . nothing. Also notice, the lateral markings are slightly elevated."

"The wings?" Amy cocked her head to one side. "If the nose impacted first, the stress on the wings would be tremendous. Would they pop up?"

Sivara shook his head. "Remember the engine on that DC-10 went down in Chicago? MD-11 is basically the same plane. The engine mounts in the front are stronger than those in the back. If the engine gets torn off, it flips up and over the wing instead of dropping back and tearing out the hydraulic lines."

"Okay . . . the nose hits first, the stress hits the engine as well as the wings." Amy tried to visualize the results. "The engine mounts in front are stronger, so . . ."

Sivara finished for her. "So the engine tries to keep going forward, the rear mounts rip out, the front ones hold . . ."

She saw it. "The engine tilts up and hits the wall."

"Maybe," said Sivara, underscoring the care that needed to be exercised at such an early stage. *Just the facts, ma'am, just the facts.* "From the difference in elevation between the nose and the engine, we might be able to calculate how fast the whole plane was going."

"I doubt it." They both turned toward Jack. "Not unless we rip an actual engine off an actual plane, while it's turning at high speed. The strength of those mounts is specified as a minimum. Normal manufacturing variances alone could make it look like big speed differences. Maybe as much as a hundred knots."

At their skeptical looks he added, "Look at the markings again. The left one's higher."

Amy shielded her eyes against the sun and looked once more at the ridge. "So maybe it wasn't a straight-on hit."

Jack remembered the sectional in his pocket, and the letter that had arrived the previous morning, and the incident at Bellingham. "I'm betting it was."

"Well, anyway, it would only be a cross-check," said Sivara. "The throttle quadrant is a mess, but the levers got fused in place at impact. Since all three of them are pretty much together, I figure they might have frozen where they were set."

"Can you tell roughly what the setting was by eye?" asked Amy.

Sivara pursed his lips. "Maybe, very roughly, something a bit over two hundred knots."

Amy whistled. "I'm surprised there's even this much left."

Jack knelt down to finger a piece of aluminum. Its signature curvature indicated a piece of the fuselage skin rather than a control surface. "Actually, you'd guess there'd be a lot of the aft sections. Normally, it slams into the ground and tears itself to pieces trying to come to a stop. Here"—he swept a hand out in front of him—"it hit once and drifted down. Ground's soft. There'll be a lot buried."

"Funny you should say that," said Sivara, pointing farther down the ridge line. "Tail's over there. You can't see much from here only because the engine assembly snapped off and landed on its side. But it's pretty much intact."

"The ship was mostly empty, right?" said Amy.

"Yeah," said Sivara. "Otherwise there'd be a lot more crap lyin' around."

"But that means the whole body of the plane acted like a shock absorber for the rear. It crumpled and cushioned the impact."

"So?"

"The black boxes." Amy looked at Jack. "They should be in good shape."

"Who's looking for them?" Jack asked Sivara, who turned and looked over toward where the tail lay.

"Kapadia and Schumacher. They'd hoped to have them by now, or at least get to where they were supposed to be. Gotta tell you, though . . ."

"I know," said Jack. "Straight in, no turns, normal settings. Like they had no idea the damned wall was even there."

Sivara looked quizzically at Jack but said nothing, then squatted down and trailed his fingers in the mud, staring into the distance. "What I can't figure is why. Unless one of 'em was sleeping or they were both suicidal, and had a pact to boot, only thing possible is their instruments were lying. All of 'em."

"Wouldn't be the first time a plane got off course," Amy offered lamely, not enjoying the deception and wishing Jack would tell it to Sivara straight.

"That's why we need the boxes," said Jack.

"Lemme go see where we're at on those." Sivara stood and brushed off his hands, then turned and walked toward where his two staffers were hunting for the boxes.

"What gives, boss?" Amy pleaded. "Why keep him in the dark? Seems like a good guy."

"He is. That's why I want him investigating without knowing the answer in advance. Keep him objective. I don't want any of us jumping to conclusions too early."

"He's waving at us. Looks like they might have found them."

The black boxes are the only devices on board a plane that have no useful function unless there is a crash. They don't aid navigation, or provide information to the pilots, or serve any other interim purpose. They are like EKG tracings reviewed during a postmortem, the last desperate flickerings of life before the spark is sucked out and sent to whatever heaven or hell sits reserved for complex pieces of machinery. They are there for one reason only: to tell investigators what the plane was doing in the last seconds before it died.

They are not black at all, but bright, international orange, with highly reflective stripes, to make them as easy as possible to spot amid wreckage.

One of them, the more sophisticated of the two, is the FDR, the flight data recorder, which steadily absorbs instrument readings collected from over two hundred sources while the plane is flying, and records them on slowly turning reels of tape. All the navigation instruments, airspeed and rate-of-climb indicators, hydraulically actuated control surfaces, temperature, turn and bank, angle of attack, throttle settings . . . everything to give accident investigators as much information as possible to understand what went wrong and why.

The FDR is powered by the plane's electrical system, the theory being that in any crash consequential enough to warrant removing the boxes, said crash would be significant enough to disrupt electrical power and stop the machine from rerecording over itself as the tape exceeds its twenty-five-hour capacity and loops around to the beginning again. The theory had never failed.

Analysis wasn't easy. It used to take weeks, but special computer programs now allowed investigators to get the basic readings out in days, sometimes hours, with listings and plots of the various data channels. When the situation warranted the effort, it was even possible to reconstruct the flight in animated form, factoring in known weather conditions, other traffic in the area, the engineering characteristics of the plane itself, reported visibility and even the surrounding terrain, resulting in a realistic re-creation of the aircraft's death throes that could be speeded up, slowed down, advanced frame by frame and turned in three dimensions.

The other box was the cockpit voice recorder. The CVR was a simple device, a fairly ordinary tape recorder capturing the voices of the crew. It took a special hardening of the senses and a deep commitment to one's craft to tolerate repeated hearings of tension, anxiety, panic and resignation that were clearly evident in the voices of the crew, but even the hardest of them cringed and drew back involuntarily when the screaming and the praying started. Almost always the crew died fully aware of what was happening to them, saw the ground spiraling crazily up to meet them, knew with ineffable certainty that in several seconds they would be dead, wondering what the first microseconds would feel like as the nose of the plane slammed into the ground and wondering also if there really was a heaven or a hell and, if so, what kinds of lives they had led in the eyes of God.

"You were right," Sivara said to Amy as they approached. "They look perfect."

Honore Kapadia finished disconnecting the input cables to one of the boxes and was handing it up to Sivara. "Should tell us a lot," she said. "Remarkable what good shape it's in. Still *ping*ing, too." Amy could hear the sonarlike tones emanating from the device, a sonic alarm that would allow searchers to locate the boxes even if they were under water.

"What about the cockpit voice recorder?" asked Jack.

"Have it up in a second. It looks good, too."

"I'll go make arrangements to send them to D.C." Amy turned to go, but Jack gently grabbed her arm.

"I'll take 'em myself."

"But, boss, they gotta go *now*."

"I'm going now."

With a backward glance at the confused NTSB field people, Amy led Jack a few steps away.

"Hell are you talking about, Jack?"

He reached for her shoulder and squeezed it. "You stick around. Learn something. Try to be helpful." He looked back out over the field. "We know what happened. We know why. Let Sivara and his team do their job, gather all the data and physical evidence. They'll set up an engineering team in

Washington. But I don't need to be here, and I want you back in two days."

"Gonna look suspicious," said Amy.

"Handle it."

With a half wave in Sivara's direction, Jack walked away, back toward the farmhouse and the rental car, toward the huddled townspeople and the police cordon, toward the airport and toward NTSB headquarters in Washington, where the righteous indignation of a cabinet secretary, a senator, a handful of senior DOT officials and one (at least) of the most powerful airline executives in the country surely awaited him.

All of their free-floating anxieties, the featureless dread of a briefly glimpsed sort-of threat, would have coalesced into a sharper fear by now, fed by the horrific reality of their bluff being called, given shape by the unmistakable manifestation of their worst fears that lay behind him as he walked away.

He wasn't supposed to be part of this. That was the deal.

CHAPTER 14

Jack looked at his watch for the tenth time in as many minutes. He hardly needed the ceiling lamps to illuminate its face. The glow cast by the hardened glares around the table was almost enough.

What they had been up against before was unnerving because it was daring and unprecedented, its technical brilliance even worthy of grudging admiration. It was all a matter of perspective, as Jack saw it, whom you rooted for in any contest of brains and wills. From whose point of view was the story being told?

Theft capers were among his favorite subjects in the movies. Despite the official role he played in his government, he had rooted along with everybody else for the jewel thieves in *Topkapi*. All that cunning and planning. They deserved to win, didn't they? Not really. You just got it from their perspective, that's all. A good director could manipulate you into rooting for a paid assassin, a mass murderer or even the whole of organized crime, as a spate of sympathetic mob movies made abundantly clear. Made you wonder about the generic distinctions between good and evil.

There was a case to be made that the government's side

had agreed to a deal and then welshed. Captain Marvel wanted five million dollars to cease disrupting air traffic operations. They started paying, and the trouble stopped. They reneged before all the money was paid out, and Marvel saw this as breach of contract, an implied release of his own obligations. So while the circumstances surrounding the bargain may have been a little unorthodox, a deal's a deal, right? *Marvel held up his end and we didn't.*

Jack's head whirled with thoughts half grasped and ideas that died aborning before he could think them through. *What we had been up against before had been unnerving. Okay. Somebody had us by the short and curlies. Didn't feel real good, but at least we understood what was going on. Had a grasp on it conceptually and took comfort in what we perceived as its finite extent. Knew we were outsmarted, but hey, what the hell, soon it'll be back to business, we take our lumps, life goes on.*

But this. This is different. Like being a lifelong atheist and then catching a half-second glimpse of God, not a long look, but just enough to know absolutely, irrefutably, that it was really Him. Then it's gone, but in that transitory, evanescent moment everything you ever believed about anything changes forever. All the old rules are gone and it's a whole new game. *Gotta cut a guy some slack if it takes him just a little bit of time to grab on to it.*

The little lights dancing in his brain made it difficult for him to think straight. He was only joking with himself when he thought that Marvel had a point, that his deal had been broken, right? Just some self-deprecating irony there, didn't really mean it, right? *'Course not, the guy's a fucking psychopath, what am I talking about?*

Except that while they were making payments, a giant airline was only losing a few pennies, amounts so small relative to its bloated balance sheet that they wouldn't even be considered a rounding error by the accountants. For Chrissakes, they spent more than that in toilet paper, so really, what difference did it make? Well, when they'd withheld the toilet paper money, three good people lost their lives, a hundred-million-dollar airplane was pulverized and frightened sleeplessness would haunt a small town in Indiana long after the officials had forgotten all about it.

No, no, that's still not right. What the hell am I thinking? He glanced at his watch yet again.

"Think of it as buyin' time, Abelard," Secretary Letitia May Hubbard was saying to Senator Fedder. "A little loss in our self-esteem is the price we're gonna pay to buy some time."

Preston Stanley, while technically blameless in all of this, was not going to let Jack swing in the breeze alone. "We asked you all to keep up the payments until we caught the guy. Now, as you can see—"

Hubbard's eyes flashed at the FBI agent. "Now, don't you be revisin' history on us here, Mr. Stanley. That request was to enable a capture, not to prevent a disaster. We were assured that the latter was no longer a possibility, so don't be confusin' means and motives."

Before anybody else could take up the fruitless argument, she continued. "People, I'm not interested in blame. Yet. So let's not start preenin' and flutterin' around. We miscalculated and underestimated the man. We'll worry about why later. Right now, we gotta figure out what's really goin' on, make it stop for good. You don't got somethin' constructive to say, pipe down!"

After an uneasy silence, Sam Cavanaugh spoke. In marked contrast with his bluster at the last meeting, walking out and pronouncing the matter closed, he was more subdued now, his former physical expansiveness now metamorphosed into a posture of implosion. His hands were folded in front of him, his elbows close to his body, he met no one's look with his own. The skin around his eyes seemed tighter even while his cheeks seemed to sag. What remained of his sparse hair was disheveled, as though he had somehow abandoned the cosmetic niceties in the face of a higher imperative. His voice was low and tentative, distrustful of itself even as it formed words.

"What do you know about my plane, Webster? What can you tell us?"

There was an embarrassed shifting around the table. The question was out of line. Many others had had cause to want to ask similar questions over the years, but each had held silent pending at least the preliminary opinion.

But Cavanaugh's eyes pleaded. This wasn't just a case of something that had been done to his airline. The possibility hung in the air that there might be culpability on *his* part, as on the parts of the others involved, all of whom had concurred in the decision to halt payments to the extortionist. Nobody had realized it was a life-and-death determination. A million angry voices, when they became aware of the circumstances, would not hesitate to express indignation that this *ad hoc* assemblage could have thought anything else.

Jack looked at Cavanaugh and shrank from the pain he found there. The executive was no soda pop salesman turned CEO, but an aviator himself, who had borrowed to buy his first plane and fought to build a company of substance grounded in dreams. This was no time to play by the book. Captain Marvel had seen to that.

"Off the record?" Jack looked around at all the faces and found nodding assent. He gestured to Amy Goldberg.

"The MD-11 seems to have been in normal approach configuration when it hit the ridge. The lab played back the cockpit voice recorder and everything sounded completely normal, except for a loud click and then a fraction of a second of silence before the tape stopped."

The interval between the time the nose of the plane touched the ridge and the cockpit microphone was crushed in the collapsing cockpit was less than a twentieth of a second, just long enough for the sound of impact to begin registering on the tape. The final moment of silence was caused by the tape recorder's reels turning for another quarter of an inch with no input from the microphone, until the loss of electrical power shut down the recorder.

Nobody in this room would ever actually hear those tapes, including Jack and Amy. They were open to too much interpretation and were heard only by the NTSB's laboratory experts. Once, a judge had ordered that a cockpit voice recorder tape be made available to litigants in a lawsuit. An act of Congress in 1990 put a stop to that. Now, all anybody got was the lab report, and no judge in any legal forum short of the Supreme Court could alter that.

"The plane flew through a thunderstorm and radioed Indianapolis approach control for weather conditions at Mepham. They told Indie they were on final approach, but they were too low for the controller to see them on his regular radar. He wasn't too busy, so he called a maintenance facility on the field to see what the weather was. By the time he got back on the radio, he was unable to raise the crew."

"Were they in trouble?" asked Hubbard.

"Not really," replied Amy, "except that the controller said they seemed to be off course before they dropped below his backup radar. They were wrestling with turbulence but reported nothing else out of the ordinary. It looked like they were going to have to abort the landing and head for their alternate. It's when they didn't pop back up on the screen that the controller got worried, because the guy he spoke to at the field thought a landing was out of the question."

"How come the controller didn't just call the field back? See if the plane had landed?" Stanley's investigative instincts were at work, and he wondered why the controller had waited until he failed to see a blip on his screen.

"He did," said Amy. "Got no answer. Apparently there was a big lightning strike right near the field. The guy he was talking to went to see what had happened. But it wasn't a lightning strike."

Fedder looked up, missing what everybody had already grasped. Amy looked at him levelly.

"They heard the MD-11 hit the ridge and explode. We have the phone conversation on the radar room's tapes."

Jack opened a manila folder on the tabletop in front of him and spread out several sheets of paper in overlapping fashion. Looking from one to the next, he said, "Very preliminary readings from the flight recorders seem to indicate that all instrument readings were normal for the approach. There's no instrument landing system on that field—"

"Then what were they doing landing there in the middle of the night during a storm?" demanded Fedder, thinking he was beating everybody else to an insightful question.

Jack looked up at him. "You don't need an ILS to land on instruments, Senator. That's just one kind of navigational aid. A good one, because it tells you not only if you're to the left or right of the approach path, but also if you're above or below it. But it's not necessary, just better."

"Mepham's a VOR approach, isn't it?" asked Deputy Undersecretary Davison, referring to a less expensive but also less precise navigation instrument. "I used to work for a regional that operated in there."

Amy nodded. "It also has a radio beacon to cross-check distance from the field." She turned toward Fedder. "Private pilots without distance-measuring equipment use it mostly, but the commercials sometimes turn it on just as an additional precaution and to stay in practice."

"But I don't get it," Cavanaugh said plaintively, almost as though he might be able to argue the crash out of existence. "The radio beacon's not hooked into the autopilot. How the hell could this sumbitch fiddle with the beacon readings? Why wouldn't the pilots have noticed a discrepancy?"

Amy turned to Jack. It was a damned good question. Even if Captain Marvel had complete control of the VOR, which fed information directly to the autopilot, the low-technology beacon wasn't part of the on-board navigation database and had no influence on the autopilot. It was an independent device.

Jack fingered the stubble on his chin and drew the wrinkled sectional map out of his folder. On it he had drawn the correct approach path in pencil and the erroneous path followed by the MD-11 in red ink. Several of the participants gathered around to look.

"The beacon instrument is really just a simple direction finder, a needle on the panel pointing to the radio station." He indicated the spot on the map. "At Mepham, the station is way off to the left of the approach path.

"So as the plane moves down the approach, the needle keeps swinging farther to the left as the station passes. You read how much the needle is deflected, you can tell where you are on the approach path."

He put the tip of his index finger on the penciled line. "See here, for example? If the needle points exactly to your nine o'clock position, the station is directly off the left wing and you're right here on the path: three miles from the runway.

Another ten degrees of swing and you're only two miles away."

"Sounds simple enough," said Stanley. "How come they didn't see they were off?"

Jack tapped his pencil on the sectional. "Because the beacon readings were completely normal."

"Holy shit," blurted Amy, forgetting for a moment where she was. "The false path is parallel to the real one!"

She grabbed the pencil out of Jack's hand and drew a line from the radio station through the true path, continuing on until it intersected the false path. "The station makes roughly the same angle with both approach paths. It can't tell you how far away you are, only if you're in a straight line."

"The beacon isn't very accurate to start with," Jack said, "and they were wallowing around in turbulence, so the needle swinging around from all the shaking was greater than the slight error."

He looked up. "They never had a chance. There was no way for them to figure it out in the dark, no outside visibility, even if they were checking the beacon. Odds are they didn't even bother to tune it in."

The people who had drawn in to see the map settled back down onto their chairs.

"Any chance it was an accident?" asked Secretary Hubbard.

Amy picked up the photostat of the fax they had received the same morning and held it up in the air. "None. And it also seems that our evidence is a little more solid this time as well." She pointed to the folder in front of Jack, who pushed it toward her. She removed several sheets covered with lines of obscure symbols and some graphs.

"Webster said the instrument readings were normal, and that's true." She picked out two sheets and set them side by side. "Now this is preliminary. There's been very little time to cross-reference all of the data, and there's a lot of work yet to—"

"Ms. Goldberg." Cavanaugh leaned forward, still working his hands around each other nervously. "We already agreed we're off the record. Please: what have you got?"

Amy cleared her throat and put an index finger on each sheet, holding her point of reference as she spoke. "The instrument readings were normal, at least in the sense that the navigational fixes were where they were supposed to be. But I ran a quick simulation of the flight path, making some assumptions about the wind conditions at the time. Maybe it'll work better on the board."

She rose and went to the whiteboard, and everybody turned on their seats for a clear view. Referring to the two sheets, Amy started drawing with a felt tip marker.

"I'll oversimplify to make the point. The approach into Mepham looks like a U with squared-off corners. The plane flies down one leg of the U, parallel to the runway but in the opposite direction of its intended landing, then it turns ninety degrees left, the bottom of the U, and then turns again to line up with the runway." She drew the lines as she spoke. "Up the other leg.

"At each of the corners, there's a waypoint, kind of an electronic street sign tells the plane where it is so it knows when to turn. For less sophisticated aircraft that can't read the waypoints, you use the radio beacon to tell you when you're at the fix."

"But if the instruments were reading right, maybe there was something wrong with them," Fedder offered. "Or maybe the equipment on the ground was malfunctioning."

Amy shook her head and started to dismiss the suggestion abruptly so she could get on with her point, then remembered Jack's lessons in diplomacy. "That's a good suggestion, and the most likely explanation, so we checked the equipment and everything's working to specs." She turned back to the board.

"What happened was this: We know from the flight recorders that the plane was traveling at two hundred ten knots. In still air, they should have been finished with the base leg— the bottom of the U—in about ninety seconds. Allowing for a thirty-knot headwind, one hundred seconds at the most."

She tried to juggle the papers in her hand and finally set them back down on the table and hunched over them. "Now if I read these graphs correctly, they spent nearly three minutes on that leg. That pushed them out about three miles. When they made the final left turn, they were heading straight for the ridge."

"What's all of that mean?" asked Hubbard.

"It means," said Jack, "that Captain Marvel doesn't have to tamper with the database at all, and probably never did."

"So what in Christ's name is he doing?" Cavanaugh was having trouble controlling his anxiety.

Amy felt sympathy toward him despite his blustery behavior at their first meeting. She spoke without inflection, giving him the facts as she thought he'd want them. "He's beaming a signal to the on-board navigation units that triggers some kind of an override. The units then ignore the real data coming from the legitimate ground equipment and take his false information instead."

Jack explained further. "All he has to transmit are slight discrepancies, just enough to stretch out an approach leg for a minute or two, and then more data that makes the equipment think it's on the approach path. It's actually simple as hell if you can just get the nav unit to ignore the real signals. Can even be done with a hand-held unit if you're not too far away." A new thought occurred to him. "Maybe that's how he hit the 727 and not the Lear in Bellingham. Just enough power . . ."

He was instantly sorry for speculating out loud. "Forget that," he said. "Too imprecise."

"Well now, hold on just a minute here." Cavanaugh's face was a mixture of anger and confusion. "What override? There's no such thing as an override in a nav instrument!"

"Yes, yes, I'm sorry." Amy took off her glasses—she'd forgotten that she hated to wear them in public—and rubbed the bridge of her nose. She had been up the entire night running the analyses. "I forgot that part." She put the glasses back on. "Somehow, he must have managed to get a special circuit into the nav units that responds to whatever frequency he's transmitting. That's all we can figure."

Tired and worn out, and having delivered the news so casually, Amy was surprised at the dumbfounded expressions she found as she looked around. She felt uncomfortable in the ensuing silence and thought maybe more explanation was warranted.

"Uh, it's most likely in the microchip, the, um, little computer that controls the unit."

Sensing her discomfort and fatigue, Jack jumped in. "Pretty much the nav unit's real brain is in the one control chip. Our guy may have been on the design team and slipped this little extra feature in without telling anybody."

"How long ago?" asked Ferguson.

"No way of telling, although it's virtually certain it only affects Autonav units." *Which have a 73 percent market share*, he declined to add out loud.

"How old were the devices in that 727 over Bellingham?" asked Hubbard.

So much for softening up bad news. "Four years."

"Jesus!" Cavanaugh ran a hand through his hair and did a quick mental calculation. "We could be talking half the commercial U.S. fleet here, people!"

"Sure makes my job harder," said Preston Stanley. "We've got to expand our check of their employees going back—I don't know—how long since the last major redesign of the chip?"

"We're checking that out now," said Amy. "But the 'mole' circuit could easily precede even a big revision. It might date all the way back to the last from-scratch design."

"All right, what are we looking at here?" Secretary Hubbard uncapped her eighty-nine-cent disposable ballpoint pen and looked around the table for a piece of scratch paper. Amy handed her a manila folder after removing the few sheets of paper inside.

"First, to clean out the junk for sure, Autonav would have to build a new chip from scratch and then replace every unit in every plane. How many we got?" She knew the answer but was trying to resurrect some sense of teamwork.

"Figure maybe three, four thousand commercial planes alone," said Cavanaugh. "And there's two units in every plane—"

"I already crunched a few numbers, Madame Secretary," said Amy, leafing through her notes. "You're looking at two years, maybe as much as two hundred million dollars, figuring installation, down time and everything else."

"Right. So let's go to Plan B." That drew a nervous laugh and a suggestion from Davison.

"What if we contract with the other manufacturer and install *their* units in every plane?"

"It's a thought," said Amy. "But all that buys you back is the design time. Still gonna take eighteen months, and the cost won't change that much."

Hubbard put down the pen and folded her hands in front of her. "Okay, we all know where this is goin'." She turned to Jack, with a glance at Preston Stanley. "So how you gonna catch the guy and his little friends?"

Jack pushed his chin forward to free some pinched skin from his collar, which seemed to have gotten tighter since he'd put it on that morning. It appeared to him that Stanley was having the same problem.

"To start with, we've resumed making payments." He looked around the table. "I assume nobody has any problem with that." There was a good deal of squirming—people like these did not suffer extortionists gladly, especially ones who seemed to be smarter than they—but no protests were raised. Even Senator Fedder thought better than to make a symbolic issue of it at this point.

"We seem to be outsmarted, at least for the moment. Short of some massive, covert surveillance of automated teller machines, which is probably impossible anyway and is guaranteed to result in one hell of a mess when word leaks out, we're not going to nail the guy with straight police work."

"There's maybe another thing." Cavanaugh fidgeted with his fingers and seemed reluctant to continue.

"What's that?" Stanley prompted.

Cavanaugh took a breath and looked up. "One of my PR guys got a call from a lady says she dreamed the whole thing before it happened. Scared hell out of her husband. Says she called a psychic who can help us find out how it happened if they work together."

Stanley looked nervously at Amy.

"Turns out we got a bunch of calls from people who dreamed the thing," Cavanaugh continued. "The psychic said something about pooling all the energy, like through a channel." He appeared to run out of steam and was looking for help. "I don't know diddly about this crap but why don't we try it?"

Jack stepped in quickly to preempt any serious discussion that might have ensued. "There's no way in hell we're gonna bother with that, Sam."

"But why the hell not?" the executive protested. "All these people having these dreams, what's the harm, we get these people in on—"

"Forget it," Jack said. "It's horseshit and we're not going to waste our time."

"Look," Amy interrupted, placing a calming hand on Jack's arm. "Let me explain something so we can move on. There are about, I don't know, maybe two hundred fifty million people in this country old enough to talk, okay? Let's say, being conservative, only half of them have dreams they can remember the next day, and they each have maybe four a night. You with me so far?"

Cavanaugh nodded. "So what? Some of these folks who called are probably honest people, and—"

Amy held up a hand. "Bear with me here. Let's assume every one of them is honest. Except the psychic, who is full of baloney, but hold that aside for a second. So far we got half a billion remembered dreams every night, right? Now one of the most common themes in dreams is disasters, and especially air crashes."

"Is that true?" Hubbard asked.

"Trust me on this," Amy answered. "So let's say, and again let's be conservative, that only a hundredth of one percent of all of those dreams is about air disasters. Anybody got a problem with that?"

She was answered with agreeing looks around the table, and went on. "Good. Because that leaves us with at least fifty thousand people *every single night* who dream about airplanes crashing. And it's not a great leap to see that a whole bunch of those are going to match a lot of details if there happens to be a real crash, so what I'm telling you is, the real miracle would be if *nobody* dreamed about the crash, not that hundreds of people did." She sat back to catch her breath after the impassioned lecture. "Most of them are honest. But it's proba-bility, not psychic powers."

Cavanaugh, ever the hard pragmatist, was helpless before

implacable logic, and didn't pursue the dream angle. "But what about the psychic? Isn't there a possibility—"

Amy shook her head tiredly. "Preston, you ever come across a case, anywhere, where one of these bozos ever really solved anything?"

"Not even one," Stanley answered without hesitation. He turned to Cavanaugh. "Don't get me wrong, Mr. Cavanaugh. I'm not saying that there may not be something to this. I'm just telling you that Dr. Goldberg is right. There's never been a single, provable case where one of these frauds ever really contributed anything other than the occasional lucky guess. And the number of times they've screwed up investigations with phony 'evidence' is too large to count."

"Didn't mean to be so hard, Sam," Jack said. "But we don't have time to play games with professional bullshit artists. I guarantee you it's a waste of time. Okay?"

Cavanaugh slumped back on his chair. "I got it. Just clutching at straws." He smiled and tried to lighten up the atmosphere. "Imagine a hard-ass like me playing patty-cake with witch doctors anyway."

Jack laughed and turned to Stanley. "We've got to step up the background work. It's our best chance for a possible ID."

"I've got a meeting with the director following this one. He's already heard from the president"—he nodded an acknowledgment toward Hubbard—"and all he needs now are the details. He's even prepared to pull trainees out of the academy for the more mundane legwork."

"You know," said Cavanaugh, now resigned to the fact that only practical approaches were worth considering, "at some point we're gonna have no choice but to open this thing up, risk going public and mobilize an all-out manhunt. I don't see how he can escape that."

"He probably can't," Amy said. "And he knows it. He's counting on us to want to avoid that at all costs. Maybe that's why he's kept his demand so low: makes the trade-off clear-cut."

"What else, Webster?" Hubbard asked.

"There is another thing. We've got the FBI's cooperation on it, too." He swiveled his chair around halfway and indicated

Amy with an outstretched palm. "We need to start playing with his head."

Having solicited her reluctant cooperation before the meeting, Jack briefly outlined for the gathering some of the highlights of Amy's background, leaving out details that were classified, which were nearly all of them.

Jack's first experience working with Amy Goldberg had come on the heels of the crash of a transport aircraft over Holland. The plane had been operated by the CIA's "Air America" cover corporation, which might have been an awkward rationale for asking the Dutch to invite the NTSB in, an invitation from the foreign sovereign being a requirement before the board could get involved. Fortunately the transport was of American manufacture. Evidence pointed to a Red Brigade splinter group, but it was an expensive operation and they couldn't figure how it was financed.

Amy was brought in, from an agency Jack was ordered to forget after the case was closed, and connected it up with a Belgian national lottery scam in which the suspects had somehow figured out how to spot winning scratch-off tickets. They had one suspect, a young man named Dieter Warschein, but the only evidence against him was, as was so typical, an anonymous telephone tip.

The established local authorities were assured by Belgian lottery officials that discerning winning tickets was impossible, which led them to assume the perpetrators had someone on the inside.

Amy assumed nothing and did not consider coincidental the fact that Warschein's father had been badly wounded during an American counterterrorist operation in East Germany. She also was intrigued that Warschein worked as a lowly technician despite possessing a doctorate in physics from the prestigious Max Planck Institute. His job was maintaining a PET scanner, a positron emission tomograph, a highly advanced medical imaging device.

Amy, after days of fruitless analysis on the winning tickets, and much to the irritation of both Interpol and the Belgian security police, insisted on using sensitive and therefore expensive checks for radiation. When the tests came up positive, the rest fell into place easily.

Warschein had worked out the exact frequencies and calibrations necessary to cause the inks below the scratch-off clay to resonate at levels that could be stimulated by the PET scanner. From there it was an easy matter to pick off an imaging "slice" and feed it to the machine's display tube. Once he had the technique down pat, he could scan thousands of lottery tickets each hour during those portions of his tedious night shift when he wasn't making largely mindless adjustments to the machine.

Getting the tickets involved nothing more clever than bribing the night manager of the biggest lottery retailer in Brussels, who was well compensated for nothing more than letting Warschein "borrow" boxes of tickets at night and return them in the morning, minus a few tickets here and there. These were subsequently cashed by Warschein's compatriots through intermediaries, who asked no questions in exchange for a percentage. Patience and care resulted in sufficient working capital in less than a year.

Interpol made short work of tracing back through the people who cashed in the tickets.

Of course, Amy had had a lot more data on Warschein's gang than was available on Captain Marvel. Which gave her the beginnings of an idea, or at least a direction. . . .

Jack finished his prepared speech, and its general nature was not lost on the meeting's participants. "One other thing," he said. "I'm going to start having Florence Hartzig sit in on some meetings."

Amy and Preston Stanley exchanged quick glances—*Say what?*—and hoped nobody had noticed. They were supposed to be a team, after all. But this was news to them.

"The FundsNet lady?" asked Hubbard. "Why?"

"No offense to the lady," said Undersecretary Davison, who was perpetually leery of *civilians*, "but what makes her any better than one of your Bureau people?"

"Couple things. First, our only communications link with Captain Marvel is the cash machines, and Hartzig can play those like a violin. She designed 'em.

"Second, this is a highly technical scam, and none of us are sufficiently up to speed on this stuff." He sought, and received, answering nods from Amy and Stanley. "I doubt anyone on our staff can match her, so we get two for the price of one with Hartzig."

Amy kept her face impassive and hoped Jack was keeping a good grip on himself. She'd sensed his growing fascination with Florence Hartzig, a brilliant and strong-willed woman, and wondered if the contrast with Jack's own wife, or at least his perception of apparent contrast, wasn't what was drawing him to her. Amy had always felt that she herself had been sought out and hired by Jack for similar reasons. But the two of them had always had a clear understanding regarding her unavailability, and no such understanding existed with Florence. Besides, Amy liked Betty Webster a good deal and knew without a doubt that she was underappreciated.

Sam Cavanaugh was less concerned with bringing on a newcomer than he was with what Amy's role seemed to be evolving into. "This from a guy tells me psychics are fulla crap?"

The smiles around the table flagged some sympathy with this position, which Jack sought quickly to stem. "She's not a psychic, Mr. Cavanaugh. She's a psychologist."

"Again," said Davison, "what's the matter with the FBI? Your Behavioral Sciences Section has had a lot of success in that area."

Damned right! thought Stanley, but he was a team player and he stayed silent. At least in front of this crowd.

Jack shook his head and looked at Stanley. "Nothing wrong with your people—our people—but they're used to dealing with serial murderers, bank robbers and stuff like that. Violent people, not afraid to stick a knife in somebody. Our guy isn't a violent type."

There was an immediate and loud jumble of protesting voices. "Not violent?" yelled Fedder above the noise. "What do you call knocking an airplane out of the sky? Killing three people?"

"There's a difference between long-distance, remote-control destruction and the direct and immediate taking of a life," explained Amy. "What we're guessing, our guy is reticent, maybe even squeamish about conventional murder or physical violence." *Or at least he used to be.*

"Why do you think that?" asked Cavanaugh. "We don't know a damned thing about this guy."

"This is where I get in over my head." Jack swiveled his chair around to face Amy. "Doctor?" he prompted, throwing in the title to underscore her qualifications for the skeptical among them.

As Amy was about to respond to Jack's invitation to continue the rough analysis of Captain Marvel, there was a knock at the door. After a respectful pause, the door opened and an administrative staffer handed Jack a note on folded paper. It was only two lines long. He read it, read it again, rubbed his forehead and read it once more.

"Basically," said Amy, "we know very little, so we have to make a few assumptions, test them and see what happens."

"What do you mean, test the assumptions?" asked Hubbard.

"I have no idea."

Cavanaugh let out a loud exhalation between pursed lips and looked around the room, turning his eyes upward momentarily. His display of impatient exasperation met with sympathetic looks.

"I've hardly started," Amy protested. Seeking to deflect attention from herself, she said to Jack, "What's in the note?"

"Sorry?" Jack looked up, puzzled. Then his face cleared and he held up the piece of paper. "Oh, this. Our friends just shifted gears again. South Dakota. One of them worked the western side of the state this morning and now it looks like team two is in the east."

Stanley shook his head. "Two of them again, and it—"

"You know," said Amy, purposely cutting him off to prevent any conversation about the two teams, "this is now in the board's jurisdiction. There's been an accident, so it's ours."

Hubbard sensed some tension. "Who's the board member in charge, then?"

"Pressman. He'll fly back soon as he can. I spoke to him earlier"—she ignored Jack's head jerking in her direction—"and he requested that Webster handle it in the interim." Well, he'd sort of grudgingly agreed to it after Amy had pressed the point. She wanted Jack not because existing board investigators couldn't handle it, but because he was FBI, just like Stanley, and if he were in charge, then Stanley would be less able to insist on going down paths her instincts were telling her were pointless. Assuming, of course, that Jack wouldn't do the same, especially under pressure from his much more experienced colleague.

All of these implications were lost on Hubbard. "You have any ideas, Dr. Goldberg?" The secretary was used to making selections from a menu of alternatives presented to her by staff. This situation was frustrating in that no such choices seemed available.

"Maybe." *But I'm not about to speculate aloud in front of bureaucrats, politicians and the middle-management protective association.*

"Not good enough." *Give me something, for heaven's sake!*

Amy's answering look said it all: *You got any better ideas, let me know. Right now, I need some time.* She didn't add that returning to this sort of work was the last thing she wanted or needed in her life.

"We're in an awful lot of trouble, aren't we?" asked Davison, a plaintive note in his voice. He needed some reassurance, needed to be told there'd be a good end to this eventually.

Jack looked slowly around the room. "We need some space, folks. This is not your garden-variety misfit."

CHAPTER 15

1962

Bo wasn't much for news. Like most people, prior to 1962 he had little idea of what was transpiring in the southeast Asian country of Vietnam. Likely couldn't even have told you that there were two Vietnams.

It is a matter of some curiosity how important events are sometimes obscured by the weight of even greater events happening simultaneously. Few marked the death of Aldous Huxley, coming as it did on the day of John F. Kennedy's assassination, or the devastating hurricane that battered the northeast American coast while a Soviet coup threatened to abort the new democracy aborning.

So it was toward the end of World War II regarding the largely unknown and inconsequential southeast Asian country of Vietnam.

Like the United States, Vietnam had its roots in revolution, dating back to the honored ancestors who rose to repel a Mongolian invasion. Also like the United States, the country found itself the subject of colonial domination by a European power, in this case the French, who for a while effectively repressed rising anticolonialism. The only real organization of any threat was the Indochinese Communist party, but it

was organized *outside* the country, in 1930, by Nguyen That
Thanh.

After living in the Soviet Union and China during the 1930s,
That Thanh returned to Vietnam at the outbreak of World War
II. France had fallen to the Germans by then and was nominally under the command of the collaborationist Vichy government, which was in no position to resist the demands of its
occupier or its occupier's allies. One of these was Japan,
which demanded joint occupancy of Vietnam.

In response, That Thanh organized the League for the Independence of Vietnam. Also called the Viet Minh, it led the
resistance against the occupying Japanese during the war,
motivated by both ancestral precedent and Lenin's theory of
national liberation struggles. As the defeat of Japan became
imminent, the Japanese government tried desperately to establish its colonial presence in Vietnam, seizing French garrisons
and convincing the Annamese emperor Bao Dai to declare
Vietnam's independence. This action took place the very week
that Bo Kincaid fought his last battle over the skies of Berlin.

Bao Dai made only a halfhearted try at governing his country, and made it easy for That Thanh's Communist-led insurgents to emerge dominant. At the close of the world war in
August, Hanoi fell to the Viet Minh and the Democratic
Republic of Vietnam was established, with That Thanh as its
president.

That same month, the great powers meeting in Potsdam
were planning to divide Indochina at the sixteenth parallel,
the north going to China and the south to British forces.

It would be more than twenty years before Bo Kincaid took
any note of these occurrences. By that time the world would
know That Thanh by his new name, Ho Chi Minh.

The peace conference in Geneva following the 1954 Battle
of Dien Bien Phu had resulted in partition of the country at
the seventeenth parallel, partitioning being somewhat of a
universal solution in the post–World War II period, even
despite the bad press accompanying the last abortive split
proposal at the Potsdam Conference nine years earlier and
one degree of latitude lower. The agreement stipulated eventual free elections and reunification. The first major actions
of Ngo Dinh Diem, the U.S. replacement for the formerly

exiled but repatriated Bao Dai, were failing to hold the elections and failing to reunify.

Among Diem's many other transgressions was the return of land to local land barons, a reversal of the more egalitarian agrarian philosophies of Ho Chi Minh's Viet Minh. If his previous actions brought the populace, at least those who weren't Christian, to the edge of rebellion, this act pushed them over. Diem's dictatorship found itself under attack from a variety of rebel groups, upon whom he hung the collective and contemptuous moniker "Viet Cong." By 1960 the Viet Cong, perhaps taking a cue from the single name Diem had bestowed upon them, consolidated themselves into the National Liberation Front of South Vietnam.

Now there was a real enemy around which the United States could coalesce a policy and a real hero to serve as its focus. Ngo Dinh Diem, like the sultan of Kuwait over thirty years later, was a ruthless dictator bent on the self-aggrandizing suppression of his people, but his failings as an American ally were outweighed by shared hatred for common enemies, so the United States stepped up military aid to the anti-Communist hero. This was ostensibly for the defense of a friend against attacks from the outside, many of these "undoubtedly" of Chinese Communist influence.

Many scratched their heads over official policy descriptions of North Vietnamese involvement in the south's growing civil disorder, seeing very little evidence of it. What they did see was a hue and cry from the local citizenry owing to the repressive behavior of the Diem administration. Nevertheless, at that point in America's history it was generally not a good idea to ask too many questions about rationales for fighting the Reds, and the inconsistencies were brushed aside easily in the face of the national paranoia that still wafted from the effluvia of the McCarthy era.

In 1962, citing violation of the Geneva Accords by the North Vietnamese because of their infiltration into the south and their support of the Viet Cong, President John F. Kennedy decided to significantly boost the number of U.S. advisers, still without direct combat roles. The commitment ramped up to eleven thousand troops, two-thirds of them army personnel. The huge growth in U.S. personnel during 1962, tripling the number directly engaged in the advisory effort, made it possible to assign personnel to South Vietnamese army units in battle zones. Green Berets were dispatched to train civilians in combat, including Montagnard tribesmen in the highlands and other groups in remote regions.

By 1963 the repressive Diem regime became so hated that acts of protest took on bizarre proportions. In June of that year an elderly Buddhist monk named Quang Due calmly sat down in the middle of a Saigon intersection, poured gasoline over himself and lit a match.

Things got so bad that the U.S. supported an ARVN coup in which Diem was killed.

Three weeks later President Kennedy was assassinated. Three hours later Lyndon B. Johnson succeeded him and took over management of the Vietnam conflict. Twenty-two months later, after having already authorized covert missions into both North Vietnam and Laos, Johnson exploited a dubious "attack" on two U.S. naval vessels in the Gulf of Tonkin to goad Congress into granting him the right "to take all necessary measures" to prosecute the war.

Along with the rest of America, Bo Kincaid watched the developments with interest. It was doubtful that his neighbors' reasons were the same as his own.

June 11, 0925 MST

> This is Jack.
>
> Is everything being done to your satisfaction?
>
> Please press 1 for Yes or 2 for No.

1126 EST

"Hot damn!" cried Preston Stanley as the minidrama started playing out on the NTSB monitor.

"He's hesitating," said Amy. "That's good. Very good."

"Why?" asked Stanley.

"Because he's scared," answered Jack. "Thrown."

"Exactly." Amy was leaning over the back of a chair, her face inches from the screen, peering into it as though to see if there were more there than only the green letters and numbers.

Captain Marvel had withdrawn two thousand dollars. The money had started dropping well before the phone connection with the FundsNet computers had been completed, but the preplanned message had shot back across the wires within a second of that and appeared on the ATM's display screen.

Jack had composed the message. Amy, the psy-ops mastermind, had tried to do it herself but became so enveloped in the intricacies, so caught up in nested encirclements of what-ifs within what-thens, that she had finally turned to him in exasperation and said, "What's the most innocent, most innocuous way you would simply ask this guy, is he satisfied with the arrangement? Don't think! Say it right now."

The message delivery was confirmed on the monitor, and then nothing happened. Normally, Marvel would have hit another key less than a second after the last twenty-dollar bill was delivered, but there was no key press this time, even though the cash machine was still active. He was still there, but not doing anything.

"Frozen." Amy's eyes didn't turn from the screen. "Like a kipper in the icebox."

It stayed that way for thirty seconds now, an incredible span of time for the extortionist to stand and do nothing. Amy could feel his panic and confusion. The longer that nothing happened the better, as far as she was concerned.

Jack shifted his weight from left foot to right and back as the seconds ticked by. When Marvel pressed the 1 key in response and it lit up on the monitor, Amy banged the back of the chair and stood straight up. "An amateur!" She spun around and faced Jack and Stanley, eyes alive with excitement. "Tell that to Hubbard! Testing the assumption, see? Scored on the first swing, and now we know something."

"Know what?" asked Stanley in puzzlement. "I don't get it." Jack's expression indicated that he felt much the same.

Amy took Stanley by the arm and sat him down, then motioned Jack to draw closer.

"Suppose this was a professional. An experienced terrorist, maybe soiled his pants first time he blew something up, but since then, a veteran, loaded with self-confidence. Probably looking forward to the nooky he's gonna get from the fawning females he's surrounded himself with in 'the cause.'" She spat the last words with contempt and tried to ignore the look on Stanley's face at her candor. The Bureau had changed in lots of ways, but not in some.

"You, me, the whole government? Like fleas on his old dog. So—" She pointed her chin at Jack in challenge. "What's this all about today?"

Jack scratched his cheek and considered the question. "Well, my guess, he doesn't communicate unless he absolutely has to. Seems to me he went to a lot of trouble to make sure he never had to talk to us directly at all."

"Precisely!" She turned to Stanley. "He's so in control, why answer us? This"—she jerked a thumb at the monitor—"this is *loss* of control. Confusion. The tables turned suddenly, and he's not coping very well, is he?"

She stood up and went back to the terminal, then turned and faced them. "This thing goes off again today, dinner's on me."

Stanley wasn't convinced. "Um, what about—"

"Wait a minute," Jack interrupted. "I'll take that bet. What makes you so sure?"

She turned back to the monitor, eyes still shining, looking at the screen as though looking at Marvel himself. "Before it was like you said, Jack, everything far away, like remote control. Press the button, crash the plane." She seemed to be talking to herself rather than to them.

The pieces were beginning to fall into place for Jack. "And all of a sudden, we've communicated. Real people talking to each other, even if only in code and only through a machine."

"That's why you had Jack use a name," said Stanley.

"And even if he knew it was possible technically," said Amy, turning to face them, "now, the reality of our link to the ATMs hits him over the head like a hammer." She paused and turned back to the monitor. "He never wanted to talk to us. He's going crazy, thinking, Am I doing the right thing? No way to know the answer. Frightened. An hour ago king of the skies, now not so sure. No more money today, Captain."

Stanley was skeptical that so much significance could be attached to all of this. "What should he have done? What response would have scared us instead of him?"

"Nothing," said Jack. "I see now. Shoulda just banged away for a few more withdrawals and never answered the message."

Amy nodded in confirmation, pleased that he caught on.

Stanley remained unconvinced. "What about the other one? The other team?"

Amy only shrugged slightly.

"Well?" He was annoyed at her lack of concern.

Amy ignored it. "No. No more money today." She folded her arms across her chest and let her head drop down. "An amateur," she muttered. She was talking to herself again, not to the others.

"An amateur."

CHAPTER 16

January 2, 1967

In the minds of U.S. military commanders, that which came to be known as "guerrilla warfare" was dismissed as just another in a string of techniques that failed against the mighty United States of America, which sat at the right hand of God and had never lost a war. That was before the carnival of insanity that was the Vietnam War.

When the Viet Cong fought their war using the classic guerrilla model, the term entered the lexicon as something to be despised rather than feared. Ultimately it had to be dealt with.

It is an essential objective of war to remove anything in the environment that is advantageous to the enemy. The new antiguerrilla strategy in southeast Asia was designed to tip the military balance by removing the VC's one major advantage in the Vietnamese environment, the environment itself. This had never been done before, but that was because the means hadn't existed before.

The new strategy was aimed quite literally at the land, and America had the technology to do it, thanks to better living through such chemicals as napalm.

But it took more than hardware. Before 1962 the national

mentality essentially consisted of a profound and ineffable faith that, at least as a group, national political leaders could do no serious wrong in matters of broad policy. A firm tenet of the culture was the notion that a loving mother would pack her only son's duffel and send him off to fight a war on the opposite side of the planet, asking no more reason than a politician's offhand statement that it was a necessary thing to do. Good citizens believed that the lives of their children were as nothing compared to the obligation to submit to the government's bidding. They equated the president with God, the legislature with America and the military with freedom, and they knew with certainty that a soldier's death in battle was an honorable and just sacrifice that ensured the rights and the dignity that were their birthright. To refuse to kill an officially declared enemy was an irreligious affront to the very meaning of America, an affront that was in no way mitigated by any critical examination of the merit of such a declaration. That it came from the government was all the verification needed.

That America could lose a war, or would stoop to wage one under any but noble conditions, were concepts so alien as not to rate even a questioning mention.

Thus, technology and apathy teamed together, and the rape of the Vietnamese countryside began in earnest. It was a gratifying plan. While the death of Viet Cong soldiers could rarely be witnessed because of the jungle cover and the impersonal saturation techniques being used, the explosive combustion of hundreds of thousands of verdant acres could be savored over and over and shown on the evening news as evidence of imminent victory, a more tangible measure than the daily body counts that added up to more than the total number of people in the whole country.

In order to do this, and everything else that the strange little conflict demanded, it was necessary to lift the war out of the jungle and into the air. Aircraft had been used in battle since the First World War, but not since the Second on the scale or intensity of Vietnam.

In the early stages of the war, American generals were frustrated in their attempts to pinpoint rich targets in Indochina. Finally a list of ninety-four targets was drawn up that consisted mostly of infrastructure rather than military sites. Declining the recommendation to conduct a massive strike against these targets, President Johnson elected to proceed more slowly, and a set of complicated restraints was imposed on American flyers. The North Vietnamese had no trouble divining the nature of these constraints and did such things as build antiaircraft emplacements on dams, which they knew were out of bounds because the Americans would not risk flooding downstream fields and villages. Airfields housing Russian-built MiGs were also safe havens, because of the American suspicion that Soviet technicians might be working there. Even SAM batteries laden with surface-to-air missiles were forbidden targets unless they fired first.

But that was still early in the game. By 1967, 350 attack sorties a day were being flown over Khe Sanh alone, and SAC B-52s from Guam, flying nearly seven hours in each direction, arrived every ninety minutes to carpet bomb five hundred acres at a time until the area looked not like lush rain forest, but like the surface of the moon.

Now what the military needed more than anything else was not aircraft or ammunition or supplies; what it needed was pilots. And by the time 1967 rolled around and there were hints that the Vietnam War was not about nobility of purpose or grand heroics, but about attrition and survival, the air force was not too particular about where those pilots came from. Or exactly how old they were.

The black military pilot was no longer a novelty. Although it took the threat of lawsuits for the U.S. Army Air Corps to establish the Tuskegee training program in 1941, the outstanding performance of its graduates ensured a continuing role for blacks in the flying military. Seven years after the National Security Act resulted in the creation of the air force as a separate service, Congress authorized an air force academy, which opened on its permanent site near Denver in 1958. From its inception, the academy included blacks in all its programs virtually without official restriction.

So it was no big deal when Bo Kincaid showed up at his local air force recruiting office. His apparent age raised more eyebrows than his capabilities, but there were still some advantages to the military's heavy reliance on blacks for its more menial tasks. A combination of cleaning people with keys, bored and angry clerical types and sympathetic old-timers conspired to readjust Bo's military records to obscure the fact of his years and to do so in such a manner that the arithmetical inconsistencies inherent in his claims of World War II fighter experience and his purported age were never manifested by two opposing pieces of evidence at the same time.

"You can yank a college boy outta the reserves or you can have a combat-proven veteran ready to go," he had said to the air force rep desperately behind quota. "It's up to you."

Classmates in jet training looked askance at the older man and had no idea he had used the last of his savings renting time in a restored Korean War–vintage F-104 Starfighter at Chino Airport in Southern California. He paid for lessons and was soon flying by himself, getting the feel for jet-powered flight until the familiar sensation of unity with the plane settled on his shoulders like an old coat. It was nothing like an F-4 Phantom was going to be, but it put him well ahead of his fellow trainees.

By the time Bo soloed in the T-28 trainer, students stood in awe of his skill and his commanders stopped asking questions. He adamantly refused requests that he remain stateside as an instructor, relying on his right in time of war to request a combat tour if he could demonstrate his fitness, about which there was little question. Technically, or at least legally, no state of war existed, but there wasn't anyone in the armed services who would dare try to make *that* argument.

In deference to his extraordinary abilities, he received first choice in assignments. He chose to fly the F-4 Phantom, and he chose to fly out of Danang, and he arrived, trained and ready, in time to take his place in the massive operation known as Rolling Thunder. This bombing campaign had begun with a tentative step over the seventeenth parallel on March 2, 1965, to destroy an ammunition dump, and continued for three years, making it the longest continuous aerial bombing campaign in history. Measured by the total tonnage of bombs dropped, it was also the largest.

That same month, Marine Corps Battalion Landing Team 3/9 became the first U.S. ground unit committed to combat in the war, its primary mission the protection of the vital air

base at Danang. It was a foregone conclusion that the air
incursion into North Vietnam rendered U.S. installations in
the south legitimate military targets, and it was no longer
possible to keep hidden the widespread belief that ARVN
regulars were incapable of providing adequate protection.

Rolling Thunder was temporarily halted in its first year on
Christmas Day, President Johnson having determined that the
North Vietnamese were being so badly mauled that they would
leap at the conciliatory gesture and sit down at the negotiating
table.

It was particularly ironic that the most awesome display of
destruction in the war thus far served only to demonstrate to
the American generals just how firmly resolved the North
Vietnamese were. Rolling Thunder was originally conceived
as a short-term strategy, a display of power and capability
that would make the enemy cower and eventually concede.
Five weeks after the Christmas pause, Rolling Thunder had
to be resumed, with even greater intensity.

While the operation rained enormous amounts of high
explosives on the north, the absence of concentrated infrastructure and military targets naturally limited its effectiveness. This situation was not well recognized early in the
campaign. The next time such a bombing strategy would be
employed, twenty-five years later in the Mideast, the military
would be equally successful in convincing the people at home
that the number of tons dropped and the number of sorties
flown was a success indicator every bit as useful as what was
actually being destroyed in the process, which was precious
little from a military perspective. Mostly just civilians who
didn't count.

But it made for a lot of employment for pilots. It would
be several years before stories leaked past military censors
of what happened to pilots who were shot down over enemy
territory, so there was still glory to be had and death to be
laughed at and one-on-one dogfights to be waged high above
the insect-infested wetlands. While poor and minority American youth were marching bravely to filthy and lonely death
and dismemberment below, the knights of the air provided
the heroics above. What happened to them upon capture was

a good secret to keep. Had it been learned sooner, the war might have ended earlier for lack of interest.

Bo Kincaid arrived on New Year's Day, 1967. Stepping off the transport, he stared curiously at the hundreds of pallets awaiting shipment back home, wondering what sort of gear required black plastic wrapping and couldn't be stacked in the more convenient containers. Small shifts in the wind, and the inescapable compromises of field embalming, provided the pungent and sobering answer.

There was no ceremony, no welcoming smiles or hand-shakes, no traditional, purposeful bustle of activity, only a somber air and a grudgingly laconic attention to administrative details by the clerks who processed him in. He could have understood resentment. There was always resentment against the big-shot flyboys who got the good food and did no manual labor. But there wasn't any resentment, just a pervasive who-gives-a-shit attitude that was present even among some of the higher-ranking regular officers.

His first night at mess, he sought out the maintenance chief who would be responsible for the care of his Phantom and struck up a friendly conversation, trying to show no surprise when the more junior man offered him a hit off his joint.

"No thanks," Bo said. "Gotta fly tomorrow."

"Yeah," growled Top Sergeant Devon Marsh, his voice raspy with the effort not to exhale. " 'At's why I thought y'might wanna toke. Y'know where you goin' yet?"

Bo shook his head and looked at the dimming sunset. "D'you?"

Marsh kept his lips pressed together and nodded. "Better take some of this."

"I'll pass. Thanks." He turned to look at the young black mechanic and wondered if he'd be high when he serviced the Phantom. "Marsh, what the hell is goin' on around here? I mean—"

"I *know* what you mean, man." He blew out a cloud of pale gray smoke, and its sickly-sweet smell was strangely alluring in Bo's nostrils. "Don't worry too much about it. Doesn't matter so much to pilots, 'least not fighter guys. 'Cept sometimes." He smiled, and Bo couldn't tell if it was friendly or sly or sarcastic or, in this strange atmosphere, sardonic.

"Meaning what? Exactly?"

Marsh took in another great wallop of the powerful local dope and held it. He felt no malice toward Bo, but he had been here for nearly a year and had learned not to get too close to anyone engaged in the actual fighting. He was by nature congenial, and made friends easily, and had a tendency inappropriate in wartime to care just a little too deeply about those friends. He was liked by his pilots, and they treated him well, and when they went down he prayed fervently that their parachutes had opened and that they were alive, but then one time he had helped drag a Special Forces officer from a swamp at the border, an intelligence agent who had spied on prison camps, and he put beer and reefer into the poor shaking bastard and listened as the man cried and spoke just before the higher-ups came and took him away from the troops who still had time left to serve and shouldn't be listening to that kind of thing, and lately every time he heard of one of his pilots going down above the seventeenth he found himself praying that they had died before reaching the ground, and now this new guy wanted to know what the hell was going on around here. It made no sense to tell him, because what was he going to do? Turn around and go home? So he decided to tell him something terrible but not too terrible, so he'd be scared enough to watch his ass but not enough to turn chicken. If he watched his ass he might actually survive and go home, but if he turned chicken he was dead from the start. Because there was nothing, *nothing* in this God's world, nothing remotely approaching the degree to which paralytically terrified soldiers abhorred anyone who gave open vent to that terror, because in the act of loathing that boneless coward and heaping unreasoning derision on him, they took the edge off their own nightmares and gave themselves some small comfort that they were not yet at the limits of their endurance because someone in their midst was more fearful even than they themselves.

"You in Rollin' Thunder, y'know that much, right?"

"Sure. Bombing campaign against the north."

Marsh snorted. " 'Campaign,' yeah. Like runnin' for the Senate." He cackled at his verbal agility and took another hit on the joint, whose glowing red tip stood out in the dying light. That someone might see it didn't seem to trouble him.

"Was this guy last year. 'The Deacon,' we called him on accounta his bein' a good church boy, y'know? Daddy was a Baptist minister, so prouda his boy fightin' the good fight and all." Marsh shook his head and smiled to himself, leaning back against the corrugated steel wall of the Quonset hut. "Flew Thuds." The F-105 Thunderchief, by the mid-1960s considered the best fighter-bomber in the air force. It carried only a single pilot, whereas the Phantom Bo would be flying also used a weapons systems officer, affectionately know as the GIB, or guy in back.

"Back when this Thunder shit started, they had rules. Still got 'em, still fucked up, but nothin' like they was when it started. Don't hit no dams, don't hit no MiG fields, stay away from this, stay away from that. Christ—" He dropped his head into his hands and scratched his ears with his thumbs, then looked up. "You'da thought it was some kinda goddamned high school football game."

Bo had no idea where this was heading and, despite his impatience, let Marsh find his own time.

"So one day he's comin' back from the north. Bright, sunny day, he looks down 'n' he sees this SAM site, right? Now, he knows he can't shoot at the thing, on accounta the rules say *they* gotta shoot first. Fuckin' Wyatt Earps we got runnin' the gummint! Did I tell ya' every single mission's gotta come from Washington?"

"You're kidding me."

"Nope. Like they was right here, only they don't know shit. So the Deacon, he's thinkin', Hey! first goddamn target I ever seen looks like somethin' worth hittin'! Only he can't shoot."

Marsh smiled in remembrance, his affection for the pilot obvious. It was a wistful smile, and Bo began to get a feeling that the Deacon didn't make it out of this one. But if that was the case, how could Marsh possibly have known what the man had been thinking?

"So what's he do?" Marsh spread his hands out. "He turns around! Square shit! The crazy fucker honks that mother over and runs right back over the SAMs again, only this time low and slow so they can see him! Meanwhile, the wing jerk-off is yellin' 'n' screamin' at him to cut it out, and the other guys circle back and see the site is only half-built and all'a missiles are still lyin' onna ground. Nuthin' even for the slopes to throw up at 'em."

Marsh's face was lit up with excitement. "All of a sudden, flak's poppin' up from the jungle. The VC din't have no missiles loaded up yet, but they had the guns in place t'shoot cover, they're heavin' up a shitload of stuff at the Deacon, 'n' he's thinkin', Hallelujah! 'cuz now he can shoot back, and he heads for the deck and he's got all his twenty millimeters bangin' away, and the wing puke is still hollerin' cut it out on accounta ain't no missile been flung his way, 'n' the Deacon says, Well, fuck that, they shootin' at me, ain't they? 'N' there's shit blowin' up all over the place, gooks runnin' ever' which way, even construction stuff is explodin', and then— get this!" Marsh punched Bo on the arm to make sure he was paying attention. "One of the fuckin' SAMs goes off! It's lyin' on its side, 'n' wham! Fire'n shit starts comin' outta one end, the thing starts whizzin' around on the ground like a Fourtha Ju-ly nigger chaser, bangin' into trees and control panels and more SAMs, and then pretty soon ain't hardly nuthin' left a'tall, and the Deacon pulls back up and rolls victory three, four times."

By now tears had formed in Marsh's eyes and started trickling down his cheeks. Bo couldn't tell if it was because of how funny the story was or because he was crying for his friend or a combination of the two, helped along by the powerful marijuana.

"He make it back?"

Marsh wiped his eyes, took one more small hit and then ground the roach beneath his heel. "Hell, yeah, he made it back. Came back fine. 'Cept next day the D.C. pukes find out about it, start makin' phone calls all over the place, 'n' we find out they gonna bust 'im. Full court-martial, make an example, the whole show."

"For destroying an enemy installation?" Bo stared at Marsh in disbelief. "What happened? What'd he do?"

"He never found out about it. Word came down, he was on his way to another mission." Marsh looked into the distance, then stood up and dusted off the back of his pants. "SAM got him over Thanh Hoa Bridge."

Marsh put his hands on his thighs and leaned down toward the still seated pilot. "True story."

He clapped Bo's shoulder and walked away toward the barracks. In a hoarse whisper, he called, "Welcome to Vietnam!" over his shoulder and disappeared into the night.

The loss of the Deacon was not totally in vain. Hundreds of messages had caromed back and forth between South Vietnam and Washington. The ones issuing forth from the government finally convinced the on-site commanders that their elected leaders had completely lost any sense of perspective. It was as though the military recommendations were being put through a fraternity hell-night gauntlet staffed by escaped lunatics representing Congress, newspaper editors, veterans' groups, movie actors, student demonstrators, weapons manufacturers and anybody else who had both influence and an opinion.

For their part, the leaders at home believed that their people in the field failed to comprehend the unique nature of this war and the extreme delicacy attendant to the politics thereof. That no war had been formally declared was still a hot issue in the halls of Congress, and there were many who believed that a negotiated solution was still a possibility, if they could only figure out who the real enemy was. If those generals over there thought that they should be free to prosecute the conflict according to the standard, time-honored rules of engagement leading to total capitulation, well: we need to add a few more courses at West Point and inculcate our fighting people with the new realities.

At the base bar one night, as Devon Marsh would tell it, the commander of the Second Air Wing at Danang finished off his ninth beer and muttered, "Goddammit, if we're here, let me fight the fucking thing," and then went to the base commander and told him that if SAM sites continued to be off limits, he couldn't promise that his pilots would keep reaching their targets and wouldn't it be a damned shame if they kept dropping their loads in the ocean for safety reasons and in case anybody was thinking about convening a court-

martial to consider the matter he should know that some of
the boys were thinking about having some conversations with
The New York Times. Whatever the reason, the taboo against
hitting a SAM surface-to-air missile site before it fired a
missile first was lifted shortly thereafter.

Now pilots could try to take them out, but the ferocity of
the SAM attacks increased. New sensors installed in the planes
alerted the pilots to the presence of a live missile, and there
were two basic options at that point: The pilot could dive and
level out at treetop height, risking gunfire from the ground,
or he could try to outmaneuver the missile in the air.

The latter choice was feasible but risky. It depended on the
fact that the plane could make a sharper turn than the missile,
and that the missile didn't know how far above the ground it
was. So it was all a matter of timing. Jink too fast, and the
SAM made a wider turn but still had enough left to come
around and get you. Wait too long, and its proximity fuse
went off and the nearby explosion could still take your plane
out.

The trick was to initiate a dive at the exact right moment
and head for the ground, pulling up sharply at the last possible
instant. The missile would try to follow but couldn't pull up
in time and would hit the turf instead. If you had uncanny
skill and enormous brass, you could even get the missile to
hit its own launch site, or so they said.

Unfortunately, eluding SAMs was a strictly Darwinian process in which the best pilots stayed alive to fight them again
and the less than best rarely got the chance to ponder their
technique and try again.

SAMs were effective and terrifying, but they were not
the only problem. Russian-built MiGs constituted an equally
disruptive influence on American air operations.

U.S. pilots owned the skies above twenty thousand feet.
Their planes flew higher and faster than most MiGs, although
the MiG-21 could hit Mach 2 and outpace an early-model
Thud or a Phantom loaded down with heavy bombs. And
while the antiquated MiG-17 was slow, it had astonishing
maneuverability at lower altitudes and presented a surprisingly
serious threat to American planes.

Standard technique for the enemy was to hover just above

the ground until the American strike force passed overhead, then barrel in from behind and begin taking out the rearmost aircraft. While the ensuing dogfights were technical wins for the Americans, they required that the fighter-bombers jettison their bombs before engaging. They might win the fight but would fail in their bombing mission.

All of this was becoming a serious annoyance. U.S. Command in Washington decided to do something about it and to do it on January 2, 1967, Bo Kincaid's first full day in-country.

Colonel James Pontiac walked up to Bo a few minutes before the briefing. "You Kincaid?"

"Yeah," Bo answered warily, the inquiry yet another reminder that he was, for the second time in his military career, the new guy. "Yes, sir."

Pontiac grunted. " 'Sir.' Yeah. Well, least somebody in this fuckin' war's still got some goddamn respect." He pulled out a pack of cigarettes, shuffled it until a few poked out the top, and offered one to Bo. "Heard you can fly."

Bo took a cigarette, tapped the filter end on his watch several times to tamp down the tobacco, and put it between his lips. "I can fly."

Pontiac lit both cigarettes with a brass Zippo, holding it long enough for Bo to catch the inscription on the side. Superimposed over an outline map of Vietnam was the message, "When I die I'm going to heaven 'cuz I already been to hell."

The colonel inhaled and squinted his eyes against the smoke and looked at Bo, who returned the stare evenly. "You don't look like one of these hotshot, ass-wipe kids think they're gonna win this war in a coupla-three days." He exhaled to the side. "Why's that?"

"Because I don't care about winning the war."

This seemed to surprise Pontiac. "What *do* you care about?"

Bo seemed to smile slightly, but Pontiac couldn't tell for sure.

"Why don't you take me up and let's find out?"

Pontiac exhaled a cloud of smoke and shook his head. "You may be a little new for this one, sport. Just take a seat and listen—"

"Let's do it!" yelled the administrative staff sergeant, calling the assembled pilots to order. He didn't care about winning the war, either, only about starting meetings on time and readying the room for the next batch.

With a last, searching look at Bo, Pontiac strode to the front of the room and took his place at the podium. He waited for the hubbub to die down and began the briefing.

"Morning, ladies. I do hope you all had a pleasant sleep." Standard opening line before a dangerous mission, and it sparked the usual nervous humor, catcalls and mumbled griping.

"I've got some good news for a change. We're leaving the heavy stuff home, going after those shit-ass MiGs."

The announcement brought the expected reaction from some of the pilots. They whooped and clapped their approval, but the more cynical and beleaguered Rolling Thunder veterans seemed to deliberately temper their enthusiasm.

Bo nudged the weapons systems officer, the guy in back, sitting next to him. "Sounds good. What's the problem?"

Benjamin Ross turned sideways on his seat. "You Kincaid?"

"Yeah." *Now what*?

Ross grinned and stuck out a hand. "I'm your backseat."

Bo took the hand and shook it, hoping he was transmitting some of his confidence to the other man. "So what's the problem?"

"Problem is the little bastards don't like to come out and fight in the open. We've gone after 'em before, but—"

"I know, I know," Pontiac was saying. "Some o' you hardasses are thinkin', So what, we done it before. Well, we're gonna do it a little different this time. . . ."

Pontiac started by describing only the technical details, not the overall strategy, waiting to see if anyone would take the bait.

Bo raised his hand and stood up. "We fly above the overcast, their ground stations are gonna see us, but we won't be able to see SAMs igniting."

"Well, getta load o' that doofus fuck!" Jack Hardegreave whispered to his GIB, loud enough for several other men to hear. "Us? Where the fuck does he think *he's* going?"

Pontiac smiled. "Izzat so?"

And as he described the mission, several things became obvious to the more savvy among the men in the room. First, this was new. Second, it might work. Third, sure as hell nobody in Washington had authorized it.

Finishing the briefing, Pontiac began to hand out flight assignments by name. When he got to Bo, he paused momentarily. "Kincaid . . ." He looked up at Bo and Ross. "You got wing." Standard operating procedure: new guy flew alongside the skipper until he settled in.

What wasn't SOP was taking the new guy up on a hot, risky mission when he'd barely hit the turf.

"What the hell—" began Jack Hardegreave, one of the more senior pilots. He hadn't liked being commanded by a "damned Indian" in the first place, and he was unable to suppress his annoyance at this apparent expression of confidence in a colored pilot, especially a mouthy new one who didn't know his place. Pontiac cut Hardegreave off without acknowledging him before he could voice his complaint.

"Let's go fly."

The huge strike force took off from Danang and headed north, crossing into Laotian airspace before reaching the seventeenth parallel. Flying at thirty-three thousand feet, they looked like a typical U.S. airborne mission with a typical mix of aircraft. North Vietnamese regulars tracking the aircraft from below had no reason to believe that this group of planes, in standard strike force formation, was anything but what it appeared to be.

There would be F-105 fighter-bombers, fully laden with five-hundred-pound bombs. There would be reconnaissance aircraft with sophisticated cameras, platform-stabilization devices and powerful telescopic lenses. Several specially equipped F-4s would be along, "Wild Weasels" whose job it was to detect antiaircraft radar emissions on the ground and dispatch Shrike missiles to fly down the radar beam and destroy the tracking station, at least those manned by crews who hadn't yet learned to turn on the radar only intermittently and for very short intervals of time.

Colonel Pontiac turned the formation and guided it toward Phuc Yen airfield, otherwise known as "Phuc You" to the pilots, who were well aware that the base held most of the north's arsenal of MiG-21s. The base was hidden by a seven-thousand-foot overcast, so Pontiac turned the formation around and flew back over the field, then turned them around again, and yet again, until the North Vietnamese ground trackers managed to get a good fix and several MiGs poked up through the clouds for the usual hit-and-run attack.

A single, highly capable ABCC Airborne Command Center radar plane, precursor to the AWACS, was flying over Laos, tracking every MiG and relaying positions to Pontiac's men. Soon four MiGs were above the clouds, and fourteen more were on their way up. It was a much larger contingent than usual. The ABCC crew gleefully confirmed that, based on their movements, the enemy pilots seemed to think the huge squadron above them was ripe for attack, especially those F-105s pregnant with enormously heavy bombs, laboriously lumbering their way to the target, each as maneuverable as an anvil because of the full complement of stores.

Pontiac ordered his flyers to hold formation. The MiGs continued to climb in preparation for falling in behind the U.S. aircraft. Some of Pontiac's flyers were beginning to get nervous. Bo craned his head to either side as the enemy aircraft turned from pinpricks to flies to planes in his vision.

"Ponty nuts or somethin'?" Ross's voice, tinged with fear, rasped in his headset.

Bo took a breath before answering, to get his voice under control. "Relax, Ross. He knows what he's doing." *I sure as shit hope, anyway.*

"Stand by—" Pontiac's commanding voice was heard in all the planes simultaneously. "Arm all systems."

As did all the other pilots, Bo reached to the upper right corner of his cockpit panel, flipped up the red safety cover and depressed the arming switch, being careful to keep the fingers of his left hand clear of the various firing buttons. A red warning light began flashing, not obtrusively enough to be distracting, but insistent enough to keep reminding him that he now controlled live weapons.

"Easy now . . ." Pontiac's confident voice held just the right timbre to convey to his pilots that he was in control, he knew what he was doing. The MiGs were now well above the twenty-thousand-foot mark, the magical altitude above which the Americans held all the advantages. They would let the

MiGs climb a little more, as reported by the ABCC, but not so high that they could look at the underside of U.S. planes and catch on to what was going on.

Pontiac miscalculated, but only very slightly. "Leveling!" the ABCC radioman screamed into his mike. "They're leveling!"

"Now!" Pontiac yelled into his own mike. "Now! Now!" The triple call was standard military procedure for beginning an action. As soon as the cry was heard, the squadron broke into four groups. The two to the left and right peeled off laterally from the body of the formation and rolled inverted into power dives toward the rear flank of the loose MiG formation. The front and rear groups did the same in the remaining two directions.

By the time the U.S. planes began descending on the MiGs in a four-way vise, the North Vietnamese pilots had very little time to notice that all fifty-six of the rapidly dropping aircraft were F-4 Phantom fighters and none of them was carrying bombs. What they couldn't see as easily was that each of them was loaded to the hilt with Sidewinder heat-seeking missiles, radar-guided Sparrows, and cannons mounted on the wings and nose, an advantage not available in the early models, nor could they tell that the planes had flown in slower than usual not only to enhance the deception, but to conserve fuel. The Phantoms had all day.

The ensuing battle was long and savage. The North Vietnamese scrambled more MiGs with incredible speed, and soon the sky was filled with more than eighty planes.

Bo heard the high-pitched squeal in his headphones that meant a MiG had radar lock on him. At the same time Ross yelled, "Five o'clock, even!" and Bo knew that the attack was coming in from the side.

He fought the instinct to turn away from his pursuer and instead banked hard over to the right, pulling back slightly on the stick so as not to lose altitude. Flying laterally, he could see the missile drop from the MiG's wing and start to arc back up as its guidance fins bit into the air. He waited until the last possible moment and then rolled upright, pulling back hard on the stick at the same time. The missile passed harmlessly beneath the plane. He remembered that morning's briefing and had banked on the proximity fuses remaining unarmed because the enemy would know there were too many planes in the air and did not want to risk accidentally shooting down one of their own.

Still pointing upward, Bo kept back pressure on the stick until his plane looped over the top and headed straight down. In less than four more seconds he was nearly wings level and he found the MiG in his windscreen. Bo knew that the Russian-made missiles emitted a huge cloud of smoke that momentarily blinded the MiG pilots. Occasionally the smoke even choked the engines for a split second, which could give the opposing pilot an edge in position if he acted quickly enough.

However it happened, Bo was now behind the MiG, who figured it out and headed for the deck. As they approached the cloud cover, Bo lined up and waited for the growl in his headphones that would tell him the Sidewinder had a lock on the MiG's engine heat. It came, but not full-throated, and Bo let the missile loose anyway just as the MiG disappeared into the clouds. The orange glow of a hit never appeared.

"Damn!" came Ross through the intercom, and Bo kept the F-4 pointed right where the MiG had disappeared.

He expected Ross to go crazy and start screaming for him to pull up and was surprised instead to hear him say calmly, "He's pulled to the right, about twenty degrees."

"Got it." Bo focused on the instruments as the thick clouds enshrouded the plane and made it impossible to fly visually. He eased the stick over gently until the gyrocompass indicated twenty degrees of turn, then leveled out but kept diving. In another few seconds they popped out underneath the overcast and found themselves directly behind the fleeing MiG.

Good call, Bo thought as he centered the MiG on the crosshairs of the pipper on his heads-up display. He got a loud, clear growl and squeezed the thumb button on the control stick. The Sidewinder dropped off the underwing pylon at the same instant its solid fuel engine ignited, spewing a brilliant line of sparkling yellow-orange flame. It dropped slightly and then found its course, lancing forward with tremendous speed.

The MiG was so close that the pilot barely had time to attempt an evasive maneuver as the missile headed for its engine as if guided by rails. He managed to jink just as the

Sidewinder tried to enter his exhaust duct, but it mattered little. The missile banged into the aft part of the nacelle, and the impact was transmitted almost instantly to the sensor mounted just inside the nose cone, sending a spark to the high explosives packed just behind and occupying most of the bulk of the slim body. The explosion tore into the left wing, the vertical stabilizer and the engine housing all at the same time, slamming the MiG violently to the right.

As air continued to rush over the largely intact right wing, the lift it generated met no countervailing resistance from the shattered left wing, and the plane rolled over rapidly and continued to do so as it fell, corkscrewing its way toward the ground. Burning shards from the collapsing engines found their way into the exposed wing-mounted fuel tank and touched off a massive explosion that shot pieces of the fighter plane in all directions. Now fully stripped of all aerodynamic integrity, the airframe sections stopped their forward motion and dropped nearly straight down, leaving smoking trails to mark their passage.

It was Bo's first kill of this war. On his first day of combat.

"Nice shot, Kincaid!" Ross was exuberant. Recognizing the critical role of the guy in back, the air force awarded kills to both crew members.

"Nice work yourself," Bo answered. But that wasn't why he was here. "What's above?"

Ross fiddled with his instruments, then answered, "Come to about two three five and head on up."

Bo turned the plane as Ross had directed, aimed it upward and reentered the cloud. Just as they emerged, Ross called again. "Hey, Hardy's in trouble!"

The blips he had seen and directed Bo toward turned out to be Jack Hardegreave, vertical stabilizer damaged and smoke trailing from one engine, being pursued by a MiG-17, an obsolete aircraft but still dangerous at low altitude because of its agile maneuverability. Against a crippled F-4, it was little contest.

The '17 hadn't fired yet. There was no reason for him to risk wasting a shot. The two planes were well away from the main battle, and the F-4 had no chance of successfully evading the attacker. The MiG pilot had the luxury of lining up for a clean, sure kill.

At first he didn't see Bo's Phantom rocket up from the cloud deck. Then he caught a glint of sunlight reflected from the windscreen as the plane appeared in front of Hardegreave's F-4 and headed directly toward him. As Hardegreave managed to nudge himself off to the right, Bo held course, waiting to see what the MiG would do.

The North Vietnamese pilot had to give up his chase in light of the fully capable plane heading his way with a combined closing speed of over two thousand miles per hour. It was a deadly game of chicken with scant seconds to plan strategy.

"The hell are you doing, Kincaid?" Ross demanded.

Without answering Ross, Bo radioed Hardegreave. "Hardy, down and to your right, as much as you can!" He looked out his window as he saw Hardegreave lower his nose. The elevators were apparently unaffected by the damage. *Good. Gives me maneuvering room.*

Ross got no answer from his pilot and tried again. "Kincaid, goddammit, what are you doing!"

Bo held steady. The two planes were on a direct collision course, closing fast. When he was certain Hardegreave was out of harm's way, he tapped his stick as lightly as he could to the left and down. When the MiG pilot saw the F-4's nose start to move, he pulled to his own left and up, assuming the U.S. pilot was calling off the deadly game. He was thus astonished to see the Phantom's nose come quickly back up, reestablishing a new collision course so that the nose was pointed directly at him but not vice versa. Before he had a chance to consider the meaning of it all, a burst of cannon from Bo's Phantom caught his wing and sent his plane spinning out of control. Bo and Ross saw the canopy pop off and the ejection seat come shooting out, followed shortly by a billowing parachute disappearing into the clouds.

Not dwelling on the victory, Bo pulled hard over and headed back in the opposite direction. They found Hardegreave's plane, and Bo keyed his mike.

"Hardegreave, Kincaid. You all right?"

"I think so. You get him?"

"He sure as shit did," said Ross before Bo could answer. "You shoulda seen it."

"What've you got left?" asked Bo. He heard a blipping sound but couldn't identify it.

"Rudder's fucked up, but I can make slow turns with ailerons. Elevators are okay." He paused. "Robbie must be hit. I can't get him on the intercom. Can't see anything."

"You also got smoke outta the left." Another blip. "How's the pressure?"

Hardegreave checked his oil gauge. "Holding steady. Doesn't look serious."

"Okay—" That damned blip again. "We're gonna follow you home. Ross?"

"Turn right heading two five zero." Ross would bring them back in through Laotian airspace and head them toward a Thai air base. "And let's get back upstairs if you can."

"The hell is that sound?"

"It's a radar sweep. SAM site below. Blips every time the beam comes around and hits us." Ross looked at his 'scope and saw the strobe line coinciding with the sweeping beam. It gave him a good idea of where the ground station lay but no sense of distance. "Twenty degrees off the nose but can't tell how far away."

The surface-to-air missiles contained no tracking instruments of their own but were guided by ground-based radar. Once the radar locked on to a plane, the sweep-search beam would be replaced by tracking radar and the blips would change to a steady buzz.

Hardegreave eased the stick over and kept his feet off the rudder pedals. The resulting turn was uncoordinated and seemed to take forever, but eventually he was facing in the right direction and leveled his wings. Bo and Ross followed slightly behind and above. Twenty minutes later they were at thirty-one thousand feet, forty-five miles from the border.

Bo dropped in closer without saying anything to Hardegreave. He eased over until the rear seat of the damaged plane was in view. Rips in the skin were visible where cannon fire had hit, just above the wing line at the rear of the double cockpit.

Ross switched over to intercom and said to Bo, "I see some

blood. Robbie doesn't seem to be moving. By the holes I'd say it was his legs."

"He may be alive," Bo said just as the buzz replaced the blip. "Probably bleeding like crazy. We might be—"

Suddenly the buzz was gone, and in its place a piercing warble like a European ambulance siren shot through Bo's brain. Ross didn't bother to explain that the SAM station had switched to high PRF—pulse repetition frequency, used to guide the missile to the target plane.

"We got a SAM!" Ross's voice leaped out of the intercom speaker. "Ahead, two o'clock!"

"Fuck!" Bo yelled involuntarily. He stretched his neck forward. The telltale puff of steam was clearly visible in the distance. The plume rose and grew even as they watched.

Hardegreave was in no position to do battle with a surface-to-air missile. Bo made an instant decision and pushed the stick forward, dropping the nose of the plane.

"What're we doing?" asked Ross, but got no answer. *I got a bad feeling about this*. An appropriate thought.

"Hardegreave, start a shallow dive!" Bo commanded. "Aim for two o'clock if you can!"

Ross tried to focus on his instruments and let his pilot do what he was paid for, but he was only half-successful. *Oh shit, oh shit, oh shit* . . . He grabbed the side rails and planted his feet firmly on the cockpit floor.

Bo pointed the Phantom down toward the incoming missile in a flight path that paralleled Hardegreave's, only much faster. Having started at thirty-one thousand feet, they had a few seconds of slack, but SAMs accelerated as they climbed. The fighter pilots could watch it grow in the windscreen.

"Don't change direction, Hardy!"

Ross heard Bo's voice and he closed his eyes, planting his head firmly back against the padded headrest. He tightened his grip on the handrails.

With about three miles still separating the F-4s from the SAM, Bo pulled the stick back into his belly with all his might. As the plane struggled to transition from dive to climb, their bodies resisted and tried to keep going in the same direction as they had been. The resulting inertial forces slammed both pilots back against their seats with savage strength. Even as his G suit automatically inflated with air to keep blood from pooling in his legs and robbing his brain, Ross strained to continue breathing with the M-1 maneuver taught to every fighter pilot; but Bo had initiated a pullout he could never have prepared for. The awful crushing pressure was like a house sitting on his chest, and Ross felt himself at the edge of consciousness as his vision narrowed as though he were looking through a tunnel. He could feel the airframe shake, and he knew for certain that Bo had strained it beyond design limits.

Just as Ross thought he might be able to hang on, that maybe the tough little plane would hang together, Bo managed to raise his left hand and let it drop on a small black button, exposed now because he had raised the safety cover before the pull-up. As his hand dropped and the switch contacts beneath the button connected, a small pump mounted outside of the midsection of the turbine engine began turning. As it did so, raw fuel was driven under pressure down a tube to the aft of the engine, where it was atomized and released downstream of the spinning turbine blades, directly into the hot exhaust. Plenty of oxygen remained in the superheated gases blasting out of the engine, and the fine spray of fuel was ignited instantly.

Rather than spill uselessly out the back of the engine, the fuel was contained for a split second by special baffles called "flameholders," which increased the turbulence of the mixture and gave it time to burn more fully. The temperature climbed to well in excess of three thousand degrees Fahrenheit before the furious tongues of blue flame finally shot out the exhaust nozzle with tremendous force.

Because the fuel was burned after the turbine blades had done their work with the main flow, the device was called an afterburner, and the added shock of its murderous punch kicked Ross over into unconsciousness even as it propelled the Phantom higher into the sky.

In several short seconds Bo had shot below and swung up and around his crippled comrade and placed his own craft between the ground station and Hardegreave. The radar thus saw only one target and fixated on it, sending new signals to the rising missile, which altered its course in pursuit.

As the Phantom's upward climb stabilized, the pressures inside the cockpit receded and Ross quickly came to. He was relieved to find Bo still in control but knew without having to look that they were being pursued by a flaming missile whose only objective in this world was the obliteration of their plane.

To confirm it, Bo jinked downward and watched the plume behind the SAM. In almost comical reaction—like "Look at all that water!" exclaimed by first-time visitors to Niagara Falls—Ross yelled, "Ah, shit!" the time-honored epithet uttered whenever a SAM angled in response to a test maneuver, which was what this SAM did in response to Bo's.

Sure now that he had diverted the missile from Hardegreave, Bo rolled the plane inverted and dove. The maneuver was designed to keep the G forces in a downward direction. Had he simply pushed over the top, it would have forced blood into his head, which his G suit couldn't fight, and might have resulted in a dangerous "red-out."

The SAM followed dutifully, swinging wide at first owing to the momentum built up at Mach 4, but reacquiring the Phantom quickly in response to the high-PRF guidance pulses coming from the ground station.

Ross nearly tore the muscle off his bones twisting and squirming on his seat to keep the missile in sight while the crushing G forces from Bo's violent maneuvers hit him. There was no other way to know where it was. And he knew what was coming next.

They'd had a couple of seconds' head start on the missile while it changed targets. Otherwise they would already have been hit. Bo continued the dive, and Ross sneaked a quick glance at the ground in front of them as they screamed toward it, the SAM closing in fast. He wondered if anyone had ever managed to tear the wings off a Phantom in a high-speed pull-up because, if not, it sure as hell looked like they had a good chance of being the first.

He resisted the urge to scream as Bo passed the point at which the hapless guy in back would have believed it possible to recover. He squeezed his eyes shut in a desperate attempt to stay conscious as Bo smoothly pulled the stick back to the stops, and he felt his spine compress as the plane shuddered and groaned under the impossible strain.

The low altitude made it difficult for the ground-based enemy radar to maintain a good lock, so there was a momentary hesitation before the encoded pulses told the SAM to pull up and try to climb; but it was enough.

Ross didn't get a good look as the missile's tail fins brushed the tops of a stand of trees, kicking the nose down very slightly but just enough to compromise its climb. Although the SAM's warhead was normally triggered by a proximity fuse, its collision with the ground was so powerful that it ignited the compact explosives and sent up an easily visible shower of bark, leaves and rapidly expanding, glowing gases.

Their joy at this display was short-lived because a Viet Cong insurgent named Troc Vinh saw it, too, from his vantage point just below the flight path of the escaping Phantom. From this distance Troc couldn't tell if the SAM managed to hit any of his village, but he wasn't waiting to find out.

He lifted a heavy, bazookalike contraption onto his shoulder, pointed it in the general direction of the F-4, shut his eyes and squeezed the trigger. The resulting kick knocked him off his feet, so he couldn't see the Soviet-built SA-7 Grail heat-seeker shoot forward, way off course, and waste a precious second before it was able to find and lock on to the tailpipe exhaust of Bo's plane, now nearly two miles away.

Ross saw it, climbing out of the wreckage left behind by the SAM, and he yelled to Bo and pointed.

They were at the border, over a geological formation consisting of low hills and deep ravines. Ignoring the possibility of being trapped in a box canyon, Bo dropped the Phantom into a long, narrow valley and leveled out at six hundred feet.

By this time Ross had regained enough of his senses to get back into the game. "Three thousand feet and closing, right on our six." He kept his voice calm. What Bo needed was information, not emotion.

Bo jinked the plane left and right and up and down, which would make the Grail do the same. That might make it slow just enough to buy a precious half second while he looked for what he needed. The valley curved sharply to the right, but not so much that the missile couldn't also negotiate the turn.

"Two thousand, Bo, now at the five." The SAM needed that extra moment to realign itself after the turn and had slipped a few degrees off to the right.

As they rounded a set of hillocks on the right, Bo saw it. Dead ahead, rising up from the valley floor, a cone-shaped hill at least a thousand feet high. He took a deep breath and aimed for it.

"Down to a thousand, buddy, you got any ideas?" Ross raised his head from his screen for a fraction of a second, just enough to see the hill looming up ahead. *Oh, yes, he does,* he thought in alarm. *Oh shit, oh shit, oh shit . . .*

There would be only one chance, and it had to be done right. Bo pulled back on the throttle, which was the last thing Ross expected. "Five hundred feet!" he yelled, his professionalism eroding rapidly as the hill came at him from the front and the missile from behind.

The slower the plane was moving, the tighter the turn it could make. But the timing was critical. The SA-7 was practically up their tailpipe, and it was still several thousand feet to the hill.

"Call it, Ross!"

"Four fifty, four, three fifty—" He was guessing, but it was close enough for what Bo needed. "It's closing faster!" As it should have, since it wasn't slowing its speed as the F-4 had.

Bo wrapped his left hand around his right and firmed up his grip on the stick. No mistakes, sweaty hands or not.

"Two hundred . . . one fifty . . . ! Jesus Christ, Kincaid!"

Bo shoved the stick hard to the left, then quickly back to center. The Phantom was now flying on its side and started losing altitude immediately with no horizontal wings to keep it aloft.

"One hundred! Oh, shit! Oh, shit! Pleeaase . . . !"

Bo yanked the stick back with all his might, sending the sideways plane into what it thought was a climb but in reality was a hard left turn. It missed the hill by less than three hundred feet, but the missile, even lightened up by all its spent fuel, could not match the track. It hit the hill at an oblique angle, and its warhead and all its remaining fuel exploded at once, sending burning shrapnel and rock shooting off at high speed. The supersonic shock wave spreading out from the point of impact, propelled by the explosive forces, quickly enveloped the F-4 and shook it as though by some giant unseen hand, but it passed quickly and the plane managed to keep flying.

The entire encounter, from the time Bo had placed his plane between Hardegreave and the SAM, had taken twenty-three seconds.

"We're hit!" Ross watched the red warning light flash on and off. "Right wing, fuel tank!"

"Switching to left tank and crossfeed." Bo reached under the panel and found the throwbar, pulled it out and then turned it to the left until it clicked into place. The crossfeed would also draw fuel from the right tank until it was gone, relying primarily on the left so the flow wouldn't stop completely at any point. He also switched from intercom to radio.

"Hardy, you with me?"

"Yeah, what's going on? What happened?"

"We lost the missile," Bo answered calmly. "We're over the border, so let's rejoin and take it home. Ross?"

We lost the missile! Ross said to himself incredulously. *That's all he has to say? We lost the missile?*

"Ross!"

"Uh, yeah, come to heading two three five."

They rejoined Hardegreave's damaged Phantom and flew without further incident into Thai territory, turning south to Ubon Air Base, which housed the Eighth Tactical Fighter Wing. The emergency equipment was called out, but Hardegreave took advantage of the windless day and managed to set his plane down with a minimum of maneuvering. Weapons Systems Officer Robbie Rubin, still alive but unconscious from the loss of blood, was lifted out of the rear cockpit and taken to the base hospital.

The day's battle turned out to be the largest of the war thus far. Seven MiGs were confirmed downed. The North Vietnamese fighters would stop taking American formations for granted, and by May the U.S. government would take enemy airfields off the restricted list. Shortly thereafter, strike forces would destroy twenty-six MiGs on the ground before they even managed to get their engines started.

Bo didn't make it to the high-spirited celebration that night, electing instead to be alone with his thoughts, which were as uplifted as they had been at any time in the last twenty years.

Early in the evening, there was a rap on the door jamb of the small barracks where the pilots were being put up before returning to Danang.

"Got a minute?" Ross was holding two beers in each hand and held them up in the air.

"Sure." Bo swung his legs out over the edge of the cot on which he'd been resting and sat up. Ross sat opposite him on another bunk and handed over a beer. They clinked bottles and drank.

"You know, you fly pretty good for a colored guy. Old colored guy, at that."

"You think?" Bo took another swig without taking his eyes off Ross.

"Mmm-hhmm." Ross polished off what was left in the bottle and reached for another.

Bo leaned over and pulled a pack of cigarettes out of Ross's flak jacket, taking one out and lighting it with the matches stuck in the cellophane wrapper.

"Scared the shit out of you, though, didn't I?" Bo's eyes crinkled in amusement as he eyed Ross through the plume of smoke.

"Me? Scared the shit out of me? Are you kidding?" Ross took back the pack and pulled out a cigarette for himself. "I don't know what the fuck scared me more, the hill, the missiles or you, you crazy fuck!"

They laughed and then fell silent, content to just sit, smoke and drink some beer. Bo Kincaid and Benjamin Ross, knights of the air, had jousted with death and won, for a most noble cause, one that had little to do with why this war was supposedly being fought.

Ross finished his cigarette and dropped it into the empty bottle he was holding.

"Well." He came creakily to his feet, arching his back, still a bit unsteady owing to the roller-coaster rides his circulatory system had taken several times that day. Bo did the same, but steadier, glad he'd stayed in shape in anticipation of the enormous demands modern jet fighting put on the pilot and crew, and not willing to show his age.

"Gonna go drink me some glory." Ross hitched up his pants in preparation for leaving.

"Do it, man. You got it comin'."

They stared at each other just a moment longer, then Ross turned and walked out. Bo sat down and lay back on the cot, staring up at the ceiling, thinking about everything and nothing.

As he neared the officers' canteen, Ross could hear the loud and raucous voices raised in the kind of celebration that only the release of unbearable tension and fear could produce. It was difficult to make out any individual words, but he thought he heard someone yell, "Tell it again! Tell it again!" followed by a chorus of approving shouts and catcalls.

He opened the door, and by then the noise had died down. A large group of pilots was gathered around an oak table, most holding beers, some smoking cigarettes. Behind the table, standing with one foot propped on a chair, was Jack Hardegreave, his neck arched back as he drained the last of his beer. Excited faces watched in anticipation.

As Ross stepped in and closed the door, Hardegreave wiped his mouth with the back of his sleeve and looked up at the assembled pilots.

"You shoulda seen him, man." He shook his head in wonder and awe and spread his hands before him in a gesture of supplication. "Just like a goddamned angel. . . ."

CHAPTER 17

June 12, 1310 EST

"Yeah. Uh-huh. But shouldn't you tell— Uh-huh. Okay, see you in about—"

Amy pulled the phone away from her ear and stared at it comically, then turned toward Jack with an amused look on her face.

"What?" asked Jack.

Amy turned back toward the phone, still holding it out at arm's length. "That was Florence Hartzig. Didn't know she was capable of getting that worked up. Says she's got something and'll be here in half an hour. Asked me to get Preston in, too." She looked up questioningly.

Jack shrugged. "Sure, what the hell. Give him a call."

"Sure, what the hell."

"Ah, c'mon, Doc." Jack grinned at her discomfort. "Can't handle a little flak from the FBI?"

She crossed the room and resumed running her eyes down the printed log. One of the Marvels had started up again in Red Oak, Iowa, and had already hit Council Bluffs and Omaha, Nebraska. Amy had been firm that no more messages were to be sent just yet, and Jack and Stanley, slightly mystified, had complied. There wasn't much choice, since they wouldn't have known what to say without her anyway.

"I'm thinking Captain Marvel isn't from the Midwest, and I don't relish arguing with Stanley about it."

"Why?" Jack walked over to the window, where sunlight was falling on the printed pages. "Why not from the Midwest?"

Amy looked out the window. The air was still and hazy, almost shimmering. She could *see* the heat. She turned back to Jack and said, "You don't shit where you eat. He's smart enough to know that."

Jack narrowed his eyes slightly. "Say again?"

Amy stuck her hands in the back pockets of her jeans and walked to the display monitor. She seemed to spend a good deal of time staring at it, as though it represented a link to their quarry and helped her try to connect up with whatever thought patterns were compelling the mysterious terrorist, which was how Amy thought of him now.

"Suppose you wanted to rob a bank, Jack. Think about it. Plan."

Jack was silent for a few moments, then said, "Okay. And?"

"Where do you do it?"

Jack stroked his chin before answering, then nodded slowly. "Anywhere but home."

"Yeah. A terrorist doesn't foul his own nest. It defeats whatever bullshit purpose he dreamed up as his justification."

"Terrorist?" asked Jack.

"Best way to think of him. He's banking on not being recognized, or accidentally bumping into any of his old friends."

"But doesn't that make him a stranger?" said Jack. "Out of place, easily pinpointed?"

" 'Course, but that's part of the challenge, see? Fitting in, fooling the citizenry? And the contempt, whoa, that's the best part! Knowing how stupid everybody else is. It makes the killing a bit easier, like he's doing the world a favor, removing a few more idiots." Trying to suppress her growing anger, she walked back to the window and leaned against the frame, looking down at the main entrance to the building. "Stanley's coming, huh? Good. We gotta make him understand."

"When are we going to send another message, Amy?"

"Soon. Hartzig's here. Just coming in the front entrance." She walked to the conference table and sat down.

"Forgot to tell you, by the way," Jack said tentatively. "She's been in touch with our tech guys out west, working on—"

"You think that's wise?" Amy interrupted. It was a stupid question, and she regretted it the moment it came out.

"No, I think it's dumb, that's why I did it."

"Didn't mean it that way. It's just, this whole thing feels so complicated, and every new element only adds to it." She was having enough trouble drawing Preston Stanley into her thinking without loading on more baggage.

"Understood. She's just on the technical end, so don't feel any pressure to explain what you're doing."

Shortly thereafter, Hartzig burst into the room. "How's it goin'?"

"Hi. What's so important?" asked Amy, trying to hide her pique.

"Where's that other FBI guy?" Florence said, breathless. "He here yet?"

"On his way."

"Then come sit down. This can't wait."

The three of them gathered around the table, Florence so excited she could barely contain herself. She drew several papers out of her tattered briefcase.

"I'm positive we're on the right track, how this guy can throw planes out of whack. Some of the Autonav designers have been going over the specs and they couldn't find anything out of place."

"This is news?" asked Amy.

"No, no, listen. For the hell of it, I had them express me the chip, the one that came out of the Bellingham 727, and brought it to the University of Maryland, a physicist I know there. Ever hear of a guy named Beeler?"

Jack raised his eyebrows in surprise. "Gregory Beeler?"

Amy looked at him, puzzled, postponing for the moment her beratement of Florence for this apparent breach of security in bringing in yet another outsider. "How'd you know that?"

"We've used him before. An expert on microtechnology."

"Everybody uses him," said Florence. "He's even on retainer to FundsNet, for our privately designed chips. And don't worry," she said to Amy. "He hasn't the slightest idea what this is about."

"But—"

"Hang on a minute," said Jack, cutting Amy off. "What about Beeler?"

"Well, uh, we had a few beers, talked over old times, and then I asked him to put the chip under the electron microscope."

She reached for one of the sets of papers she had taken out and unfolded one sheet until it covered almost half of the table. "This is the design spec."

It was incomprehensible, like a model railroad laid out by a lunatic or the output of an electronic plotter gone berserk and allowed to run unchecked for a year. The twenty-four square feet of paper were covered with hair-thin lines laid so close together that it almost took a magnifying glass to discern that the graphic was anything but a solid blotch of light purple. The diagram was punctuated occasionally by dark memory blocks, circular junction points, dense arrays of jagged peaks and troughs signifying arithmetical control units, and connecting points that would allow the impossibly detailed web of submicroscopic components to communicate with external circuits.

"This represents layer three of a seven-layer design that essentially contains the brains of the Autonav unit."

Jack looked up at her in disbelief. "This is only one of seven layers?"

"Uh-huh. They're—"

"Hold it, hold it," Amy interrupted. "How the hell did he take a picture of just one layer? I thought you couldn't do that."

Florence fixed Amy in her sights. "That's *his* little secret, okay? Makes us even." She waited a moment to see if Amy would object further. "Anyway, the chip is built up layer by layer, and each level is connected to the others by these junction points." Florence indicated the circular markings. "Remember, thirty years ago a device that could do the work of this chip would take up a whole room four times the size of the one we're sitting in. They didn't reduce the number of components, just their size."

"What are we supposed to make out of this?" asked Amy, still annoyed.

"Look here." Florence stood up, took out a pencil and pointed just to the side of one of the dark boxes. "According to the Autonav techs, this is the signal integrator. Basically, it's the part that first gets the incoming nav signal, figures out roughly what it's trying to say, then directs it to the right part of the chip to handle it. I've got a transparency of this section."

She opened a manila folder and took out a piece of film the size of a sheet of letter paper and clipped it to the wall-mounted viewer normally used for examining X-rays of fatigued metal. She flipped a switch on the side of the unit, and the internal fluorescent light flickered on and steadied.

Amy got up and switched off the overhead light. The film sprang into sharp relief in the darkened room, and the portion of the circuit design in question was plainly visible.

"Now," said Florence, reaching for another piece of film. "This is the photograph Beeler took with the electron microscope of the actual chip that was built, the one from the 727." She clipped the film to the side of the design photograph.

Jack and Amy stood and huddled around the viewer. Florence held up a finger to the design photograph. "Look here"— she held up her other hand and pointed to the corresponding spot on the micrograph—"and here."

They peered closely until Amy said, "There's a little boxy thing on the micrograph."

Florence dropped her hands and smiled triumphantly. "Precisely."

"Precisely what?" said Amy. "What is it?"

"It's a difference. The chip in the nav unit doesn't match its technical specification. Something's wrong." She paused and looked at Jack. "Something was added."

Jack moved in closer and put his face inches away from the micrograph. "Well, I'll be damned."

"It's getting a signal? Somebody's sending a signal?"

"Definitely. And somehow that signal lets him create false readings on the instruments the pilots see, or that control the autopilot."

They each took a close look and then reconvened around the table. Jack looked uncomfortable and glanced around to see if Amy shared the feeling. She did, he could tell that. Preston Stanley walked in just as Amy turned the overhead lights back on, then they both sat down.

"Got here fast as I could. What's going on?"

Jack pointed at the viewer. "There was definitely some tampering with the chip. There's a circuit element wasn't in the original design. Has to be how he's doing it."

Stanley glanced at the viewer in an offhanded way, then looked around the table and voiced Jack and Amy's concern without realizing it. "Nice to have found it, but what's the big deal? Kinda knew it, didn't we?"

Jack leaned forward and placed his elbows on the table. "As a matter of fact, Florence, that's kind of what I been thinking. It's a great piece of work, but ... ?" He spread his hands in a questioning gesture, and Amy sensed some impending embarrassment concerning a possible overestimation of her talents.

Florence's spirit was not to be dampened. "That's not why I came over, sports fans." She jerked a thumb toward the viewer. "Slick, yeah, but like you say, hardly a breakthrough far as we're concerned."

She pulled her chair in closer and motioned for Stanley to sit down. "We know how he does it, but we still don't know how he managed to tweak the 727 and not the Lear. The cargo plane he trashed was easy, because it was the only thing flying that night. But how'd he single out the 727?"

Jack felt a tingle start up in his spine: Florence knew. She'd figured it out, and now she was going to tell them.

"We know the Lear also carried Autonav equipment, so that doesn't help. Amy already figured out that a highly directional beam wouldn't be practical."

Amy nodded her agreement. "And the point was made again with the cargo plane. No way Marvel could have aimed right at that plane in the middle of a noisy shitstorm in the middle of the night."

"Exactly. So there's only one other way."

Florence paused dramatically, knowing the effect her insight would have on the team and relishing the moment.

Amy shrugged a shoulder and scratched her nose, then shifted from one buttock to another on her chair. "Captain Marvel was on the plane, right?"

Florence jerked her head toward Amy. The wizard of FundsNet looked as if she'd been punched in the stomach. Later Jack would recall how he'd never seen that much air let out of one set of sails at one time.

The computer scientist stared at Amy. "How—how the hell did you know that?" she finally managed to get out.

Amy shrugged again and waved toward the micrographs. "We know it was a signal. If it couldn't come from outside, it had to come from inside. Not much of a mystery, I should think."

Stanley wasn't interested in the byplay, especially since Amy was the chief beneficiary, and he sought to deflect the discussion to a more productive line.

"You're telling me the guy was on the 727?"

"Had to be," said Florence, recovering, but only slightly. "There's just no other way. That close to the instruments, he could have been carrying a low-powered transmitter you couldn't tell from a portable radio."

"But why would he risk his own life?"

Florence turned up a palm. "What risk? He knew there was a high ceiling, he knew exactly where he was directing the plane. There was virtually no risk except maybe the pilots going blooey when they broke out."

"Wait a minute, wait a minute," Jack admonished, not willing to let the momentum of the revelation carry them to a too quick conclusion. "How could he possibly know the tower at Bellingham would be out of service or what the ceiling would be, in enough time to buy himself a ticket for that particular flight?"

Florence, recovering still further, brightened. "He didn't, don't you see? That was a pure gift. Even if the weather had been severe clear with a functioning tower, there still would have been little doubt he could do what he did in bad weather, whenever he wanted."

"No, not a pure gift." Amy hunched forward. "I just realized something. His letter, remember? I was sarcastic about how it was off by only a half mile and a couple minutes." She turned to Florence, who had not been privy to the details of Captain Marvel's first letter other than the payoff instructions. "But he was off because he didn't know how much good luck he'd run into, as you said. He was able to carry it much farther than he'd planned. But he wouldn't have done it in clear conditions. He waited for some bad weather, which is probably why he picked the Pacific Northwest in the first place, and got ideal conditions for his demonstration, and even though it made his letter less accurate, the point was better made."

Jack drummed his fingers on the table. "So what you're saying, he has even more precise control than we thought?"

Before Amy could answer, Stanley spoke up. "But I don't get it, how he could do all of that from the back of the plane, when they were inside a cloud and he couldn't see out."

"That's an easy one," Amy said, leaning back. "Simple timing. He knew the approach configuration, he knew by exactly how much he was throwing them off. . . . He could have brought them safely down to a thousand feet if they hadn't broken through the cloud layer at three thousand and seen for themselves."

"Then everything fits." Stanley jumped up and began pacing. "If you're right, this is great news. We can get the passenger manifest and check out everyone who was riding on that plane."

"He wouldn't be traveling under his own name, would he?"

"Of course not," said Stanley. "But everybody else would be. We find whomever he sat next to, we can maybe get a visual ID. And my guess is we can figure out what seat he was in almost immediately."

"Because he paid cash for the ticket," Amy said.

"Right," said Stanley, forgetting for a moment his annoyance with her.

Amy turned toward Florence and looked at her levelly. "That was brilliant, Florence. Some nice work."

Florence looked crestfallen again. "But you'd figured it out already."

Amy laughed and sat up straight. "You crazy? I figured it out only when you gave me the answer. Just now."

Florence looked puzzled as Amy explained.

"Sometimes, the most important thing is how you frame

the question. If you had said 'How the hell did he send up the beam?' you immediately head down the wrong track. But the way you asked it gave the answer."

Amy leaned back again and waved a hand idly. "All I did was follow where you led. It was nice work."

And nice work to you, too, Amy, thought Jack as he watched the lights go back on somewhere inside Florence.

"You haven't got anything else, I'm outta here." Stanley paused momentarily at the door.

Jack looked at Florence, who turned to the FBI agent and said, "Go get him, sport. Or them. Or what the hell ever."

"No," Jack countermanded, "stick around, Pres." He turned his attention to the indecipherable chip design still laid out on the table. "Florence, is there any chance at all, figuring out how this modification works?"

She stood and walked to the viewer where the enlargement was still displayed and considered the question. "Very difficult. It would be easier if we had the real circuit design, the one he modified, but we don't."

"Can we reverse engineer the chip itself?" asked Amy. "Work backward from the physical structure, see maybe how the thing actually works?"

Florence was doubtful. "Doesn't work that way with microchips. Not normally. Hell, you need an electron microscope just to see the damned things, and that won't tell you the values of things like transistors and capacitors."

"You know, there is one thing," said Stanley, staring in deep concentration at the diagram. "We do have the chip itself. In fact, about as many as we want, yanked out of the nav units sitting on shelves, or even in Autonav's stockpiles."

"But how do we know that all of them have been modified?" asked Jack.

"Not a problem," Amy jumped in. "We can shoot pictures of a handful in less than an hour, see if the mod shows up."

"Nope." Florence shook her head forcefully. "Taking the picture ruins the chip. The beam is too intense. But Autonav has only one template for making the chip, so you can be sure all of them on the shelves are modified."

"So what's your idea?" asked Jack.

"There can't be that many ways it could work. So what if

we identify the most likely hypotheses and set up rigs to test the chips against the possibilities?"

"How many rigs has Autonav got?" asked Jack.

"Fifteen," Florence replied without hesitation. "I got a briefing, via marketing video. You just drop a chip in, or any other key component, and you can fire any test you want through a cabled antenna input."

Amy stood and joined Florence at the viewer, then looked at Stanley. "So we set the rigs up with tested components and change only the chips. Then what?"

"Then we prioritize the possibilities and run through the most likely ones first, the easiest ones to test, really, fifteen at a time. None of those pan out, we proceed to the tougher ones."

"Why so many at a time?" asked Jack. "There can't be that many ways of doing it."

Stanley shook his head. "There aren't. But he's beaming signals, and the number of possible frequencies is very large, so we have to test each one."

Florence agreed. "Best clue we have—and it's actually a pretty good one—the signal has to be capable of being captured by the type of antenna normally hooked up to a navigation unit. That should narrow down the range considerably, probably to the band allocated for the purpose."

"Come to think of it," offered Amy, "I'd bet we could start looking at the frequencies in that band that are still unassigned. Those would be the most likely, because that way our guy would never have to compete with a ground station."

"I'm still missing something," Jack said. "How come he wouldn't just use the actual ground frequency? That way, he wouldn't have to even modify the chip. He can knock out anybody anywhere. We were thinking of that some time ago, playing with possible terrorist scenarios."

"Power," replied Florence. "It would take an enormous rig, and a generator the size of a tractor trailer to power it, in order to make sure he overrode the ground station."

Amy nodded in agreement. "Not only that, but a station that size would affect every plane tuned to it over twenty thousand square miles. Then everybody could tell something was screwy, and air traffic control would shut it down and broadcast an out-of-service message within minutes."

Jack was satisfied with the explanation. "We find out how it works, how difficult would it be to defeat?"

Amy smiled. "Depends on how it works. If it's really triggered with a standard frequency? Uh—"

"Might be possible to filter it selectively," Florence suggested.

"Maybe," said Amy, "but that means fabricating a device and installing it on a couple thousand planes."

Florence had another idea. "It might be easier to install transmitters on all the ground stations. They'd broadcast a signal on the triggering frequency, but without any information in it, just jamming Captain Marvel's device, really. That would be pretty inexpensive to do, and could probably get done in a hurry."

"How would you know it could really defeat the mod?" asked Jack.

"We test it on the rigs first."

"Okay," said Jack, placing his hands on the table and ending the discussion and also signaling the start of an action plan. "Amy, we got a good man in the Northwest? NTSB, I mean." *Damn, gotta stop that!*

"Not for this sort of thing—"

"The guy at Autonav I spoke to on the phone?" said Florence. "Top-shelf engineer. We hit it off well together."

"Good. Let's not waste time anybody getting on an airplane. Coordinate by phone and pull together a test plan, and make sure you have a Bureau staffer fax a confidentiality agreement to that engineer first. Arrange for some newer stock chips to get pulled and identified. Do a lot more than you need in case we need to test any to destruction."

He next turned to Amy. "I want you to work with Florence once the test plans are laid out. Start with the best possibilities and figure out how we engineer a defeat if they come up positive. You better get an FAA engineer in on that part, since we're gonna need to move mountains if we have to dick around with operational air traffic control equipment."

"We still need to try to catch the guy," Stanley reminded Jack.

"I know that. It's the other reason I want Florence and Amy to stay and work here." He turned to Amy. "Tell Admin we're commandeering the conference room next door, tell them we want a secure line to Autonav set up immediately, with a fax machine."

He waited until those taking notes were finished. "And unless there's anything else, let's get cracking."

Amy and Stanley left the room, and Florence began clearing the conference table and retrieving the photo images from the viewer.

"Coffee?" offered Jack.

"Sure, black."

Jack poured the coffee into two foam cups and returned to the table, handing one to Florence and sitting down heavily.

Florence stared down into the cup for a second. "Am I supposed to drink this stuff or fill my pen with it?"

"Wait a few more hours. You could fill potholes with it."

She got up and, to Jack's surprise, left the room with no explanation. She returned a minute later, closed the door and resumed her seat, reaching into her jacket pocket and withdrawing two cigarettes and a book of matches. She held them up in the air.

Jack grinned, wide-eyed. "Well, goddamn! From Freddy?" Freddy was a summer research intern from George Washington University who sneaked smokes in the lavatory and blew the exhalants down an airshaft so nobody would notice, but everybody did and nobody said anything so they could bum cigarettes from him.

"Face like a turnip?"

Smelling the length of the cigarette and placing it between his lips, Jack nodded. "That's Freddy."

Florence struck a match and offered it to Jack first, who closed his eyes with the first inhale. He exhaled luxuriously and considered the cigarette. "Pretty damned funny coming from a reputedly intelligent woman."

Florence didn't smoke anymore and didn't miss it at all. Didn't even enjoy it when the situation called for her to have a cigarette. Like now. "One of those big-shot FAA guys, he said you were in the military. Carriers, right?"

Jack took a sip of the stale coffee and grimaced, whether from the coffee or the memory, Florence couldn't tell.

"Yep. Philippines. Skipper of the *Constellation*, actually, out of Subic Bay."

"Skipper? Didn't know you were such a big deal."

Jack shrugged. "It's all relative, I guess. Aboard ship, I snap my fingers and five thousand uniforms jump. I go ashore, get my shoes shined? Just another schmuck."

"You miss it?"

"I miss a lot of it. I miss the flying. 'Course, as soon as you get a command, you can't fly anymore. Like taking the best doctor in a hospital and making him director. No more medicine, no more patients, no more doctor."

"It's like that with a lot of professions. Why'd you leave?"

Jack stared at her a long time before deciding to answer.

The command tower of the aircraft carrier *Constellation* sits some seventeen stories above the deck, atop a series of steep, switchbacked staircases. The enormous ship, its population larger than that of many towns in America (although the average age of the crew is all of 19½), seems to the casual observer the very essence of stability, incapable of any but straight-ahead motion as its mammoth engines propel it through the submissive seas, the centerpiece of a twelve-ship, eight-thousand-man, eighty-aircraft armada.

But for all its mass and presence, the ship is still afloat, resting on water and rising above it, by virtue not of the wings of angels, but of the fact that it weighs less than an equal volume of water would. The same laws of physics that buoy a child on an inner tube on a calm lake are at work on the carrier on the high seas.

When those seas are calm, the deck of the ship is not much different from the street of a city, feeling anchored to the very bedrock of the earth, solid and immutable.

In heavy seas, such as the ones battering the great ship at this moment, the wave-induced differences in water height along the length of the keel translate into a raising and lowering of portions of the deck, called "pitching" when the motion is fore and aft, and "rolling" when it is side to side. Often, in particularly fearsome storms, the two motions are combined into a demonic ballet of indeterminate periodicity, making even the simple act of walking extremely hazardous.

The higher up on the ship one went, the more pronounced the effect as distance from the center of gravity increased. The very top of the command superstructure could sway back and forth as much as ninety feet, whipsawing the stairs leading up from the deck and anyone foolish enough to be on them.

Which is why Lieutenant Clarence Prendergast was out of breath and slightly pale when he reached the topmost level and burst through the rubber-sealed door, bringing in with him cold air and the caustic smell of brine.

"Captain," he gasped between puffs of breath, "we got a problem. Couldn't raise you on the bitch box." He waved toward the 19MC communications unit, used to contact the tower primarily when problems arose.

Captain Jonathan "Jack" Webster picked up the handset and held it to his ear; he heard nothing.

"You run all the way up here in this shitstorm to tell me that?"

"Nossir," Prendergast wheezed, choking down another lungful. "In the air—another Hornet—on his way in."

Webster turned and looked down at what he could see of the deck. The storm, a force 3, had arisen with alarming suddenness as warm air stirred up by a near surface inversion slammed into a colder front propelled from the north by a renegade southern dip of the jet stream. As the two swirling masses met, the colder air sucked moisture out of the warmer in a frenzy of violent turbulence. It seemed to Webster as though the entire dance were a conspiracy to mug his ship.

"Won't be easy, Lieutenant, but it has been done." *Not by me, it hasn't. Not in stuff like this. But others ...* "Does he want nets up? Make sure we have additional tie-downs on all the planes still on deck."

He reached for the phone, but Prendergast cut him off, most of his ability to breathe now recovered. "No, sir, it's not that. He's in trouble. The plane, I mean, well, there's a problem."

Lieutenant Commander Robert Baker stepped forward, careful to grab on to the railing of the map table before letting go of the overhead strap he'd been holding. "What kind of problem?"

"They're not sure, sir—the cause, I mean—but it seems he can't put his flaps down, at least the starboard side, and one side of his gear won't come down neither."

Webster stared at the lieutenant in disbelief before looking out the window once more. The F-18 Hornet needed its flaps fully extended for the slow-flight regime of a landing. Retracted, the aircraft was a three-hundred-mile-per-hour, twenty-ton bullet. Landing it in that configuration and bringing it to a controlled stop was impossible. Add the asymmetry of damaged landing gear, and this was a plane Webster couldn't let anywhere near the deck of the carrier. But how could two such disparate calamities have befallen a single craft?

Webster looked back to his remote radar screen, on which he had been watching the planes march down from the sky in procession. They used the standard Marshall pattern, each plane a thousand feet higher for every mile back, starting twenty miles out. Plenty of separation, even for a night like this. One lone blip remained on the screen.

"Who is it?"

Prendergast hesitated before speaking. "It's Slattery, sir. He stayed up until everyone else was down. One of the pilots was getting a little freaked, younger guy—you know how it is, skipper—and Slattery flew wing for him on the way down, then went back around."

Webster shook his head. It took no figuring out. A typical hotshot hero move, the kind of uncriticizable stunt that is, at its base, truly an act of unforgivable ego. The pilot would have bragging rights for a year, no doubt about that. Every peacetime fighter-jockey in every service in the world prayed for an opportunity to pull something like this, to put himself in harm's way and come up a winner. That's what really made peacetime so difficult for the warrior: not the lack of action, not the wasted training, but too few chances to be valorous, to be a lion, to test oneself under the random conditions of real battle and fling it in the devil's face.

And yet—? Webster bit his lower lip. Even with all of that, it was still real, not a game. Not some computer-simulated romp through a battlefield of virtual reality. To purposely place yourself in danger when no post hoc critique would have faulted you for doing otherwise, to walk resolutely into the demon's gaping maw for the benefit of a brother in the fraternity of flying—what was it Halsey said? There are no extraordinary men, just ordinary men placed in extraordinary situations. How true, and how wrong.

He turned back to look out the window, to drink in the vicious storm, a taunting prizefighter of a gale dancing in the oceanic arena, landing punches and retreating, howling in laughter at the sailors' puny efforts to cover up, to defend, to ward off the repeated, tireless blows. He pictured Brian Slattery in his F-18 Hornet, an insignificant speck of titanium and epoxy plastic and boron fibers, barely a penny in the balance sheet of the furious storm. Any pilot caught in this airborne maelstrom would be in terrible trouble, but in a damaged plane? Whatever his motivation, the pilot had weighed the odds and ignored the outcome, following instead the dictates of his heart. Webster knew that the fear in the boy's belly was bottomless and nameless, and he knew that only against such terror was true bravery to be found.

He put down the phone and reached for his slicker. "Let's get down to air ops. Who's controlling?"

"Sivara, sir. He's talking to Slattery and called in his mechs."

Sivara. Thank God. "What do they say?"

"Nothing by the time I left to come get you."

"Baker, you have the ship. I'm gonna handle this one myself."

"Captain off the bridge!" a bosun called loudly, in acknowledgment of Webster's exit.

Having not left the con since the storm arose, Webster was momentarily shocked by its strength as the portwise tilt of the superstructure combined with any icy blast from the northern gale through an open hatch to throw him off balance. Prendergast, more acclimated to the conditions inside the stairwell, reached for his skipper's arm even as Webster's hand shot out and grabbed the ladder chain.

"Damn, what a monster!"

"Grab on tight!" yelled the lieutenant over wind howling

through the bulkheads and hatchways that were opening and closing everywhere. "We got enough troubles for one night!"

The two shipmates made their way slowly down the staircase, pausing before the apex of each roll and moving quickly during the brief pauses before the tower changed direction.

"How long since the last plane came in?" Webster asked, putting his mouth to Prendergast's ear during a forced pause in their descent.

"About thirty minutes," he replied as their respective mouths and ears changed places. "Wasn't half this bad then."

Landing planes on carriers during the day was fun. Pilots looked forward to it, went for as many trapped landings as possible, maybe on the way toward induction into the prestigious "Von Trap" club where lifetime sea landings were measured in the thousands. There was little nervousness amid the almost carnival atmosphere, and even the always surprising violence of winding down from 170 miles per hour to zero in two seconds didn't seem to bother anybody too much during daylight ops.

Night landings were pure hell itself, as bad as it got for a naval pilot in peacetime short of a malfunctioning aircraft. The absence of visual cues, an almost complete cessation of three-dimensional context and a general sense of free-floating dread all added up to a fairly unpleasant experience for even the most hardened of pilots. Throw in a storm and each pilot's "turn in the barrel" took on the flavor of a waking nightmare. To make it even worse for Hornet pilots, theirs was a single-seat aircraft, depriving them of the comfort of another human being in close proximity, another soul as a small palliative for their raw nerves.

Thirty minutes. The training sortie had been a short one. Slattery should have plenty of fuel, maybe enough for a climb to a safer altitude and a long hold at low power. There was no land close by, and Webster wasn't about to risk putting up a refueling tanker in this weather.

"He dump his ordnance?" Webster shouted, and received an affirming nod. In addition to its MK-61 Vulcan cannon, the F-18 carried four Sidewinder and four Sparrow III missiles. Planes routinely landed on the deck with their underwing armaments in place, to be disarmed by red-suited ordnance personnel as soon as the plane taxied clear of the landing area. In emergencies or marginal conditions, several million dollars' worth of missiles were dumped into the sea as a precaution, a practice long the target of Pentagon budget watchers but one that nobody in his right mind would question.

As they neared the open deck, Webster could make out the shapes of men—no women served on carriers or any other combat ships in his day—moving slowly but with purpose, using hand signals in place of voices that would only be carried off by the wind. Each crew member wore a colored slicker that indicated his function. Now, just below where Webster and Prendergast were standing, yellow-shirts were trying to rid the deck of airplanes to prepare for a possible crash landing. Farther forward, blues were erecting the barrier nets that would stop the F-18 without giving the pilot a chance even to try to catch a wire with his tailhook. The order to put up nets was not made lightly. Aside from the possibility of damage to the plane, it was surprisingly difficult to fly a net landing: there was no more unnatural act for a pilot than to fly his plane headfirst into a fixed object.

Silver-suited firefighters were also on hand, anticipating the worst. There would be no aborted landing and takeoff on this night. Deep in his heart, Jack knew there might not be a landing at all.

They reached the bottom landing and reentered the ship's interior through another rubber-lined door, then took two more sets of stairs until reaching air operations, a smallish office from which the captain could command operations. It adjoined CATC—carrier air traffic control—a much larger, darker room, illuminated mostly by the glow of numerous radar scopes topping individual workstations. CATC was separated from air ops by a transparent wall containing an outline chart of the area. On this map, the positions of planes and ships were indicated for the captain's benefit by small props moved around by hand as updated reports came in.

"Captain in ops!" announced an ensign, who abruptly changed it to "Captain in CATC!" as Webster ignored the outer office and strode directly into the darkened control room. The obligatory salutes were dispensed with quickly.

"What've we got?" asked Webster as he doffed his slicker

and handed it to an aide in exchange for a cup of coffee. "Thanks," he said, looking directly at the man for a second, reflexively letting him know that his efficiency was appreciated.

"Not good." Gene Sivara didn't take his eyes from the display console sitting in front of Joe Guarino. He was hunched over the workstation operator, his headset plugged into the second receptacle that acted as an extension to Guarino's.

"Can we get him upstairs?"

Sivara shook his head. "Too low on fuel."

Webster looked startled. "The hell are you talking about? Didn't they go out full?"

Sivara looked up for the first time. "He's got a leak, skipper. Right tank. Didn't Clarence—" He turned his head. "Oh, shit, we found out after you left, Lieutenant. Sorry."

"A fuel leak? On top of everything else?" Webster was having trouble grasping all of this. Angrily he said, "A little too much goddamned coincidence around here for my blood, gentlemen."

"No, sir." Mechanic Andy Espinoza looked up from the chart table where he had spread a technical drawing of the F-18. Webster not only tolerated dissent from his crew, he demanded it, considered it a professional's obligation, and he considered all his crew professionals.

"I'm Slattery's mech, sir. I think everything's related. The leak came first."

Webster exchanged glances with Sivara and walked briskly to the table. "Show me."

Espinoza leaned on one arm and pointed with a pencil, his singsong Cuban accent almost like a chant. "Here, where the leading edge of the wing meets the fuselage? The fuel tank is probably punctured, most likely through this access panel where it comes in contact with the fuel bladder inside the wing."

He was pointing to one of a profusion of inconsequential-looking dots that might have been ink blots from the plotter's pens, the kinds of markings Webster thought nobody ever paid any attention to.

"What made it leak?"

"If I told you, you wouldn't believe me, skipper, but it's not important now anyway." He moved the pencil as he spoke. "Best guess, the fuel dripping down evaporated so quickly in the windstream it dropped the skin temp way below freezing. The moisture in the clouds must have frozen up on the skin, over and over until there was a solid cake of ice." Years later Jack Webster would remember this moment and crack the puzzle of a dozen "blue ice" accidents on commercial air carriers: toilet fluid leaking out of the planes and freezing into deadly chunks in the upper atmosphere.

He peered closely at the diagram. "So it blocked off the gear door?"

Espinoza nodded grimly. "And sprayed backward, fanning out and doing the same thing to the flap extension mechanism. Because everything's on one side, that's why I think it's all the same problem."

Webster looked back at Sivara. "What're we doing?"

"I got him in slow flight, or at least as slow as he can get with the flaps up. The high angle of attack may keep more fuel from spilling out the front. It seems to be working."

"What about the ice?"

"Espinoza's got an idea."

The mech stood up straight and turned away from the drawing. "I think, he snaps the plane into a few turns and works the retractor, the wing bending might crack the ice, maybe let him shake it off."

"Down side?"

Espinoza hesitated. "The wing is built to withstand stress by being flexible. If it's too stiff from all that ice, it might fall."

Webster realized as Espinoza spoke that the mechanic had gone beyond the requirements of his coursework in understanding how his pilot's plane worked. "What do you recommend?"

Sivara answered before Espinoza could. "Captain, he stays in this condition, we can't let him on the ship. And if he ditches, we can't launch a chopper. He'd have to take his chances with a raft until the weather clears."

The rest lay unspoken between them. Both men, and everyone else in the room, knew that an ejection even under ideal conditions was a grave risk. The Hornet's much admired zero-altitude escape system, which had successfully saved pilots even when they ejected with wheels still on the runway, was based on an unusually violent explosion of charges packed beneath the seat. Pilots were usually greatly relieved if they only broke an arm or had a mild concussion or maybe lost a spleen if they got banged around too much. And in a raging thunderstorm the odds dropped even further. On land, even an unconscious pilot could survive a parachute landing with generally recuperable injuries. But on water, further steps were required to deploy a raft and save one's own life.

"How's he feel about it?" Webster jerked a thumb upward, indicating the plane somewhere in the vast blackness outside the ship.

"I think you already know that."

Webster approached the workstation and made a beckoning motion with his hand. "Gimme a mike, and put him on open."

Sivara yanked off the headset and handed it to Guarino, who unplugged it and replaced it with a hand-held microphone. He flicked a switch engaging the wall-mounted speaker. Only a light hiss emerged, indicating no signal passing between the plane and the carrier.

Webster keyed the mike. "Slattery, this is Webster. What the hell'd you do to sixty million dollars of taxpayer airplane?"

He released the key, and shortly thereafter a burst of static erupted from the speaker, followed by the sound of a young man's voice. "Awful sorry, sir. You want it back or what?"

Webster glanced at Espinoza and smiled. The mechanic bit his lip and tried to stay composed, not trusting himself to say anything.

"Your mech tells me he thinks you can knock off some ice. Are you holding fuel?"

"I think the leak's a little slower, but not stopped. Right now I'm doing squat, so let's get on with it."

"Stand by one." Webster released the key and addressed himself to Guarino. "What's his altitude, Joe?"

"Angels two zero, sir. Plenty of maneuvering room." Twenty thousand feet, and even if he accidentally ejected straight down, he could survive. "He's about six miles east-southeast."

Webster rekeyed the mike. "It's your call, Slattery. Stay on freq and talk to me."

"Roger that. Stand by one."

The speaker calmed back down to its background hiss, and Jack tried to picture what was going on four miles above his head. Slattery would cycle the nose and left gear back into the plane to reduce drag, then snap the plane into a full-tilt aileron roll one way, then the other, in an attempt to bend the wing as much as possible. It was the best idea they had at the moment. *C'mon, Slattery, say something.*

The speaker squawked obediently. "I heard something! Like a crack! Can't tell if it was the wing or the ice. I'm gonna cycle the gear."

He left his mike hot as he engaged the extenders. A mechanical groan could be heard in the background, a metal-on-metal screaming sound that rose in pitch and then stopped.

"Negative! I say again, negative. Going for round two." And the speaker went quiet again.

The tension in CATC mounted, not just because of the waiting, but because the nursing of anxiety was as close to anything resembling an action they could do. All of the assembled leaders and support crew, all of the blinking lights and sweeping radar screens and other trappings of advanced technology, meant nothing across the disconnected emptiness separating them from the damaged fighter jet and its brave pilot. *So very brave!* Jack thought. Any action, however insubstantial, was still an attempt to make contact, but if no such action could be mounted, if all they could send up were ideas, then at least they could intensify their own anxiety, as though this would make it seem less like they were abandoning the pilot and taking comfort in their own assured security.

The speaker blared again. "One mo' time!"

Again the sickening groan, then a sharp crack, and then the smooth whirring of perfectly synchronized gears and pinions. There was a pause, and the speaker went quiet before coming back on, and only later would the assembled shipmates conjecture that Slattery had unkeyed the mike for a second to keep his hysterical rebel yell to himself before recapturing his composure, clearing his throat and, in his calmest, most professional voice saying, "Okay, that loosened the gear up."

Espinoza's head jerked up and his eyes narrowed with the effort to stay dry. The collection of held breaths in the room sighed in near unison.

Webster picked up his mike and, in *his* most commanding voice, said, " 'Bout time. Now extend your flaps." He motioned to Guarino with his hand, and the technician handed him a cigarette and lit it for him. The skipper's bumming was legendary, as was his tradition of periodically buying the bummees a carton.

He sat down and inhaled deeply, rubbing his forehead, enjoying the brief exhilaration in the room and wondering how best to bring Slattery back. The speaker came back to life.

"Uh, negative on the flaps."

Webster froze and felt everyone's eyes lock on him. Guarino, buying him time to think, stepped on his foot pedal and spoke into his headset's boom microphone. "Say again?"

"No dice. Still stuck."

Webster grabbed his mike. "Slattery, recycle."

"I did, skipper. Six times. Not even a budge."

Shit! Webster said to himself. *Shit! Shit! Shit!* He looked around the room and got nothing but overwhelming need from his people. The need to be directed, to be guided and led and nurtured and fed and taken care of. All from him, right now, decisively and with no looking back, as though he were some kind of God or saint or fucking genius or Lord knows what.

No. Not fair. "Any ideas?"

Sivara shook his head to snap his eyes back from their distant stare. "What about a touch-and-go, let him slam into the deck on his wheels and try to shake the ice loose?"

It was a clever idea.

"Negative. Not on this rolling deck, not with a fuel leak. Coming in that hot, he could lose it, maybe explode and take out half the tower." And a good number of crew with it. On these seas, at his speed, an upward pitch of the deck at the wrong moment would present itself to the incoming fighter like a brick wall instead of a landing zone.

"But then——" Espinoza stopped himself in midsentence. *But then you won't let him into the net, either, if all else fails, won't let him try a landing. You're gonna strand him in the sky, make him eject.*

Then the rest hit him. With the flaps retracted, Slattery wouldn't be able to slow his craft down enough for a safe ejection. He might stall the plane and send it tumbling, maybe into a spin, which would make an ejection even riskier. His only option was to do it at the lowest speed the no-flaps, swept-back wing configuration would allow and still maintain controlled flight.

Webster waited, knowing that nothing useful would be forthcoming from his people. He brought the mike back to his face. "Say fuel, Slattery."

"About three minutes, not counting the leak. Somewhat less, probably. Skipper?"

"Yeah?"

"I'm gonna punch out, right?" He sounded very small all of a sudden, very young.

Webster took one last look around. Espinoza, some irrational part of him having taken over momentarily, waited for his answer. The others waited only to see how he would phrase it.

"Affirmative. I want you to angle in toward the ship, but stay parallel and at least a thousand yards out, you got that?"

"Roger, I— Oh, Christ! Oh, Christ! Flameout on one! I say again, one's dead!"

It didn't make any difference, really, losing the engines at this point. But Webster knew that they had been keeping the pilot up in the air, and Slattery probably subconsciously felt that they could do so forever, or at least until he got himself good and prepared and did what was necessary in his own good time. But now, this way—

"Two's gone! I say again, two is gone! I'm going in!" He wasn't screaming, not hysterical, maybe just mildly alarmed, but still in control.

"Slattery, listen to me carefully. Set up for a minimum rate of descent glide." Webster looked up at Sivara.

"Two sixty," Sivara mouthed at him.

"Two six zero knots, Slattery, you got that?" It would maximize the amount of time he could spend in the air, even though the Hornet with its flaps retracted would still be dropping like an anvil.

"Two six zero, affirmative."

"Good. Now when you hit five thousand feet—no lower—pull up the nose, hard. You start getting stall buffet, punch out. Don't wait for it to heel over, y'got that?"

"I got it, sir. Five thousand."

For the first time in his heretofore charmed life, Brian Slattery, football team captain and campus heartthrob, knew real loneliness, knew it as a vibrant and heavy thing. The images and memories of his world receded until they were light-years away, separated from him across unfathomable gulfs of thick, empty space, his life now a mere pinprick in the vastness of the cosmos. The voices in his headset were detached, disembodied, and seemed to emanate not from human beings, but from the tiny speakers themselves. He was on his own, no protective linebackers, no entourage of sycophantic freshmen, no flight deck full of trained crewmen who made his safety the locus of their lives. Just himself, his sweet mother's son, just him and the storm and whatever God he had long ago forgotten and whose acquaintance he had scant seconds to resurrect. The part of him that could feel kept alive the most fleeting hope of miraculous redemption while the part of him that could think brooked no such irrational aspiration.

"Where is he, Joe?"

Guarino's eyes bored in on the radar screen, its green markings precisely tracing the plane's track. "Seventeen thousand and dropping fast, sir. He's about four miles out, but the minimum descent has him on a steep angle down. He'll be over a mile away at five thousand."

"Sivara, quick: gimme max glide!"

"Two ninety!" Espinoza said quickly. Sivara nodded his agreement.

"Flatten out a little, Brian, you're too far away. Two niner zero knots." Better to go a little faster and end up closer to the ship.

"Roger." The voice was calmer now, resigned. The reduced angle of attack would increase his downward speed but bring him closer to the ship. When he pulled up and approached the stall, the plane's speed through the air would be minimized no matter what angle he had been at before.

"Thirteen thousand, dropping faster now," announced Guarino.

Webster imagined the silence on board the plummeting fighter, the sickening absence of engine noise rarely heard except in the simulator. He imagined also that Slattery in the last few minutes had gone through all the standard phases of a terminal disease, at first denying that he was in serious danger, then angry that it had happened to him, then profoundly depressed and hopeless, and now resigned, hoping for the best but expecting little.

"Eight thousand," said Guarino. "Only two miles away now."

"Slattery, you ready?"

"Yes, sir." The voice was flat, emotionless and devoid of inflection. Dead.

"Six thousand. Only a few seconds."

"Start your pull-up now. Slowly at first, then hard when you get below one eighty."

"Got it."

"Descent's falling off, skipper." Guarino watched the blip slow as it crawled down his screen.

"Five thousand!"

The blip picked up speed again when Slattery's hands left the stick. The arrow shape of the Hornet, in the absence of control surface deflections directing it to the contrary, naturally pointed itself downward and accelerated rapidly. In a few seconds the blip suddenly stopped moving and then winked out of existence.

Florence shook her head and exhaled forcefully. "And the boy?" she asked.

"Only thing we found was his helmet."

Florence stayed silent. Webster's eyes were pointed at the table but focused somewhere underneath it, somewhere very far away, maybe as far as a distant planet or star. His coffee cup tottered precariously in his hand, forgotten and ignored for the moment, the dark liquid lapping at the rim and threatening to spill over onto his pants. Florence made no move to rescue it.

After another moment, Jack jerked his head up as he remembered where he was, and the coffee made it over the side and into his lap. It was cold, and the wet feeling shocked him and made him laugh at the same time. He jumped up and swiped at the small stain. Florence made a move to do the same but thought better of it. She hoped Jack didn't notice.

"Hey, you tell some story, sport!"

Jack flushed in embarrassment and sat back down, not quite sure exactly what he had just revealed, either of the facts or of himself. "Yeah, well . . . kind of hard to forget something like that."

Florence nodded in understanding. She could only imagine the all-consuming guilt that, years later, stayed largely suppressed but reared its head on occasion, maybe in the night, when Jack would wake up shivering and fevered, the sheets plastered to his body, trying to remember where he was and wondering how to make the pain stop. *How did it drive him now?* she wondered.

"Guilt musta been awful."

"Guilt?" Webster swung his head around to face her. "I felt no guilt."

She stared at Webster in surprise. This wasn't at all what she had expected.

Jack registered her rattled look. "There was nothing to feel guilty about. I made the right decision. Believed it then, and I believe it now."

"But a pilot was lost. A boy died. Didn't it bother you?"

"Bother me? I cried like a baby." *No, I didn't.* "Couldn't sleep for a week." That part was true. "I still think about it on occasion. But I never confused sadness with guilt. I did what I had to do. It simply wasn't my fault, and I went on."

Florence marveled at the strength of the man. She knew that cops and agents drew on guilt to force confessions out of people consumed by it, sometimes to the point of suicide, by episodes of much lesser consequence or direct connection. Parents of children dying of unknown causes ate themselves alive for somehow being the cause, when no such correlation existed. How did it happen? she had always wondered. What was it that differentiated those who suffered only from rational and finite grief from those who plagued their minds with imagined and endless culpability?

"What wouldn't you believe?" she asked.

Jack, familiar with the technique, was determined to stay even with Florence's precipitous shift in subject and was damned if he was going to have to ask her what she meant. He stared while replaying the last minutes of conversation in his mind, trying to figure out what the question referred to.

He smiled in resignation. "I give up. Not believe about what?"

Florence pretended not to get the joke and clarified her question. "The mechanic, he said you won't believe what—"

"Oh, oh, the leak? In the Hornet's tank?"

"Uh-huh."

Jack shook his head ruefully. "What the mechanics did. Or Congress. Or somebody, depending on how you look at it."

Now it was her turn to look confused. "Wrong parts? The bureaucrats stick their noses in?"

"Not exactly, but sort of."

Jack rose to fill his cup and lifted it in invitation to Florence, who waved it off. As he poured the now highly concentrated, lethal-looking brew, he said, "You remember when everybody was popping off about how defense contractors were robbing the government blind on tools, supplies, that sort of thing?"

"Six-hundred-dollar toilet seats, two-hundred-dollar hammers, that kind of stuff?"

"Yeah, all of that." Jack took a sip of the coffee and struggled to get it down. "Wish Goldberg were still here. Only one knows how to work the damned coffee machine."

He carried his cup back to the table and sat down. "Those were easy targets, but what a lot of people didn't realize, those prices weren't all that unreasonable for specialized tools made in very low quantities."

Florence stood up and walked over to the coffee machine. She ran hot water in the tiny sink and rinsed out the pot. "Two hundred for a hammer?"

"Suppose I asked you, make me a hammer with a nonstandard head size and a special grip. What do you figure that should cost?"

She pulled a clean handkerchief out of her pocket. "So let's say, fifteen, twenty bucks."

"And how would you do it?"

She punched the handkerchief in her fist until it formed a small bowl. "I suppose I make a mold, then heat some metal until it melts, then pour it in the mold. Take it out, do a little work on the grinder, make a grip somehow, you're making a very good point, my friend."

"Not just twenty bucks anymore, right? If you make a hundred, the price goes down. But people were bitching and yelling so loud, these guys didn't dare try to defend themselves. Some dingbat congressman goes out to the hardware store, buys a thirty-nine-cent screwdriver, holds it up next to the official version and embarrasses the hell out of those guys."

Florence opened a can of ground coffee and poured some of the brown powder into the center of the handkerchief, then set it down over a clean cup. "Anybody in particular, this dingbat?"

"A public servant with more ambition than brains. One of the tools he ridiculed was a special torque wrench for tightening access panels on the F-18. Cost nearly two hundred dollars, but the panel screws looked like ordinary screws, so the dingbat says, Gee, who needs the expensive one?"

"But torque is important." She poured a small amount of hot water into the center of the little mound of coffee and waited for it to seep through.

"Yes, but not always very apparently. The contractor issued standard screwdrivers to the field maintenance people and credited the money for the torque wrenches. Only now the mechs couldn't measure the tension, so they guessed as best they could."

Florence poured a little more water into the coffee. "And?"

"Over time, the metal began to fatigue from overstress. Everybody was afraid of the doors popping open, so they tightened them on the high side, just to make sure. After Slattery went down, we inspected the rest of our planes and found dozens of the panels ready to come apart."

Florence turned from her kitchen chore and looked at Jack.

"Some of them," Jack continued, "had little shards of metal

sticking inward that couldn't be seen from the outside. We figured they had pierced the Hornet's fuel bladder. In high speed, high-G maneuvering, it must have sprayed out, and in the thunderstorm it froze up surrounding moisture on the plane's wings and gear."

Florence lifted up the handkerchief, poured half the coffee into a second cup and brought both to the table.

"Here. Try this."

Jack took a sip and raised his head up with a pleased grin. "Hey, this is good!"

She shrugged and said, "Old commando secret. Mr. H. was a Green Beret, showed it to me camping once. This is what killed your pilot?"

Jack took another sip. "Maybe. It also turns out the same torque wrench was used to tighten bolts in the ejection seat mechanism. So we inspected all our planes for that. Four were so mangled they wouldn't have worked. Cost over sixty thousand each to fix."

Florence lowered her head and shook it as Jack stared into the distance and sipped his coffee. The implications were clear: it was quite possible that Slattery hadn't been lost in the inky blackness of the storm-tossed ocean, but that he'd never even made it out of the cockpit alive.

"But if you did right by the boy, why'd you leave the service?"

Jack put down his cup and looked directly at her. "Because I was getting damned tired of having to make those kinds of decisions, even if I was doing them right." And there was no way in hell he would ever allow himself to be put in that position again. He'd devoted the balance of his career to making sure.

Florence scratched her chin and stared at Jack quizzically. "Then what the hell are you doing in this cockamamie job, tell me?"

Jack laughed and folded his arms across his chest. There was no rancor in his voice, no bitterness. "That's a longer story. And a little complicated."

"That you're in demand doesn't surprise me. But why do you do it?"

Jack didn't feel like telling her that the challenges of his present job were more real and made more sense to him than maintaining a nuclear arsenal at a state of full readiness. He wasn't up for arguing about the sense of futility that overtook him when he realized that Slattery's death was not the fault of Congress or the contractor or the taxpayers or anybody other than the whole collective society of human beings that spent several trillion dollars a year preparing for war. And he didn't feel like defending the strategy of sending young men into the air in beautiful, terrible flying weapons of such mind-numbing complexity that there would always be death and dismemberment from inexplicable accidents, and how he would write letters home to the families and try to explain about how Johnny died in the service of his country and hope to hell none of them wrote back and asked him to explain how, skipper, exactly how did Johnny's dying benefit the nation because, believe you me, pal, if we had known beforehand, we wouldn't have let him go.

"The challenge, I guess."

Which wasn't it at all, actually, only there were a couple of other things that Jack didn't feel like telling the frumpy genius, who grunted once, looked at Jack and grunted again, and knew for certain the unspoken part was a good deal more important than the spoken but was smart enough to let it go. They drank the rest of their coffee in silence.

CHAPTER 18

1635 MST

> Hi, this is Jack.
>
> We're all pretty impressed back
> here.
>
> The bit about modifying the nav
> chips was a nice piece of work.
>
> Please press 1 if everything is
> still okay.

June 13, 0835 EST

By the time the first communication with Captain Marvel had taken place via the ATM, Sam Cavanaugh had managed to pull himself together as he had done after other adversity in his life. Now, two days later, his composure seemed completely reconstructed, even to the point where his damaged delusion of invulnerability was fully intact.

Dr. Amy Goldberg never failed to marvel at the resiliency of the human ego. Tear it apart, stomp on it, what the hell ever: if it was strong enough in the first place, it snapped back into shape like a surgeon's glove. Usually it came back with all its flaws intact as well.

"Dammit," Cavanaugh was railing at Amy, her earlier demonstration of calm capability all but forgotten now, "whaddya wanna go and piss him off for? I mean, f'Chrissakes, isn't the whole point now do what he wants, keep him from getting excited again?"

Jack tried to step in before Amy could answer, but she didn't let him. The strategy was hers, and she would take responsibility for it. "No, the whole point is to catch the bastard."

"Now what's that supposed to mean?" Cavanaugh thundered.

"We have nothing," Amy responded calmly. "He has everything."

"C'mon, Goldberg." Letitia May Hubbard usually enjoyed a lively and mildly obscure exchange, but she wasn't in the mood for eccentricity under the present circumstances. "Let us in on the fun."

"Simple. You need something to go on. A clue, a lead, some evidence. Maybe a big blockbuster, maybe just a mound of small, circumstantial bits and pieces. If you have very little, and nothing more seems to be coming, sometimes you have to make them come, force them out of hiding places and into the open."

"And you're saying we have nothing?" Hubbard was beginning to understand why the psychologist seemed to be rambling: she had nothing to go on and only the vaguest outline of a plan. Not even a plan, really, just an idea. Maybe Amy was one of those elliptical thinkers, the kind driven more by intuition than calculation, who liked to circle a problem and spiral in on it rather than shoot arrows straight to the middle. An artist, a musician, rather than a scientist.

And men like Cavanaugh were used to being presented with a slate of alternatives, each supported by countless hours of underlying analysis, from which they could make educated choices. Hubbard's experience of "successful" executives had taught her that most were not very good at nuance. If you told them you were sixty percent sure that the number was between twenty and forty, they latched on to thirty and ran with it as though it represented mathematical certainty. What Amy needed was time, because her approach was more trial and error than considered action, and Hubbard knew that this wouldn't sit well with the chairman and CEO of Alpha Airlines.

"Oh, I don't know," Stanley said. "We know there are at least two people, or maybe two teams. We know they're familiar with the Midwest. We know the leader is extremely clever, maybe brilliant, and has access to sophisticated aviation equipment."

Cavanaugh, apparently satisfied with this summary, turned back to see how Amy would react. But she only cocked her head to one side and looked at Stanley without speaking. The FBI agent glanced uncomfortably at Jack and hitched up a shoulder as though to shake off a flea. "We, uh, have a pretty good rundown on most of the employees of Autonav, past and present, and we've started field checks on a big handful." *C'mon, Jack, help me out here!*

"Well . . ." As though receiving the message telepathically, Jack scratched his chin and looked at the ceiling. "Sounds like we got it narrowed down to about eighteen hundred people."

"What the hell are you talking about?" Cavanaugh roared.

For the sake of efficiency, all the involved parties had agreed to pare down the overstaffed meetings and create a more streamlined task force. Secretary of Transportation Hubbard was nominal head as the ranking official, since Senator Fedder declined to participate because of the potential political down side, but she deferred to Jack Webster in all but matters of general policy. Preston Stanley was the experienced FBI field man, and he also had a close, long-standing relationship with the director. Jack was relatively new to the game and in a special unit. And in the absence of any better ideas, Amy Goldberg, Ph.D., and the person responsible for all facets of the MD-11 accident investigation until Chairman Pressman returned, was calling the shots on dealing with Captain Marvel, even as Stanley's people tried to figure out his identity.

"Autonav is a big company, lot of employees, most of them technical," Jack explained. "They've been in business almost since Doolittle made the first instrument flight. Our clues don't buy us much in narrowing down the field."

"But what about the Midwest angle?" Cavanaugh pressed on. "The company's in California, they can't have had eighteen hundred people from the Midwest."

"We didn't get a chance to talk before the meeting, Pres." Jack glanced uneasily at Stanley. "Amy doesn't think the Midwest thing is all that relevant. It's just not that hard to find out where the ATMs are. FundsNet publishes national and regional directories, and even provides street directions in some of the smaller rural areas." He didn't mention that the FundsNet directories also clearly identified which machines were protected by closed-circuit television cameras and, by exclusion, which ones were not. While the assistance thus afforded to thieves and muggers, as well as to Captain Marvel, was obvious, it also limited the company's liability: any customer knowingly using a machine without a camera would have no cause to take the company to task, since that fact was clearly spelled out in the directory, which the company purposely provided free of charge.

Stanley looked uncomfortable. "We thought of that. But why would he pick that area in particular? There has to be a reason."

"We agree," said Amy. "But it isn't necessarily the case that the reason relates to where he grew up."

Amy addressed Cavanaugh directly. "So, we know next to nothing. He's crazy. Or maybe not. Maybe political"—she doubted that—"maybe he's gonna make some big deal proposal, spring a prisoner, who knows? But hard stuff? For a positive ID? Nothing."

"Can't you even guess, Doctor?" Hubbard sensed Amy holding back. "You been through this kind of thing before. Aren't there patterns, recurring similarities? Anything?"

"Just a guess?" Amy pursed hers lips and looked at her sleeve. "Sure. It's not money. For this kind of performance, he could be getting a whole lot more."

"But it would be so hard to collect," protested Stanley. "Look how slowly it's going out now."

Amy shook her head. "There's lots of ways, some even the FBI may not know about. Ask your friends in CIA covert ops. You want their phone number?" It was a cheap shot, but she couldn't help herself.

"Okay, okay," said Cavanaugh. "What, then?"

"Our fellow wants to be in control, in command. Likes calling the shots, could be because he never did in his life. He likes to look powerful. To us. To himself. But I've got a strong feeling he's not a complete loony."

Stanley was puzzled. "Why? Because he's so smart?"

"No, no, Lord knows there're plenty of smart loonies. You got serial killers think like Einstein. No, it's because he took out a cargo plane and not a passenger job. I think maybe this guy doesn't like killing. Some morals somewhere. Maybe. And he makes up for the dearth of bodies by smashing a giant plane. No . . ." She seemed to have come to this conclusion even while explaining it but felt it a valid one. She could see in Jack's face that he agreed. "This one has some marbles left."

"Are you trying to tell me this sumbitch's got morals because he killed three people instead of three hundred?" Cavanaugh was livid with righteous indignation. "What the hell kind of morals does it take to hold up the damned government by threatening the airway system?"

"Morals, Mr. Cavanaugh," said Amy. "Plain and human. Not political, not arising out of fire-and-brimstone preaching. Big difference between three and three hundred. To you it may be black and white, but to some, and maybe to our guy, it's patches of gray." She paused to let it sink in. "Our opinion of his ethics isn't as important as our understanding of them."

"So what's the plan, Doctor?" said Stanley. "What are you trying to do?"

It was Amy's turn to look discomfited. "I'm not sure."

"Look, don't play games with us, this isn't the time."

She was too lost in thought to react to the rebuke. "We may need to ask Captain Marvel for some information."

The rest of the meeting participants exchanged confused glances, which were not lost on Amy.

"Say what?" Hubbard finally ventured.

Amy looked up, fully alert now. The ideas that had been swarming in her mind were starting to congeal—not completely, but enough to get started. She hated thinking out loud, especially in front of bureaucrats, but she drew conviction from the dawning clarity she felt. "We send messages, we get answers, we communicate even though he hates to. He keeps pressing buttons because we're giving him information. He wants to know what we know, so I'm betting he won't cut off his supply of information, even though he might be getting only a small piece here and there. He's thinking maybe it's enough to keep him one step ahead." She looked at Cavanaugh. "I think this guy wasn't really looking to wreck your airplane, Mr. Cavanaugh." *At least not before he decided to do it.*

The sudden switch in thought pattern rattled the executive, who was more used to people taking better preparations before addressing him. "What makes you say that?"

"He went too far, didn't he?" Jack had both his hands palms down on the table. "Never intended for it to happen."

"Very likely," said Amy. "He was hoping to get the money and run. But when we cut it off, he had no choice."

"But you said it wasn't about money," said Stanley.

"It isn't." Amy's voice grew animated as the pieces continued to come together and make sense, however warped. "It's about winning. About control. The five million had nothing to do with retail buying power, it was a scorecard. He hits it, he wins. He doesn't, we win. Only he decided to give us a lesson in how the game is played rather than give up."

She turned to Stanley. "And now that he's gone too far, his plan is down the can. Now every day is a new story, new rules. Some his, some ours."

"What makes you think he won't suspect our little dribs and drabs of information?" asked Secretary Hubbard.

"He already suspects like crazy. He has no idea what's true, what's baloney, only that we might have some reason for sharing information, but he doesn't know what it is."

"As a matter of fact, what is it?" asked Cavanaugh, suspicion evident in his voice.

"Whatever craziness he has, to make it worse. To make the game more, ah—" She waved a hand in a circle; only a favorite Yiddishism of her father's came to mind: *farvikelt.*

"Complex?" offered Hubbard.

Not exactly, but close enough. "Exactly. Raise the stakes

and Marvel's anxiety at the same time, maybe goad him into making some mistakes because he's trying to figure out the rules and there aren't any. Our last message, we didn't leave a way for him to respond negatively but he hit a key anyway. He made a mistake because he's a little messed up."

"You're trying to drive him nuts?" Cavanaugh ventured, puzzlement evident on his face.

"But what makes you so sure he'll keep talking to us?" asked Hubbard. "He's got to know we're not gonna give him useful information."

Jack, who had been paying close attention to Amy's extemporaneous theorizing, ventured his own interpretation of the approach. "He's a genius, or close to it, right? He can't help but be drawn into the communication, because it makes everything more personal. Without it, he has no clue to the effect he's having on us, other than we keep paying out money."

"So this way," said Amy, "he gets the satisfaction of being in control. Knowing that some high-powered higher-ups are devoting all their attention to him. That we fear him, even."

She looked at Jack, not realizing how much she was soliciting approval from the fatherly figure. It gave Jack a small twinge he couldn't place.

"What about the accomplices?" asked Stanley, deliberately changing the subject. "What about the other team? They're still moving in tandem, switching off when they're in the clear."

"I don't know." The question seemed to trouble Amy. "Sorry."

"There's another part of it I don't get." Stanley still had not gotten over what he perceived as a snub of his own department's psychological specialists. Jack had explained several times that the FBI, restricted by its charter to purely domestic affairs, had little experience in dealing with criminals of this type. And they couldn't involve the CIA because that organization was forbidden from involvement in domestic affairs. So, faced with an extortionist patterned after international terrorists but operating within U.S. borders, Jack had consulted with an old friend, who had confirmed his own notion that the one person best suited to the task was Amy Goldberg. It was just as well that Stanley didn't know that this friend worked in the Behavioral Sciences Section of the FBI.

"How come we only send a message once in a while?" Stanley continued. "Why not keep at him all the time, get this thing done?"

Jack turned to Amy and said, "It's an intermittent schedule of reinforcement, right? Like lab mice?"

Amy looked at him in surprise. "Very good!"

"So what's that?" Stanley insisted, unamused.

Amy tried to explain the analogy. "You ever see white mice trained to press a bar and get a food pellet?"

"Sure, everybody's seen that. A learned response."

"Right. And every time the bar is pressed and food comes out, the response is reinforced. It gets stronger every time, but after a while it's as strong as it's going to get and then it levels out."

"Obviously. So?"

"There are ways to measure how strong that response is. The best way is to see how long it takes to extinguish it."

"Make it go away?" asked Hubbard.

Amy nodded. "You stop giving the mouse pellets. First he presses the bar like a madman, not believing that some food isn't coming. It's really something to see, the mouse banging away maybe two, three thousand times."

"Eventually, though, he stops." Amy tapped the table a few times and then kept her fingers in the air. "He finally figures out it's all over and gives up. You count how many times he presses the bar before quitting, that's your measure of how strong the response was in the first place."

"So what's all this intermittent stuff?" asked Stanley.

"That's the best part. When he's still getting the pellets, instead of giving him one on every press, you give him one every fifth press, or every tenth, or on a random basis."

"And?" Stanley's curiosity got the better of his petulance, and he was drawn into the tutorial.

"And the strength of the response shoots practically off the charts. When the pellets stop, it can take ten or twenty thousand presses before the mouse gives up and the response is extinguished."

"So when I'm training my dog," asked Hubbard, "I'm better off rewarding her only every so often?"

Amy nodded. "You won't believe the impact."

"So in the case of our guy . . . ?" Hubbard began.

Amy smiled as she pictured it. "A little message only every so often should drive him bonkers. He swipes his card and gets no message? We get another square inch of his stomach lining."

CHAPTER 19

1968

It is an inevitable by-product of the cultural conceit that people always suppose theirs is a time of unprecedented change.

It is an inevitable consequence of the laws of probability that every once in a while, they are right.

American policymakers were certain that the Vietnamese insurgents were weakening and were therefore more than a little surprised when the NLFSV celebrated the Buddhist New Year in early 1968 by launching a massive, carefully coordinated attack on 120 separate targets, including forty provincial capitals and the old imperial capital of Hue.

The attack was not a cowardly snipe at easy marks. It included an assault at the enormous, heavily fortified U.S. air base at Tan Son Nhut. Even the U.S. embassy compound was taken and held for six hours.

The South Vietnamese insurgents suffered a staggering toll in casualties, and their intent to intimidate the United States by a show of force backfired. The Tet Offensive was officially interpreted as a clear demonstration that the removal of the U.S. presence in the region would lead inexorably to the complete domination of South Vietnam by the Viet Cong and their allies to the north.

At the same time, the Reverend Dr. Martin Luther King was stepping up his plan to organize a poor people's march on Washington, to press home the familiar theme of ending racial discrimination. This time the marchers' demands would include $12 billion to fund an "Economic Bill of Rights."

When he felt that the work was progressing well, Dr. King took some time out to provide assistance and moral support to striking sanitation workers in Memphis, Tennessee. Standing on the balcony of a motel, the youngest winner ever of the Nobel Peace Prize died anything but peacefully. Nor was his death mourned peacefully. His assassination at the hands of a white man triggered a chain reaction of anguished rioting that spread through unseen connecting filaments to ghettos across the country.

Eight days later the Democratic field of presidential candidates was reduced by one as President Johnson delivered an address on national television. Thirty-five minutes into his droning, he announced that he would not be running for reelection.

Less than two months later, on a warm and dry Wednesday, the field was reduced again. Voters in California, along with those in South Dakota, were turning out for their Democratic primary. The tired and drawn Robert Kennedy, worn out from a hard campaign, spent the day on the beach at Malibu with his wife and six of their children. Late in the afternoon they headed to the mid-Wilshire district to sweat the vote count at the Ambassador Hotel with supporters.

"I think we can end the divisions within the United States, the violence," Kennedy said, then left the rostrum through a curtain draped behind it, where a shortcut through the kitchen would take him to the pressroom. He stopped to shake hands with dishwasher Jesus Perez, and at the same time a Jordanian immigrant hidden behind two maître d's propped his elbow on a serving counter and shot him. He died shortly after midnight.

In the early morning hours of August 26, a U.S. Army transport flew steadily at thirty-three thousand feet in the skies between Hawaii and California. On board, twenty-two new

Vietnam veterans failed to sleep as the first fingers of sunlight teased at the horizon. Bo Kincaid and several of the others looked out the starboard windows to see if they could spot land in the growing light. They also picked up three of their comrades and carried them to the right side of the plane; their wheelchairs were packed in the hold along with eleven black plastic zippered bags in oblong boxes.

Bo had been uncomfortable as he drifted in and out of partial sleep. He was in many ways a shy man, had always been that way. Not much for surprise parties or a lot of pomp and circumstance, generally declining to be at the center of attention, although he welcomed his share of quiet notoriety, as would anyone.

But it was going to be difficult to avoid it this time, and he resolved to accept it graciously. For his wife's sake, if nothing else. She'd borne his pain, why not share his glory?

"Scoot me over a touch, will ya, Captain?" Sergeant Phillip Donovan's slinged arm conspired with his paralyzed legs to prevent him from maneuvering into a good viewing position.

"Sure." Bo leaned over and drew Donovan's arm around his neck, then put his own arm under the newly crippled soldier's legs and lifted him half out of the seat, turning him at the same time. When he set him back down, Donovan's arm stayed around Bo so he could hold himself upright. Thus enwrapped, the two of them looked out together for the first signs of landfall. Of home.

The full force of his new infirmity hadn't hit home yet in Donovan's mind. He knew it was permanent, intellectually, but some deeply layered piece of his subconsciousness had the feeling that his lifeless legs were part of the war experience, not his normal life, and that as soon as he got home and was discharged, his paralysis, like the war, would be behind him, a bad dream better left forgotten. Counseling provided by the military wasn't going to do him much good, either, because the idea that his was a glorious sacrifice for a noble cause would be a little difficult to internalize in the atmosphere of squalor, filth and neglect that awaited him in the VA hospital.

And since that bleak reality hadn't really sunk in yet, the badly mangled soldier smiled through his pain—remarkable how much there was when you weren't supposed to have any feeling in your paralyzed limbs—knowing that people would ask him about the hours he was able to spend with Bo Kincaid.

"They gonna treat you like some kinda hero, huh, Captain?"

"Hah! I left a damned fool and I'm comin' home a damned fool. Din't you learn nothin', Donovan?"

The black flyer was spoken of in hushed and reverential tones, as though to speak too loudly would break some sort of spell. He'd never believed in the war, although nobody could tell for sure because it was difficult to engage him in much conversation about it. More than likely he just never thought about it one way or the other. On the one hand, he didn't use the kind of demeaning slang for the enemy that was standard issue in any war, the thought-speak designed to perpetuate the kind of hatred that was required to take lives on a continual basis, since America never fought innocent people but only yellow peril, Aryan murderers, savage redskins, crazed Middle-Eastern religious fanatics, evil empires, traitorous rebels and repressive and dictatorial monarchies. It hadn't really been all that necessary in the air war, though, since the enemy was rarely seen. So in that sense Bo represented the new breed of fighter, a cocooned technologist who did his job by pushing buttons.

On the other hand, his flying was not devoid of intensity. To the contrary, his ferocity and daring were frightening and inexplicable in terms of a simple adherence to the dictates of his chosen avocation. To some who flew with him, the beginning of his tour had been a mystery, and they even suspected Bo Kincaid was a coward, afraid to mix it up in battle.

He wasn't interested in taking out SAM sites or bombing bridges or defoliating suspected insurgent encampments, though he carried out these tasks with unassailable competence, staying far enough above the required margin of enthusiasm to avoid censure, if not suspicion. In a dogfight, he never fired the opening shot or presented an aggressive stance as an invitation to battle. In the more evenly matched jousts, he was sometimes known to hover idly, almost in standby, while the rest of the squadron engaged the enemy.

Over time, they came to understand. Bo was the white blood cell of the squadron, a benign presence coursing through invisible skylanes on reasonless missions with his squadron. Harmlessly adrift, he waited.

He waited for a wound, for the entry of a parasitic invader, and then he would expand before their eyes as though in a zoom lens, and the engines on his F-4 would start to glow and the control surfaces pricked up like a falcon's tail feathers. His enmity for the invader was boundless, personal, a lifetime of bile and vitriol stored for this moment only, some secret and terrible motivating alchemist perverting his blood and his brains until he flashed out of the sun and struck at the astonished invaders with uncompromising viciousness.

By the end of his tour, the stories were legion. Pilots besieged and outnumbered, already crying their novenas and kissing pictures of their wives and girlfriends, suddenly alone in the sky as their pursuers evaporated in white-hot explosions behind them. Pilots pulling out of desperation power dives, only to see a flashing Phantom streaking upward overhead, nose cannons blazing, oblivious of the stacked odds of superior numbers and home turf advantage. Pilots in damaged planes, already in the electronic crosshairs of missiles, watching as this avenging angel interceded and drew the missile off, sometimes pointing it toward the sun to confuse it, sometimes turning inside and losing it, and sometimes, but only twice, getting struck by the relentless weapons and punching out, only to crawl back, ready to do it all over again.

The second time Bo was shot down, the U.S. military command insisted that he be taken out of action. To stem the likely riot in the ranks that would accompany this decision, the base commander at Danang disclosed that the captain was being grounded because the North Vietnamese had put a bounty on his head. It would be another three years before American naval flyer Randy Cunningham struck back by taking out Colonel Toon, the enemy's leading ace, who had blown thirteen American planes out of the air, the most kills of any pilot on either side of the war.

Bo had turned down high-level entreaties to instruct or to fly a desk and had elected instead to take an early out of his second tour, a petition that was granted reluctantly. He hoped to reenter the States with a minimum of fanfare and once again disappear back into a quiet life, a little more at peace with himself than when he'd left. He had done his job well. He hoped that Judson Greaves would understand that. Lenore never understood it all in the first place.

Now, as the first fringes of the coastline came into view, and the other men in the cabin awoke and sought out his face before they even looked out the window, he knew that he would not be able to slip back in unnoticed and hoped that he could smile his way politely through the welcome-back-hero routine and enjoy his newfound place in the sun.

"Boys, y'all look like shit," he announced. "Splash a little water on your faces and straighten out your pants, try to look partways decent for the people, okay?"

Amid grinning faces and partially successful attempts to look presentable after the grueling flight, Bo stretched his arms and legs hard, more than anything else to try to shake the tension attendant to his nervousness over the welcoming festivities. He had read the paper every day—well, most days anyway—and figured the country was still in a funk over the deaths of two of its heroes and probably needed a good old-fashioned patriotic homecoming to buck its chin up. As always, he would do his best to be obliging and not rain on anybody's parade.

The transport turned south and wheeled over the city of San Bernardino, lining up for landing at Norton Air Force Base. It was hard to spot a small crowd amid the clutter of airplanes, hangars, ground vehicles and scattered equipment, so Bo sat back and a thought struck him: *Jesus, what if they ask me to say a few words*? He closed his eyes and rubbed his forehead, trying desperately to come up with something so that he wouldn't make a fool of himself.

The plane touched down with a squeal and a puff of smoke and taxied for what seemed like a very long time. It finally came to a halt, and Bo heard the giant turbofans start to wind down. A deep rumble followed the sound of a turning hatch handle, and the back floor of the plane dropped downward until it touched the ground. A lone figure in coveralls stood at the bottom of the ramp, holding a clipboard. He held it up briefly and called, "Welcome home," in a bored and casual voice, and then he walked away as the whining of the engines continued to die away.

Bo and the men who were ambulatory stood and waited for a minute, then looked at each other. One of them shrugged and said, "Mebbe we ought to go on down."

"What about these boys?" someone else asked, jerking a thumb back toward Donovan and the others who would never walk again. "Isn't somebody supposed to come with their chairs?"

Bo turned back toward the interior. "Fuck it. Let's take 'em with us."

He picked up Donovan in his arms, and two others did likewise with the other wounded men. They all marched down the ramp together.

"Look sharp, guys!" Bo reminded them one last time.

As they emerged into the late August sun, they looked around in all directions. They were nowhere near a hangar. The serviceman who had opened the hatch was disappearing around the front of the plane.

"Hey!" Bo called to him.

He turned. "Yeah?"

"What's goin' on? Where is everybody?"

"Everybody? Oh, uh, hang on just a minute. Bus'll be here in half a sec."

"Bus?"

"Yeah. To take y'all to the hangar. We don't bring incoming transports over there until they're unloaded. You understand. . . ." He pointed to the cargo hold that contained the rest of the returning veterans.

Bo followed the man's finger with his eye. "Sure. I get it."

He turned at the sound of an engine approaching and saw a bus painted in camouflage colors approaching from the west. "Any chance of getting these men their chairs?" he asked the serviceman over his shoulder.

"Oh, yeah. Sorry."

The man opened another hatch and crawled into the cargo bay, emerging with the collapsed wheelchairs just as the bus pulled up alongside. The bus was equipped with a lift, so the wounded soldiers were placed in their chairs and hoisted unceremoniously into the back of the bus, each one sitting helpless, childlike and exposed, up in the air for the few moments it took to complete each procedure.

"Let's do it!" Bo yelled, slapping the nearest standing man on the back and herding them all into the bus. The driver waited until they were all seated and then moved the bus out.

As they neared the reception hangar close to the entrance of the base, Bo could see several cars lined up on the other side of a high, chain-link fence. Some people milled about, watching the bus. Not a lot of people. Maybe two dozen.

He spotted Lenore and waved, not sure if she would be able to make him out through the grimy window. She stared hard at the bus but showed no sign of recognition until it had nearly stopped, then she caught his eye. One hand flew to her mouth and she waved back with the other.

As each of them stepped off the bus, an enlisted man with a clipboard checked off his name, without salute or further acknowledgment. Then it would be through the gate, out into civilian territory and into the arms of whichever loved one happened to show up.

"Kincaid," Bo said to the clipboard.

The enlisted man made a tick mark with his pencil and nodded his head.

"That's *Captain* Kincaid," Bo said, stopping his forward motion and holding up the line.

The enlisted man looked up. "I got it. Is there a problem?"

Sensing some jostling behind him, Bo replied, "No. No problem." He moved out through the gate.

His reunion with Lenore was pretty much the same as had been played out thousands of times by thousands of other returning servicemen. He was glad to be home, glad to see her, to feel her once more in his arms. But even as he hugged her, he picked up his head and looked around. Back toward the transport plane, he could see a forklift disappearing behind the opened ramp, ready to unload its cargo away from the eyes of witnesses. He shifted his head around as discreetly as he could and saw no welcoming committee, no crowd of well-wishers, no speaker's podium or news photographers or banners or little schoolchildren carrying presents on behalf of a grateful nation. There was only a street with passing cars, none of which paused as they drove by the scene. A small hair wiggled somewhere deep within Bo's belly. He barely felt it.

Lenore hustled him into the car, and they drove off.

"Hey, y'know what? I'd like to stop and pick up a six of beer, whaddya say?" He looked over at Lenore and grinned.

She smiled back, but only with her mouth. "Tell you what, why don't we get on home, you get in the shower, I'll run out quick and pick some up."

"Aw, hell, you don't have to do that. Here, just pull in over here"—he pointed to a convenience store just coming into view—" 'n' I'll jump right in and out."

Lenore kept her foot firmly on the accelerator. "Really, I don't mind. Really, I mean it."

The store shot by the window, and Bo looked over at Lenore, confusion registering in his features. But he had no wish to start anything, so he kept quiet and wondered what the problem was, and he looked down and remembered that he was in uniform, and the little hair in his belly got larger.

They exited the freeway when they were well to the northwest of Los Angeles and stopped for a red light. A motorcycle pulled up alongside. The driver was about twenty years old, with hair down to his shoulders, wearing a beaded shirt, sunglasses with round lenses and a black felt, wide-brimmed hat. The girl gripping his waist had unshaven legs and enormous breasts that jiggled, unencumbered by any undergarments, out to the sides of her loose-fitting tank top.

Bo regarded the pair idly, and then the driver turned his head and eyed Bo's uniform, with its profusion of medals for bravery, valor and the various campaigns in which he'd fought. Bo enjoyed the intimidation that this display was sure to engender.

"Hey, soldier boy, murder any babies lately?"

What? Couldn't have heard that right. He rolled down the window. "What was that?"

"What are you, fuckin' deaf? I said—"

But Lenore had stomped down on the pedal and started forward before the light had even turned green.

They drove the rest of the way to Santa Paula with no further stops or perfunctory conversation. No banners on the house, just a small American flag over the mailbox. Lenore drove all the way into the garage, which Bo never remembered her doing before, and they went in through the back door, and the hair became two hairs and inside there was no surprise party, no gathering of admiring friends, and Lenore told Bo she had fixed a wonderful little breakfast for just the two of them, and then tomorrow he could go see Joe Cutter because Joe knew all about Bo and said his job was still open if he wanted it because Joe wasn't like the others, Joe still knew what it meant to fight for your country and he was a true friend, but, hey, it might not be such a bad idea if maybe you hung that uniform up in some back closet somewhere, honey, 'cuz, after all, you're not in the service anymore, not really, not after your honorable discharge. You're a civilian now, even if maybe not in your heart, but in your heart people can't see it, can't stop and stare, but if it's right there on your uniform, well, then everybody can see it and you know what? You wanna know something really interesting? This isn't exactly the most wonderful time to be letting folks know you're in the military, and, well, especially not if you're a pilot. You understand, don't you? And the hairs disappeared and were replaced by a fist, which gripped the walls of his stomach and turned as it did so.

They made love, because it was first things first no matter what else was going on, even though in the middle of it all Bo had a strong foreboding that the last two years of his life, far from being the start of long overdue expiation, would be an ironic Magi's gift of convoluted happenstance that turned inward on itself, and as his Lenore moaned, he understood the fist but denied it in case he was wrong.

That night they sat in front of the television, as did many millions of their fellow countrymen, and they watched the opening of the Democratic National Convention in Chicago. The year before had been the "summer of love," the coming-out party of the disaffected whose only common interest was the one-upmanship of vaunting alienation. Like a glowing white pearl that resulted from an irritation, the flower children thought they could fashion a utopia based on driving away from all that they hated rather than toward something that they loved. The summer of 1967 had been a pretty and fleeting thing, and by the following year a political voice had precipitated out of the music and drugs and become heir to the same corruptions that befell all things political. Without Vietnam there would have been no ad hoc unification of countercultures, but this genesis also doomed the movement, because it was an amazingly short time before it became politicized to the point that it was the subject of exploitation by anybody who could afford a mimeograph machine.

Until this year, this week, the war was a distant thing, fought somewhere else on another planet by other people who appeared like ghosts on television every night, playing to the numbness of Americans who believed the daily body counts like they believed pro wrestling.

Until this week, antiwar protestors were Communist dupes, dirty, smelly drug users misled by foreign provocateurs and afraid to face their final exams. They were the misbegotten, poorly reared issue of someone else's loins, ungrateful for the sacrifices of generations of soldiers who would die before they let the flag touch the soil.

But this week, as Bo Kincaid and his wife watched television, all that would change. Robert Kennedy was dead, Martin Luther King was dead, Richards Nixon and Daly were alive and a political convention was going to proceed as though everything were normal. The week's body counts were reengineered to make the country look strong, as though it were winning, and people gathered in Chicago to let their leaders know that fighting senseless and undeclared wars with impunity was no longer an option.

In an abysmally stupid and misguided demonstration of municipal power, the mayor of Chicago denied the protestors a permit, as though that would send them home quietly. Determined to march to the convention hall, the demonstrators convened at the Hilton, three thousand strong, where they were surrounded by riot-equipped battalions of Chicago's finest.

The police warned the demonstrators to disperse. Then they waited for uniformed reinforcements to arrive, which they did by the busloads. When the police phalanxes were fully manned, the okay was received, and for the rest of the night the country watched as its children brought the war home to America's own soil.

The police waded into the crowd like hunters into a field of fur seals, crushing heads and breaking bones with grinning zeal, wallowing in a cathartic orgy of bloodletting. A breakaway squad trapped 150 demonstrators against the wall of the hotel until a plate-glass window gave way and a dozen of them fell over the shards into a lounge. The police jumped in after them and beat them mercilessly.

By this time it was clear that the police were rioting, caught up in a feeding frenzy, out of control and unstoppable. Maintenance of order and the enforcement of laws had lost all meaning as those charged with the public peace clubbed the young protestors into senselessness. The demonstrators themselves were no longer interested in making a point, only in escaping. Bloodied men and women scrambled desperately to enter the Hilton lobby, and McCarthy aides on the fifteenth floor did their best to jury-rig an emergency ward for the more grievously wounded.

Police rioting? Bo wasn't sure what to make of what he was seeing. Cops were the ultimate symbol of authority. If they spun out of control, engendering mistrust and disrespect, then who was to argue with the legitimacy of civil disobedience? Who guarded the guardians, who even now were crossing the line from enforcement to adjudication to punishment, crushing due process beneath their heels?

Bo watched it and tried to think, to think past the pabulum served up in the military's captive news services, to try to remember the radical headlines he had passed off as enemy propaganda, to try to recall the slogans sloppily painted on the protestors' placards.

He racked his brain to put together half-remembered bits of rumors he'd picked up in-country, rumors he'd dutifully dismissed as his commanders had ordered him to.

"Lenore, y'all here at home ever hear anything about a place called My Khe Four?"

No, but she'd heard about My Lai. Was that the same thing?

March 16 of that same year. For reasons everyone would have trouble recalling years later, one of the most hotly contested areas that spring had been Quang Ngai province on the northeastern coast of South Vietnam, long thought to be a Viet Cong stronghold, perhaps for as many as ten years.

U.S. troops were helicoptered in, under the command of Captain Ernest L. Medina and Lieutenant William L. Calley, Jr. They entered the village of Son My and proceeded to the hamlet of My Lài 4. They were nervous and tense, nearly on the edge of hysteria, not knowing from where the enemy was going to spring. They went after anything that reared its head, which turned out to be mostly children, women and a few old men. They herded some into ditches and shot them there. In all, Calley's Charlie Company killed three hundred unarmed, defenseless and innocent people, all within sight of the lenses of military photographers.

At the same time, in a less celebrated but no less grisly massacre, Bravo Company was perpetrating a similar atrocity in the hamlet of My Khe 4. This operation would have no Lt. Calley to take the blame. The incident was never pursued, and no soldiers were punished or even accused.

It was the loss of America's innocence, the surrender of the moral high ground, the end of her right to ask, with shaking head, How can people do such things? The conduct of Charlie Company came to be seen not as isolated and anomalous behavior, but as the perfect symbol of an errant policy, the progressive brutalization of good boys in a bad environment. And it tainted every fighting man without regard to motivation or character.

American soldiers had wanted their enemy to behave as they themselves would, fighting out in the open as God had intended, treating prisoners of war with dignity and respect. Now, Americans tortured captured VC, burned their villages and threw them screaming out of helicopters to their deaths. They slaughtered innocents who, but for an accident of local geography, might have tended their buffalo and milked their goats and been alive and watched the scorched countryside grow back over time.

Bo watched it all, and he knew why there were no parades, no welcome home parties, no banners bedecking the front porch. He knew why the invitation to speak at the local VFW was delivered in a plain envelope and why it wasn't advertised in any newspaper.

The worst part of it was that Bo couldn't explain to anyone about how he really didn't give much of a damn about what the war was about anyway, that it didn't make a difference to him why we were fighting, and that killing the enemy wasn't the point. He couldn't talk about the Americans who would be going home to their families to rake leaves and fix toilets and have Christmas because Bo Kincaid had been there.

He couldn't talk because to do so would cheapen the whole point, and besides, nobody would listen anyway. They were too angry and too scared and too enraged at the government that had betrayed their trust. Every backpack-toting grunt became a sadistic junkie, every administrative clerk a monster who sewed heroin shipments into the cadavers being sent back to the States for burial. Pilots were the worst of all, naturally, because they rained liquid fire that stuck to the skin and inflicted incalculable pain as the lives of unsuspecting farmers and peasants were terminated, sight unseen, in the thick jungles below. The citizenry at home even turned its back on the plight of American POWs, men whose greatest crime was doing their job the way they were brought up to do it, naively flying off to war because their government said they should.

Bo watched it all and had no idea, as he couldn't have at the time, that America had not yet learned how to still love its soldiers despite hating the war and the elected officials who sent them there. That would take many years beyond the war's end, and by then, for him as for many others, it would be too late.

He sat in the attic one late afternoon and opened the trunk that he'd hoped might have stayed closed forever. He looked briefly at the medals, the bronze bas-relief P-51 Mustang profile with the signatures from the 332nd on the back, his leather flying helmet and all the other memorabilia of what should have been a proud and heroic time but lay like a choking and heavy thing in his memory.

He found the picture, taken by an armed services news organization photographer in 1944, when the squadron was beginning to earn its mystical reputation over the skies of Europe. It had never been published, the smart thinking being that the folks back home were not ready to hear that their strapping white children were being protected by people who last week were fit only to shine shoes.

Judson Greaves sat in the cockpit of his Mustang, canopy rolled back, chin straps hanging down from his helmet. The smile on his face was slight, a major concession to the photographer who couldn't know of Jud's self-appointed mission. It was taken three days before he died in the skies above Berlin. Bo looked at the photo and wondered if those Nazi bastards had been planning the death of the *schwarze Engel* even as the picture was being snapped. Then he wondered if those same bastards were any different than *he* had been in Vietnam, doing their duty as citizens even while their leaders cynically manipulated world perceptions to their own ends.

He knew that the only reason the Germans had wound up in Nuremberg was that they had lost the war, and the history books were always written by the winners. *Who's gonna win this one*? he wondered. *Where will my Nuremberg be*?

He looked down at the gentle face, the kind eyes that held not malice toward the enemy but compassion for his friends. He felt a shocking pang of jealousy, because Jud had died a pure hero in the last pure war, while he—?

He cried out Jud's name in his mind even as tears formed in his eyes and dropped onto the glass frame. *I tried so hard, Jud, really I did. For you, for me. Mostly for me.*

He pictured for the millionth time Jud's plane erupting in flames as the bullets from the pursuing Messerschmitts hit its wings, while he could only scream and pound his console in helpless agony.

He'd made up for it dozens of times in the last two years, giving pilots and guys in back a chance at another springtime in a series of now legendary feats of unprecedented bravery, daring and skill. And nobody cared, nobody talked about it. Everybody who had said thanks had disappeared and gone home.

And it's worse than that, Jud. Much worse.

He held the photo at arm's length and stared at it through the blur of his tears.

And wondered if he was not only not a hero, not the object of the boundless adoration of almost-widows and a grateful citizenry, but maybe—was it possible?—something worse, something dark and sinister and loathsome. He wondered as he looked at his dead friend's face if he wasn't in fact what those children in the streets were saying he was.

A war criminal.

* * *

Captain Webster kept his eyes on the radar screen but could feel the shock of his dumbstruck shipmates, sensed more than heard the sniffling from mechanic Andy Espinoza, felt assaulted by the thundering silence broken only by the creakings of the eighty-six-thousand-ton vessel as it rolled in the storm.

The bright green bar on the screen continued its clockwise sweep, uninterrupted by the characteristic glowing spot that signaled the presence of an aircraft. Webster watched it through several more circuits, like a poker player staring at his cards in the distant belief that if he looked long enough, maybe one would change. At some point he would have to tear his eyes away and meet those of his crew, each of whom badly needed to be reassured, patted on the head and told, *There, there, it's all right. Don't be frightened, and grieve only for the loss, not the guilt, because this is the way it is, folks, it's not an amusement park ride, and people don't only get killed in war, they get killed getting ready for war, even if there is no war to get ready for just now. Thus has it always been and thus shall it always be, you know that, so take a few minutes and then snap out of it, and I, your captain, your leader, I am telling you that this is an appropriate way to feel, giving you permission to curtail your sorrow, ordering you to rein it in and get on with it even while parts of me are dying as I stand here and other parts are making me strong so you don't see it. . . .*

"Right call, skipper," Sivara said solemnly, and several others nodded their concurrence.

Webster looked across the room and did what he had sworn never to do, single out a crewman for special concern in front of his shipmates, but he did it because Espinoza was Slattery's mech and he needed it and that's why he did it and the shattered mechanic understood it perfectly.

"Espinoza, you okay?"

He forced a smile through his tears. "Hell, no, skipper, I'm not okay." Then he stopped talking for a moment so he wouldn't lose it.

Webster continued to stare at him. *Tell me.*

Espinoza dropped his head, looked at his shoes for a

moment and then slowly began rolling up the airplane spec sheet. "No other way, Captain. He knew that. I could hear it in his voice."

Thank you. Bless you. "You're off the line for now." It was SOP and Espinoza nodded, gratefully.

Webster looked briefly around the room, met the eyes of his officers and poured strength into them, flooded them with his confidence and his wisdom. He could feel their shoulders start to rise from where they had slumped, could feel the laws of thermodynamics at work as the reservoired excess of his icy control flowed into the bottomless cavity of their need, and he hoped and prayed he could get out of that room without any of them seeing that they were suckling from an empty and withering breast.

They watched in admiration as he strode through the door, his posture uplifted by his acceptance of the way things were, his spine unbowed by any weak, cowardly refusal to acknowledge the basic facts of life and death. No sniveling disavowal of the laws of the universe for their leader, nosirree, and that's why they worshiped him and envied his advanced level of self-possession. *He can take it like that, then dammit, so can I,* and they all stood taller as he disappeared down the corridor.

The captain of the *Constellation* closed the door to his cabin and leaned heavily back on it, his breath suddenly exploding in heaving rasps not only from the pain that lanced at him with brutal insistence, but as a result of the effort to maintain his outward equanimity until he was alone. Rivulets of sweat materialized on his brow, but his hands and arms trembled too much to attempt a swipe at them.

The severity of the anxiety attack surprised him. He'd been through worse than this, so why the overreaction? Only later, in calm reflection, would he realize that his soul could suppress but not erase, that it could put things in bottles and containers in secret places, but they were there nevertheless, accumulating and growing like an infection until the pressure found a weak spot and burst it open and through the hole poured the totality of all that had been shoved in before, no matter how far back. His ability to cram the last great tomato in the itty-bitty can was gone, and the whole gooey, ugly mass threatened to come apart in his head.

He knew what he had to do.

When Jack was in the naval academy, he had taken a two-week trip to Italy. He'd come across Michelangelo's *Pietà* in St. Peter's, not having known in advance that the sculpture was housed there. He'd walked through the huge main doors, turned to his right and gone around a corner, and there it was, with no warning, just a few feet away.

The beauty of it floored him and he couldn't move, nor could he sort out what about the sculpture affected him so deeply. Maybe it was the humanly impossible artistry, the sublime perfection of the sculptor's craft. Or perhaps it was the enormous gulf between the subtlety of the expression on the Madonna's face and the depth of the emotion it evoked, through some mechanism Jack had never even known existed. Maybe it was the majesty of the tragedy it represented, a mother cradling the son who had died in unspeakable pain before her eyes, her hands outstretched in a gesture that encompassed all of humanity in its profound grief.

Whatever. All Jack knew was that it haunted him beyond all rationality. For days he thought of nothing else, going over each detail in his mind, trying to picture a mortal man in the act of actually creating such a masterpiece and failing to understand how such a feat was possible. He had never seen anything so beautiful, and it depressed him terribly. He was convinced that nobody in the hundreds of years since its creation had ever been affected quite like this.

He knew what to do. He had done it before.

He deliberately overdosed on it.

He spent hours with it, walking around it, looking at it, drinking it in. He bought books of pictures of it and stared at them without letup, until the sensory overload had so pummeled him that he became numb to its effect. The statue no longer scratched at him with its ethereal beauty, and he found peace. That he had also lost something important was less obvious.

Now, here, on his ship, he replayed the loss of Slattery over and over in his mind, the biting pain of the young flyer's demise receding slightly with each repeated cycle. His defense mechanisms kicked into high gear and began serving him, as they were designed to do, but at the same time important

pieces of Jack Webster began to shut down like automated
safes in a bank during an earthquake, steel doors slamming
into place and sealing off their hurtful innards.

It was the latest, and most dire, in a lifetime of such pro-
cesses, critical for averting a psychic meltdown but exacting
an appalling price. While his sanity was being protected, the
coin of his salvation was his ability to feel pain, and with it
his capacity to know real joy, for the two were not opposites
but quantum mechanical complements, obverse sides of the
same coin. And in his quarters on that dark night, Jack will-
ingly bade farewell to an essential component of his humanity
in order to spare himself a pain he knew could crush him.

His wife could feel it the second he walked off the gang-
plank at the end of his tour.

She loved him deeply, and the reticence and distance he
brought back from this trip troubled her, but she was a proper
military wife, and the center of her world was not herself but
her husband. There was a protocol in career military mar-
riages, not written down anywhere but as compelling as any
voted into place by Congress. It was the same protocol that
conferred on a military wife the rank of her husband when
she was among other military wives.

Jack's career was of paramount importance, and his mental
health, and hers, shrank into insignificance beside it. For that
matter, psychological well-being was a given, any mention
to the contrary an automatic career death sentence liable to
no commutation. For Betty Webster to have whispered a word
of her concern to anyone, anywhere, would have been a breach
of propriety tantamount to a public declaration that both of
them wore each other's underwear.

So she kept her own counsel, and prayed, and loved him,
and was prepared to go to her grave under those circumstances
with nary a breath of suggestion that he seek any assistance.

For his part, and without quite knowing why, Jack sought
to blast through to his shielded core by brute force. The
antiterrorist stint helped, although Betty had not taken well
to his repeated temptation of fate by volunteering for the most
dangerous assignments. She didn't know that her husband
had come up against the worst kind of wall in a military

leader's career, the point at which he would rather take his own life than be called upon to sacrifice someone else's. The only good thing to come out of that particular assignment was Jack's meeting Dr. Amy Goldberg.

The key opportunity arose when he was approached by the NTSB following his successful battle to regain his pilot's license. It was Gene Sivara who brought his name to the board's attention.

Colleagues were surprised by the speed with which he accepted the position and totally immersed himself in the world of crash investigations. Never before considered a quick study, Jack read voraciously and buttonholed his new colleagues at every opportunity, driving them to distraction with his persistent interrogations on data-gathering techniques and interpretation, absorbing vast amounts of information on flight theory, metallurgy, forensic examination, construction technology, civilian airway rules and regulations and the whole cornucopia of esoteric arts and sciences that coalesced and intertwined to answer the questions, What happened? and, How do we prevent it from happening again?

These were all but prelude to his real objective, investigating in the field.

He did them all, no matter how much he had to travel or what he had been doing when the disaster struck. Staff investigators began to take his presence as a given and relied on him to provide strong leadership and a confident presence. The press, at first put off by his refusal to speculate idly about possible cause, eventually understood and accepted his caution, knowing that he would be cooperative when the time was right. It actually had a benefit for them: if the sleaze-mongers began dribbling out unsubstantiated rumors with subtle intimations that they originated from official sources, the more reputable media representatives could counter them instantly, knowing that Jack Webster didn't play favorites and that if he had something to say, he would tell them all. Eventually they learned to ask only what they knew he would answer, which consisted only of the facts as known ("It came down here, it broke into four pieces, there was a fire, no explosion was reported. . . ."). Conjecture was reserved until after scientific analysis and then was accompanied by probability ranges, and God help the reporter who didn't mention the uncertainty factors in his report.

What nobody could see, though, was the nature of Jack's self-administered therapy and how badly it was failing. Like a junkie whacked out on sense-numbing methaqualone who stabs at his skin with broken glass in a desperate attempt to feel something—anything—Jack immersed himself in the volcanic horror of the violent death of innocents. He walked among the smoking wreckage and tried to open his pores and let the magnitude of the cataclysm find his center and assault it. In invisible desperation he sought to assimilate the visions of mangled bodies, children's bloodied toys, a shoe, a book, and let them pluck the strings of his compassion.

Because if such sights as these could not move him, was he then not lost forever?

CHAPTER 20

June 17, 1640 EST

There are few things that better epitomize the shape of the Organization in the twentieth century than the Meeting.

The Meeting is characterizable as a singular entity because regardless of subject matter, venue, time of day, participation, seating configuration, lighting, catering arrangements, duration or accoutrement, there are certain ineluctable patterns that underlie most meetings and give those doing the meeting an uncomfortable feeling, a sort of businessman's déjà vu: *Say, I've been here before, one or two million times*.

Of all the disparate pursuits of man, the Meeting is one in which it is inconceivable that the meeting itself could possibly be the point. The Meeting is always "about" something else, and it is easily demonstrated that, while the Meeting is going on, that which it is about, isn't. Therefore, in the vast majority of cases the Meeting is an avoidance of all that is productive, useful and meritorious, hated by those who would rather do than not do, beloved by those for whom doing is an unforgivable concession to the common and the tasteless.

The Meeting is what one does when there is little else to do so, given the practical exigencies of human endeavor; there

will always be the Meeting, spawning like protozoa in the
brackish waters of business and government.

Jack Webster's core team of investigators was meeting in
Conference Room B of the National Transportation Safety
Board facility in Washington, D.C. They were reviewing progress. More correctly, they were reviewing movement. Progress
is definable only in terms of demonstrable headway toward
a stated goal or objective. Movement is the next best thing,
the comforting feeling that while one is not necessarily making
progress, something is certainly going on that might not have
been were they not doing something useful, which may or
may not at some fortuitous moment be transformed from
movement into progress.

Four days had passed since Amy Goldberg, Ph.D., had
explained the theory of intermittent reinforcement, while
admitting that she had no plan other than a clever way to
shake up Captain Marvel and whatever band of merry men
he was commanding. None of the others on the team had
succeeded in drawing her out on the subject of multiple perpetrators. She had been obstinate in her refusal to discuss the
matter, as though in refutation of the clear evidence before
them, and it was starting to wear on some people. Mostly on
FBI special agent G. Preston Stanley.

Jack had invited Florence Hartzig to this full review session
as a courtesy, even though she wasn't technically part of the
team. This also rankled Stanley, a believer in protocol and
procedure, who was already troubled by the computer expert's
de facto inclusion in all of the team's activities. But he couldn't
deny the value of Hartzig's technical insights and elected to
keep quiet for the moment. In any event, it helped to deflect
some of the credit from Amy, who was from outside the FBI
family and may have had, in his mind, a dangerous propensity
for ignoring relevant evidence.

"We think the messages are starting to have a definite
effect," Amy reported. They had gone out on a limb revealing
their knowledge of the chip tampering, but it seemed to have
worked: Captain Marvel had stayed with one machine for
nearly four minutes, apparently desperate to get more data
out of the investigators.

"He has no idea what we're monitoring or what we can

read from the console, so he kept slamming keys. We thought they were random, but they weren't."

"He used a code," said Jack, "probably figuring that's what we were expecting."

"What kind of code?" asked Florence.

"Simplest sort, really. Touch-tone keys stand for the same letters they usually do. Number of presses tells you which of the three letters is being referred to. 'Hello' is 44-333-555-555-666. Same way you program your cellular phone for alpha characters."

"What'd he say?"

Jack grinned in spite of himself. " *'Pleasure doing business with you.'* Then three machines later, *'Keep it up.'* Hardly inspired, but the point was made."

Stanley looked puzzled. "You call that rattled? Sounds to me like the sonofabitch is in complete control."

"No." Amy shook her head and sat up from her slouch with an almost audible creaking of tired joints. Sleep was coming to her lately only with great difficulty. "No, this is not control."

"That so?" Stanley leaned forward on his elbows. "Sounds like a wise-ass joker to me, having a good time at our expense."

"That's what it's supposed to sound like. That's why we're making progress."

Stanley looked around the room before *harrumphing* his disagreement. "How do you figure?"

Amy rose and stuck her hands in her back pockets, pacing idly in varied directions. "When he started, Marvel behaved like he was deadly serious, icy hard. Cold water instead of blood. He was frightening to us."

"I didn't find him so frightening," Stanley said matter-of-factly.

"Well, I did," Amy said.

"Why? Because he had the power to disrupt air traffic?"

Amy shook her head. "No. Because he sent the message here. To the NTSB."

"Yeah, so?"

"Why not to Alpha Airlines? Why here?"

"Because it wasn't about Alpha in particular, it was the whole system."

Amy shook her head harder this time. "Bullshit. It was only five million crummy dollars. Alpha could've handled it."

"Why, then?" Florence asked.

"Because," said Amy, "we had the power to keep it quiet and avoid pressure for a confrontation. We had the means to keep it from the flying public. The board has the tightest security imaginable, and we're the only ones could play the game on his terms without it getting out of control."

She stood up and walked to the monitor, looking into its blank face. "If we had to, we're the only ones could play this game forever, knuckling under to his every demand."

"So what's so scary?" Stanley asked innocently.

Amy turned around to face him. "The pathology behind his motivation. I thought the most terrifying thing was not understanding it, but I was wrong. It's even worse when it starts to surface."

They were quiet for several moments before Florence asked in a low voice. "Where's this going, Doc?"

Amy shivered slightly and came up out of a faraway place. "All of a sudden, he's into happy conversation with us. Joking, almost. Still contemptuous, sure, still the upper hand."

Jack stood and walked to the window, looking out at the sunset just beginning to turn the air from white hot to softly golden.

"He's communicating with us. Why? For what reason? And not just hello, top o' the mornin' to you. He stayed at one place four minutes." He stretched out the phrase, punching his fist in the air to accent how long a passage of time that represented. "Four. Long. Minutes. What a risk! And for what? For games? Had we known, we could have had someone dispatched to spot him."

Florence watched Jack, caught up in the flow of his and Amy's thinking. "Why? Why does he take the chance?"

Jack turned back toward the table and spread his hands out before him. "We think he's lonely."

Stanley looked at Webster, then back toward Amy. "Lonely? Are you serious? He needs someone to talk to?"

"Yep," Amy replied. "He has no friends, no person he can trust. It's not about the money. It never was. It's something else. Something worse."

"Like what?" asked Florence.

"Like something to prove. And someone to prove it to. Someone who's paying attention to him, even if the attention is at gunpoint."

"Us," said Florence.

"Like I've been saying. Except we started out as government buffoons to be toyed with, and now it's possible there's some grudging respect coming our way. Now he has someone he can show off to, someone worth the energy to frighten, to control. And I'll bet any amount of money he visualizes us as a single person, not a group."

"So what are we now," asked Stanley with a tinge of sarcasm, "his friend?"

"Oh, yes," said Amy, as though the question were so obvious it didn't bear asking. "Oh, yes, we're his friend, very best friend. Close, like brothers."

"And then what?" Florence was surprised and confused by this explanation. "What do we do now that we're his friend?"

"We do what so many friends do." Jack smiled a sad smile. "We betray him."

Amy's silence communicated her agreement.

"Isn't that a little risky?" Stanley asked her.

"Very risky. Only as a last resort, if we can't trick him into a mistake. We're losing and he has too much control? We piss him off and we get ready and we have this all over with, one way or the other. It's the last thing in the world he expects because it's the one thing he's been trying to avoid."

Stanley was trying to maintain his equilibrium and continue evincing a professional demeanor. "A lot of people could get hurt. What makes you think he's gonna force us to do something?"

"It's not money. I know it. The money's gonna become boring, and there's got to be something else."

"Like what?" asked Florence.

"Maybe more money. Some other demand—"

Or maybe no more demands. Amy knew that whoever Captain Marvel was, he wasn't the same as before he crashed an airplane. There was a barrier that every practicing terrorist or extortionist crossed sometime in his career. It was the same one a soldier or a mob button crosses the first time he takes a life. It was possible that Marvel crawled into a closet and threw up for an hour following the MD-11 disaster, went to confession and tortured himself for days and maybe came close to giving up the game.

But it was also possible that the taste of taking away what only God had the jurisdiction to grant was the instant addiction it was for many people, an intoxicant no more resistible than heroin or political power.

Amy wasn't ready to put that on the table yet.

"—more and more until we can no longer agree and then there'll be a confrontation. We don't catch him first, it's near certainty. . . ."

Seeing that Amy had again drifted into some private meditation in the middle of her soliloquy and believing the point to have been made, Jack sought to switch topics.

"Pres, what've we got on the employee rundown?"

"Yeah, that's what I'm anxious to hear," said Florence.

The FBI agent shuffled through the papers in the manila folder before him. "We've been running traces on all the manufacturer's employees to try to narrow down the field to some qualified suspects. Technical expertise, access, right time in the position, that sort of thing. We were tracking time they might have spent in the Midwest," he said, glancing quickly at Amy but turning away before the psy-war specialist could catch the look, "but got disabused of that notion pretty quick."

Florence was nodding enthusiastically. "Good idea. And?"

Stanley stopped shuffling and slumped his shoulders. "And nothing hard yet."

"Nothing?" Florence looked surprised. "Almost unbelievable. The guy had to have been inside. There's, like, no other way."

Tell me about it. "We're not through yet. Look, Autonav's got over eighteen hundred employees, and when you add in—"

"Autonav?" Florence's head jerked up as she looked at Stanley in disbelief.

The agent looked around to see if anyone else understood her reaction. "Yeah, Autonav. Who'd you think we were looking at?"

"What the hell are you looking at Autonav for?"

Jack sat up straighter. "What are you talking about, Florence?"

She turned to Jack. "They don't make chips, Webster. That's a highly specialized craft. Takes millions of dollars of equipment and a ton of people."

"I don't get it," said Stanley. "So who makes them?"

"Somebody else makes them, that's who. A fabricator, like MicroFab or Custom Semi. Autonav designs them, and then the fabricator builds them on contract, according to Autonav's design."

"So okay, somebody else makes them, but only according to Autonav's design, right?"

"Wrong," Jack breathed in sudden understanding, thinking back to the diagrams Florence had laid out on the table days before. "The modification wasn't in Autonav's design."

"Of course it wasn't," said Florence, an edge of anger creeping into her voice. "I showed you that. It was added later. By the fabricator."

Stanley looked so stunned and disconsolate, nobody had the heart to berate him for the error. Besides, none of the others had seen it either.

Amy chortled, shaken out of her funk by the intensity of the repartee. "Lookin' up a dead horse's *tuchis,* Agent?"

"Well," said Stanley as he rose and went for one of the phones next to the display monitor, "only remedy for a screwup? Unscrew it." He punched in the digits from memory.

"If it *is* MicroFab," said Florence, "I know the director of the design department. Woman named Phyllis Dalek. We shared some classes back at—"

Stanley held up a hand for her to be quiet as someone came on the other end of the line.

"At least he's being a man about it," Florence whispered as Amy returned to the table.

"Yeah," Amy was forced to agree.

"Schoenberg? Stanley. Listen, we gotta redirect your guys, and pronto. We've—What? No shit? No shit!"

The rest of the meeting participants exchanged amused glances at Stanley's agitation as he cupped one hand over the mouthpiece and turned toward the table.

"We may have found the seatmate!" he said.

"No shit?" exclaimed Amy in mindless repetition of Stanley's own witless *bon mot*.

"Put him on the speaker!" Jack commanded.

Stanley pressed the speaker button as he hung up the phone. A red light appeared on the tabletop unit, and he said, "You there, Schoenberg?"

"Yeah. Everybody cleared?"

"My authority, Larry. Let's hear it."

They crowded around the little box, as though to do so would enhance their immediacy to the source.

"Three passengers paid cash, so we checked them all out. Two were for real, no trace of the third, but we know the seat assignment, so we tracked down the person in the next seat. He's in Europe. . . ."

"How do you know?" asked Jack.

"Again, it's not a for-sure, but we contacted people we know in Interpol and asked them to track him down while we send a guy over. They caught up with him somewhere in Belgium, and get this: He's a professional photographer—observant type, y'know?—and first thing he says is, 'Yeah, sure I remember: laughed like hell when we got knocked off course by those fighters.' You believe that?"

"Is he gonna cooperate?" asked Stanley.

"I think so, but we didn't want the Interpol guys doing the interrogation—woulda had to tell 'em too much—so we sprang for a good hotel, and he should be on his way there now."

"Well, I'll be damned," said Stanley, slumping back on his chair.

"Agent Schoenberg, this is Amy Goldberg of the NTSB. Tell me, what name was used on the ticket?"

"You're gonna love this. 'J. Doolittle.' You believe the brass?"

"That it, Larry?" asked Stanley, sensing that all the valuable information had been transmitted.

"That's it."

Stanley looked around before he said, "Thanks, fella. Nicely done."

"By all means," added Jack.

The field agent clicked off, and the line went quiet.

They sat back on their chairs and took deep breaths, looking at each other with satisfaction and amusement.

Only Amy remained on her feet, a look of intense concentration on her face. "J. Doolittle?"

"It's a joke, Amy," Stanley started to explain. "Jimmy Doolittle was one of the greatest—"

"I know damned well who he was," Amy said, waving off the explanation. "Why would he pick that name?"

Stanley was also annoyed, at what he perceived to be a useless avenue of inquiry. "It's just a joke, Goldberg. Why make a big deal of it?"

"Maybe it tells us something."

"Yeah, maybe, but meanwhile we've got something a lot harder to go on than some Freudian clue."

"That so, huh? And what are you gonna do about it?" There was a sardonic glint in her eyes.

"Are you serious? We're gonna—"

"Preston," said Florence, "I think you forgot something on that telephone call."

"Like what?"

Amy started for the door. "Gonna go bum a smoke."

"Forgot what?" demanded Stanley.

Amy opened the door and stepped halfway out, then turned back only briefly to the FBI agent. "Forgot to tell your man on the phone where to look." And then she was gone.

"What?"

Jack punched him lightly on the arm. "You called Schoenberg to tell him to drop Autonav and go after the chip fabricator, remember?"

Stanley looked confused for a moment and then smiled sheepishly. "That I did."

"It ought to be easy," Florence observed. "Especially if we get a decent visual ID from Europe. I suggest your guy gets to the director of the department as quickly as possible and bypass the brass."

"How come?" asked Stanley.

"Chip design is pretty intense stuff, and the staff tends to be a bit inbred. The director's usually the one with the best handle on what's going on, and on the people. Tech weenies don't like executives much, and so whoever they report to always tries to protect them. Especially in Silicon Valley—those companies are always trying to steal each other's employees."

Stanley took in the confidently delivered speech on the realities of the high-tech business world. "You said you know one of the design managers . . . ?"

Florence smiled. "Yeah. If it is MicroFab, which is probable given their size, let me know. Phyllis Dalek, the design director? Your guy doesn't kiss her ring, she's likely to chuck him out a window, but I get along with her fine. It's also likely the execs will try to not let you get to her."

"I'm sure we could handle it, but I'll keep your offer in mind."

Florence felt that the present circumstance outweighed protocol, and she reacted to the transparent brush-off. "I know what I'm talking about, Stanley. Even if you find the guy another way, maybe from the visual, Dalek's gonna be the only one can help us neutralize the danger if you don't catch him right away."

Stanley nodded dismissively. "You don't even know for sure it's MicroFab, so why don't we postpone this until we find out, shall we?"

Florence saw that further debate was futile and chose to stay quiet until the situation warranted a more spirited rebuttal.

Amy, coming back into the room with two cigarettes as this last exchange took place, stifled the urge to comment on Stanley's unproductive turf pride, she herself having been the target of it once before. As the agent rose to leave, she stopped him and poked him lightly in the chest. "Try to find out if our guy flies airplanes."

"Airplanes? Why?"

Amy handed one of the cigarettes to Jack, who looked around embarrassedly as he took it. Florence gave him a scolding look, then another to Amy.

"Just ask. A favor to a difficult broad."

June 18, 0835 PST

"Agent Schoenberg, my name is Pavel Chulowski. I am the president of MicroFab Corporation."

"Pleased to meet you."

"And this is Marlene Simmons, head of human resources, and Otis Easterlund, director of administration."

They shook hands all around and sat at the round conference table in a corner of Chulowski's office. A personal computer sat at one end, its screen glowing.

"We are on-line to our corporate records," explained Chulowski. "In very short order we can search through the databases and try to come up with a list of names. We will do everything to try to cooperate."

"That's much appreciated, sir. I'm sorry to have been so circumspect on the phone, but this is a matter of some delicacy."

"Is that why we had to sign those forms?" Simmons asked with a resentful tone.

"I'm afraid so."

"Look," said Chulowski, "we have all blocked the entire day, if necessary, to help you. What do you need?"

Schoenberg stood to remove his jacket. "We're looking for a former employee, but we don't know how far back." He unbuttoned his cuffs and began rolling up a sleeve. "He would have been associated with the Autonav account and had access to your physical design and fabrication process."

"May we ask why?" Simmons said.

"I'd appreciate it if you didn't."

"We can easily put together a list like that," said Easterlund, "but it might help if you told us how far back to go. Our records have only been automated for the past three years."

Schoenberg smiled, trying to put them at ease. "Really? I thought you were a computer company?"

Chulowski smiled back. "I am afraid the shoemaker's children often go barefoot. And I fear this list is going to be quite lengthy. Silicon Valley is notorious for turnover among the technical staffs."

"I assumed that," said Schoenberg, rubbing his eyes. "Could go back as far as five or six years."

Easterlund turned away from the PC. "You can't be serious."

"Is that a problem?"

"Not for us, no, we're happy to comply. But for you. Autonav is our largest customer, and one of the oldest. This list could have over five hundred names on it."

Schoenberg took his hands from his eyes and looked at Easterlund, speechless, and then at Chulowski.

"Perhaps," said the CEO, "you might give us some more information, to help narrow the search. For example, you said *'former'* employee. Would he still be working here?"

"Doubtful. It's also likely he would not have had many friends on the staff, probably didn't partake in many social situations—"

Simmons was shaking her head and smiling. "You just described ninety percent of our technical staff. Unfortunately, that isn't the kind of information we keep on a database, computerized or otherwise. Although"—she leaned forward conspiratorially—"Lord knows I'd like to."

"Look," said Schoenberg, hoping to convey by posture and tone of voice both the gravity of the situation and his growing frustration, "is there any reason why I couldn't meet with the manager of the design department directly? Wouldn't he be in the best position to help me?"

"She." Chulowski ignored a giggle from Easterlund and an amused gasp from Simmons. "Perhaps. But I would submit that we in this room might be of better service. Now, while I understand and respect your wish to keep this confidential, perhaps you could hasten matters along by divulging more than you seem to be willing to." He held up a hand before Schoenberg could make any apologies. "Don't misunderstand. No offense is taken. But it does limit our ability to be of assistance."

Schoenberg listened politely and let a silent moment pass before he spoke. "Is there some specific reason why you're unwilling to let me visit with your design manager . . . what was her name again?"

Chulowski sighed. "Phyllis Dalek."

Marlene Simmons stifled another laugh while Otis Easterlund giggled out loud. Schoenberg turned to each of them in turn before speaking. "What's so funny?"

Chulowski intercepted the conversation before they could answer. "Agent Schoenberg ..." He leaned back and drummed a finger on the arm of the chair. "Ms. Dalek runs the entire design area, knows every cubic centimeter of the operation and keeps close tabs on the staff. It is very likely that she might be able to help you."

"I'd like to be a fly on the wall for that one," Easterlund said.

"Please, Otis," Chulowski, chided him gently. "She's not all that bad."

"Yeah, she is," Simmons said with some amusement. "Arrogant is one thing. We got plenty of those, all high-tech operations do. But this one? Tough. Very tough."

"Then why are you laughing?"

"Are you kidding, Pavel?" Easterlund said to Chulowski. "You're gonna sic this unsuspecting guy on Phyllis?"

"She's gonna want to know your grandfather's underwear size before she'd agree to cooperate," Simmons said to Schoenberg.

"That bad?"

Chulowski made a helpless gesture with his hands. "An undeniable talent, truly. Without her, we would not be what we are today. But difficult."

"And not here, either," said Simmons.

"Why?" Schoenberg asked. "Where is she?"

"Her hours are her own," said Chulowski. "So long as she continues to be effective, we don't keep tabs on her."

"That's not it, Pavel." Simmons sighed and turned to the FBI agent to explain. "She's a workaholic, see? And the more she works, the more miserable everyone around her gets." She turned back to Chulowski. "Pete—that's our executive VP for technology, Mr. Schoenberg—Pete told her to get lost for a week."

"Why?"

"Seems there was a design conference on a new sputterer for the research section, and he overrode one of her recommendations."

"So?"

"So, Phyllis stood up and told him to—and I quote—'stick it in your ear.'" She turned to Schoenberg. "Pete's got ears like Dumbo. We'll never know if she said that as a generic insult or specifically for him."

"Unusual," said Chulowski. "Normally, her insults are more refined—and more clever, I might add."

"That's probably why he told her to take some time off. I'll give you one thing, Pavel: she sure as hell knows her stuff, and her people."

"Yeah," Easterlund said sarcastically. "Breathes over their shoulders all day long."

"Now, now," Chulowski scolded, as though to quarrelsome children. "Agent Schoenberg, I do not know what your situation is, although I suspect there is great urgency. I must confess that, if this indeed involves a current or former MicroFab employee, Phyllis Dalek will be invaluable. She is fiercely dedicated to her craft and intensely aware of its value in actual use. . . ." He paused and got affirming nods from his colleagues. "But if you want her help, you're probably going to have to tell her why."

"I'm not sure I can do that. However, if we have to, there are certain measures—"

Chulowski was singularly unimpressed by the veiled show of official power. "With all respect, higher up than you have tried. We have many military applications here, and it is my suspicion that Ms. Dalek knows national security regulations better even than you yourself."

Schoenberg decided to risk a slight security breach in the interest of expediency. "Do any of you know Florence Hartzig?"

Chulowski brightened noticeably. "Most certainly! We tried to recruit her many times. To little effect, I am sad to say. Why do you ask?"

Schoenberg shrugged and tried to minimize the importance of his inquiry. "One of my people knows her. Maybe Hartzig might have some sway with Phyllis Dalek? You know, another woman in the same field?"

"Possibly," said Simmons. "Very possibly, in fact. Not a bad idea."

Having achieved his objective, Schoenberg wanted to end

that part of the discussion and go on to more practical matters. "Do you know where she is?"

Chulowski looked at Simmons and raised one eyebrow.

"No," she said. "But she'll more than likely check for messages on a more or less regular basis. Whether she responds to them . . . ?" She made a rocking motion with one hand.

"Mr. Schoenberg," asked Easterlund, "do we—MicroFab, I mean—do we have anything to worry about here?"

Schoenberg cocked his head to one side and considered the question. "Maybe just some work on your security procedures. Incidentally, does your database track who among the staff flies airplanes?"

"No, although it would be a relatively easy matter to check with the FAA for pilot license records. However, I can tell you that most of the technical people working on the Autonav chips are pilots. Saved us some learning curve on the actual application. Why? Is that important?"

Schoenberg waved off the question. "Probably not. Just curious. May I use your phone for a minute?"

1546 CST

```
Hi, this is Jack.

Today's financial news:

MicroFab Corporation up one and
seven-eighths on news that it is to
receive a huge order from Autonav
for newly redesigned chips.

Film at eleven.

Have a nice day.
```

CHAPTER 21

June 19, 1205 MST

Phyllis Dalek cursed the rental car as she had cursed so many in the past. More correctly, she cursed the agency that had rented it to her, the company that had built the piece of junk, the auto workers' unions that had contributed to the ubiquitous malaise in attitude toward the quality of American-made products, management's dehumanizing treatment of labor that had resulted in their cynicism toward their own work in the first place, the entire capitalistic system of unregulated greed and, before she made it out of the parking lot, most of those portions of Western civilization that had conspired over the last four thousand years to make sure that the ill-designed console frame rubbed the outside of her right knee as she drove.

She pulled into a gas station as soon as she left the small airport, since this was one of the new breed of rental companies that didn't provide a full tank of gas. Phyllis had tried to explain to the agent that this made very little sense, since how could anybody be expected to guess the exact amount of gas they were going to use and then buy just that amount? What if I fill the tank and then have to cut my trip short? What then? The clerk had not had the presence of mind to explain to her that one of the reasons their rates were so low was that they didn't have to bother with the administration of a refueling service, which explanation wouldn't have satisfied Phyllis anyway.

She put six and a half gallons of the cheapest low-octane in the tank and handed her credit card to the man in the glass booth, which is how she had come to think of the cash register operators who hid from their customers in hard-shelled cocoons.

"Ooh ack shebbin keckah?" rasped the speaker while the attendant did nothing with her Visa. "Eh eeh."

"What?" she said in annoyance, her face screwed up with the effort of trying to decipher the auditory hieroglyphics.

The attendant, of unknown ethnic orientation, rolled his eyes at this stupid woman's inability to comprehend a clear question delivered with flawless diction. He wordlessly conceded the possibility that four feet was not an optimal distance between mouth and microphone by stepping forward to where the round metal ball hung from the ceiling by a frayed wire. "You. Like. Chevron. Credit. Card?" he said slowly and with exaggerated clarity, evincing bored disdain for her initial non-comprehension, which had necessitated his movement toward the mike. "It free."

"Why do I want one?"

Sensing a possible score, which would net him a five-dollar premium from the company, he condescended to explain. "Use for buy gas, oil, other stuff."

"Don't you take Visa?"

"Yah, sure, but Chevron card free."

"But I already have the Visa card. What's the benefit of the Chevron card?" She didn't care a whit, knowing full well that the only benefit was for the gas company, which would avoid charges from the credit card company, but she had this guy outclassed by better English, a good forty-five IQ points and a lifetime of bristling cynicism honed to razor-sharp perfection. She could feel this poor bastard's member lose half its length as her tongue bit off great gobs of his rapidly dwindling masculinity, which he sought to rescue with the only weapon remaining in his arsenal.

"Hey, lady, fuck you! You don' wanna card, bust someone else chops, hah?"

Phyllis Dalek was not having a good day, although it was a fairly normal one. As she proceeded north in the rattle-bound heap that drove as if it had turned over the odometer more than once but really only had seven thousand miles on it, she fumbled at her purse on the passenger's seat, trying to find her cigarettes. "If you're so goddamned smart," her father had asked, "how come you smoke?"

"If *you're* so goddamned smart," she snorted back, "how come you ask?" She saved some of her best shots for him, not because she didn't like him, which she did, but because he was one of the few people she knew who was clever enough to appreciate her wit, such as it was.

She got angry at the purse and shook it hard, spilling its contents onto the seat. Among the tissues, various keys, eye-glass case, aspirins, pencils, address book, small change, wallet, memo pad, pocket calculator and other absolute essentials, a miniature photo album fell open to the snapshot she loathed more than any other and that she was never without.

She was seventeen years old, housed in a dress that was timeless in the sense that it would be out of vogue in any age and therefore provided no clue as to the year of its creation. She had often wondered what could possibly have passed through the mind of its designer, as it was inconceivable that any traditional notion of gracing the female figure could have played a part in its production. Phyllis had long suspected that there was an entire infrastructure out there geared specifically toward ensuring that girls like her had an endless supply of depressingly sensible shoes, horrid dresses, brassieres to make them look like their grandmothers, eyeglasses that would do a flounder proud and jewelry that, when no longer needed, could easily function as reasonably priced decorations for a second-grade Christmas pageant, all financed not by the wearers thereof, but by their fogged-in parents, paleolithic aunts and uncles and misogynistic neighbors.

Next to her in the photograph, sitting on a table, was a wooden slab about twice the size of a record album, topped with a tangle of wires that sat linguini-like over an assemblage of electronic gadgetry. A small antenna poked out of the mess, and affixed to the apex of the miniature mast was a blue ribbon with gold lettering too small to be readable in the photo.

She had waited quietly through the presentations by her high school classmates of their own science projects, stifling a series of yawns as Justin Wiener waxed eloquent on the subject of crystal radios. In keeping with the appropriately enlightened theme of helping others rather than science for its own sake, Justin described in detail how radio communications was of inestimable aid to people beset by catastrophe, distracting his listeners from the stultifying blandness of his project concept, the ineptitude of its construction and the decidedly nonutilitarian fact that it could not transmit but only receive, and do that only if his particular device even worked, which it didn't.

Prior to that, Ashley Lumbrowski discoursed passionately on the correlation of air temperature and salmonella poisoning among eastern South Dakota picnickers, a thesis of blinding obviousness backed up by statistics graciously supplied by one Mr. Stasz Lumbrowski of the state health department.

Phyllis's own project was in actuality a multiband radio scanner, built of parts scavenged from a variety of transistor radios, high-technology refrigerators (plenty of those in junk-yards—Phyllis had often wondered why a manufacturer would go to the expense of building a complete "diagnostic center" into an appliance with a mean time between failure interval normally measured in centuries, a feat of reliability surpassed only by old rotary-dial telephones and attested to by the fact that about the only thing that was ever broken on the junked refrigerators she kept finding were the diagnostic centers, which endeared the average American consumer to her even more), old click-style television remote controls, lamp dimmers and the finely printed back pages of Radio Shack catalogs.

The scanner could monitor the frequencies of seven radio bands at once, halting on any frequency that happened to be transmitting at the moment, in a priority set by the user from the choice of police, aircraft, weather, civil emergency, fire department and two local taxi companies. Phyllis pondered this accomplishment as Scarlett Hanamura finished her dissertation on the finer points of pest control in the Lesser Antilles or something like that, and the teacher, who had sat through all of the presentations with the patience of a tranquilized sloth and about the same level of comprehension, finally called her name.

Phyllis rose and moved toward the front of the class, exhibiting the typical close-limbed, tentative shuffle of the terminally self-loathing. She went over her prepared remarks in her head and discarded them by the time she reached the third row, having come to a decision that in other times, other places, might have been viewed as risky but that she knew presented little such danger in this setting.

Mrs. MacAvoy smiled and nodded her head in encouragement. Phyllis folded her hands in front of her, lifted her chin and began.

"My science project is a positron emission tomograph for use in medicine to help people with diseases difficult to diagnose." She went on to illustrate the basic process by which the antiparticle analogues of electrons were created and poured over the afflicted body segment, synchronizing their frequencies with the body's own natural electronic emissions, the discordancies presenting themselves through later analysis and indicating likely tissue pathology. Watching as Mrs. MacAvoy's eyes crossed slightly, Phyllis delved into the more arcane facets of particle physics, conveniently neglecting to mention that the technology she was describing would not be available as a commercial product for another twelve years, would cost a minimum of two million dollars for the crudest of prototype units, would require a room the size of a small warehouse to contain all the equipment and had nothing whatsoever to do with the radio scanner sitting on the table by her side.

Which is how she won the blue ribbon, her insight having been related not to the science involved, but to the inescapable conclusion that while the teacher might have had difficulty awarding top honors to something she couldn't understand, stated contrapositively she also had no basis for denying them, either, and could easily work the justification end by citing the extraordinary machine's potential for social good. Mrs. MacAvoy having come down on the side of confrontation avoided rather than good work rewarded, Phyllis got the ribbon. One could make the argument that this was a just result anyway, since hers was clearly a superior piece of science. However, if one were to consider as a criterion the degree to which the student stretched preexisting capabilities and actually learned (and taught to fellow classmates) something new as a result of the effort, Phyllis was the least qualified candidate, since the multiband scanner for her took about as much stretching as it would for Albert Einstein to balance his checkbook.

The sudden blast of a car horn in the next lane startled her, jarring her out of the childhood reminiscence. She swerved back into the center of the lane and tried to refocus her concentration on the here and now.

1447 EST

Special Agent Preston Stanley arrived at the L'Enfant Plaza offices at the same time as Florence. As they entered the lobby together, he said, "Good news and bad news."

"So?"

"The good news is, it *is* MicroFab and there's no doubt your friend Phyllis Dalek could probably help us zero in on the guy."

"And the bad news?" prompted Florence, already suspecting the answer.

"A, she's still as much of a flake as you remembered and we'll probably have to tell her the whole story, and B, we don't know where she is."

"Golly," said Florence. "She one of those nut cases doesn't believe in national security rules above all?"

The sarcasm was not lost on the FBI man, well acquainted with the details of Amy Goldberg's first encounter with Florence. "We can debate her politics all day long, but before I bother to launch a manhunt, I have to decide if our guys can lay it out for her when they find her."

"You already know the answer to that one."

Stanley nodded. "I know. She's our biggest hope right now.

And get this: Most of the MicroFab people who've worked on the Autonav account were pilots."

"No kidding?" said Florence. "Amy was right?"

Stanley's lips were set in a straight line. "Yeah, but so what? If nearly all of them were, what does it do for us?"

"You don't like her much, do you?" asked Florence.

The question seemed to startle Stanley, as though Florence were saying something that everybody else seemed to know and he refused to admit. His step faltered slightly. "Why do you say that?"

"You do sort of rag at her all the time," Florence said, then seemed to think better of it. "Sort of, you know what I mean? Little things."

"She's high-handed, holds more stock in her theories than in the evidence, but isn't sure enough to just lay it out for us."

Florence shrugged. "It may be just a front for not knowing very much when everybody's leaning on her."

"I think she's dangerous. I met people like that back in training, MI-5 psy-war guys. They don't pick 'em for their table manners, believe me."

"But she seems to be getting a line on how this guy thinks," said Florence, surprised to find herself actively defending Amy but wanting to retain an appearance of objectivity. Stanley seemed to have forgotten his objections to her presence on the team, and she didn't want to jeopardize her status.

"I just don't want us to get off track," Stanley said, hitting the stairs and taking them two at a time. "She's completely ignoring the other team, the other collectors, like they don't exist."

Florence struggled to keep up with him. "They're an anomaly to her, Preston. It goes against the grain of everything she believes about how people like this operate."

Stanley stopped as they reached the top of the staircase. He turned to look at her.

"I can't deal with her theories when they contradict the facts. The facts are, at least two people or groups are yanking money out of cash machines, perfectly synchronized so they aren't operating at the same time. We nab one, the other starts crashing planes. And Goldberg's got everybody ignoring that second team."

He turned and began walking down the hall. "Now you tell me how in the holy hell I'm supposed to deal with her goddamned theories."

"You got a point there," said Florence, but not so the agent could hear it as he retreated down the hall. She bit her lower lip. *Something doesn't click here, and we're not seeing it.*

She walked into Conference Room B just behind Stanley. A pile of cigarette butts nearly overflowed a small ashtray, coffee cups littered the floor, and one wall was covered with sectional maps of the American Midwest, multicolored push-pins scattered over its surface.

Jack Webster and Amy Goldberg were sitting back on their chairs, feet up on the table, whatever work they had been doing obviously concluded.

"Jesus," Florence exclaimed. "You guys been interrogating somebody?"

"Only our muses," said Amy.

"Guess what?" Jack said.

"Wait," said Stanley, holding up his hand as he walked into the room. "Let me look first."

He went to the maps and studied them closely. The colors of the pins apparently delineated the two different collectors or teams. Green pins indicated Detroit Lakes, Minnesota, and then Fergus Falls and Morris, a clear line down the western part of the state, which then picked up again in Idaho. Red pins pierced the little towns of Brainerd, Little Falls and St. Cloud, and then they, too, reappeared in the neighboring state. The pattern was repeated in several locations. About every third pin there was a circle hand-drawn in felt marker around a printed symbol consisting of a tiny white line or two in a round magenta field. Zigzag marker lines joined the circled symbols across the map.

"What're these little purple symbols?" Stanley asked off-handedly.

Jack and Amy exchanged amused glances. Florence walked up behind Stanley and looked at the map, then said, "They're airports, aren't they?"

Stanley reexamined the map in light of this new piece of

data until its significance sank in. He turned slowly to look at Amy. "Well, I'll be damned," he said quietly.

"What?" Florence said with some irritation, apparently the last in the room to be let in on the game. "What the hell's going on?"

Jack put his hands behind his neck and looked at Stanley. "Don'tcha think a little honor is due the good doctor here, Preston?"

Stanley started to take a step toward Amy, his hand out, but then he stopped short. "Maybe. Maybe not. It's still a theory."

"Oh, Jesus, Preston!" Jack said. "Can't you admit it when you're licked?"

"Yes," said Stanley, withdrawing his hand. "When we know for sure. But I will admit it's a nifty piece of brain work. Nice thinking, Goldberg."

"Tell him," she said, indicating Jack. "He figured it out."

Stanley shook his head. "No. He may have figured out the method, but you knew about it all along, didn't you?"

"No. I just knew something. But"—she gestured at the board—"not this. Nice you should mention it, though."

"Hey!" Florence fairly screamed. "When the mutual admiration society is through meeting, somebody wanna tell me what the hell everybody else already knows?"

Jack leaned forward and folded his arms on the table. "There's only one, Florence. One Marvel. Acting alone."

Florence looked at the maps, and then she saw it. "He's flying an airplane."

She peered at the wall for another moment. "He drops in on a small airport, sometimes even a grass strip. Uncontrolled, no tower, sometimes not even an FBO. Nobody to log comings and goings."

"What's an FBO?" asked Stanley.

"A fixed base operator," Amy said. "They provide gas, maps, fast food, sometimes flying lessons and other pilot stuff."

"He rents a car if there's a service nearby, maybe calls a cab. Who knows, he could even carry a bicycle in the plane and ride around for a couple of pleasant hours, hitting up cash machines before hopping back to the airport and taking off."

"Incredible," Stanley said in undisguised amazement. "He makes us think there's more than one person involved. If we were sure"—he looked at Amy—"we could nail him."

"But we didn't know. I only suspected. It wasn't enough. I wasn't sure enough."

"But surely now," Florence said excitedly. "I mean, hell, all we have to do is go after MicroFab employees with pilot licenses, and then we'll know, right?"

"That's it," said Jack, triumph in his voice.

"Uh, not exactly," said Stanley.

Jack froze. It might have been more petulance on Stanley's part, but something in his voice told Jack it was more than that. "What do you mean?"

"Oh, shit," said Florence, thinking back to their hallway conversation, knowing what was coming.

"It seems that nearly everybody at MicroFab who worked on the Autonav account was a pilot," said Stanley, no gloating in his voice.

As Jack's shoulders started to slump in disappointment, Florence said, "But shouldn't it be relatively easy to go after the plane? How do you hide something like that?"

"You don't." Jack turned away and walked slowly back to the conference table, where he sat down heavily and began picking at his lip. "You abandon it."

"Or maybe you just rented it in the first place," added Amy.

But Florence wasn't to be dissuaded. "Assume he owned it. Why abandon it? Why won't he stick to the same MO?"

"You told him, didn't you?" asked Stanley, observing the glum look on Jack's face. "In one of the messages, you told him what we know, isn't that it?"

"Not exactly, but close." Jack exhaled heavily. "We let him know that we were on to MicroFab, to rattle him good, but that was before we figured out he might have a plane. Now, he probably knows we've figured it out. If we're right."

"So how come we don't just try to nab him?" asked Florence. "There's no danger of alerting an accomplice anymore, is there?"

"Probably not," answered Amy. "But we still don't want to make him mad unless we're sure."

"What do you suggest?" said Stanley, pleased that she was allowing for some doubt.

"Waiting. One, maybe two more days. Let's see how the pattern changes. We're not in such a hurry, and your people will have time to do some more checking."

"Checking? Christ, Doc, if the pattern changes and confirms the MO, and we get a visual from the seatmate in Europe soon, what more checking do you want?"

"We might learn his name. We'll know where he lives. But we don't know *him*. We're not gonna catch this one by knocking on his door and saying, 'Excuse me, we're from the FBI, will you come quietly?' We have to know more. Much more."

Chastened, Stanley said, "We can track down his family, even his friends, such as they are."

Amy nodded vigorously. "Yes. That'll be good. Bring me something."

"What? Bring you what?"

"I don't know. Something I can use. About him. Something he doesn't want us to know."

CHAPTER 22

June 20, 1245 EST

"**A**ctually, uh, I wanted to take you to lunch by way of an apology, sort of."

"What on earth for?"

"For getting you into the middle of this mess. I'm sure you had better things to do with your time."

Florence eyed Jack with a disarming and penetrating stare, as if trying to reach a decision. "It's not enough."

"Sorry?"

"Lunch. Not enough apology."

Agents of the Bureau, even relative newcomers, are supposed to keep their calm, no matter the circumstances but most especially in highly personal confrontations. It is a sin of the first order for an agent to let an adversary get the emotional upper hand. That's why they make such good witnesses under cross-examination. It's what made Jack's present face-reddening discomfort so satisfying to Florence.

"What then?"

Florence tapped two fingers on the table. "A wee drop o' the grape—"

"Aahh . . ."

"—and not cheap local swill either, sport."

"No, no, you're quite correct. Something special."

"And expensive, so there's a little suffering, you catch my drift. But not so much it can't be cured by the wine."

Jack had not had an alcoholic beverage at lunchtime since leaving the naval academy, but he signaled the waiter for the wine list, sensing that this was an appropriate time to break the rule.

"Any favorites?"

"Red. Bordeaux. Sixty-one if you're feeling like a Rockefeller, seventy-eight if not."

"I'm partial to seventy-nine myself."

"Acceptable."

They ordered a Lynch-Bages and sat back to await its arrival, both of them guiltily anticipating the indiscretion.

"So, would you mind telling me, please: Why now the sudden contrition? Which, as we both know, is ridiculous."

Jack scratched at the linen tablecloth with a fork. "You're very good at what you do."

"This from your own observation?" asked Florence, knowing that this wasn't the case and wanting to see how honest Jack was going to be.

"Not exactly. I did a little background check." He stopped scratching and looked up at her. Since she'd come on the scene, Florence had lost weight, her clumsy gait had become more graceful, hair better kept, even some of the puffiness in her skin had dissipated and she was dressing better.

To any disinterested observer, of course, nothing about her had changed at all.

She was unique in his experience, except for maybe Amy, but even the redoubtable Dr. Goldberg was somewhat enigmatic, often a mass of contradictions and swirling emotions, not unusual for someone who'd spent years doing what she did.

Florence was new. Strong, smart, self-confident without being overly arrogant, seemingly in command of her own life and her place in the world, sitting at the top of the ziggurat in her chosen field. As far a cry from his wife as he could imagine.

"Tell me something, Jack."

He lifted his chin in permission and waited.

"I'm curious. You've paid your dues. Some would say several times over. Why do you continue?"

Jack waved a hand in the air and decided to be as candid as national security regulations would let him. "This isn't continuing. This is easy."

"Easy? Are you serious?"

Jack allowed an indulgent smile to cross his face, as though lecturing an innocent child. "And so easy."

"But how? I don't find it easy at all."

He spread his hands. "There's no personal danger to us. Our government is backing us. All of the laws're on our side. The very staff of righteousness is with us. No ambiguity, no moral equivocation, a nice, binary question of right and wrong, with us being the good guys. Easy."

"But what if we have to do something hard? What if we have to flush him out?"

"We're heading down to Columbus for my nephew's birthday party Tuesday."

"Marvelous! How old is he now?"

"Six. Damnedest little kid. Plays baseball with eight-year-olds, can you believe it?"

"No! Takes after his uncle, huh?"

The waiter had approached the table with the wine several seconds ago, and as he came into earshot Jack had automatically switched tracks without a ripple in the flow of the conversation, and Florence followed suit. The waiter pulled the cork, unscrewed it from the opener and handed it to Jack, who felt the tip to make sure it was moist, indicating the bottle had been stored on its side, and then dropped it on the tablecloth. He didn't sniff it.

"Good for you," the waiter whispered in approval. He poured a thimbleful into Jack's glass.

"Let my aunt taste it, too," said Jack, pointing toward Florence's glass.

They swirled the ruby nectar to raise a bouquet, lifted the glasses and sniffed the ambrosial vapors redolent of minor sin, and closed their eyes in delighted expectation of the first sip.

"*A votre santé,*" said Florence.

"*Gesundheit,*" answered Jack.

They sipped, approved, the waiter poured and then left.

"So," said Florence. "Tell me really."

He'd never told anybody, except Amy. He wondered how much to tell Florence.

The new position with the NTSB seemed to work for Jack for quite some time, each on-site investigation adding to the layers of emotional scar tissue, until he and Betty went fishing in the Blue Ridge Mountains of northern Georgia.

The trip was cut short by an unanticipated front of embedded thundershowers that overnight turned their campsite into a bleak, Stygian place, cold and unwelcoming. They awoke and struck camp in misery, piling the soggy mess into the station wagon with little attention to neatness and heading down the steep, winding mountain road.

It hadn't rained in the area in ten months, which made the storm all the more surprising, but right then the primary significance of the first rain after such a drought was its effect on the road. Grease and oil from the undersides of vehicles had accumulated on the asphalt road bed and lain unmolested for nearly a year, building up in minuscule layers and posing little threat while pressed into the rough surface.

But as soon as the first drops of water fell, they began to find the microscopic fissures and depressions of the roadbed. Being heavier than oil, the water naturally insinuated itself beneath the grimy layers and forced the hydrocarbons upward to the surface, where they soon reliquefied, pooled and merged with other pools to form a slick lubricant on the road. Drivers in the cyclically arid Southwest were acutely aware of this phenomenon and treated the first seasonal rains with great respect, but it was new to the Blue Ridge.

Jack drove cautiously. You didn't need to tell an aircraft carrier veteran what rain did to a grease-stained surface. He was surprised when a dark green, early-model Corvette shot past them at a rate of speed that would have been questionable even in dry conditions. Betty leaned forward and looked past Jack to catch a glimpse of the cocky driver, barely out of his teens, if even that. Jack kept his eyes focused on the road as he squeezed to the right to give the idiot as much room as he wanted.

The Corvette disappeared around a bend.

"Hope that jerk knows there's a hairpin up ahead," Jack muttered even as the trees reflected the Corvette's suddenly lighted brake lights.

The boy had reacted like an amateur, locking the wheels and thus ensuring that they would lose their already tenuous grip and float on a thin layer of road grease. The back end of the car fishtailed wildly, and he struggled to steer back to a straight line, but the sharply angled wheels further ensured that no traction could be recaptured. The car careened sideways at a high rate of speed and hit the stone embankment, pushing the driver to the side and back, and then it ricocheted and spun back across the road, slamming into the mountain wall head on.

The young boy's head, which had been thrown back like the hammer of a cocked pistol, tried to maintain the forward momentum of the car it rode in even as that car was brought to an abrupt stop, and it shot forward with slingshot force into the steering wheel.

Jack's later-model car had antilock brakes, and he stomped the pedal to the floor, concentrating on his steering as the system pulsed the brake pads and brought the station wagon to a stop some fifty feet behind the crumpled—or, more correctly in the case of the fiberglass Corvette, shattered—sports car.

Jack threw his car into reverse and began backing up as fast as he could.

"What're you doing?" Betty yelled without taking her eyes off the wreck.

Looking at the rearview mirror, Jack said, "Going back to that straight section of road."

When they had rounded the bend, Jack maneuvered the car so that it lay across the road, blocking both lanes, headlights on and emergency flashers blinking, creating an obstacle that offered plenty of slack for drivers coming down the road to stop. Had he left the car farther down, nobody would have been able to see it in time.

He jumped out and ran to the back, opened the tailgate and fished around for a blanket and some tools.

"You stay here," he yelled to Betty. "First car comes along, send them down for an ambulance, then come and help me."

Betty nodded and got out of the car as Jack ran back down the road. A pickup truck appeared almost immediately, and Betty flagged it down and repeated Jack's instructions. The driver nodded, then proceeded slowly until he was past the wreck, pausing to see the blood on the windshield and Jack as he came up to the driver's side of the Corvette.

Jack looked up and shouted to the driver, "He's unconscious. Get going!"

The driver waved his acknowledgment and took off.

By the time Betty reached the wrecked car, Jack had already smashed the window, as the door was too deformed to open. He felt for a pulse, which was fairly strong and steady, and ascertained that the driver was breathing without difficulty, but blood was flowing freely from a gash in his left arm where a piece of the metal window frame had pierced it.

Jack wrapped a rag around the arm above the wound, then twisted the ends around a screwdriver and turned it until it squeezed tightly and stanched the flow of blood. Betty came around the other side and opened the undamaged door. She reached for the boy's head, which was resting face first on the steering wheel.

"Don't move him!" Jack warned sternly. "His neck may be broken. Wipe the blood away from his nose, but gently."

Betty pulled a handkerchief out of her pants pockets and began dabbing at the blood where it was starting to congeal. The driver groaned.

Jack put his free hand on top of the boy's head and held it steady. "Take it easy, fella. Don't move."

An eye opened, full of fear and confusion. He shifted his head very slightly to escape Betty's ministrations, then seemed to realize what she was doing and kept still.

"Can you move your fingers?"

The boy clenched and unclenched his fists in response.

"Toes? Feet?"

Nothing.

"Can you move your feet at all? Give it a try."

Still no response. The boy worked his hands again, harder this time, as though the exaggerated movements might somehow compensate for the trouble he was having with his lower extremities. Jack saw his eyes shift to his legs, but there was no movement of any kind below, and he saw the boy's chest begin to heave and his shoulders tremble, and then his hands were flailing wildly at his thighs and Jack had to fight to keep his head still as the newly born paraplegic struggled in vain to feel something in the legs that now hung useless from his shattered spine. Tears dripped from his eyes, mingling with blood from his nose and splattering onto the steering wheel.

Through it all, Jack alternately loosened and tightened the tourniquet, making sure that sufficient blood coursed through the arm to prevent irreversible tissue damage, and he kept reminding the boy not to move. He knew for certain now that there was severe spinal damage and that one wrong move could further destroy vital pathways and rob the victim of even more capacity. Betty talked to him and tried to keep up a steady stream of idle conversation. His name, how old he was, where he lived . . .

They stayed that way until the ambulance arrived. Two paramedics eased themselves out—Betty was always surprised at how slowly emergency personnel seemed to work—and approached the car on the driver's side.

"Whatta we got?" asked one.

"One occupant," said Jack, "nineteen-year-old male. He's conscious, pulse seventy-five, breathing freely, good color. Seems to have lost sensation in his legs."

The paramedic took note of the makeshift tourniquet, the blanket, and Jack's hand restraining the driver in position, and he nodded his approval. "Okay, we'll take it from here."

Jack eased his hand back as the paramedic took over.

"Gotta take off now, son," Jack said. "You take care now, y'hear?"

The boy turned his eyes toward Jack as best he could. He was in too much shock to offer verbal thanks, but Jack read both his fright and his gratitude, and there was something else in there that was more difficult to articulate.

It was the acknowledgment of a shared intimacy, that Jack had been there at the moment his life had changed, profoundly and forever. The stranger had held his head while the life had drained out of his once strong legs, had ministered to his wounded arm and stood by at the very beginning of his new existence as a wheelchair-bound cripple, for which he would eventually find many euphemisms but none of which could comfort him now. *A cripple.* The central fact of his life from now on. And this stranger had shared its genesis, maybe even saved what little was left of him. Maybe he would wonder at times if the stranger had done him a favor or a disservice, but for right now, right here, it flickered between them, and his eyes conveyed all this to Jack. Or tried to.

"Say, what's his name?" the paramedic called out as Jack and Betty headed back toward their car.

Jack stopped and turned. "I dunno." It seemed to surprise him that he didn't know.

"It's Hank," Betty called back. "Lives over near Allatoona Lake."

They pulled up to a motel, registered and parked the car in front of the door to their room.

"Well," Jack said as he turned off the ignition, "guess we did our good deed for the day. Hungry?"

Betty stared disconsolately through the rain-splattered window but forced herself around to face Jack. "Yeah, I guess."

"Let's get this stuff inside and spread out to dry, go find some greasy spoon."

As he rummaged around through the tailgate, Betty leaned against the doorpost and said, "I guess we did that boy some good, didn't we?"

"Hell, yeah, I'd say so," Jack answered without stopping what he was doing or looking up.

"You were so . . ." She seemed to fish for the right word.

Jack smiled to himself. Masterful? Heroic?

"Efficient," she said finally.

Jack's hands froze, and the smile vanished from his face. Something stabbed at him, a forgotten memory, maybe several. By the time he leaned back and stood up slowly, Betty already had the room door open and was stepping inside.

Jack stood still for a few moments and stared after her, mindless of the rain that fell on his uncovered head.

They ate a light supper, saying little of consequence, toying with the idea of maybe calling the local hospital to see how the boy ("His name is Hank, Jack") was making out, but dropping it by tacit agreement once they had left.

Perfunctory conversation continued while they got ready for bed, they kissed good night and turned out the lights, and shortly thereafter Betty fell asleep.

Jack lay on his back and stared at the ceiling. The thunder-showers had stabilized into a steady rain that tapped softly on the roof of the one-story motel. Larger drops collecting and falling from the gutters and railings made gentle splashing noises at irregular intervals. Once in a while the room lit up from car headlights pointed directly at the thin shades as other guests drifted into the parking area and maneuvered into the closely spaced spots.

He couldn't shake the boy's face out of his mind. One minute he was just a brash and cocky kid, stupid but without malice, barreling his way joyfully down a rain-slicked mountain road, showing off, as was his proper birthright. Now he lay in a hospital bed somewhere, cowed and disbelieving, probably as frightened of his parents' reaction as of his dire condition. Maybe he had a girlfriend. Maybe he'd just spent the night with her, making the kind of mindless, frantic, teen-age love that he would have looked back on nostalgically in his later years, not realizing that it was the last time he was ever to taste those pleasures.

That wasn't what was bothering Jack. What bothered him was that it wasn't bothering him.

Efficient.

He had held the head of a guileless youth—his name was Hank—while all that the kid cherished was streaming out of him and disappearing into the mists by the side of the road. He watched him weep in newly mature understanding at the distortion and collapse of his own personal cosmology, while he—Jack Webster, hero, as tomorrow's local paper would be sure to pronounce him—tightened and loosened the tourni-quet, periodically checked his pulse and made sure he didn't move. All proper, all correct, all ... *efficient.*

Jack conjured up Hank's eyes, the pupils dilated with terror behind the brimming tears. When he'd had enough, he blinked to make them go away, but they were still there, large and wanting as they begged Jack, the closest human being, to make it otherwise, to help him deny the inevitability of his situation. But Hank had found only neutral competence in Jack's face, and he had wanted to turn to Betty's soft voice and find his solace there but Jack wouldn't let him because it might cause further damage and that was correct and proper but Hank couldn't tell that at the time and so he kept looking at Jack, hoping to crack through and find Jack's soul but he never did.

Jack felt his heart speed up and his breathing deepen.

He knew what he had to do.

He stared into Hank's eyes, replaying the scene over and over, willing it into the distance with each showing, waiting for the gauze to appear between the two of them and to thicken into the blessed opacity that would signal his release.

But the kid wouldn't let go. His pupils widened even more and became pools, black holes of escalating gravitation that exerted an unmistakable tug on Jack, slight at first and then more insistent, and Jack struggled mightily but the more he strained against the pull the more Hank's eyes compelled him and his breathing became labored with the effort of it, and then he started to panic and he could feel his mind slipping, like the car on the wet, greasy road and he was sliding down toward the black pools and he knew he had to summon up every last scrap of psychic energy to escape. . . .

And then he did the bravest thing he had ever done in his life, a life already full of brave and heroic moments: he let go. Abandoned himself completely into the hellish maw of Hank's eyes.

His capacity to distinguish between himself and the bloodied youth vanished in an instant. Their neuronal intertwining was as enmeshed and irreversible as whiskey diffusing through a glass of soda, and Jack was crushed beneath the full weight of Hank's pain and fear. The force of it exploded in his chest and rocked him violently, and some small piece of him wondered if he hadn't brought the very structural supports of the cheap motel room down around their heads.

From the locked and sentried vaults of his tortured subconscious other visions seeped out and joined the fray, apocalyptic phantasms of twisted and bleeding bodies, ill and dying friends and relatives, a twelve-year-old niece who had lost her first junior high school love, all the damned and hurting people who had presented him with their suffering and agony and had received proper and correctly solicitous sympathy but little of substance, little of aching empathy, little of Jack Webster.

And then carrier pilot Brian Slattery hove into view, his handsome face bravely composed as he hurtled toward the depths that awaited him, and the keening began far back in Jack's throat, distant and restrained at first, but building swiftly as the images assaulted him without mercy. A light came on somewhere, a real one, and his frightened wife shook him, but he was too far gone and too immersed to respond to her. She might have panicked, might have called for help, but that good woman listened to his babbling and tried to make sense of it, and a vestigial instinct long dormant not only in her but in her species told her what to do, and she held him close and rocked him while the demons tore at him from the inside.

It went on most of the night, Betty arising periodically to moisten a towel for his forehead, until even the fearsome power of his pent-up nightmares succumbed to the dissipation of his physical energy and sleep took him in its infinite mercy.

It was near noon before he awoke, blinking and startled, his eyes rimmed with red. The rain had stopped earlier in the morning, and a determined sun broke through the clouds, suffusing the room with a calming orange glow.

He remembered everything right away and gasped, steeling himself for another onslaught; but it didn't come. While he knew who he was once again and was able to think, the profusion of memories raced at a furious pace, and he knew it was useless to try to sort them out.

Betty sat cross-legged on the bed beside him, consternation creasing her normally smooth features. "You okay?"

He looked at her, and tears sprang to his eyes before he could stop them. He reached for her and pulled her down and held her so tightly that she could barely breathe, but she hugged him back anyway and didn't let go until he did, and when he looked at her he could tell that she had been crying too.

She got up and made some instant coffee with the little kit that passed for room service in cheap motels, using less water than the instructions called for. Jack marveled to himself at the taste. It was the Bordeaux of coffees (it was the most cut-rate mud the proprietor could find), the most arresting nectar that ever crossed his lips and caressed his tongue.

The burned bacon, runny eggs and soggy toast in the coffee shop were equally sublime (Betty could hardly stand more than a few bites of the gloppy mess), and he wondered how this culinary palace had stayed hidden for so long.

They stayed there two more days, walking in the nearby woods, picnicking along small streams, dropping a line or two in a tiny pond a few miles back up the road and tossing back the flashing sunfish.

Jack talked, incessantly, ostensibly to Betty but really to himself. He talked about people he had known, people who had suffered pain both physical and psychological or who were troubled by vaporous presences they couldn't understand. Some were civilian acquaintances, some were relatives, many were service colleagues. Some had died and were beyond his ability to ever go back and comfort, and he cried unabashedly at the thought; but others were alive, and he noted them all in his memory as he plotted the balance of his redemption.

Betty listened, she paid attention. She made no attempt to assuage his discomfort. Nor his guilt, which tangibly receded in the telling and was gradually replaced by a purer sorrow where it made sense or by accepting resignation where that was appropriate.

At night they made love, often and slowly, and felt transported as much spiritually as physically and rediscovered, or maybe learned for the first time, what it meant to live in each other's mind.

By the end of their last day Jack was drained and spent, and they returned to the motel from a hike where they had watched the sun go down from the top of a small hillock. A car they had not seen before was parked by the office, and the day manager waved them over as they passed by. Sitting on a fraying, nylon-webbed chair was Hank, his legs flung forward at an odd angle. He looked up as Jack and Betty stopped several feet away.

Upon recognizing them, he smiled and reached for a cane

propped against the wall next to the chair, stood awkwardly and took a few wobbly steps forward.

In his shock and amazement, Jack stared stupidly at Hank's legs. Betty let a small squeak escape before her hands flew to her mouth.

Hank stopped and his smile vanished. "What'sa matter?"

Jack couldn't speak, and Betty answered, "You're walking!"

Hank looked down and then back up. "Don't worry. Doc said it was okay long as I don't overdo it."

Jack found his voice and said, "But—we thought you couldn't, Walk, I mean. We thought—"

Hank regained his smile and laughed. "Yeah, I thought so, too. Couldn't feel a damned thing. Scarier'n hell, y'know? Musta just been the shock." He shook his head at the memory and then forgot about it. "I, uh, wanted to see you both, to say, you know . . .".

Jack looked up at Hank's face and met his eyes, held them and saw the gratitude and his own relief reflected there. Hank seemed to understand the effect the misperception must have had on Jack, and it concerned him. Jack searched for words to allay the boy's consternation but quickly realized that they were not needed.

"We're very glad you're all right, Hank," said Betty.

"Doc said, you hadn't held me still, I mighta been a real mess. Little fragment in my spine, or somethin' like that. They got it out okay." He paused for a moment. "Guess you know I'm thankful to you guys."

Jack waved a hand. "No big deal."

Hank swiped at a stray lock of hair. "So, what're you doin' hangin' around this burg?"

Jack looked at Betty. "Just killing a little time before going back to work."

She squeezed his hand and smiled at him.

Hank nodded with an awkward shyness that now substituted for some of the cockiness that had been knocked out of him. "Well, gotta run." He tried another step and smiled in self-deprecating embarrassment at the stiffness in his legs and the careless bravado that had caused it. "Y'all take care, huh?"

"You too, Hank," said Jack. "You gave us a bit of a scare, there."

"Sorry. All okay now, right?"

He hobbled away and was gone.

A week later, at the gentle urging of his wife, Jack discreetly solicited the name of someone who could help him sort out the final pieces, maybe someone who'd dealt with people with a similar history, someone who could relate directly to his experience. Two days later he was on a plane to spend three excruciating weeks in the company of one Amy Goldberg, Ph.D., late of the Central Intelligence Agency's officially non-existent psy-ops division.

Several days after his return, a Royal Oceanic passenger jet lost an outboard aileron on approach to the Dallas–Ft. Worth airport and slammed into the freeway in a hail of disintegrating metal. Later that same morning, Jack Webster resigned from the NTSB and accepted an offer from the FBI to join a special investigations unit, an offer he had been actively soliciting since the day after his and Betty's return from Georgia.

Some time after that (a few weeks after meeting Florence Hartzig, to be completely accurate), as an unforeseen and misguided consequence of his own odyssey of self-exploration, he had gone to Betty and asked her why she hadn't opened a pottery shop or run for city council or gone to law school (or been more like Florence Hartzig, he wanted to know but didn't ask) or any of the hundred other standard things you were supposed to want to do to avoid the worse-than-death fate of being labeled a housewife, as embarrassing an example of modern womanhood as you could possibly be except for a *military* housewife, which, by the way, she also was.

And Betty had thought about that for a full minute, actually thought about it for less than a second, the other fifty-nine being taken up with trying to control the anger that tore through her nervous system and tried to goad her into strangling the monumental clod standing before her. Straining to keep her voice even so as not to compromise the clarity of her answer, she told him that not everybody was cut out to save the world, not everybody's destiny involved the undertaking of what were traditionally and unthinkingly held to be "important" activities, not everybody suffered an egotistical compulsion to spend the majority of their time proving something to the world so that people—people they didn't even *know*, for Chrissakes—would think better of them. For some, for the very few, fulfillment came in the form of perfectly complementing only one other human being, nurturing several more into the world so that they hit it fully prepared, and achieving that special state of grace that came with knowing that you may not have won a war, or commanded a goddamned hundred-thousand-ton hunk of floating nuclear death, or discovered a cure for cancer or written the Great American Novel, but, dammit, you made your own small corner of the world brighter than you found it, sacrificed many of your own simple pleasures without complaint, cried yourself to sleep at night every single time your husband went up to fly a fighter plane built by the lowest bidder, and never voiced a single note to complicate his life, which was a damned sight better than most people could say, you flaming, fucking, ungrateful sonofabitch.

It hadn't gone well, in other words.

It never did when he behaved like a flaming, fucking, ungrateful sonofabitch.

He'd never loved her more than at that very moment.

He left the last part of the story out.

Florence was too mesmerized to speak and too afraid to break the spell cast by Jack's account of events in his past. The freshly poured wine sat untouched.

Jack swirled up from his reverie and reached for his glass, and only then did Florence do the same.

"Jack!"

Glasses poised at their lips, they turned toward the shrill cry to see Stanley waving from the doorway as he made his way to their table, then turned back toward each other as they set their glasses back down.

"Anyway, that's about it."

Florence stayed silent, resenting Stanley's intrusion.

Jack turned toward the entrance of the restaurant. "Wonder what he wants."

"Better be damned good," Florence muttered as Stanley reached the table, out of breath.

"Sorry, guys. Jack, you gotta come back to the office."

The two of them knew better than to ask any questions. Jack looked up toward the waiter and raised his hands in an apologetic gesture. "Can we at least take the bottle?"

"Nope. Our license is for on-premises consumption only."

"Right away, Preston?" Jack asked hopefully.

"Definitely."

"Fine. You pay the check and we'll meet you back there."

Both of them were gone in a flash, leaving the befuddled agent to settle up with the waiter.

They reentered the NTSB building and made their way to Conference Room B, where a grim-faced Amy Goldberg sat and entered keyboard commands to retrieve a printout from the terminal. She turned to Jack and Florence as they entered the room, too distracted even to throw him a rebuking look.

"Bad news. Somebody's collecting money in Florida."

Jack shrugged. "So he moved. What's the problem?"

"The problem," Amy said, straightening up from the table and holding the end of the paper as it emerged from the printer, "is that they're still collecting from the Midwest as well."

Jack stopped in his tracks. "You're shitting me."

"I shit you not." Amy tore off the sheet and handed it to him, looking as stunned as he'd ever seen her.

Jack was still staring at her as Stanley entered the room. Jack quickly filled him in, then said, "What's it mean, Amy? What the hell is going on?"

Amy turned to the monitor and looked at it. A small tremor was visible along her back. She leaned against the counter to steady herself. Stanley opened his mouth to speak, but Jack cut him off with a hand wave. The FBI agent backed off, suppressing a smile, a little ashamed that his first thought on hearing the news was to gloat. He resolved to be as gentlemanly as he could, seeing from Amy's cowed posture that his point was well enough made without his needing to rub it in.

"It makes no sense!" Amy hit the table once with her fist.

"Dammit!" She was talking to herself, needing no help from Stanley to berate herself.

"Okay, look," said Jack. "We need to rethink here. Integrate this into our assumptions." Amy didn't move, didn't seem to have heard him. "C'mon, Goldberg."

She stayed quiet a moment longer, then straightened slowly and turned, sat back against the edge of the table and folded her arms across her chest. Stanley misread it as defensive body language and found himself even less interested in her interpretations than he had been before.

"So what now, Doc?" he asked, trying not to sound snide as he verbally underlined her title with a note of derision.

"Maybe not anything," she said.

"I'm not in the mood for riddles," said Stanley, bristling.

Amy turned to look in his direction, but her gaze was someplace past him. "Something is very wrong. All my thinking, all my assumptions . . ." She put the tips of the fingers of one hand together and pulled them apart quickly, realizing too late how that gesture exposed her misery. She put her hands in her back pockets and focused on Stanley, seeing in his face how he all too rapidly began to discard everything she had ever conjectured about their quarry. She knew without a doubt that unless she intervened somehow, he would issue an unconditional arrest order on the next ATM payoff.

She tried to reinject some confidence in her voice. "Sometimes, not often but sometimes, it's necessary to ignore evidence. It may be false, misleading. Makes us give up a good theory, a right theory. Maybe fate, well, maybe it's playing a trick." She winced inwardly as she saw that statement fail to have its intended effect on Stanley.

"Fate?" the agent exploded, slapping the back of his hand on the printout sheets, his contrition of the day before already forgotten. "Fate, my ass! How the hell you call somebody with the right card, the right code, fishing dough out of cash machines using the right procedures—how the hell is that fate?"

Amy shrugged and looked suddenly sad. "Maybe not the best choice of words."

"What do we do now?" Florence asked.

"I need to think about this," said Amy, rousing herself to

her former posture of assertive expertise. "His pattern has been too tight, too well defined for us to shit-can everything and abandon our approach without some more thought." She dared Stanley with her eyes.

Already annoyed with himself for losing his temper and not yet in possession of a better plan with which to argue with Amy, Stanley glanced down at the brown paper bag he forgot he had been holding. He set it on the table and carefully drew out the recorked bottle of Lynch-Bages, holding it up with one hand on the bottom and a single fingertip at the top, much like a sophisticated *sommelier*.

"Now, how the hell'd you do that?" asked Jack, a surprised and delighted look on his face.

"Little green friend of mine named Abe Lincoln," Stanley answered, rubbing the tips of his fingers together in the age-old gesture of the greased palm.

Amy saw no need to be angry with him. She had to buy some time. She tried not to dwell on the fact that her analysis may have been dangerously misguided and thrown the entire investigation off track. "Now come the answers to all questions," she said as she gathered some Styrofoam cups from the coffee counter. Her best move was to accept Stanley's implicit temporary truce and be a good sport about it.

Florence closed the door as Stanley poured and said as she lifted her cup, *"In vino veritas."*

"What's that mean?" Jack asked.

"In wine there is truth," answered Stanley as he sipped, his irritation with Amy momentarily forgotten.

"Delicious." Jack smacked his lips lightly, then set down his cup. "I think we ought to try to establish some direct communication."

"Agreed," Amy said without hesitation.

"You mean with Marvel?" Stanley said. "Talk to him directly? How do we do that?"

"It's easy." Jack took another sip and rolled the wine around in his mouth. "Pump out a message telling him to call. We can actually just use the second line on the terminal table. Nobody outside knows that one yet, so nobody could fake a call."

"What makes you think he'll do it?" asked Stanley.

"Who the hell knows? Worth a try, though, isn't it?"

"Only to the Midwest," said Amy. "The message."

Stanley looked up from his cup but tried to stay calm. "What about Florida?"

"Forget Florida."

Florence saw the detonation welling up from somewhere in the agent and sought to ward it off as quickly as she could. "What do we say to him? Who does the talking?"

"Why, our own Mr. Webster," said Amy, turning to Jack. "You have experience chatting up hijackers, don't you?"

"Sure, but that's a little different, isn't it?"

"No," Amy said simply.

The excitement level began to rise in the room, as it always did upon the creation of something to do in place of waiting. The ensuing conversation had an air of inevitability about it, as the team headed toward the realization that they would have to take a chance, and maybe more than one, in precipitating a confrontation of some kind. Right now Captain Marvel was proving to be an unusually capable adversary, and there was every expectation that standard police work would ultimately prove ineffective. He had thought it all out and had all the bases covered.

"What if we piss him off?" asked Stanley, nervously peeling the Styrofoam rim off his cup. "What if he gets mad and starts going after planes again?"

As the discussion swirled around him, Jack thought back to the 1976 Winter Olympics in Innsbruck. Franz Klammer in the downhill, almost literally falling down the mountain in a frightening display of out-of-control skiing, hovering on the edge of a potentially disastrous fall every second of the trip.

"This cat-and-mouse bullshit, it's time to give it up," said Amy. "We need to escalate up from the fun and the games, start to get serious."

When Klammer reached the bottom safely, in a time that it was clear nobody could possibly better, a TV newscaster asked him to comment on his performance:

"To win," he said, still shaking from his only fright, *"you must risk losing."*

"Let's do it," said Jack. "What should the message be?"

"Something intimate," said Amy. "Maybe not exactly intimate, but something that hints we know about him, as a person. Or that we know something of his method."

"But do we?" asked Florence. "What if we're wrong?"

Stanley paced in front of the window, then stopped. "We gotta get clever, folks. It has to be something a little ambiguous, so if we're wrong, there's a possible second meaning. Otherwise he's gonna know we're bluffing."

"Let's let him know we know he flies a plane," said Florence, turning to Jack. "You said before he might suspect we know. Let's tell him outright that we know something about both him and how he's doing it."

"Not outright," Stanley insisted. "In case we're wrong." He turned to Amy, expecting a rebuke but not getting one.

She stood quietly, lost in thought, tapping a finger against her cheek.

1646 EST

So you've slipped the surly bonds
of earth?

Call 202-555-1825 and ask for Jack.

CHAPTER 23

October 1972

They finally found it on the third day of searching, as winter's advance team hissed frigid air in an early intimation of the coming cold. Each night, the humidity hanging in and about the trees surrendered to the dropping temperature and settled as crystals on the pine needles, only to recede and vanish by midmorning under the sun's breath.

They had no doubts that it was there somewhere. The report from the father-and-son hunters had been corroborated to their satisfaction by a pair of hikers and was consistent with the story told by older inhabitants of the town below. The altitude and relative inaccessibility of the area would have made inadvertent discovery unlikely, even if the Bureau of Land Management hadn't declared the site off limits. The lifting of the ban had attracted a few hardy souls who wished to tread on virgin territory before "they" got hold of it and ruined it, whoever "they" might be.

Joe Cutter saw it first and pointed without saying a word or making a sound, as though to avoid scaring it off. Bo Kincaid and one of Cutter's restorers, Kurt Bakal, came up behind him and stopped, looking at the spot where he pointed.

It lay at the feet of two Douglas firs, under a blanket of

pine needles, moss and various kinds of leaves, the detritus of the forest's life, which had continued around it for some forty years following the violent intrusion. It was distinguishable by a tail section that rose vertically from the forest floor and the bulge of a canopy now covered with lichens and mud. When they held their heads at just the right angle and used some imagination, it seemed that the rotting organic material around these two features also outlined a pair of wings.

"Let's have a look," said Cutter.

Most of their restoration work came from others, people who had themselves scouted likely locations or heard rumors and pursued them. The sources were endless. One customer had found a wingless, gutted T-38 Talon supersonic trainer sitting on the ground as a jungle gym in a children's playground in South America. Its airframe was still intact, and he'd bought it, shipped it to Cutter's and had it back in flying condition after two years and an enormous amount of money.

Incidents like this didn't sit well with the U.S. Air Force, which was ill disposed to its discarded aircraft falling into the hands of civilians, for reasons never made terribly clear. The air force maintained official aircraft graveyards scattered around the country, mostly in deserts away from the corrosive effects of humidity. Some planes were kept intact, for possible sale to Third World nations as trainers or active combat planes. A very few were retained as possible museum pieces.

But the rest—Cutter didn't like to think about that. The air force had a huge crane and a seven-ton slab of metal shaped like an ax head with a sharp blade. For the planes they no longer had a use for, they would haul the monstrous iron knife high into the air, poised above the midsection of the plane, and then release it to free-fall and smash into the aircraft, effectively breaking its back and tying it forever to the apron strings of Mother Earth. They would rather destroy it than have it fall into the seditious hands of some crazed aviation enthusiast.

But there wasn't a damned thing they could do when you found one broken and forgotten in the wild.

"Can you tell what it is?" asked Bakal.

Joe shook his head. "I can't."

"Single-seater, by the size of the canopy." Bo walked wide

around it, unwilling yet to risk stepping on something vital. "Tail's broken, with a lot of crap hanging off it."

They completed a full circle, then started slowly for the plane, probing the ground with their walking sticks and only stepping where they got a soft response. They approached from the right rear quarter, the place least likely to harbor any protruding pieces.

Bakal reached it first and began carefully lifting pine needles off the canopy. Bo swiped at the mud-encrusted fuselage. For now, the extent of the plane's structural damage was as important as its identity. If the frame was broken or bent too severely, the best they could get was a display model to grace some underfunded museum, in which case they would simply take a few pictures and leave the craft unmolested. It wouldn't be worth the money to salvage it.

Bakal reached a hand under the muck topping the rear fuselage and ran it backward, feeling for surface features and protrusions. Bo did the same on the underside and was surprised to feel the shape of the body suddenly narrow as his hand slid back toward the tail. He looked up at Bakal, whose hand had been brought to a stop by what might have been an antenna mount.

Bakal was a recent graduate of the Smithsonian's restoration facility in Silver Springs, Maryland. Only in his mid-twenties, he was such a hard-core fanatic of antique and vintage airplanes that his encyclopedic knowledge was already well-known in aviation circles. The protrusion he had just discovered triggered a look-up somewhere in his mental index. He looked down at Bo.

"What?"

"Feels like an air scoop underneath. Ends right about here. What've you got?"

"Antenna mount. Right where the scoop ends."

They looked at each other, neither willing to voice his thoughts. Bo turned to the nose of the plane, where Cutter had worked his way by stepping gingerly around the hidden wings.

"Hey, Joe. Stick your hand in there—no, about a foot back—what've you got?"

Cutter scraped away some leaves plastered together in the

melting ice and felt around as best he could. "Feels like an exhaust pipe. Couple of 'em. Could be just busted plumbing, though."

"How many?" asked Bakal.

"Hang on."

Cutter withdrew his hand and worked on the leaves and muck, clearing away a larger space. After a few minutes, the years of accumulated gunk began falling away in larger slabs, and Cutter was able to clear a large section of the forward fuselage.

"Looks like six. Gotta be exhaust. Very symmetrical, all facing aft."

Bakal and Bo looked at each other for only a second more before they stepped to the tail section and began scraping away at the organic covering. The vertical stabilizer was cracked and bent, but the trim tab was clearly visible on the rudder, as was a trapezoidal access cover on the stabilizer itself. Soon the original shape and form of the tail section was visible, and the two of them stepped back.

"Well, I'll be dipped in shit," said Bakal.

Cutter had cleared away more of the nose, exposing the large, bullet-shaped propeller hub. He looked back to where Bo and Bakal were standing and stared at the exposed tail, then turned back to the six in-line exhaust pipes.

"It's a Mustang," he barely whispered to no one in particular. "An honest-to-God, no shit Mustang."

Bo didn't speak but came toward the canopy. He cleared away the needles and fungus from the rear area, revealing that the canopy had been pulled back and was broken off its tracks. The pilot had wisely cranked it open before submerging below the treetops of the forest and was able to haul himself out of the plane and eventually down the mountain.

"It's a D," he said, based on the shape of the canopy, which was of a single-piece design and elongated toward the rear.

Further effort through the long morning revealed that the basic airframe structure was intact. One wing had largely torn from its mount, probably snagged by a treetop or a thick branch on its way in. That would have slowed the plane and lessened the eventual impact with the ground. It appeared that the landing gear remained retracted, another wise move by the pilot, and it meant that the underside stood a good chance of going relatively undamaged. Two blades of the four-bladed prop were found nearby, torn from their mounts, while a third hung straight down from the bottom of the hub. The fourth likely had spun off and been flung as much as a mile away.

There was no question that it could be restored.

Cutter eyed the dense surrounding forest beneath the towering trees. "But how the hell do we get it out of here?"

They were in central Colorado, close to the Roaring Fork River where it passed the western edge of the Maroon Bells, forbidding peaks devoid of roads. Six more weeks and the snows would have deposited enough on the slopes in the nearby resorts of Aspen and Snowmass to start the ski season and to render impossible any salvage of the plane this year.

As Cutter and Bo looked around them, Bakal looked up. "We gotta fly it out."

They all looked up to try to visualize a vertical path out, as Bakal spoke. "We gotta knock down these two trees and get a chopper in here. The wings'll have to come off. That's easy. One's practically off already, and the other can be disassembled."

He turned his attention back to the plane. "We sling it— here and here." He indicated the fuselage sections fore and aft of the wing spar. "Should balance perfectly. Haul it down to town and truck it out. Shouldn't take but two hours of chopper time altogether."

At five hundred bucks per, thought Cutter. *Not to mention what we'd have to do to it once we got it home*. He ran an expert eye over the plane from a distance of several paces and shook his head. "It's practically a rebuild, boys."

Bo hadn't said much since their discovery of the plane's identity. It had never occurred to him that there was a decision to be made, but now he knew that Cutter was in the process of formulating one, and he had a moment of disorientation.

The plane sat in squalor, with little visible evidence of what adventures it might once have known. No doubt that the military had known the location of the accident, but back then there was little unique about the plane. After all, many thousands had been built, and it was as ubiquitous as the Piper Cub. There was not even a thought of climbing the Maroon

Bells for something as ridiculous as salvaging a Mustang. The cost of the operation would likely have exceeded the value of the plane.

But now things were different. Among aviation enthusiasts, the P-51 was as prized as a Fabergé or a Stradivarius or a van Gogh. It was the greatest piston-powered fighter ever built, and the plain, simple fact of it was they weren't making any more.

And now one sat before them, repairable and theirs for the taking, albeit at an alarmingly high eventual cost, one that Cutter seemed unwilling to suffer.

"Joe?"

"Let me guess."

As Bo stared at the plane, he knew that he had to have it, and that the means by which he could do so had to be found. It was a question not of a decision, but of a method.

He knew that most of the expense involved in restoring an airplane related to labor. Parts and materials were surprisingly plentiful, and custom fabrication when parts were not available was largely a matter of professional time and not materials.

After his years with Cutter, Bo had picked up a great number of skills. He could reshape metal, rewire electrical systems, reconstruct structural members and even work lathes and milling machines when necessary. He was still a little green on paint and other surface finishes and only marginally competent in power plants.

"I got some saved up, Joe. Enough for a chopper and a truck haul, enough for some parts and other stuff."

"What about labor?"

"I'm the labor."

"It'll take you forever."

"I got forever, too, Joe." *A forever of nights and weekends and holidays and sick days, and for whenever else you turn your back for a couple hours and don't pay too much attention to exactly what I do when business is slow.* "What I need is some hangar space, spare time on the machines, bugging rights on the guys."

"You don't know engines, Kincaid."

"I do," said Bakal, forgotten during the interchange as he cleared off the cowling stays and struggled to raise the metal panel. "I know engines real good." He could practically feel the giant Merlin thrumming beneath his hands, pouring power down an iron shaft to the massive propeller and blasting the lithe aircraft through the air at over four hundred miles per hour. "I got forever, too, Bo."

It took more than a few hours. It took the entire winter and had nothing to do with the physical burdens of removing the plane from the hostile environment. Recovering the Mustang and restoring it looked to be a piece of cake compared with the burden of dealing with the entrenched bureaucracy.

First they had to obtain a removal permit. While there were no legal prohibitions attendant to moving the plane, a permit was nonetheless required.

"Think of it like a visa to visit Yugoslavia," the federal BLM representative had said. "The point is not that it's difficult to get. Hell, it's yours for the asking. So why is one required? you ask. Simple. So it can be denied to you if there's a reason. See?"

Then they needed another permit to chop down the two fir trees. This was much tougher and was vigorously opposed by an environmental activist group that could not see the benefit of destroying two perfectly healthy trees in order to save an airplane. They could also not see the trees, which were invisible from anywhere but the forest itself, which had been visited by a total of eight human beings in the last forty years, one of whom was the unknown pilot of the Mustang.

This problem was solved when it was discovered by a concerned citizen and former pilot that the chairman of the environmental group was planning to destroy six also perfectly healthy aspen trees in his backyard in order to improve the view of his beloved mountainside forest. A quid pro quo of sorts was reached when both Cutter Aviation and the chairman agreed to plant a stand of twenty Ponderosa pines surrounding an abandoned mining camp near the outskirts of town.

Permits were also required to overfly Pitkin County with a helicopter, owing to noise restrictions meant to preserve the peace and tranquillity of the valley township. Waivers on restrictions on interstate travel were needed because the wrecked airplane was still legally classified as military hardware. Furthermore, an inspection was required to ascertain that no live ammunition was present on the plane, despite the fact that it had been lost on a peacetime training mission, as official records had disclosed following discovery of the plane's tail numbers.

By the time everything was quite in order, the P-51 was thoroughly buried under five feet of snow, and even if Cutter and Bo had decided to dig it out and proceed, they couldn't because all helicopter traffic in the valley was now prohibited in order to prevent the triggering of avalanches.

But by May it was safely in the hangar at Santa Paula. It would be six years before Bo Kincaid flew it into the clear mountain air one chilly morning.

It had been more than an avocation with him, it had been an obsession. He had felt at various times like Michelangelo, Henry Ford, and Orville Wright. Mostly he felt like Dr. Frankenstein, robbing graves for a piston or a seat back or a rudder pedal.

But after the first two years the Mustang began to feel less like a random assemblage of scavenged parts and more like its unique self. The airframe and the engine (most of it, anyway) were original to this aircraft, as were most of the wings. Other key components, such as the propeller, ignition system and ailerons, were at least original to the breed, if not this particular plane. Only a few pieces had to be made from scratch.

Bo's attention to detail and authenticity bordered on the compulsive. He had ordered Kurt Bakal to dismantle the engine and replace a crankshaft following the young man's reluctant revelation that the part had come from a B rather than a D model. The refit had taken over a month.

Bo himself had stripped three brand-new paint jobs off the skin because they didn't look right.

"Jesus Christ A'mighty, Kincaid!" Cutter had bellowed in exasperation. "It's the same specification, the same weight, the same goddamned everything!"

But Bo had shaken his head calmly and proceeded with the harsh chemical wash to remove it. "Hell with the specs, Joe. I flew one, and it din't look like this."

Eventually they got it right. And they all had to admit on

the day they rolled it out into the sun, not even fresh from the factory had it looked this good.

There was not a wrinkle on the skin, so that the shiny fuselage looked like poured glass. Even the rubber wheels shone and reflected the sun, dappling the underside of the air scoop with watery smears of golden light.

The huge water-cooled engine kicked over on the first crank, without even the normal burst of sooty black exhaust. It settled quickly into a smooth, throaty rumble as the four giant propeller blades bit into the air and tried to drag the plane along, a thoroughbred overeager for the starter's bell.

They started with taxi tests, gradually increasing speed to near takeoff velocity. The Mustang was technically an experimental plane, uncertified for general aviation use and subject to a strict set of testing guidelines, beginning with taxiing.

The plane behaved so perfectly that Bo and his helpers had to guard against complacency as the days passed. Before long they had the necessary paperwork in place for the first flight.

A crowd had turned out to watch. Santa Paula was often referred to as the "airport of the stars," as it was the home of many antique and vintage aircraft owned by entertainment industry denizens from down the road in Los Angeles. A goodly number of these enthusiasts showed up to stare in wonder at the born-again Mustang.

They waited for a windless day. While a headwind was highly desirable for both takeoff and landing, Bo opted for no wind, to guard against a possible shift to a direction across the line of the runway, which was tricky under any circumstance but dangerous for a newly restored craft of untried handling characteristics.

He taxied to the very end of the runway and held short while he went through preflight and checked for other traffic in the vicinity, broadcasting in the clear to nobody in particular, warning of his impending takeoff.

Moving onto the runway, he turned smoothly on the left wheel by braking it until he was pointed down the centerline, the morning sun at his back. He eased the throttle forward slowly until the manifold pressure gauge rose to the maximum-permissible setting of forty inches, his confidence building as the rumbling engine rose in pitch to a constant roar. The airframe bucked and vibrated until he released the toe brakes, and then it leaped forward down the tarmac.

The slipstream swirling clockwise from the whirling prop corkscrewed down the length of the fuselage and slammed into the left side of the vertical fin, trying to turn the plane off its track. Bo applied pressure to the right rudder to counteract the effect, pushing the stick forward slightly to get the tailwheel off the ground and level the body out as the plane picked up speed. He was amazed at how quickly it was accelerating, and soon he was at rotation speed.

He eased the stick back until the nose pointed slightly upward, and then he waited patiently until the plane found its own moment to leave the ground. The sound level dropped a bit as the engine noise bouncing back up from the ground faded away, and soon he was climbing into the sky, unaware of the cheering back on the runway.

He tried some simple turn-and-banks, getting the feel of the controls before turning back toward the airport. He started his descent from two miles out and trimmed for 130 knots. One minute later, with no throttle adjustments and hardly any motion on the stick, he touched down lightly, ran it out for about a hundred yards and then pushed the throttle forward once again to retake the skies.

Forty minutes after that he landed for the third and final time and taxied the Mustang right up to the hangar door. Reluctantly he throttled back and pulled the manual choke, robbing the engine of air so that it sputtered and died.

Cutter and Bakal ran breathlessly toward him as he slid back the canopy and pulled off his leather helmet. Spectators on the other side of the runway waved, their smiles so wide that Bo could see them clearly. Soon a ladder appeared at his side with Bakal's excited face atop it.

"Oh, Bo!" was all Bakal could manage to blurt. "Oh Lord, oh Lord," and there were tears in his eyes and he didn't have any questions really, nor anything much to say, but the time seemed to call for some expression and so he tried but he couldn't get much of anything out.

Bo wasn't a lot of help, either, just kind of sitting there and grinning stupidly, looking back from Bakal to the instruments and back to Bakal again, until he wondered where Cutter was, and he stood up to peer over the side of the cockpit to see him sitting on the ground next to one of the landing struts, an arm wrapped around it, not doing much of anything except sitting there, just sitting and kind of . . .

Bo cocked his head to one side. Cutter was hugging the plane, was what he was doing. Not hugging, maybe, more like pals arm in arm enjoying each other's company.

The plane became a linchpin in their lives, the bond that held them together and provided meaning and significance. The question of ownership never came up, was never discussed, and even though the registration papers were in the name of Cutter Aviation, well, that was a convenience only.

They never stopped working on it, never stopped admiring it or talking about it. Bo flew it at air shows and gave the fees back to Cutter, who kept the money out of the general business fund and earmarked it for maintenance of the Mustang.

The plane was widely admired and featured in magazines as emblematic of the breed. There were many offers, some of them moderately exorbitant, but all were politely declined.

Even Lenore Kincaid, who had grudgingly indulged her husband's passion for the project despite more misgivings than she could count, had to admit that the fighter plane was a thing of unusual beauty, a perfect blending of form and function that could be admired as vehicle, weapon or even art. And even she admitted to herself, though not to anybody else, that seen in the right light, in the right position and in the right frame of mind, the P-51 seemed to possess a certain spark that transcended the fact of its genesis in aluminum and rubber and steel. To say that it was alive would be an overstatement. To say that it possessed a personality would not.

In any event, whatever it was, the group of friends who had breathed that essence into it were buoyed by their achievement, something most people would never experience in their lifetimes. It wasn't a possession. It was part of who they were. It defined them, even comforted them, just to know it was there.

CHAPTER 24

June 22, 1530 EST

"**H**ello? This is Jack."
Amy huddled close while Preston Stanley flicked on the speakerphone, keeping the volume low to avoid feedback.

"Like I said, my name's Jack. What's yours?"

Amy winced.

"I mean, what should I call you?"

The speaker stayed silent, and Stanley fiddled with the controls until he was satisfied that everything was working properly.

"Okay, I understand. No problem. I'll talk for a little while."

Amy nodded her approval and kept staring at the speaker.

"I'm glad you called. I'm hoping we can come to some kind of reasonable accommodation on this. Frankly, you have us over a barrel and—"

"Me!" Amy mouthed to Jack in exaggerated mime as she pointed to herself. "I!"

"—and I'm ready to talk about how to get this resolved."

Silence.

"It's not the money. That doesn't bother me all that much. Mostly I'm worried about more people getting hurt. I have a feeling you didn't really mean to kill those pilots, and we might be able to put that aside."

Silence.

Jack took a deep breath and gritted his teeth. Amy waved for him to continue.

"But what I need most of all, I need some assurance that you can't tamper with the system anymore. That's necessary right there. So why don't you tell me what you're thinking, what you want, and I promise I'll do everything I can to—"

Click.

"Hello?"

The door opened and Florence came in, pulling off a headset and motioning for Jack to replace the telephone.

"Line's dead. He hung up."

"Did we get a trace?"

She shook her head. "Only a partial. He knows what he's doing: hung up five seconds before the trace was complete. It came from midtown Minneapolis."

1830 EST

Secretary of Transportation Letitia May Hubbard's eyebrows arched above her inquisitive eyes as she sat up straighter and looked at Jack Webster. "Why just the senator and me?"

They were meeting in Conference Room B, Jack and his team, along with Florence Hartzig. He explained to the two officials that their investigation, despite the pending identification of the extortionist, was bogged down in trying to actually put an end to his activities, as well as those of any accomplices. If there were any.

"You both should know we've got some disagreement on the team concerning how many people are involved here," said Stanley.

"What kind of disagreement?" Fedder asked.

Stanley looked over at Amy. "May I?"

Amy nodded her assent, and the FBI agent explained, as evenhandedly as he could, the differences of opinion regarding the cash machines being hit in Florida.

Hubbard turned to Amy with a frown. "And you really

don't believe this is significant? How do the rest of you feel?" she asked before Amy could answer.

Jack and Florence looked around uncomfortably. They found it difficult to ignore compelling evidence, yet they also felt a strong affinity for the psychologist and a deep respect for her insights.

"I think," Jack began for them, "that we all feel ambivalent. Except for Agent Stanley, obviously. On the one hand, there can be no doubt these Florida hits are related to our guy. On the other, there might be some question as to its significance, and the degree to which we should let it interfere with progress."

He took a breath and forced himself to stop speaking, hoping nobody would notice how shallow an answer he'd given.

"Well, that's clear as a summer's day," said Hubbard. "Which scenario are we proceeding under?"

Amy sat up and put her elbows on the table. "I feel very strongly this guy is a loner. He isn't one to take people into his confidence. I don't understand how it's possible someone like this is part of a team."

She leaned back and didn't try to hide the self-doubt and confusion evident in her face and manner as she continued.

"Sure it's connected up somehow. A coincidence like that is impossible. But I'm wondering, maybe it's a mistake of some kind." She held up a hand quickly. "And what kind, I'm far from knowing, Preston."

Stanley, embarrassed at the anticipatory rebuke, sought to dissuade the cabinet officer and the senator from any notion that the internal dispute was anything but cordial, a reasonable and necessary professional disagreement on the way to the construction of a workable theory.

"There are some indications that a significant deviation from the preestablished fact pattern exists now."

Hubbard dropped her chin and looked at him over the tops of her bifocals. "Come again, son?"

Stanley swallowed and scratched his chin. "It's not like it was before. It's very different. When they—he—whatever—when they started, the two teams alternated, as though each was making sure the coast was clear before the other started up."

"Y'know," said Hubbard, not waiting for the rest, "I always wondered about that. What's so damned clever? If we'da spotted one of 'em, we coulda held surveillance for as long as we wanted without grabbing him. When we had 'em both, we move in simultaneously." She looked around. "Isn't that right?"

"Not entirely," Stanley replied. "Only if you're sure there's only two. And if you're sure at least one of them is actually the guy. What if he was masterminding from a distance?"

Hubbard nodded in understanding. "And now?"

"As soon as he knew we were on to him," Amy jumped in, "the two-team business stopped abruptly. Then there seemed to be only one person operating."

"Furthermore," said Jack, "he started holding it down to little more than a minute per machine, and spacing them out more. We figure he knew we were no longer afraid of moving in."

He added another note. "And Dr. Goldberg figured it was part of his plan. He knew we'd catch on eventually, and he had an adjustment ready and waiting."

Hubbard nodded thoughtfully at Amy. "That's what you meant about testing assumptions, I take it. You assumed he was just one guy, and the change in his act confirmed it. That about right?"

"That's it. Or at least it was."

"Hold on here," said Senator Fedder. "Whaddya mean he knew we were on to him? How the hell'd he find that out?"

Amy, looking greatly discomfited, said, "From me. What these good people aren't telling you, I'm the idiot who told him."

"Come again?" said Fedder, preternaturally alert to any intimation of admitted culpability.

"I wrote a message for him saying we know where he works. It gave away more than I realized at the time."

"So you gave him too much information," said Fedder.

"We thought so at first," Jack said quickly, fending off an ad hoc investigation by the veteran politician. "As it turns out, it wound up helping more than it hurt. We think we got 'em rattled now."

Hubbard idly tapped her fingers on the table before remembering the earlier thread of the conversation. "You said the pattern had changed."

Stanley picked up where he had left off. "It did. First, there's the fact that they're no longer trading off. That's probably because they know it's a useless maneuver."

Amy didn't let the implication pass. "Or maybe it's because they don't know about each other."

Stanley fought the temptation to terminate one of Amy's vital functions and simply said through clenched teeth, "You can't be serious!"

"What else?" asked Hubbard. "What else is different?"

"The biggest thing is the amount of time they're each spending at the machines," said Jack. "The one still operating in the Midwest has kept it down to only about a minute."

"Can't be pulling in much dough that way," Fedder suggested.

Hubbard did a quick mental calculation. "Ten machines a day, six grand a pop . . . Not a bad way to make a living."

"But Florida's been downright sloppy," Jack continued. "Sometimes spends as much as four or five minutes at a machine. That's why we think he's losing it, getting desperate."

"Couldn't we grab him pretty easy, then?" asked Hubbard.

Jack looked at Stanley and mentally threw him the ball.

"Uh, actually, that's why we wanted to talk to you and the senator," the agent said.

"Oh, Lordy," said the secretary, waving her fingers in the air in a dead-to-rights impression of a Pentecostal minister, "here it comes!"

"No, no!" Stanley began in earnest denial. "That's not the point, Madame Secretary, all we——"

" 'Course it's the point, Preston," Jack said with a sarcastic and self-deprecating smile. He turned to Hubbard. "We think we have to make some moves, and we need some kind of authority. It's classifiable as an emergency situation, so we can eliminate a lot of red tape, but we need high-caliber involvement. It's also a national security matter, and that's why we wanted just the two of you."

"Senator," he said, addressing Fedder directly, "you're head of the Aviation Policy Committee. There isn't any Civil Aeronautics Board anymore and the FAA is purely regulatory, so as far as we're concerned, you represent Congress as an expert.

"Madame Secretary, you've got to go to the president. Directly. I trust you to play this one close to the vest, but I'm less certain about some of your colleagues. We need to get the president's help on an idea."

He turned to each face in the room as he continued. "There's no time to stand on a lot of ceremony here, folks. We are it, far as I'm concerned. We either proceed by consensus or open it up to half the government and watch it all go to hell."

"Agreed," Hubbard said without hesitation. "Senator?"

Abelard Fedder came from a political family and had spent virtually his entire life under the klieg lights of public scrutiny. He had raised the art of evasion to new levels of ambiguity and was a master of double-talk and the veiled accusation. He held a third-degree black belt in verbal assassination and had the survival instincts of Rasputin.

But: Senator Abelard Fedder was not a stupid man. Nor was he necessarily particularly venal unless threatened. He had known from the beginning of his career in politics that there might come a day when he would be called upon to put aside the hard-won trappings of his heavily layered public persona, cut through the purportedly impenetrable strata of his psyche and actually try to do the right thing for once.

"Forget it. I say we take it to Congress."

"Abelard . . . !" Hubbard sputtered in shocked amazement.

Fedder held up a hand and smiled. "Just kidding, Letitia." He turned to Jack and Preston Stanley. "What's the plan?"

Jack thought back to Franz Klammer. "We gotta flush him out. We can move in on Florida. He—or they—is sloppy and stupid, and a collar should be easy.

"Our big problem is the main guy, who we're pretty sure is handling the Midwest directly. I don't think we're gonna catch him on the wing. Pres?"

Stanley shook his head reluctantly. "He's too smart. He has to have anticipated a standard bust and prepared for it."

"Exactly. So what we have to do, we have to tick him off in a big way, get him to act and hope we can deal with it."

"What do you propose?" asked Fedder.

"First, I want to move this command post to O'Hare. Right away. Overnight, if possible."

Amy and Florence exchanged glances. This was news to them.

"Why, Jack?" asked Amy.

"Because I want to be able to hook into any radar or air com system in the country, and nobody can handle that better than O'Hare. It also happens to be closer to where he's operating." *I hope*.

"Soon as that's done, we want to pinch Florida," said Stanley.

"But what if Dr. Goldberg is right?" asked Hubbard, harboring a strong suspicion she would be. "That won't do anything."

"True," said Stanley. "But we might learn something. And if they're in collusion, it might be just the trigger we need."

"And if it's not?" asked Fedder. "How do you flush him out?"

"We have another idea," Jack replied, turning to Amy.

"We need to stick a pin in his balloon, in just the right place. Using any information the FBI can get us. Something he doesn't like, something that tells him we know more about him than he might suspect, not just his identity and standard background information."

"How do you know there *is* something?" Hubbard asked.

"Because," said Amy with authority, "there's never been anybody, ever, who's pulled something like this guy's doing and didn't have at least one great walloping sore spot in his closet to drive him crazy."

"He called us, Madame Secretary," said Jack. "On the phone."

Hubbard stared at him but said nothing as Amy explained the significance.

"There isn't a single rational reason in the world why that was an advantageous thing for him to do. Dumb. Beyond belief, dumb. But he needs to communicate, or he's afraid not to, and this tells us a lot. We know money isn't the motivation, and this is good for us. If it was only money, we wouldn't have any ammunition."

Hubbard grew thoughtful. "Does it make a difference which we do first? Florida or the Midwest?"

Stanley shrugged and answered without looking at Amy. "Depends on which version you believe. Under the circumstances, maybe not."

"Why the president?"

Jack stood up and stretched his back. "We can't take a chance turning this guy loose on unsuspecting pilots."

"We need a cover, Madame Secretary," said Stanley. "Some insurance in case he takes to the airways before we can grab him."

"And you have an idea?"

"To tell you the truth," said Jack, "it's not a great idea. It's just the only one we've got. But we can't spring it until we have some more information to go on."

Hubbard looked increasingly uncomfortable with the preponderance of highly speculative theory in light of the glaring lack of hard evidence. "Agent Stanley, you got any word at all on the location of that woman, the one that runs the MicroFab design section?"

There was no evading the question. "No. But we have an idea, if everything goes right, it might work." He nodded at Florence, who explained further.

"It's likely she's going to need some folding money wherever she is. The FBI checked out her bank account and other financial history . . ." Florence lifted a conciliatory shoulder at the apparent invasion of a citizen's privacy. "National security, right? Turns out when she travels she always uses her credit card to get cash from ATMs, and her bank is on the FundsNet system. It's a relatively easy matter for us to detect when she's using her card and to send a message to the screen of the ATM, much like we're doing with Captain Marvel."

"I use those machines," said Fedder. "I never bother to look at the screen anymore."

Florence nodded. "True, but what if your card didn't pop back out when you expected it to? Or you didn't get your money? You'd look at the screen to see what the problem was."

"You can do that?"

It's just a computer. We can make it do anything. "It's not too difficult."

"Still doesn't mean she's going to answer, though, if she's that much of a management problem," said Hubbard.

"We'll put something suitably alarming in the message," said Amy. "Besides, the next time she uses her card, we'll know exactly where she is, and we can get some local law on her." She prayed that Stanley would stay silent for once and not point out that Phyllis Dalek hadn't broken any laws that would warrant police intervention.

Hubbard seemed satisfied. "And your agent in Europe?" she said. "He debriefed the seatmate yet?"

Stanley looked at his watch. "Should be there in a few hours. The guy's a photographer on assignment out in the boonies. There's a phone, but it's a party line and we didn't want to chance anybody listening in, so we're moving him to a hotel. Our guy will debrief him there."

"How's your man going to report in?" asked Fedder.

"Portable satellite link unit with scramble."

Hubbard seemed satisfied with at least the immediate plans. "Then we're adjourned. I suggest we meet again morning of the twenty-fourth, at eight. Anything else?"

CHAPTER 25

"We're looking for major clever here, Goldberg."
She nodded. "I know. And I'm tired. You take a crack at it."

"No problem." Jack walked to the whiteboard, picked up a felt marker, unscrewed the cap, picked up a paper towel, wiped a section of the board clean, positioned himself in front of it, screwed the cap back on, picked up another marker, unscrewed the cap, then stood there staring at the board.

"Okay," said Amy. "Moving right along. Let's start with Phyllis Dalek. That should be easier."

"Why?"

"First of all, she's never gotten a message like this one on an ATM. It'll probably spook her a little, get her attention. She's the intellect she's supposed to be, she'll get interested and at least check her company's voice mail system for messages."

Jack looked at the board for another few seconds and then wrote:

```
Phyllis: urgent you call office at
once. Matter of utmost urgency.
```

"Not 'Phyllis,' " said Amy. "Too personal. It would just be someone from the office, maybe playing a joke or over-reacting."

"How about just 'Dalek?' "

"Make it 'Phyllis Dalek.' Sounds much more official, like an imperial command or something. And give her our phone number here, so she doesn't connect it with her office."

"I like it." Jack screwed the cap back on the marker. "I'll call Florence and tell her to get it out right away. Why don't you work on the message to Captain Marvel?" He started for the door.

"Oh, sure, like you did your part already?"

" 'Course, look at the board."

"Very funny."

He was back in five minutes and looked at the board to see what Amy had written.

```
Call in and let's figure out how to
finish this.

We can't keep it up forever.
```

"Nice sexual overtone. As in, 'neither can you.' "

"Didn't even occur to me," Amy said. "Seriously."

The phone rang. Jack picked it up. "Yeah?"

He covered the mouthpiece with his hand. "It's Stanley. Get him on the speakerphone."

Amy jumped toward the table and hit the switch.

"Go ahead, Preston," said Jack. He replaced the receiver on the hook.

"We busted Florida."

Jack looked at Amy, who stared at the phone, dumbfounded. "You out of your fucking mind?" she hissed.

"Relax. That's not the bad news. Or the good news, depending on your point of view."

His seeming lack of urgency was puzzling. "We're listening," said Jack.

"One of our agents took the call when the guy started up on some machine near a racetrack. Didn't think much of it since they've never made it to a machine while he was still there anyway. But this time there he was, stuffing bills into a backpack. Careless, oblivious, about as much of an amateur as you can imagine."

"And he pinched him?" asked Jack.

"No. Tailed him and made his plates. Listen to this: Remember that guy at FundsNet did the actual reprogramming? The one we didn't have time to vet?"

"Uh-oh," Amy said *sotto voce* to Jack.

"This guy's his cousin."

The implications were immediately apparent, and Stanley voiced them without hesitation. "You were right, Goldberg. There's only one. Don't think there can be any doubt about that now."

"Understood," she said, taking care not to sound as though she were gloating. She forced herself steady, thought hard for a second and then hit the mute button on the phone. Emboldened by Stanley's news that the theory to which she had so tenaciously clung was probably correct, she turned to Jack. "That's it. I say we go."

At his answering nod, Amy released the mute and said into the speakerphone, "Can you get here first thing in the morning? It's going to hit the fan, we should all be in one spot."

"What's gonna hit the fan? You were right: Marvel has no idea it was even going on."

"We're gonna *make* it hit the fan," said Jack. "We have to bank on a loner, and we've got to start flushing him out. Got a couple messages to shake him up, and as soon as we get the ID we're gonna go full bore."

Stanley let it digest before speaking. "I'll be there first thing."

They heard the click as he rang off.

Jack hit the off button on the speakerphone and looked at Amy. "Send the Marvel message right away. I don't see any reason to hold off. We're gonna hear from Europe in the next couple hours."

"I agree." Amy reached for the phone. "I'll call Hartzig and tell her to get it out. But let's just hope to hell we locate Phyllis Dalek and figure out who this guy is before the day is out."

June 23, 0746 MST

If I drive through one more hick burg, eat in one more IHOP, Arby's or McShitsville, read another Hog Times Press *or hear another "Howdy, ma'am," I'm gonna blow something up.*

Her body contained few of the beneficial chemicals and endorphins that contributed to one's ability to relax, Phyllis having made a lifelong avocation out of ensuring that at least fifty percent of her caloric intake came from fat, in rebellious contravention of all that was holy to the four-food-groups authority figures she detested. Her surfeit of midabdominal adipose was testimony to her success and once had even given her another opportunity to use her intelligence as a psychic bludgeon. It had happened in high school. . . .

"Y'know," said her classmate Yvonne Gikow, ostensibly to be helpful but at least partially to get one good poke into the otherwise unpokable Phyllis Dalek, "there's lotsa ways to reduce that cellulite."

Phyllis fixed her with a baleful glare. "Reduce what?"

Yvonne shrank visibly from the *"what hump?"* tone of voice but persevered. "Cellulite. You know—" She dropped her eyes and indicated some nonspecific part of Phyllis's body. "Cellulite." Her eyes came back up and met Phyllis's with, despite some part of her knowing better, a hopeful look.

Phyllis regarded Yvonne and squished the key elements of this conversation into her decision-making pulp processor, where, like most choices in her life, it would get crushed and spun into some gelatinous mess, liberally laced with whatever malicious ingredients her progressively eroding persona had available at the moment. Whatever compassion she might have been able to muster up was lost as she pictured Yvonne sitting in front of the television, watching some "infomercial" that the FCC had failed to suppress because it was too busy cackling its approval of douche ads, enraptured at the silky body lines of some thespian nymphette of minimal mental faculties who was swooning in gratitude at the manufacturer of the twentieth-century equivalent of snake oil whose avowed mission on this God's earth was to rid the thighs of women everywhere of the scourge of cellulite, which, like cold fusion and Dillinger's bejarred penis, was not so much of this earth as of some cynic's fecund imagination.

"It's fat, Yvonne." Phyllis pinched a fold of Yvonne's between two fingers. "Fat. You can dress it up in Armani, rub swamp scum over it all day, and it's still fat."

"No, no," said Yvonne, slapping Phyllis's hand away in rebuke for her quite understandable misconception. "See how this has a sort of ripple . . . ?"

Phyllis knew that for reasons as yet unclear, it was a fact that people who predicted the end of the world were rarely disappointed when it didn't happen. As it turned out, their warped beliefs got even stronger every time their prophet's prediction failed to materialize. Nobody knew exactly why. She figured that Yvonne had been laying out money for this junk for years, and that every time it didn't work it strengthened her faith in it, to the point that any demonstration of its ineffectiveness was a severe blow to her sense of self.

Exactly the ordnance Phyllis needed.

"Yvonne, listen to me. There's no such thing as cellulite. It doesn't exist, do you get what I'm telling you? It's fat, and they only give it a cutesy name so that pea-brained ditzies like you will go out and buy a lot of useless, expensive shit to rub on themselves and then feel guilty when it doesn't work because maybe they didn't follow the directions right so they go out and buy more and try again."

Tears formed in Yvonne's eyes. She not only wasn't stupid, she was actually fairly bright, compared with anyone else but Phyllis. Her brain struggled between the towering forces of self-preservation and inarguable logic as Phyllis showed her, with Nobel-class precision and irrefutable sophistry, what a worthless and self-deluding excuse for a human being she was. It was made worse by the fact that Yvonne wasn't fat at all, just thought she was, at her age the perfect formula for making manifest the latent anorexia that lay just beneath the uppermost level of awareness of most of the residents of her peer group. Her only fault in the present situation was being a teenaged girl, a crime that was its own punishment but usually didn't carry with it a Phyllis Dalek. *That*, nobody deserved.

"Call it what you want," Phyllis said as she slapped

Yvonne's shapely thigh, choosing the one that wasn't bearing the poor girl's weight at the moment, thereby highlighting the jellylike shaking that even a Schwarzenegger would feel if the leg were hanging loose but that felt to Yvonne not like unengaged muscle but like a flesh bag containing horrible, pustulating fat cells. "It's still fat."

Whereupon Yvonne turned and fled, tears flowing uncontrollably, in all probability to forcibly disgorge whatever harmless lunch she had allowed herself before encountering her classmate Phyllis Dalek.

Phyllis chortled happily at the memory as she reached across the console to the passenger seat, fumbling for her cigarettes while trying to read the highway sign and drive at the same time. Claire City, South Dakota. *Christ, almost like some hick asshole had purposely tried to outhick the next town over*. What the hell had made her think of Yvonne Gikow at this particular moment? *Needed a lift, I guess*, she smirked to herself.

Hers had not been a happy life, and she believed it was the fault of every living creature in God's kingdom except herself, a proposition she was prepared to defend if anybody were to ask her, which nobody did. Her parents were at the root of all her many and varied tribulations, a miserable pair of misbegotten, hopelessly out of touch, unfeeling and insensitive Cro-Magnons with a deep-seated and cementlike inability to act appropriately in matters of their only child's welfare.

Actually, outside of Phyllis's private reality, their only real crime lay in their perfect normalcy, since Joe and Moira Dalek put the lie to the notion that the typical American couple did not exist. Nielsen or Yankelovich would have killed to find these two, and whatever special problems were attendant to daughter Phyllis lent credence to the theory that we are shaped by our genes rather than our environment, for parents such as these would have easily survived any formal inquisition regarding their parenting, which, while not always perfect, was certainly reasonable. The problem lay in those most mysteriously circuitous loops of logic that swirled in the minds of young females, that no matter what their parents did, they were wrong, but would have been right had they done something else, except that, had they *really* done that something else, it would have been wrong as well.

Moira Dalek's sense of correctness was grounded firmly in the Bible, King James version, the New Testament taking priority where it conflicted with the Old, convenience winning out where it conflicted with itself. Moira believed that the King James was the very word of God, and never mind those subsequent modernized versions, issued by the various Churches of What's Happening Now. An intelligent woman, she was willing to entertain Phyllis's questions on the subject of her beliefs, patiently enduring the innocent blasphemies emerging from the mouth of the babe who was, after all, merely trying to comprehend, maintaining faith that her sole progeny would eventually grow into the kind of deeper understanding that transcended earthly logic and accepted the blessed state of grace for its own sake, although the probability of a divinely inspired transmogrification seemed to decrease exponentially as Phyllis got older.

They sat in front of the television and watched as an old and frail woman was pulled from the burning wreck of an automobile. A passing short-order cook had witnessed the car drive off the side of a curving mountain road and come to rest on a rock outcropping after bouncing along a pitted field for several hundred yards and bursting into flame.

The cook had jumped over the embankment, spraining his ankle in the process, and had limped to the car, beaten back the flames with his jacket and reached in to drag the terrified woman to safety, sustaining burns on both his arms.

As the news cameras gathered, the woman started to regain her composure, looked directly at the cook and said, "Thank God! Thank God for saving my life!"

Phyllis sat up straight. The woman found her rhythm and continued to express gratitude to the Good Lord for pulling her out of the burning wreck.

After several more minutes of this, the cook spoke up. "Hey, lady, what about me?" He held up his newly bandaged arms. "I mean , f'Chrissakes, *I'm* the one who pulled you out, ain't I?"

Over the next several days, the hapless cook was excoriated repeatedly for his implicit denial that his act of extraordinary heroism was anything more than a bit part in a performance directed by the Almighty. Phyllis was enraged by this and demanded to know why everybody credited God with all acts gentle and decent yet exonerated Him from blame for disasters and tragedies, yet all the while professing His absolute control over everything, and she attempted to make the argument that, if anything, it was the Almighty that got the old woman into that mess in the first place, and that she would likely have died if the cook hadn't decided to intervene.

"Well, in that case," intoned Mama, "he was interfering with heavenly intentions and is damned anyway."

"How do you know which it was?"

"Read your Scriptures, daughter. All answers are within its pages."

"Mama, that Bible is the word of God?"

"It is."

"All of it?"

"Every bit."

"Y'mean even Habakkuk, Sirach, Thessalonians One *and* Two? Philemon, Colossians?"

"All of them."

"God speaks English?"

"He speaks all tongues."

Young Phyllis nodded thoughtfully, eliciting a sweet smile from Moira, an intended reward for even the slightest hint of dawning faith, which did not actually exist, nor did any sense of pleasure from the proffered smile.

"So let me get this straight, now. We've got versions in Syriac, Coptic, Armenian, Greek . . . some of them even pre-date the Christian era. We know that some of the Targums—" Seeing the crease in Mama's brow, she stopped to explain. "Free translations? Paraphrases? Stuff that wasn't in there but which somebody thought ought to be?" Mama nodded hesitantly, ill equipped to do intellectual battle with the tyro at her feet. "We never got to English until the Middle Ages, and we all know what a circus of enlightenment that period was. And we're still issuing revisions to this very day." She tapped Mama's own beloved, leather-bound King James. "Sixteen eleven there, Mom. Two hundred years after Coverdale's.

And also after Matthew's, the Great Bible, the Geneva and Rheims-Douai. And you think this is the word of God?"

Phyllis expected no cogent response, believing that one of the great benefits of religion was that it came packaged with its own rules of logic, along with a built-in refutation to any possible counterargument that essentially said that if the Good Lord created logical laws, he/she/it could sure as heck violate them. Believers believed that the laws that governed our daily lives were a mere subset of all those that existed, and that the ones hidden from us were those we could not possibly hope to understand. As the Hindu explained when asked why Jesus had killed the olive tree for no apparent reason, "Become a God and you will understand." Phyllis knew this and, accomplished sophist that she was, could easily have taken her mother's side of the argument and done a much better job of it.

But Moira wouldn't be shaken. The Romans couldn't do it with lions, and this little snippet of a nonbelieving sinner wasn't going to do it either. Moira loved her anyway, and the power of her faith, disregarding for the moment the merit of its theoretical underpinnings, was such as to make her a forgiving, loving mother who consoled herself with thoughts of the future, when Phyllis would see the light, and Moira would be thankful that she had been patient, nurturing, and resistant to the temptation to scold or berate her. Phyllis appreciated this, which was why she usually stopped short of completely eviscerating the poor woman, but she wished her mother would mount a better argument instead of retreating to propositions that, while serviceable in the defense of the Creator, could just as easily justify the existence of marshmallow people on the planet Zorp.

She finally located the half-crushed pack of Ultra-Super-Low-Tar & Nicotine Lites, the smoking of which made about as much sense as reading a blank book, and managed to fish one out while careening only halfway into the oncoming lane. She stuck it in her mouth and punched the dashboard cigarette lighter in a touchingly hopeful expression of faith in U.S. manufacturing technology and was not disappointed when the little knob with the precious line drawing of a burning cigarette remained in its own version of a fetal position, as though afraid to snap back out into the hands of the misanthrope at the wheel. Phyllis stared at it, wondering how much time had passed and whether it was sufficient to assure that the little piece of junk was actually inoperative. She pulled it out manually and stared at the spiral ribbon of metal within, cold, dark and nonfunctional, and tossed it out the window, just in front of a sign that read "Sisseton, 5 Miles." She fumbled some more until she found her own disposable, forgetting the open window and the windstream that blew ashes into her eyes. She dropped the lighter back onto the seat and looked at the photograph again.

Dad wasn't a bad guy. Hell, he put up with Mama, didn't he? Loved her, in fact, and did so without question or criticism. Phyllis occasionally wondered why and eventually figured out that it had nothing to do with her brains, or her ideas about life, or her body, which was a good deal like Phyllis's and therefore not a suitable candidate in this line of inquiry. It was simply because something in Moira touched something in Joe, and vice versa, a something that transcended whatever outward trappings the world might see when it looked at them but that they themselves had long ago stopped noticing.

Gurus of the New Age (Phyllis preferred to pronounce it "newage" because it rhymed with "sewage") spent endless hours in fabricated exposition of the secrets of love, as people had done with little useful result since the beginning. It annoyed her that her parents were so smugly satisfied simply to have that treasure with no attempt at fathoming it. It annoyed her even more when one of them would do something that should rightfully have incurred the wrath of the other but evoked nothing more than a loving smile and a mildly chiding shake of the head. Her friends, of which there were few, would remark on how wonderfully her parents seemed to get along. Even after twenty years of marriage Joe would sometimes run up the stairs because he couldn't wait to see his wife and the elevator was too slow in arriving. "I get cavities watching this shit sometimes," Phyllis would say, embarrassed at how uncool it all was.

Joe was an engineer by trade and not a very good one. His perpetual excuse was that the vocational things he had to do to put food on the table were not sufficiently challenging to stimulate his best work. Instead he reserved his vast storehouse of real creativity for himself, for his tinkering, because he may have been a mediocre engineer, but he was an Olympic-class dreamer, of the variety that never lost faith no matter how many setbacks there were and who was better off as a failure because he knew how to handle that, had that one down pat, but would likely have crumbled under the weight of success, although Lord knew that a couple more bucks each month could have been accommodated easily.

Joe Dalek fancied himself an inventor, and by the technical definition of that term, he was. He did invent. He created things where there were no things before. He took ideas and components and melded them in ways that had not been considered previously. And he was creative, no denying that.

The conventional notion of an "inventor," however, went beyond these qualities. For one thing, most inventors were at least mildly attuned to the concept of necessity, understanding that some element of need was usually present if someone was going to go out and buy whatever it was that had been invented. At the very least, such need was required to induce someone to actually produce the thing and to share in the risk that the perception of need was correct.

Joe was relatively untroubled by such concerns, believing as he did that the essence of true utility was in the creation of a need where none existed before. "Philo," he used to say solemnly after the precocious tyke was old enough to start asking why Daddy was bothering to create a device that automatically dialed a telephone when using the device required more key presses than dialing the number itself unless the party you wanted to talk to happened to be in Kuala Lumpur, "remember that nobody in Canada thought they needed underarm deodorant until American advertisers taught them that they stink."

"But Daddy," she protested, whining as only a five-year-old who had recently earned her brat wings could do, "they *do* stink," thereby getting to the very heart of, and at the same time undercutting, the major part of Joe's take on life.

He felt strongly that Phyllis needed to be more than he was and equally strongly that a young child could have no say in such matters, it being the responsibility of the parent to make such decisions pending the arrival of sufficient cortical material in the little one's head to take over the execution of its life. The only flaw in his plan was that Phyllis was born a girl, an eventuality that he was at first unprepared to reckon with. A boy would have worked in so much better.

Where other children had worshiped DiMaggio or Roosevelt, Joe had grown up in awe of P. T. Farnsworth, who, at the age of fifteen, designed the image dissector, forerunner of the television, obtaining his first patent six years later. By 1935 he had demonstrated a complete television system, four full years before David Sarnoff did it at the New York World's Fair and actively discouraged both Farnsworth and Allen DuMont from entering the field. By the time he died in 1971, he had 165 patents to his credit. Now *there* was a dreamer, and who knew television was a need back then? (*Practically everybody*, Phyllis would argue, which Joe perhaps suspected but denied anyway.) It was why he insisted that both he and Moira refer to Phyllis as Philo, Farnsworth's first name, which she detested with a passion beyond all understanding, likening it more to a type of Greek pastry dough than her father's hero.

It was Joe's hope that "Philo" could be reared into a technical genius and bring some recognition to a family that had known love but not much public pride. She attended public school, as there was simply no money for a private institution, but the Daleks sacrificed to hire private tutors occasionally, mostly in the hard sciences. Since this took up most of their spare cash, there was none left to clothe Philo in anything remotely fashionable, which was just as well since Joe felt that such frivolities were not only superfluous but distracting, and he sincerely believed that his little girl was above such petty foolishness anyway. No little girl was, ever, and one might have thought that Moira could draw on her own experiences and muster up a little sympathy, but she had never been in a public school, only Catholic girls' school, and over the years she had unconsciously sublimated the torture of a school uniform into some kind of blessing, a gift that, had she known then what she knew now, should have seemed to her less like purgatory and more like an extra incentive to keep her on the Right Path. Surely Philo could see that now with the benefit of Mama's hindsight. And the same went for intramural athletics,

Friday night dances at the teen center and most other forms of social outlet that made some contribution, however slight, toward one's ability to interact with the other people in the real world rather than with obscure mazes of coils, relays and tubes.

Phyllis was brilliant, perhaps even a genius. Her mind was so sharp that it stormed down paths of connections and conclusions while most other people were still struggling to understand the premises. Properly channeled, it may have been a Nobel-caliber intellect, who could tell? She soaked up information on a vast array of subjects, learning being for her like an addiction. The more she came to know, the more she needed to know, because each opportunity for a connection between two seemingly disparate pieces of information expanded logarithmically into an ocean of possibilities, and it nagged at her to leave so many loose ends, even though she was smart enough to know that the pursuit of those avenues was an infinite recursion that could grow only more tangled.

Yet when she looked at herself in the mirror, what she saw was distinctly unattractive, with that special, unmistakable look that warned the world around her, "Believe me when I tell you that you really don't want to know how I feel about myself, and I promise that if you force me to confront it, I will tear off your head and shit down your neck." It was the kind of look that obese people sometimes wear as they parade their bulk with exaggerated movements, daring you to wince at what has so long ago passed beyond plump that their only recourse is to wear it proudly, even while its presence makes them sick at heart. Philo wasn't very fat, but she had the look.

All this had led to great ridicule and an unending series of humiliations at the hands of her classmates, a subspecies of human afflicted with that special affinity for cruelty that only children possessed. The last time her mother called her Philo, she was eighteen. She turned around, walked out of the house and never came back.

She hadn't been worried about her future while in high school, having assumed that both the academic and business worlds would little care that a woman was socially inept and physically unattractive. In the former case she was quite right. Colleges and universities were notoriously blind to the traditional graces, taking a good deal of self-righteous credit for that enlightened quality but generally failing to acknowledge that it was easy in academia, there being no customers to please, no executives among whose ranks the currying of favor was important (at least among the students), and no long-term outlook, since the student was there for four years and then ceremoniously shown the door. In fact, the university, even more than most corporate environments, survived primarily on its numbers: graduate exam scores, number of Phi Beta Kappas, average starting salary upon graduation, number of Nobel scholars, grant and chair awards and so on and so forth. Nobody ever came back and asked if the students knew which fork to use or could they hold an intelligent conversation (except in their majors, of course) or broke wind during high tea. Hell, there wasn't even a personal interview required for admission, just a 250-word essay on why I want to go to college.

Her introduction to business, however, was the first truly great shock of her postadolescent life. The "numbers" only got her in the door, and personal interviews were something for which she was totally unprepared.

"So tell me a little about yourself."

"Like what?"

"Like whatever you feel like."

"I don't 'feel like' telling you anything, but I'll answer questions if I have to to get the job."

Pretty much the extent of her first interview. The second, too, until she started to catch on. Finally she got hired by a semiconductor manufacturing company in desperate need of an engineer with a good computer background and not too concerned about her interface with the rest of society since they figured they could pretty much keep her in relative social isolation. This particular company, MicroFab Corporation, practiced the mushroom school of employee management: Keep 'em in the dark, shovel shit over 'em, and if they try to pop their heads up too often, cut 'em off.

Phyllis was happy as hell.

There were other women at her level, some with engineering backgrounds and others more business-oriented. Phyllis thought she'd be happy puttering around with circuit designs and fabrication technology, but she soon grew restless, especially when she saw what kind of latitude attended to higher rungs on the corporate ladder.

Several times she was considered for promotion and was passed over just as many times. Some of those who prevailed in these contests were women, none of whom could match her for raw intellectual ability but who possessed more readily discernible management styles, dressed better and generally projected brighter auras of professionalism. Phyllis assumed, quite wrongly, that these were shameless tarts sleeping with their bosses or waggling their fannies at the customers. What she failed to grasp was that technical skills were as plentiful as cellulite. Much rarer were poise, powers of persuasion and the kinds of personalities that naturally commanded great personal loyalty, often the marginal persuader in the retention of employees and customers who might otherwise just as easily desert in the face of transient problems or anomalous blips in service.

These were qualities that no amount of raw intellect on Phyllis Dalek's part could possibly compensate for. And the realization that talents less than hers, at least as she perceived them, were barreling upward through the ranks while she continued to wallow in the darkest corners of the lab opened the wounds that had lain dormant during the happy times following her first assignments. The pus of her reawakening self-hatred oozed back into her life and covered her perception of all that she saw. An idea had begun to form, but she wasn't sure what to do with it. It was too early in her career, a career that eventually did accelerate, owing to her irrefutable contributions to the company's stranglehold on advanced fabrication technology.

She was approaching the outskirts of the small community of Sisseton and tried to negotiate the exit while shoving the seatful of sundries back into her purse, which was easy because the small items barely filled a tiny fraction of the unprepossessing vinyl handbag's cavernous interior. A sign along the side of the road read "Business Section" and included an arrow pointing to eight square blocks that constituted such downtown as existed in the little community.

Phyllis parked on Lincoln Boulevard and walked two blocks

to a shopping center way too large for Sisseton alone but had been built to accommodate eleven communities in the tri-county area. Alongside the Federal Savings of South Dakota retail branch were four automated teller machines that served as the hub of financial life in the community. People were lined up three and four deep, standing a respectful distance back from the machines so that each individual could transact his business with the privacy that rightfully attended such a function. Phyllis picked a line of three people and took her place.

She watched as a dark-suited man inserted his card into the slot and carefully punched his personal identification number. When the screen flickered in response, the man put his finger to his lip and tapped, obviously lost in decision making.

Hey, asshole! Phyllis yelled in her mind. *You stood in this line for ten minutes, you couldn't have spent some of it trying to figure out what to do when you finally got there?*

Oblivious of this silent assault, the man started a tentative finger toward the keyboard, then paused and reconsidered, eventually bringing his finger back to his lip in further contem-plation, whereupon the machine spit his card back out with a scolding beep because he had taken too long.

Phyllis gritted her teeth and kept her peace, occupying her mind with thoughts of what she would like to do to him assuming she could do so with impunity.

Finally the man reinserted his card, pressed a few buttons and transacted some business Phyllis couldn't see but assumed was of sufficient weight and import to warrant the intellectual summit he had held with himself. After another ten minutes, it was her turn at last.

She stepped up to the counter, set her purse down on it and stood slightly to the right, in front of the money dispenser, reaching to the left, where she briskly and professionally inserted her card, not bothering to wait for the screen prompt before she punched in her six-digit personal identification number.

Nothing happened, and she was about to enter the PIN again when an insistent beeping drew her eye to the monitor.

0946 EST

Preston Stanley leaped for the phone even before the first ring was able to finish. "Stanley," he barked tersely.

The others watched as he strained to hear past the static, then he looked up and pointed to the phone. "Europe! Coming in now!"

Jack started for the speakerphone, but Stanley held out a restraining hand. "Hold it. Too much static—they're going to try to change satellite transponders."

"Over here!" Florence yelled suddenly. "Something's coming in on the monitor!"

Jack and Amy hurried over to look at the screen. The bottom row was filling slowly with a series of seemingly random numbers, many containing double and sometimes triple digits.

Florence grabbed at the desk for a pencil and a scrap of paper and started writing down the numbers. "He's sending a message. Must have gotten your request to negotiate." She was so excited, she could barely keep her writing legible.

Amy reached for an unused phone and snapped off the plastic plate behind the keys that showed letters corresponding to numbers. She got more paper and another pencil, hunched over the desktop and began decoding the numbers as Florence finished writing the last of them down.

"He's on!" shouted Stanley, then into the phone: "Yeah, yeah, go ahead. Yes, I got it, and . . . ?"

He straightened up slowly, jaw slack and his face quite literally gone pale.

"What?" Jack said quietly, almost afraid to ask the question.

Before he could answer, Amy stood up, staring at the paper in her hand. Her eyes met the FBI agent's and locked as Stanley held the phone away from his ear.

"What the hell is going on?" Jack yelled. "Goldberg, what's the message say?"

Amy looked down at the paper, then back up. "It says, 'Stick it in your ear.'"

Jack whipped his head back around to Stanley, who was nodding slowly. "The seatmate says the person next to him was a woman. Spent the whole last half hour of the flight fiddling with a laptop computer and a stopwatch."

Confusion and alarm mixing on his face, Jack breathed, "Phyllis Dalek?"

Florence stared, stupefied, at the numbers on the piece of paper in her hand. She hadn't known about the insult Phyllis Dalek had hurled at her superior before being forcibly told to take a week off, didn't know that the message Amy had just decoded echoed the same sentiment in identical words, didn't know any of those things. But in the few seconds that passed following Jack's uttering of the name out loud, Florence thought back to stories and incidents and half-heard gossip and rumors circulated in the rarefied upper levels of the best commercial computer scientists in the country, of which both she and Phyllis Dalek were a part. Then she thought back to her own life, and certain difficult and seminal episodes, and thought again of the ill-reputed Dalek and the number of times she had met her at conferences, and each time she had done so the phrase "there but for the grace of God go I" had played automatically in her mind, the closest she usually came to directly thanking her deity, in this case for sparing her the ignominy that had beset someone else in circumstances very similar to her own. In those few seconds everything swirled into place, and she was as certain as she ever was of anything.

Amy watched her carefully, was acutely aware of the parallels, could see the pain in her eyes, as much in sympathy for Dalek as for herself. She waited patiently.

"It's her," Florence said finally, looking up at Jack. "It all fits. Everything."

CHAPTER 26

Phyllis Dalek leaned forward toward the dispenser, resting her arms on the counter and effectively shielding the horizontal slot from casual view. Almost immediately the lid flipped open and crisp twenty-dollar bills flitted out and tumbled onto the small retaining clip that held them in place.

It took about twenty seconds for the one hundred bills to be disbursed; Phyllis lifted them out about every five seconds or so to prevent them from bunching up and blocking the outlet and tried to send her coded return message at the same time. When it was finished, she punched the OK button on the panel. As a fresh batch of bills started their downward cascade, she continued entering her reply.

She didn't look around, favoring one leg while bending the other slightly to heighten the appearance of casualness. Given the amount of time other people were taking at the terminals without visible complaint from those still in line, Phyllis hit the button a third and fourth time before pressing CANCEL. Her card popped out of its slot immediately. She replaced it in her wallet, hefted the newly laden handbag upright so the bills would settle safely to the bottom and started a leisurely walk back to the car she had left two blocks away. She would drive to a mail-order distribution center on the north side of

town, the largest employer in the region, where three ATMs
serviced the needs of the twelve hundred employees who had
no time to waste going to banks to cash checks on payday
evenings.

"How to finish this," my ass, she smirked to herself. *I'll
fucking well tell you how to finish it.*

It was easy to keep her anger up, to maintain the reservoir of
pure fury that fueled her madness, though she herself wouldn't
have called it that. All she had to do was remember. . . .

Three Years Ago

The flight from the San Jose airport to Redmond, Washington, would take two hours. Phyllis brought along her laptop
personal computer, one of her prized possessions. It had
been issued in standard form by her company, but Phyllis
had fiddled with its innards, adding memory, swapping out
the processor and loading on exotic software until the book-
size machine was a highly personalized, extremely powerful
marvel of cybernetic engineering. She had even considered
discussing some of its more interesting features with manufacturers who might be amenable to a licensing arrangement.

Phyllis treated herself to a first-class ticket. It seemed like
a small fortune and more than doubled the fare, but what the
hell, nobody ever liked waiting on her, so maybe she could
buy herself some decent service. And the wider seat would
give her more room to work. She'd promised the head of
manufacturing that she would transmit the results of a spreadsheet analysis as soon as she stepped off the plane, and it
would likely take her the entire two hours to get the work
done.

By the time the door closed, the flight attendants had pretty
much asked everybody for their drink orders except Phyllis.
She didn't want a drink, but it bugged the bejesus out of her
that she was being ignored.

" 'Scuse me, miss? Could I get a drink?" She didn't like
sounding plaintive, it wasn't her style, but she noticed that
passengers rarely acted assertive to the domineering flight

attendants, who controlled your comfort and the entire tone of your flight and the level of service you would receive. She hadn't even protested when she'd found all three forward overhead bins stuffed with the attendants' own belongings.

"Sorry," said the overly made-up attendant with a practiced and insincere smile. "You need to fasten your seat belt for takeoff now."

Once the plane was in the air, Phyllis pulled down the tray table and unpacked her laptop. After switching it on, she waited for the machine to complete its internal self-diagnostic routine, letting the pale blue light from the display wash over her face. She wasn't a fan of sunshine, but this electric glow was a warming substitute.

As the machine hummed and clicked, she thought back momentarily to the scene played out at the airport's security screen. "Mind turning that on for me, ma'am?" Standard procedure called for the agent to see some numbers come up on the screen as proof that it wasn't a bomb in disguise. While waiting, Phyllis had eyed the agent out of the corner of her eye and thought, *Do you have any idea how easy it would be for me to make a bomb that displayed these nice numbers on the screen*? Someday she would fill a laptop case with gelignite and do just that, just for the hell of it. Just to be able to say she had. Say it to *whom*, she had no idea.

Finally she got the double beep indicating that the computer had passed its own audition and heard the hard drive whine into life as the operating system was read and loaded into memory. Soon she was happily click-clacking the keys as she manipulated the rows and columns of the spreadsheet. To save money, the manufacturer had used keys that were nothing more than cheap springs sitting over membrane switches; thus, instead of an actual mechanical click, the machine's speaker emitted a little electronic one every time contact was made, which served acceptably as auditory feedback.

The passenger seated on her left waggled a finger at the keyboard. "That thing gonna work all the way to Seattle?"

Phyllis brightened immediately. "Oh, yes. It's got a long-life battery. And for longer trips"——she reached into the side pouch of the carry case and pulled out what looked like a black-vinyl-covered cigarette pack—"I can just pop in this spare."

The passenger nodded slightly. "Damned annoying sound."

Phyllis's face dropped involuntarily. She had completely misread his question, mistaking his irritation for technical curiosity. Momentarily at a loss for words, she tried to size him up.

Businessman, executive probably, used to flying in the front cabin. The short-cropped hair and thick-soled shoes told her he was likely ex-military. Thin lips, Republican, WASP, steel-rimmed glasses, still wearing his jacket, and buttoned, too. This was a man used to giving orders and having them obeyed instantly. Despised civilians (meaning both nonmilitary or not working for his company) and anybody else not under his control. His copy of *Business Week* was rolled up tightly and held in one hand, and he was tapping it on the armrest.

"Uh, I'm sorry about that." She resumed her work.

He continued tapping the magazine. "I have to listen to that in my office all day. Shouldn't have to hear it here."

She stopped typing and rested her wrists on the tray table. "Look. I'm sorry. This is what I do for a living." She looked him full on, then turned back and continued working. "I paid for this seat, and I have the right to do my work."

More tapping. His left hand was on the armrest, elbow in the air, causing his shoulder to rise in a display of building belligerence. "I have rights, too, don't I? I shouldn't have to put up with that."

She stopped again and turned to him. "Let me make this real clear: I've got two hours to finish what I'm doing, and I'm gonna do it. That's all there is to it. Why don't you change seats?"

He reached up and pushed the attendant call button. When she didn't appear in his accustomed nanosecond, he pulled it back out and pushed it again, repeating this several times, oblivious of the obnoxious gonging that resounded throughout the cabin.

"Yessir," an attendant finally hissed, not pleased to have been torn away from her paperwork. "May I help you?" Phyllis snickered silently, at both the absurdity of the man's position and the annoyance of the flight attendant called in to deal with it.

"That machine is making too much noise. It's bothering me."

Phyllis looked up at her in conspiratorial glee. "He doesn't like the sound the keys make." *Do you believe this dork?*

The attendant returned her gaze. "Would you mind not using it, then?"

"Excuse me?"

"How about putting it away so it doesn't disturb this gentleman?"

Phyllis couldn't believe she was hearing this and barely knew how to respond.

"I don't want to put it away. I need it. It's my work."

The attendant shrugged and fluttered her eyelids up and down. "Well, she *does* have the right to use it," she said to Mr. Exec, her tone conveying sympathy with his predicament and obvious frustration at her inability to stop Phyllis from bothering him.

"So don't I have rights, too? I shouldn't have to listen to that."

"Boy, I agree with you, but as you can see, she just won't—"

"Look, why don't you just change his seat and both of you can leave me alone, okay?"

"Well, miss, there aren't any more seats, as you could see if you turned around."

"Well, *miss*," Phyllis shot back through clenched teeth, "why don't you find another passenger willing to change with him?"

"Why should I have to change seats?" the big shot whined.

"Because, asshole, there's no way in hell I'm moving or stopping my work, that's why!"

"What's going on here?" A second attendant showed up, looking cross at the disruption.

By way of summary explanation meant to objectively encapsulate the whole incident, the first attendant said, "This woman is bothering this gentleman and won't quit."

"What the hell are you talking about!" Phyllis practically screamed, tears now squeezing between her eyelids at the monumental unfairness of it all. "I'm not doing anything! This jerk doesn't like my computer, so why's it *my* fault?"

"No need to get abusive, miss. That's uncalled for."

Phyllis knew that "abusive" was an airline code word, invoked to release flight attendants from any pretext of smiling customer service. With "abusive" passengers, all bets were off and airline employees were permitted to protect themselves and other passengers without regard to civil niceties. Phyllis forced her voice down and her hands onto the armrests.

"I'm not being abusive," she said slowly. "I just want to do my work." She could feel her legs shaking and a tremolo creeping into her voice. "I have the right to use this computer, you already know that, so what do you want to do about it?"

The second attendant had drifted away momentarily and now returned. "There's another passenger who is willing to change seats with you, sir. Would you follow me, please?"

"Is it a window seat?"

Phyllis turned and looked at him in disbelief. As she lifted the machine, flipped the tray table back up and rose to clear the way for him to leave, she turned to find the entire first-class cabin staring at her (not him), shaking their heads in disapproval and whispering to one another. When her new neighbor arrived and she was resettled on her seat, she mumbled, "Thank you," to the flight attendant, who replied with a hard and reproving look and walked away without a word.

Phyllis folded her hands together to make their trembling less obvious and fought to regain her equilibrium. Her powers of concentration were shot, at least as far as her ability to work on her spreadsheet, and she sat in withering isolation and despair, not even lifting her computer back up in front of her.

Instead she considered her life, which appeared before her now as a collection of incidents like the one that had just occurred. She knew with certainty that had she been pretty or more poised, this unforgivable treatment would have been spared her, as would so many others in the past. "Unforgivable" was the operative word here, and she dwelled on it obsessively, rolling it around on her tongue like a living thing.

"Sorry?"

She turned, startled, at the sound of the elderly woman

newly seated next to her. "Wha—? No, nothing. Just, uh, rehearsing a speech."

Unforgivable. She liked that. She closed her eyes.

Her parents had told her often that her intellect would be her undoing, and "You're too smart for your own good" would be a refrain played to her frequently by casual acquaintances, teachers, guidance counselors, employers, colleagues and a vast array of people whom she would only meet on a single occasion but who nonetheless were treated to a dollop of her galactic, condescending contempt.

It was not unusual for someone so terminally bright to wander through life in a state of perpetual frustration at the infinite variety of logical contradictions that constituted everyday living. Challenged once during a presidential election year in her high school cafeteria by a self-styled young conservative senior, Phyllis the sophomore took him on and maliciously grabbed his arguments, twisted them inside out and flung them back in his face one by one. In helpless rage before her battering, in which she put forth no agenda of her own but only tore his to bits, the senior finally blurted out, "Well, I got a right to an opinion, don't I?" to which Phyllis responded, without really thinking about it in advance:

"Yeah, and so do I, right?"

"Of course y'do," he agreed, thinking that she was offering a gracious end to the fight.

"So what if my opinion is, you don't have a right to yours? Then what?"

Stopped dead in his tracks, her adversary fumbled for a moment and then said plaintively, "But that's not a valid opinion!"

"So are you telling me I have no right to it?"

"Yes! No . . . I mean, you have a right to any opinion you want, only—"

"Only what?"

And so it went. She'd stumbled on the conundrum by accident, and it haunted her for days, to the point where she realized that the only opinions worth having were those about opinion itself, and until you got that one solved, there was no sense expressing any thoughts about anything else. Her attempts to explain this were generally met with blank stares, and her analytical mind never figured out that the nature of human social intercourse was a matter of the sacrifice of mathematical precision in favor of being able simply to get things done. Her peculiar brand of "analysis paralysis" also was to have a deleterious impact on her effectiveness at work later in life, which she sublimated into discrimination against her gender, her weight, her clothes and anything else handy except what it really was.

Propositions grounded on fallacious reasoning put forth by the proponents of various causes also added to her cynicism. If a bellowing politician "proved" that his people were discriminated against because so many of them were thrown in jail, Phyllis would rise and ask him if it wasn't equally likely that they just committed more crimes. If someone complained about the garbage he was forced to watch on television, Phyllis asked him why he didn't shut the set off. If someone argued in favor of limiting political terms, Phyllis would ask him why he would pass a law that so directly contradicted the will of the people. And why, she would demand when feeling particularly feisty, do we demonstrate against the clubbing of fur seals when thousands of lobsters are plunged live into boiling water every day? Because the seals are cute and furry and have big, sad eyes? How come the guy marching against fur coats is wearing a leather jacket? Would he feel better if we ate mink meat instead of throwing it away?

At first Phyllis anticipated hushed reverence at this parting of the veils blocking people's vision of the truth and was amazed that her delivered revelations were about the only thing that could unite bitter foes as they ganged together to shut her up. This blatant denial of incontrovertible logic at first stunned her but soon made her angry, smoldering at first but fanning into a blaze by the time she entered college, where she survived by retreating into the unassailable symmetry of mathematics and computer science.

By the time she graduated, she thought maybe it was possible to insulate herself from her seriously defective fellow citizens, but then she had to find a job and actively interact with people and it all began to unravel again.

She knew she was brilliant, a genius, and probably off the standard scales, but she was never able to take solace in the way other people of equivalent mental dexterity managed to survive and even prevail, because she had decided early on that nobody who was happy in this world could possibly be as smart as she was, by definition. If they were, they would have no choice but to retreat into similar pathology as the inevitable result of their recognition that everything around them was basically absurd and preposterous.

All this streaked through her mind before the plane crossed the Columbia River separating Oregon from Washington. Before *it* happened.

She wouldn't be able to tell afterward exactly *when* it happened. More than likely there was no specific point, no discernible center of the bridge before which she was on one side and after which she was bound inexorably for the other. Not a binary kind of thing, *I used to be there and now I'm here*. Not like that.

She found herself for the first time on an airplane actually listening to the sound of the engines, surprised at what a loud, encroaching presence they presented. The body's amazing compensating mechanism usually blocked them out, so effectively that their sudden cessation at the end of the flight was a surprise, a soothing quiet following a period of forgotten noise. But she heard them now, and the tenor of their shrill mixture of frequencies was a raucous intrusion at first, until the noise began to seem less like a sound than a semaphore transmission of the turbines' power. The currents of that energy entered her through her back and buttocks and twanged at the organs hanging free in her body, and she felt those, too, for the first time, as they vibrated in willing sympathy with the engine noise.

She opened her eyes and drew a sharp breath as the seat back in front of her jumped out in crystalline relief, each thread in each line of the corduroy fabric separately visible. The tubular frame of the seat bottom, the emergency running lights on the floor, the grimy wheel of the beverage cart, each cube of dripping ice in the wrinkled plastic bag sitting on the rolling server . . . everything within her vision extended in space with exaggerated dimension and surrealistic clarity.

"Surrealistic" was the wrong word. It was real, only more so than she had ever seen or heard anything, ever, and she marveled at how it was possible to have missed it all her life. The power of this perception frightened and thrilled her simultaneously, and while it seemed as though the unfiltered sensations, by virtue of their perfect correctness, could never recede once experienced, she was suddenly fearful that it was only a temporary phenomenon, a teasing whiff by a cynical god, like a peak sexual experience never to be repeated but only wistfully and imperfectly recalled.

That fear gave her the courage to tear away from the simple objects in front of her and to chance turning her eyes to something unfathomably complex, to risk exposing her unshielded senses to the great outpouring of signals that constituted the interpersonal radioactivity of a human being. She angled her head upward and found the face of the flight attendant who had earlier embarrassed her into shaking rage, and the full impact of that face slammed into her with such palpable force that she stopped breathing momentarily.

Great, crashing waves streamed from the attendant, and Phyllis tried to remain outwardly calm while she processed it. She saw with perfect lucidity the seething hostility the woman harbored for her, the easy willingness to take her life if there was no possibility of being caught, how every second of her waking consciousness devoted itself to the perfection of Phyllis's pain and humiliation. She understood now how every movement of the attendant's hand, every inclination of her head, every telling flicker of her glowing eyes, telegraphed her roiling disdain, her preoccupation with Phyllis.

It all became clearer by the second. Phyllis could see the reddish tinge of the aura that connected the attendant to the man several rows behind her, the one who had started all the trouble. An entire conversation was going on between the two of them, and probably had been for some time now with no interruption, a conversation about her, strewn with insane lies that they both believed and filled with grisly scenarios they passed back and forth with shared malice.

As the engine exhaust screamed into the cabin and coursed through her arteries, the power grew, and Phyllis watched in mounting terror as more was revealed to her, the red-orange connecting vapors extending to the other attendant, and then to other passengers, until the totality of the collective consciousness in the first-class cabin was in complete communication and was able to focus its single presence directly on her.

Phyllis didn't know whether to be stunned more by the fact or by the certainty of what she was learning. The strength of the conspiracy overwhelmed her and tried to crush her in her seat, and she began to gasp. The first flight attendant turned toward her and said something, outwardly solicitous but secretly gleeful and triumphant, and Phyllis didn't answer, too distraught by the explicit acknowledgment of the plot that up until now had only been a hint in the red cloud. The attendant sneered and shrugged, making a show of moving the cart along since the bitch in 2B was too self-concerned to answer her, and this actual confirmation of Phyllis's fears reeled her sense of balance even farther.

But the energy from the engines continued to flow into her, and the coursing vibrations steadied her and began a steely solidification in her marrow. The hard edge in her vision began to dull slightly, taking with it some of the paranoia that had exploded like psychic TNT and threatened to engulf her. As the boiling black waters of her revelation began to recede to their normal state of adumbration, they were replaced by the concrete pilings of a new fortitude, firmly resolved but only vaguely directed.

Phyllis blinked, as though in waking from a dream. She looked around hesitantly, and though her world had largely returned to its former blunted roundness, a slight sparkle of iridescence still danced along the hard angles of the armrest, the jawlines of the people across the aisle, the handles of the overhead bins.

She blinked again. The iron in her bones was still there. Something inside of her had determined to do something, had decided on a course of action, but was going to feed it to her consciousness in small doses. She'd know what it was soon, in the next few minutes, actually, and a smile played around her lips, not happy but sardonic. Her breathing steadied and her hands no longer shook. Like most epiphanies, legitimate or pathologically delusional, it eventually ended, and few details remained, but the damage was done. The arcs of circles long nascent began to find one another and connect, forming ever larger sections, the seemingly disparate elements of her life seeking each other out and completing a demented teleology she had no idea even existed. She felt herself floating slightly above the seat and hoped nobody would notice, and still the strength inside her grew.

"Ladies and gentlemen, in preparation for our descent into Seattle, please return to your seats, fasten your seat belts and bring all seat backs and tray tables into their upright and locked position. We anticipate landing in—"

Unforgivable.

As she headed for the exit door, overnight bag on one shoulder, the laptop and her attaché on the other, the flight attendant fixed her with a contemptuous stare. "I thought you were going to work the whole flight."

Phyllis, the ingot of resolve firmly ensconced deep within her belly, the first glimmer of an idea scratching at the cells of her cerebral cortex, looked back at her, dry-eyed and strong. "I thought you were gonna go fuck yourself."

The attendant's jaw dropped as Phyllis kept walking without turning away from her.

As she reached the end of the jetway, an animatronic airline representative holding a sheet full of connecting gate information smiled at her and said, "Thank you for flying Alpha Airlines."

Alpha Airlines. Unforgivable.

Walking easily and radiating self-confidence, Phyllis rented a car and drove out of the lot, smiling politely to the gate attendant who checked her contract before raising the black-and-white-striped gate arm.

"Excuse me," she said lightly. "Can you give me directions to the Autonav Corporation?"

That was a long time ago. Like most seminal life events, the details remained carved into her memory like scars from a knife fight.

She shook her head to clear it, then took another look at her map. The town couldn't be more than two miles ahead. She lit another cigarette and sighed. It had seemed so easy when she'd first planned it. Walk up to an ATM, knock out a couple-three grand at a time, go hit another one. Few hundred trips and *voilà! I'm a millionaire.* Piece o' cake. Beat working, anyway.

But it was exactly like working, only harder on the feet, the back and the general constitution. The first waterfall of bills was exhilarating. Now, it was just a job. She had always wondered how those people working in the federal mint could stand to be around so much raw cash day after day. Now she knew. After a remarkably short time, it was just a job, no different from tightening bolts on an assembly line.

She began to look for ways to occupy her mind in order to combat the road hypnosis that made these sleepy little one-horse dorps all look the same, even more so than they did in reality. Solving partial differentials in her head worked for a while, except when she got lost in them and missed some turnoffs.

She had to stay alert to preserve the timing of the plan. Many of these roads were labeled like those in her native California had been before both out-of-towners and new arrivals complained so bitterly that they were changed. Instead of saying "north" or "south," the directions were labeled with the ultimate destination, like "Bakersfield, left lane" and "Irvine, right lane," which didn't do a damned bit of good to anybody who didn't happen to know where those places were to begin with.

Out here it was even worse; the assumed familiarity was taken to absurd lengths so that often the only clues as to the road's direction were labels like "County Seat" or "Fairgrounds" or "4H Headquarters." She'd learned to be vigilant for subtle clues, like stores named after the town.

So she turned right, off of what passed for a highway out here in the boonies, at the first available road following the "Centerville Pharmacy" billboard. Keeping her eyes on the move in case there was any unusual police activity or possible surveillance (this was another situation she had missed in her planning: there was no way to spot surveillance out in the sticks because every stranger was under surveillance all the time, from everybody. It was only if they *moved* to follow you that you were in trouble), she drove toward the center of town, being careful not to exceed the speed limit.

Oh, boy! The two automated teller machines attached to

the Iowa Chartered Savings & Loan were both unoccupied, and both showed the green "Open" sign through the Plexiglas display windows. She wouldn't have to rub patched elbows with the *lumpen proletariat* in a forced display of democratic good citizenship but would have the electronic geek all to herself.

She looked around as she parked the car, because later her head would remain forward and relaxed as she walked toward the machine. Carrying her satchel lightly in one hand, she reached into her coat pocket and withdrew the ATM card. She had a bunch of them, aware that the delicate magnetic stripe could be damaged by anything from an eelskin wallet to an accidental brush with a television just as the set was turned on and the picture tube automatically degaussed with a powerful magnet. Making duplicates was easy.

She inserted the card into the receptacle and punched her code without bothering to look at the screen.

It had taken her a surprisingly long time to recover from the shock of the first message they had sent her. As the bills were falling from the slot, she had been surprised at hearing a triple beep emanating from the terminal just before the flow ended. That had never happened before.

The beeping had sounded again, and she'd frowned, turning her head to look at the screen. The standard welcome screen with advertising tripe had been cleared, and Phyllis had frozen as she read what replaced it, not even aware that several bills had gotten past her and fluttered to the ground.

She'd read it again and again, not that it had been difficult to comprehend. That wasn't it. So what was it?

The screen had read:

```
This is Jack.

Is everything being done to
your satisfaction?

Please press 1 for Yes or 2 for
No.
```

That was it. That was all of it. She remembered her reaction: *Why do I all of a sudden feel the skin crawling on my neck?*

She'd continued to stare at the screen, at a total loss for what to do. The sound of footsteps had startled her, and she'd looked around quickly, seeing the bills that had fallen. After stooping quickly to pick them up, she'd spun around to see if anything else was amiss and had fumbled the top of the satchel closed before its contents were made visible to whoever was approaching.

The screen had not changed, its blinking cursor alive with expectation of an answer. *What's the big deal, here? Why the panic?* It shouldn't have been so much of a surprise. She'd known that they could quickly locate the machine she was using, so there shouldn't have been any trick to sending a message, although the fact that it had happened that fast was a little disconcerting.

She'd known she had to get out of there, and quickly. Maybe they were already on the phone to the local yokel police force. Maybe those steps about to round the corner were those of an FBI agent. Maybe . . .

Relax! Think! They wouldn't nab her, not with the dual collection arrangement, not while they thought there was more than one person involved. Too risky. But they could have gone for a visual ID. Phyllis had known from the beginning that this was a possibility. But they wouldn't have done it by having someone walk right up to her and say hello. Then again, he wouldn't have had to say anything, just drunk in her features with practiced eyes or a concealed camera and gone about his business as if nothing had happened.

But it would have been impossible for them to have found her, the way she'd been moving. Wouldn't it?

She'd looked at the screen again. Maybe it was a sincere question that was being posed. They were running scared, didn't know if their compliance was pleasing her (hah! pleasing *him*, they were probably thinking), maybe needed a little reassurance. *So why am I so panicked?*

Her gloved finger had hovered above the keyboard for an eternity before she'd pressed 1, spun on one foot and hurried away, not even bothering to see who had been approaching.

But that was then. This was now. And now there was a new message.

No problem. It didn't bother her at all.

* * *

The hell it didn't.

Phyllis sat with her head bowed, hands white with stretched flesh gripping the steering wheel. An animal sound rose from somewhere deep within her, crescendoing into an anguished scream.

Her primal explosion was interrupted by a tapping on the window, and she turned her head to see a leather knuckle as the cause of the sound. She raised her eyes to mirrored sunglasses beneath a blue helmet, as the gloved fingers made a downward, twirling motion. A sign language command, which she obeyed by lowering her window, slowly, to give herself time to try to construct a temporary veneer over her pockmarked psyche.

"Yes, Officer?"

The policeman, satisfied that the woman's hands were firmly planted on the wheel where he could see them, glanced quickly and professionally at the passenger seat, the under-dash floorboards and the backseat before replying.

"You okay, ma'am?"

She smiled weakly, as though bravely laughing off pain. "Just a cramp."

He smiled back with the kind of sympathy meant to commu-nicate that he, burly male and symbol of authority, was sensi-tive and not above empathy for the kinds of things most men couldn't hope to comprehend but he certainly did. "Sure. I understand."

Fuck you, you understand. You understand shit. "I'm okay now."

"You sure?"

Fuck you again! What if I'm not? "Absolutely. And thanks for asking."

"You bet." He touched his helmet with two fingers, the trucker's half salute to a kindred spirit. "Drive careful now, y'hear?"

"You bet," Phyllis replied in sarcastic repetition the cop failed to catch, as she started the engine of the rented car and drove off slowly, checking both sides and the rearview mirror in obedient acknowledgment of the policeman's watchful stare.

When she was about two miles out of town and certain

that the patrolman was no longer a threat, she pulled off the
main road and down a side street, stopped the car in the soft
embrace of a towering elm and killed the engine. The new
message replayed itself in her mind. She leaned her head back
and tried to make sense of the new information, to sort it out,
to make a plan.

She was no fool. She knew the best laid plans of mice and
terrorists were as nothing against the caprice of happenstance.
The measure of her mettle was not the flawless execution of
a careful strategy, but how she responded as the situation
changed. She knew it would and thought she had been prepared.

The first message on the ATM screen had shaken her badly,
but she had recovered quickly. In fact, her adversaries' apparent dim-wittedness thus far had been a pleasant surprise that
only increased the level of her disdain for them.

But this?

```
Hi, this is Jack.

Today's financial news:

MicroFab Corporation up one and
seven-eighths on news that it is to
receive a huge order from Autonav
for newly redesigned chips.

Film at eleven.

Have a nice day.
```

To have figured out *that* quickly that she had worked for
the chip fabricator? *That* was incredible.

She fought back against the shock and tried to think. Their
most obvious train of thought should have been that she had
simply duplicated a ground station, a simple idea that had
even been a plot element of a popular motion picture. Anyone
with a general electronics background could do that, and it
was a wonder that it hadn't been tried before. She knew from
the background briefings by Autonav executives that it was
even a standard scenario in CIA, MI-5 and Mossad training.

Picking out isolated aircraft was part of her strategy. She had checked the schedules carefully and knew that only one airliner was due in to Bellingham when she'd zapped the 727. Was it possible that another aircraft had been inbound at the same time?

That had to be it. That one plane was disrupted, and another in the vicinity wasn't, that would be the giveaway. Couldn't have happened in Indiana: that plane went down with no survivors, so how would they know? Must have been Bellingham.

Fuck it. Fuck them. She knew that swapping out the affected units would take a very long time, and they knew that, too. That part of the operation was safe.

But now they knew she worked for MicroFab, or at least had at one time. What did that mean? Lots of people worked there, and they couldn't know how long ago the modification was planted in the design. Not without pulling units from selected airplanes to see how far back the mod appeared. They may not even know how to tell if a particular chip *was* modified, wasn't that right?

She rubbed her forehead. Wrong. If they'd already figured out the MicroFab angle, these were not your garden-variety GERBs, the government-employed rat bastards held in such low esteem by the *hoi polloi* of private high-tech. This was a bunch of serious overachievers motivated by some dumb, shit-ass sense of civic duty. Christ, she hated assholes like that.

Her only alternative was to assume that they knew exactly who she was. Had to be. As soon as they asked who would have been smart enough and mad enough at the world to pull something like this, her name would have popped to the top of the queue. And that meant they would quickly find out that she owned a plane, and what its tail numbers were. Maybe they'd even realize that its navigation unit contained the very first modified chip, the one she'd used to test the whole idea. Then they would gasp with the realization of how many of these things there were out in the world. . . .

The thought gave her a moment of satisfaction, but it passed quickly. God, she was going to miss that plane. Would likely never see it again.

Have to think, dammit. Replan.

Her thoughts raced back to the small green display on the

cash machine. It was the face of the enemy, of all her enemies. Pieces of her mind were disintegrating and re-forming in new patterns, severely traumatized by the unexpected intimacy engendered by this unholy form of communication. It had a name—*Jack*—and some part of her had the unshakable feeling that it wasn't a made-up name, not a neutral moniker selected by a committee as the personification of their collective presence. Jack was a person, she just knew that, and it bothered her a great deal because, without realizing it during the years of planning, she had subconsciously counted on dealing with a faceless and inept bureaucracy, not with a breathing human being. It made it hard to think, and she had to think, hard, about what she was going to do next.

Jack. It had a nice ring. Hard, abrupt, no frills and right to the point. The sick and crumbling part of her mind, which was reaching the turning point in its debauched competition with what little remained of her more normal self, mulled over the implications of dealing with a representative of everything it hated about that subset of the human race it labeled as non–Phyllis Dalek. There was somebody to show now, somebody in whose face to rub her titanic contempt and the loathing she sought desperately to shift away form herself.

This was going to call for something special when the time came. The time *would* come. She was no idiot, no self-aggrandizing self-deluder stupid enough to think that she could simply disappear and be happy. Her odyssey was an addiction of the worst kind. Not to drugs, not to sex, but to power, to that fragrant, jasmine perfume of absolute control and authority over people and institutions that, often as not, was a sublimated, failed mastery over oneself.

Its ultimate demonstration wasn't in the day-to-day dictate of trivial acts, the mindless redirections of inconsequential activities so prized by corporate executives and prison guards. For Phyllis Dalek, the apocalypse would be larger than the laughable gathering of dimes from bank machines. It would be writ large on the psyches of her enemies, her classmates, her bosses, flight attendants and the myriad other unwitting sculptors of her tortured soul.

If she could only get that goddamned, condescending, sono-fabitch bastard of a cash machine to quit bothering her.

CHAPTER 27

June 25, 0700 EST

> Emergency NOTAM 007-13245
> 25JUN, FAR 23-98
> TO: Commercial pilots—scheduled
>   carriers, charter and cargo
> FROM: Director, Federal Aviation
>   Administration
>
> ///NOTAM begins.
>
> With regard to the upcoming South American
> peace conference being hosted by the
> President, the Agency has received
> notification from the Director of Central
> Intelligence that threats have been made
> against the U.S. Air Traffic Control system
> by heretofore unknown terrorist
> organizations.
>
> While it is impossible at this time to determine

the credibility of the threats, or how ATC might be affected, it is the policy of the Agency to take all such threats seriously. Notice is hereby given to all pilots to be alert for anomalous navigational instrument readings when flying in instrument meteorological conditions.

You are directed to immediately report such anomalies to the controller handling your flight and to switch to timed dead reckoning navigation if at all feasible. If you are unable to maintain radio contact, proceed on your flight plan until reaching VFR conditions and remain VFR—do not reenter IMC.

This NOTAM is in effect until further notice.

///NOTAM ends.

June 26, 0815 MST

Phyllis Dalek had the cigarette halfway to her mouth when the news came over the radio. It ended so fast that she couldn't catch all of it, and she flipped through the channels, trying to find another news program.

> " . . . were handed an unusual regulatory notice
> from the FAA today as they filed flight plans
> throughout the country. The emergency
> notification, or NOTAM, as it is called, warned
> that terrorists had made threats against the
> nation's airway navigational systems in protest
> of the upcoming South American summit. The
> notice warned pilots to be wary of erroneous
> instrument readings, although it gave no details

about what kinds of problems might be expected.
Local FAA representative Vernon Mulcahy had
this to say to KBNK reporter Ashley Rodriguez:"

"Ah, don't let's be making a big thing of this
now. We issue these kinds of warnings all
the time. As a federal agency we have to take
every darn fool threat seriously, and all
we're saying is, Pilots, stay on your toes for a
while until this thing blows over."

"KNBK will keep you posted if there are any
further developments."

Phyllis switched off the radio and wiped away the ash that
had fallen from the forgotten cigarette onto her lap.

Terrorists?

It seemed awfully coincidental, coming as it did so soon
after the flurry of information from "Jack." *Wonder if he's
FBI?*

She pulled off the main highway just outside Fargo, North
Dakota, and considered what it might mean. All the pilots in
the country on alert. Commercial pilots, not private.

No. He'd said it was a NOTAM. That meant every single
pilot in the country would have access to it, even though it
may not be applicable to private flyers. But why exclude them
in the first place? They certainly flew "hard IFR," deep inside
bad weather, and were in just as much danger as a commercial
carrier if somebody . . .

Who am I kidding? It has to be me! They excluded private
pilots because they knew she wouldn't bother with them.

The thought gave her a sudden rush, as though her limbs
had gone weightless in some gravitational perturbation. The
dizziness made it difficult for her to think, to sort it out. Why
would they go public with it, knowing full well that there
was no risk while the money kept flowing? Why now? What
the hell was going on?

By the time she reached the Custer Savings & Loan headquarters building on Black Hills Avenue, she was nearly shaking from her inability to construct a scenario that fit the

available information. Up until this point, she had been more or less in control, or at least knew what was going on and why.

Now, between the time she heard the news on the radio and the twenty-three minutes it took her to reach the cash machines, she could feel her equilibrium dissipate like frost on the window as the sun came up. Her teeth were so tightly clenched that they hurt, and she had to force her eyes to stay focused. She felt as though the slightest misstep could resonate with her crystalline fragility and shatter her as the jeweler's hammer shattered a flawed diamond.

She eyed the cash machine from inside her car. It was an inanimate object, hard steel and some quartz glass. She knew that.

All along it had been a benign dispenser of extorted largesse, a trained goose disgorging golden eggs at her behest, delivered with the flick of a plastic card and the touch of a few buttons. Thoughtless, obedient, mechanical. She *knew* that, dammit.

There were no other people around. *Just you and me, machine.*

It dared her. She thought she heard it humming in feigned nonchalance, demonstrating its nervelessness. A child's game of slap hands. *Touch me and I may slap you. I may not. If I get away with it, I get a point.* The night deposit drawer was a grinning mouth, the display monitor an inscrutable, electron-pumped eye. *Wanna play?*

Phyllis put the side of her hand into her mouth and bit down on it. It hurt like hell, so she bit harder and held it until she couldn't stand it anymore, then she opened the door and stepped out, clutching her oversize handbag. She slipped on her white dress gloves and was glad nobody was around to see the small drops of blood that oozed through the fabric. The sidewalk felt like a trampoline, and she slowed to stop the bouncing.

She found it difficult to breathe. Her chest shook as she tried to inhale, and then she was at the machine. The plastic card wobbled in her hand, but it steadied as it entered the slot. She had to rest her wrist on the base of the panel so she could hit the keys, and then she closed her eyes, opened them and looked at the monitor.

Nothing there. She almost cried out in relief and then turned back to the rush of bills that threatened to overflow out of the wire receptacle because of her inattention.

In her near delirium, she stayed a full three minutes for her largest single withdrawal to date, then realized how foolish and dangerous that was. She walked confidently back to the car and forced herself to stay under the speed limit as she drove away.

It was easy. She just drifted into her favorite way of relaxing. All she had to do was conjure up the memory. . . .

There had been nothing but dead silence on the radio for nearly fifteen minutes now.

For the past hour, rain *ping*ed on the roof of the rental car with varying intensities as the powerful embedded thunderstorms moved eastward, slowly and mysteriously, in the darkness somewhere overhead. When they were directly above, the volume of water at the end of its four-mile fall was so great that it seemed as though the roof would buckle under the onslaught. Afterward, the background cascade, though significant in its own right, seemed a pleasant interlude before the next wave. Lightning, cracking and booming with Olympian majesty, periodically illuminated the roadway and stood the surrounding trees in stark relief. She could prolong the retinal afterimage by blinking, but she began to have difficulty separating the real scene from its chemical analogue and it spooked her, so she stopped.

Almost four o'clock. Getting toward zero hour, but there was no precision to it. Not in this weather. Turbulence up there must be awful. Nevertheless, as the minutes ticked down she found herself shifting back and forth on her seat. Not uncomfortable, exactly. Not exactly anxious, either. More like expectant, a little nervous. It was somewhat of a new feeling, not altogether unpleasant, come to think of it. . . .

"Indie Approach, Alpha Cargo three-niner Charlie."

The static-ridden voice blasting out of the portable scanner jolted her so badly she banged her wrist into the steering wheel as her hand flew up in an involuntary defensive reaction.

Glands she barely knew existed injected a microscopic droplet of adrenaline into her system, and her whole body flared from the sudden heat. Her limbs grew light and her fingers splayed open as she sucked in a quick breath, an ancient reflex designed to scoop up as much oxygen as possible in preparation for escaping a threat or fighting an enemy.

It was over in a flash, only the pounding thump of her heart as a reminder. The chemicals and the extra air and the stepped-up coursing of blood through her system, all unnecessary and unused, made her feel so light that she thought she might faint. But she couldn't allow herself to do that. Not now.

The bright blue aura from the screen of the portable computer on the passenger seat cast an eerie glow in the car, adding to the otherworldly atmosphere of sitting dry in the middle of a raging storm. Phyllis had no time to think about that now, although the strange little feeling, boosted by the adrenaline charge, was unmistakable and new, and she would have liked to savor it a little.

She reached for the scanner and turned down the volume just as it scratched out another transmission.

"Three-niner Charlie, this is Indie Approach, go ahead."

It was time.

She had the whole program preset into the computer. All the frequencies, probable timings and positions. All she had to do was push the right buttons as things progressed, stay alert for position clues as the radio chatter proceeded, and be prepared to get creative if need be.

She reached for the keyboard, but the little feeling intruded and she stopped for a second to try to figure it out. Her breathing seemed a little deeper, a little faster, maybe, and that was unusual, but what was even more unusual was that she noticed it at all. Mouth a little dry, too. But that was understandable. Standard anxiety reaction.

Except this wasn't anxiety. Noticeably different, but she couldn't quite put her finger on it.

She touched one of the buttons on the keyboard, the one that would initiate the correct procedure. As the key reached the bottom of its travel and she felt more than heard the confirming click, a small charge of electricity shot through her and her breathing stopped momentarily. Not painful. Not at all. Pleasant, even.

She sat back, mystified. Nothing to do for sixty seconds anyway. Her lips were parted and her eyes half-closed, arms lying limp at her sides. She blinked to try to clear her head, to make it go away, but it did and she didn't like that, so she tried to relax and make it come back.

The laptop beeped and some symbols appeared. She glanced at them. Everything was in order, and her breathing deepened even further. The planned correction to the program would not be necessary, and she had another minute. Her face felt warm, and she suspected that if she looked in the mirror, it would be flushed red.

"Request weather update on vicinity Mepham, say again, vicinity Mepham."

Oh, God, fantastic! She had little doubt that the pilots were going to try to bust minimums before aborting their landing. She only needed them to do it just a little bit.

The computer beeped again and displayed a new set of numbers, and Phyllis put out a trembling hand and pushed a few more buttons, barely able to pick out the correct little keys from their neighbors, but she managed and then let go and slumped back and her breathing grew shallower and more labored.

"Alpha Cargo, Indie Approach: Say altitude and squawk." The voice was puzzled, demanding. This was just too good.

Against the sonic overload of the rain, something else made itself apparent, a steady whining, a sound of power, growing closer from somewhere behind the car. Phyllis let out an involuntary moan, and her head fell back against the seat. Her head was spinning and she was scared and elated at the same time, and as the sound grew louder a pressure began to build inside her.

"Squawking one-two-five-niner, three thousand and . . ."

She figured out that pressing the buttons and watching the perfect numbers arrange themselves across the screen was all part of it, and she couldn't let any piece of the whole thing go or none of it, whatever it was, would work at all, and the pressure built and built as the sound of the massive cargo plane came blasting down at her from above and she heard the approach controller say, "Alpha Cargo, stand by one . . ." and she was almost weeping with the bliss of it and then the sound of the enormous turbine engines started to soften ever so slightly as the plane passed her position and she opened her eyes just a bit and her rasping breath steadied in rhythm as she tried to rest and prepare herself—for what, for pity's sake!—and for a moment the whole world was still and expectant and then—"I say again, Alpha Cargo, this is Indie Approach. Acknowledge!"—the sky lit up in a sulfurous fireball and seconds later the countryside was rocked for miles around and the shock waves hit the car and rippled through the frame and into Phyllis's waiting body and her neck snapped back and her spine arched into an impossible shape and the fevered pressure broke and exploded and escaped through all her cells, the guttural moan in her throat escalating into a deep, long, unstoppable primal scream that had lain dormant for years, and tears streamed from her eyes in a strange mixture of pain and ecstasy that drowned her travails and anguish until the kerosene-fueled glow in the sky dimmed and the sound of the explosion died away.

She turned her head on weakened neck muscles and was barely able to lift an arm to switch off the radio. For some reason, the frightened voice that had affected her so powerfully a few seconds ago now failed to stir her quite as it had before, but the voice—"Alpha Cargo, Indie Approach: Do you copy?"—urgent and a little scared, felt to her like a warm afterglow, and she basked in it until her breathing was mostly back to normal.

She put her hands on the steering wheel and pulled herself more upright. The glow continued to suffuse her, a warm, pleasant aftertaste. She felt embarrassed, even though she was alone, and swallowed hard several times. She reached for a cigarette.

It was still raining as she opened the door and stepped out gingerly, turning her face upward and letting the droplets hit her and trickle down her cheeks. She stuck out her tongue and licked at the delicious water, which ran down her collar and onto her back, the coolness a thrilling and refreshing sensation.

No longer afraid of the feeling, and realizing how comically

clichéd the cigarette was under the circumstances, she started
to giggle. It caught hold of her and grew until she was laughing
uncontrollably, and she had to lean against the car, sliding
down helplessly until she was kneeling in the leaf-strewn
mud.

When she was too weak to continue, she looked toward
the ridge, unseen in the darkness, where the MD-11 had disin-
tegrated at her command. It had been so easy. And so pleasur-
able. Something deep within her told her that she had known
it would be like this.

Could be like this again.

She clambered to her feet and wiped her muddy hands on
her jacket. Composure restored, she got back into the car.

No time to fool around. Gotta go send a fax.

She reluctantly let the sweet memory go, shook herself
back into the here and now and tried to concentrate on her
driving. *Now* she had them by the balls and wasn't about to
let go. Control was her weapon, the ability to keep it together
when all around her were flailing themselves into chaos.

A few minutes later she drove without stopping past the
Great Plains Feed Co. teller machines, past the Hovey Savings & Loan, past the United Farm Workers Local 61 Credit
Union, not even slowing down as the Federal Bank of North
Dakota hove into view and then disappeared in her rearview
mirror. She pulled over to the side of the road, slid over to
the passenger side, opened the door and vomited onto the
gravel.

How could she have miscalculated so badly?

Really, what the hell kind of sense did it make to plan for
everything and forget that there would be real people on the
other end, experts, and not just a bunch of tech weenies,
either, but professionals who really knew their business, knew
how to deal with mad extortionists and other affronts to the
public well-being?

Did she really think they would stay in the background,
faceless and mechanical, pursuing a barrelful of thin leads
and treating her like an automaton? Did she really think that
she could plan perfectly, execute flawlessly, and not have

these guys come to the realization that they needed to go after her mind? Why was she losing sleep, weight and nerve in a three-way footrace toward a nervous breakdown?

At first it made her confused, then depressed, then paranoid. Eventually it made her angry, in a mirrored parallelism of her whole life. Anger was good for her. Her tortured introspection sublimated into plans for countermeasures, even though some retained grain of rationality should have told her that, in actual point of fact, no such measures were necessary. After all, if she could just ignore the personal swipes, was it not the case that the information they were passing her was useful? If not for them, she'd be flying around in a marked airplane even at this very moment.

But the mission had taken on a momentum of its own, too big even for her to stop. That was the one thing she hadn't planned on, how to stop. There was no way. The modified navigation units were in place and would be so for at least two years. That meant she was a threat, even if she decided to stand down the mission, because there was no way for her to demonstrate the permanent cessation of her activities.

And then lives were lost, and a hundred-million-dollar aircraft, and the game stepped over a boundary line etched deep into steel. She hadn't intended for that to happen, but it was necessary, because the faceless bureaucracy she had set out to engage in battle had assumed a corporeal form. It even had a name.

Jack.

She wiped at her mouth and threw the tissue out the window as she pulled away from the shoulder and back onto the highway, whipping the rear end of the car around as she sailed across the double yellow lines back in the direction from which she had just come, flooring the pedal and not letting up until she saw the Great Plains Feed Co. teller machines.

She left the engine running as she jumped out and ran to the machine, with barely a glance to ensure that she was alone, plunged the card into the reader and punched her code.

There was a moment's hesitation before the bills starting dropping into the wire holder, and then they overflowed and fluttered to the ground and blew in the wind as Phyllis, frozen like a deer caught in headlights, read the message on the screen.

    What's a nice girl like you doing
    in a job like this?

      Call 202-555-1825 and ask for
    Jack.

Bank of the Grange. One site, no branches. Purely local savings and loan. One FundsNet cash machine hidden toward the rear, facing the parking lot. Eight cars. None in or out for the last twelve minutes. Promised herself to wait twenty, but that was twelve minutes ago.

She inserted her card and punched the code, and her mouth went dry as bills failed to materialize. A blinking cursor sat alone on the display monitor. Maybe she'd punched the wrong code.

She inserted the card again and typed in the code, then tried it two more times, looking around to make certain she wasn't being watched, even though she knew that she was unlikely to spot an experienced tail.

Either way, it was time to get the hell out of there, to find a place to figure it all out. Maybe they were calling her bluff, figuring they were real smart now and had a way to cut her off at the knees.

She turned to go and got three steps away when the terminal began beeping insistently. She stopped and turned slowly, seeing the letters forming on the screen but too far away to read them.

She considered leaving anyway but knew that this would be an impossibility, so she stepped back as slowly as she could, until the blurry characters clarified and swam into focus and then bit into her brain as no scalpel or bullet could ever hope to do, and she felt the anger, the secret anger that only surfaced every once in a great while, she felt it erupt from its lair with a great and terrible roar and engulf her before she could mount any sort of a challenge to it, assuming that she would want to in the first place, which, as she read the message over and over, she realized that she didn't. Not this time. Not to save those fucking bastards or any of the other fucking bastards or anyone in this entire country or the whole world, for that matter.

She read it once more before turning to leave.

```
Philo?

What kind of name is that for a
campus sweetheart like you?

 Philo?
```

CHAPTER 28

1342 MST

"Iit's too quiet."

It had been more than five hours since Phyllis Dalek had received the message on the Bank of the Grange ATM. They were very surprised that not a single attempt had been made after that.

All except Amy Goldberg. She said that she would have been amazed had there been even one more try.

"Isn't it possible she thinks we're not really cutting off the money?" Stanley asked her. "That we're just goosing her?"

Amy smacked the heel of her hand lightly on her forehead several times. "How many times I have to tell you? It's not the money!"

They were in a private office on level eight of the control tower at Chicago's O'Hare Airport. Letitia May Hubbard had exercised her considerable authority and had wrought a near miracle of logistics. Their biggest worry had been the installation of the phone lines, but all the lines were not only in place, they had the same area code and numbers they'd had in Washington. Secretary Hubbard had helped the phone company to understand the likely consequences of their procrastination and substandard procedures as they pertained to a matter of national security and also offered to reconsider for them whether the day-to-day installation of long-distance switching equipment constituted the carriage of goods across state lines as per federal commerce statutes. Thus motivated, their cooperation was commendable.

Jack Webster was not participating in the nervous repartee this afternoon. He sat by the window and watched as the giant airplanes took off and landed, as many as one every thirty seconds, and considered how the system barely worked when everything was functioning properly and how easily its delicate and balanced interplay of people, hardware and procedures could be upset.

His morose air gradually spread throughout the room, the contagion of his melancholy settling on his colleagues until the atmosphere no longer supported the deflection of their fear through increasingly stale witticisms. They knew what he knew.

Whatever was coming was going to be as dangerous as it was dramatic. Amy theorized that Phyllis Dalek was constitutionally incapable of ignoring the gauntlet that they had flung in her path, and on this point Preston Stanley was in complete agreement. He knew, as did all of his Bureau colleagues in the field, that an enormous majority of high-profile and creative criminals could avoid capture simply by ceasing their activities, slipping back into the dark night of their own existences. But their egos and warped competitiveness usually made that impossible, as the overwhelming drive to demonstrate their superiority ultimately annihilated any sense of longer-term self-preservation. They had to win not only in their own minds, but in the minds of the enemy, in a manner that they could see, not just surmise. It might go on longer for some than for others, but, inevitably, it was their undoing. It was why they all lost in the end.

Phyllis Dalek was no different. She had proven herself a formidable opponent and one who had gone too far to give up the game or wrestle to a stalemate. Whatever was going to happen, this one was for all the marbles.

Jack wondered how it would come.

Book 3

He went down
As when a lordly cedar, green with boughs,
Goes down with a great shout upon the hills,
And leaves a lonesome place against the sky.

—Edwin Markham (1901)

CHAPTER 29

June 29, 0659 PST

"Holy Hannah, Kincaid, why don't we just adopt the little nuisance!"

Lamarr was happily oblivious of Lenore's good-natured griping, too busily engaged in inhaling scrambled eggs, toast piled high with orange marmalade, a frightening amount of bacon and enough orange juice to deplete a small orchard.

Bo watched in fascination as the skinny kid cut a swath through the generously laden table. He had often pondered the physical inconceivability of how so much food could fit inside that smallish frame.

"We couldn't afford it, Lenny. This way, we don't gotta feed the little pecker but five, six times a week."

"Aunty Len, y'got any more milk?"

" 'Course. We bought our own cow last week."

They weren't really his aunt and uncle, not technically speaking, but the only other title that would have justified the affection showered on Lamarr would have been fairy godparents, and that would hardly do.

Bo got up out of his chair, shaking his head, and went to the screen door. The sun had been up for nearly an hour, and the last of the ground haze was vanishing as the warming rays found the thin wisps and vaporized them. The soft gray above had given way to a deep blue that was beginning to lighten in the east, and the hills to the west were covered with buttery yellow light. The shadows of the hangars and the tied-down airplanes at the airport less than a mile away stretched long across the tarmac and would be gone in a few hours as the summer sun's transit carried it to a nearly overhead position.

"Nice day for flyin'."

Lamarr, mouth full and up until now seemingly heedless of the surrounding conversation, looked up quickly and emitted a choking half squeal, leaped from his chair, dutifully remembered to grant Lenore a token kiss that didn't quite connect with her cheek, and shot through the screen door, leaving a small but discernible sonic boom in his wake.

"Who said I was gonna take you?" Bo muttered uselessly as the door sprang back at him, but Lamarr was by then too far away to hear him. He turned to look at Lenore.

"Go on ahead," she said resignedly, gesturing at the table. "Maybe I can donate what he was *planning* to eat and save a starving nation."

Bo opened the hall closet and reached for his flight bag. "Back by lunchtime, sweets."

"Of that, I have no doubt," she said, watching Lamarr in the distance through the screen door as he danced and waved his arms for Bo to hurry up. She wasn't happy about her husband's flying. It made her tense and anxious, although she tried not to let it show. Besides, it was the price she was prepared to pay for the light that shone in his eyes, which had to do not so much with flying as it did with spending time with Lamarr. It helped that he wore a parachute when flying the Mustang, an FAA rule for aerobatic flight. With Bo at the controls, the sleek fighter didn't spend a whole lot of time in straight and level flight.

They'd not had children of their own. She wasn't happy about that, either, but Bo was terrified of being a parent, believing that he'd never be able to crawl out from beneath his crushing sense of failure. Lenore, with a degree in psychology and a lifetime as a professional counselor in high schools, knew enough to realize that no amount of spoken rationalization could hope to penetrate the enameled guilt that had baked into his soul. He was still haunted by the vision etched behind his eyes so long ago, and while Lamarr hadn't made him forget, he had given Bo something to head toward in addition to what he had to run from.

Bo looked at Lamarr and saw a template, a living tabula rasa whose future would be shaped by the incidents and influences of his childhood. While he had come into the world, Bo believed, already gifted with intelligence, wit and an unflappably sunny disposition, Bo also felt strongly that boys were profoundly shaped by the masculine role models in their lives. Lamarr's father was a good man and would play that part well, but Bo also knew that his own relationship with Lamarr could ultimately prove more significant. Their bond was not an artificially constructed, sticky-sweet concoction of psychobabbled endearments and endlessly analyzed interactions. Theirs was more mysterious, an almost telepathic interplay of shared perceptions and worldview that did not require a torrent of words. It was an adult relationship, one that allowed them to poke and gibe at each other in rough, barracks-house fashion, neither one ever doubting for a second the love that ebbed and flowed between them like the tides.

Most important, and best of all from Lenore's point of view, Bo's sense of responsibility toward the boy was so strong that he consciously strove to suppress his bouts of reflective melancholy. Bo was smart enough to recognize how illogical and unreasonable his decades of devastating self-flagellation had been and continued to be. While he could no more alter the currents of his memories than he could stop the moon in its orbit, he could do his best to shield them from Lamarr.

To some extent it worked, but the luminance of their insights about each other was not easily dimmed, and Lamarr readily sensed Bo's troubled side. Bo had told him the story of Judson Greaves's final hours and of his life, at first smoothing over the disturbing parts as they related to war and the extraordinary passion men could mount for one another's destruction. But by the time Lamarr was in the second grade, Bo's respect for the boy had grown to the point where he'd told him the story head on, all of it, including his own helplessness as the cowardly enemy tortured Jud from a distance until he died.

He had recounted that part of the story only a few times. At first Lamarr had vehemently challenged Bo's assertion of his own ineptitude, but with that startling clarity of vision only a child could mount, he had come to understand the futility of that line of reasoning and grew content simply to hear the story as many times as Bo cared to tell it and ask as many questions as Bo cared to answer.

So Lamarr let Bo be strong for him and drew hungrily on that, because he knew, without consciously knowing that he knew, that Bo's strength was not a facade but was vital and real, and Lenore hoped that someday her husband would recognize that as well.

What Lenore also knew, but would never tell Bo, was that the young boy's influence on her husband was at least as powerful as, and probably more important than, her husband's was on the boy.

They looked like remora and shark as they walked together toward the field, Bo slow and dignified while Lamarr pranced around him, urging him to speed up.

The Cessna 150 two-seater was tied down outside, chained to iron loops set in concrete on the ramp. Bungee cords held wooden two-by-fours on top of the wings. The plane was so light, a thirty-five-knot wind could lift it off the ground. The pieces of wood acted as spoilers while the plane was parked, disrupting the flow of wind over the wings and ruining the lift.

Their preflight was thorough. Bo tolerated no sloppiness or shortcuts. Even if they only landed at another airport for a few minutes to get a piece of pie, they still went through the entire routine.

Once inside the cockpit, Lamarr read off the printed check-list as Bo tested the various controls and instruments.

"Parking brake, locked position?"

"Up and locked."

"Ailerons, full deflection?"

"Operating and correct."

"Gear switch down and locked?"

Bo turned and flicked his finger at Lamarr's nose. "Ain't no gear in a One fifty, pea-brain."

"Just makin' sure you're payin' attention. Choke?"

"Full out."

And so they went on until it was time to start the engine.

Bo and Lamarr looked carefully around the plane, then Bo loudly yelled, "Clear!" through the small side window and engaged the starter. It cranked for about ten seconds without starting, and Bo released the key.

"Shot of primer, Unc?"

"Go ahead."

Lamarr disengaged the primer knob and pulled it all the way out, listening as fuel gurgled into the chamber. Then he pushed it back in, sending raw fuel into the carburetor, and locked it back in place.

"Clear!" Bo yelled again, and reengaged the starter. The prop turned again, and after a few seconds the engine coughed and belched a small puff of smoke, then coughed again, then finally caught and spun under its own power as Bo released the key.

The engine continued to sputter erratically, refusing to settle into a smoother rhythm. Bo tried various throttle settings to no avail.

"Let's burn the mags!" Lamarr yelled over the din.

Bo nodded and released the parking brake, taxiing the Cessna out to the runway away from other aircraft. He slewed around by holding the toe brake on one wheel until he was pointing into the wind, then reset the hand brake.

He pushed in the throttle until the engine reached 1,400 RPM, then turned the key until they were running on only one of the twin magnetos and let it stay there to burn off any carbon deposits. Then he did the same with the remaining mag and pulled the throttle back to idle. The engine was still unacceptably rough.

Two more attempts were equally futile. Bo saw the disappointment on Lamarr's face, but there was nothing he could do. He also glanced at his watch and knew that if he didn't get in the air pretty soon, he'd miss Jerry Bradley's shift in the control tower.

He taxied the plane back to the ramp, swung it into position and killed the engine. They sat quietly for a while. Lamarr looked out the front windscreen at the lightening sky, the trees perfectly unmoving in the windless air, the shimmer of heat just beginning to flake from the hilltops to the north. He also knew Bradley's schedule.

"Whyn't you go on up in the big plane, Unc? Shame to waste this day."

"Thought we was goin' together."

Lamarr shrugged and opened the flimsy side door. "I'll get ahold of Joe, ask him can he look at the engine. Then we can go this afternoon, okay?"

"Okay. Wanna help me preflight?"

Lamarr was already out the door and running for the hangar.

"Hey, ain't you gonna help me tie this one down first?" Bo yelled after him, to no avail.

They used a hand-operated electric tow cart to pull the Mustang from the hangar. In the rising sunlight, its counterposing ambiguities were everywhere in evidence. Every line on the plane looked as lethal as it did swift, but it seemed a reluctant killer. Seen from the ground, it appeared big and imposing, the overall effect enhanced by the enormous propeller that loomed impossibly large high over Lamarr's head. Yet in the air it was a bullet, its sleek body slipping effortlessly through the air, about as fast as anything powered by a piston engine could go.

It sat on conventional landing gear, two big main wheels and an afterthought of a tail wheel at the rear. Pointed skyward even while sitting on the ground, the P-51 existed in a perpetual ache to fly, as though every grounded moment were an affront to its heritage.

It took nearly three times as long to preflight as did the Cessna, and soon Bo was in the cockpit alone, the canopy still pulled back.

"Uncle Bo?" Lamarr called from below.

Bo looked over the side.

"How you gonna teach me to fly this thing if it's only got one seat?"

Bo slapped his head with an open palm. "I never thought of that! Guess there's no way. Clear?"

"Clear!" Lamarr yelled back up, and Bo punched in the starter button.

The giant prop labored for three or four turns and then caught, sending a blast of air toward Lamarr that nearly knocked him over. Bo taxied out and headed for the east end of the runway, swiveling the tail back and forth so that he could watch where he was going out the side windows. It was impossible to see over the top of the instrument panel when the plane was sitting on its tail. Later, when the tail came up into flight attitude, his forward visibility would be excellent.

He paused at the end of the runway and performed his run-up, satisfied that everything was in proper working order. As usual, several airport workers and hangers-on had drifted out to watch the restored classic take off.

After looking up to check the skies and broadcasting his intentions, Bo cranked the canopy forward and latched it, then taxied onto the runway. He pushed in the throttle and listened carefully as the powerful Rolls-Royce engine spun up to take-off speed.

Looking out, he saw the spectators gathering and also spotted Lamarr far down the runway. *What the hell, might as well give 'em a thrill.*

He stood on the toe brakes and held the plane still until the propeller was whirling at its maximum power and the airframe threatened to come apart under the strain. He tilted his feet back off the brakes, and the suddenly freed plane bolted forward, slewing characteristically to the left until Bo corrected with rudder.

The tail came up quickly as takeoff speed approached, and when the plane was ready to fly, Bo let it rise off the ground but held the nose down. Thus relieved of the obligation to climb, the Mustang accelerated rapidly. By the time it had covered three-quarters of the runway, it was moving well in excess of two hundred miles per hour, barely ten feet in the air. Bo imagined the held-breath wonder of the gathered onlookers.

As he came abreast of where Lamarr was standing, he abruptly pulled the stick all the way back, and the agile P-51 responded quickly, rocketing upward at a perilous angle and clawing its way heavenward, G forces tugging at Bo's eyeballs with familiar insistency.

Its speed bled off at an alarming rate as it fought for altitude. Bo held it as long as he could, then pushed the nose over to get more air flowing over the wings before the onset of stall buffet. By then he was nearly out of sight and heedless of the spontaneous cheer that rose from the scattered crowd at his display; young Lamarr was the most fevered of all, currents in his spine reacting to the unexpected beauty and drama of it.

High overhead, Bo swung the plane around in a chandelle maneuver developed originally by bush pilots to escape from box canyons. Leveling eventually at eleven thousand feet, he set up for a 190-knot cruise toward the L.A. basin as he felt his arms and legs synchronize with the rhythmic throbbing of the engine and the gentle swaying of the wings.

CHAPTER 30

0835 PST

First Officer Roland Kurtzman kneeled down beside seat 14B and smiled politely at the besotted auto parts salesman. The passenger's face held a strained smile, the vestige of a more prolonged expression that he tried to hold so as not to betray his acute embarrassment at having incurred the attention of the flight crew. There was a stain on his pants.

"Mr. Johnson, we'd sure be appreciative, you toned down the partying just a little bit, okay?" Kurtzman said quietly.

Mr. Johnson looked around for some sign of support from his fellow revelers and found mainly averted eyes and distracted fidgeting.

"Not hurtin' anybody, what'sa big deal?" He looked around again for encouragement in his brave defiance of a uniformed symbol of authority, but his view was blocked by Kurtzman's rising bulk as the first officer stood and bent over, putting his mouth close to Johnson's ear.

"I'm gonna make this real clear, pal. One more disturbance and I'll have you arrested when we land for endangering the safety of a commercial airline flight, prior to which I'll probably break both your fucking arms and lock you in the lavatory."

Kurtzman pulled back a few inches and said matter-of-factly, "For the safety of everybody, of course."

He stood up and smiled politely again, removing the rest of the drink from Mr. Johnson's trembling hand. "Do we have a deal?"

Mr. Johnson looked as though a grenade had gone off in his innards somewhere, and the small part of him still responsible for the maintenance of his survival instinct kicked into overdrive and assumed command, although all it could manage was to move Mr. Johnson's head up and down slightly because the rest of his systems were concentrated on retaining control of his bowels.

"That's the spirit. Enjoy the rest of your flight."

Flight attendant Theresa Lietsch stepped from the galley as Kurtzman entered the first-class cabin.

"Thanks, Roland. It was getting out of hand."

"Close the bar down, Terry. We're starting approach in a few minutes."

He eyed the wire baskets of empty bottles in the stowage bin. "What the hell is wrong with these people? It's not even nine in the goddamned morning yet."

The attendant shrugged in resignation, surprised by little after fourteen years on the job, and looked down the aisle of the completely filled airplane. "Fourth of July weekend. They like to get started early."

"You should have cut that guy off a long time ago, Terry."

The lead attendant appeared from the galley. "Hey, it's not that easy for a 'dumb broad' to be telling Mr. Wonderful he's had enough. Most times we just let them get plowed and they don't cause trouble."

Kurtzman looked back to see Johnson sitting stock still, hands gripping the armrests. Undoubtedly he'd remain that way for the rest of the flight.

"I think I may have overdone it on that guy in fourteen B. Maybe you should go and—"

"Fuck him," Theresa spat angrily. "He's been grabbing at my ass for the last hour. Drunken bastard didn't even feel it when I spilled hot coffee on his leg." A veteran, Theresa had known better than to drop it on his crotch.

Kurtzman laughed. "Don't know why I even worry about you guys."

He withdrew his key and opened the secured cockpit door. "Let's get 'em strapped in."

Theresa reached for the microphone as the first officer disappeared into the cockpit. "Ladies and gentlemen, as we make our initial descent into the Los Angeles area, the captain has requested that you return to your seats, place your seat backs and tray tables in their full upright and locked positions, and—"

As Kurtzman resumed his seat and began strapping himself back in, reaching overhead to flip on the "Fasten Seat Belt" sign, Captain Harriet Boleyn pulled off the oxygen mask that was required whenever the other crew member left the cockpit.

"All settled?"

"No problem. Next time you handle it."

"Very funny."

She may have been the captain, but they both knew that a woman confronting a male passenger regarding loutish behavior was an open invitation to trigger his potentially destructive defenses against public emasculation. The crew's obligation was to quell disturbances, not make political statements.

"Look what we got here," she said, pointing out the windscreen at a dense and seemingly impenetrable carpet of gray fog below.

"Wow. You don't see it extend this far in very often."

Despite its postcard appearance, Los Angeles is essentially a well-irrigated desert. Even its ubiquitous and trademark palm trees are not indigenous but were imported for the 1932 Olympic Games. That made the scene before them as incongruous as it was impressive.

The rainy season is confined to the winter months, but late spring and early summer bring weather that is a perennial source of irritation to coastal dwellers. The land areas, unable to dissipate heat as effectively as the convective ocean, warm up quickly as hot weather settles in. Air above the ground rises, and the partial vacuum is filled in by cooler air sucked in from the sea, which, being moisture-laden, condenses into a thick, heavy fog called a marine layer.

Usually confined to the immediate coast, the marine layer

is so well defined that it is possible for one house in a neighborhood to be enshrouded in a cocoon of wet, gray down and another a block away to sit unmolested beneath a brilliant blue sky. Residents in high rises in Santa Monica and Marina del Rey are often treated to the otherwordly spectacle of looking down at the layer from above, the ghostly spires of other buildings poking up from the fog.

Sometimes the marine layer can expand until it is several thousand feet high and extends as far east as the San Bernardino Mountains, making the entire Los Angeles basin look less like a sprawling metropolis than a boiling, opaque ocean. Like it was doing now.

Captain Boleyn had already received the hand-off from center and had listened to the airport conditions report from ATIS, the automated terminal information system, which broadcast a recorded message without the need for a time-consuming, one-plane-at-a-time-only radio conversation. Runway visibilities were marginal but still acceptable for appropriately equipped aircraft.

"L.A. Approach," she began when there was a break in air-to-ground radio traffic, "TransGlobal three one niner heavy inbound with the information."

"Roger, TG three one niner, slow to one niner zero knots for separation, turn left heading two four eight, expect landing runway twenty-four right. Call us at the final approach fix."

"Roger, LAX. Any chance of two-five right?" Runway 25R would be closer to the TransGlobal gate area on the south side of the airport.

"Negative, three one niner. Sorry about that. We're slowed to a crawl for maximum separation in the soup."

"Understood."

"I hate taxiing around in this shit," said Kurtzman, thinking about the long ground travel from runway 24R to the TransGlobal terminal.

"Really?" Captain Boleyn said sarcastically. "Not me. Hell, I love it. Punch us in, will ya?"

Kurtzman began entering the approach information into the on-board computerized navigation system. He had flown the Airbus A310 for about six months, mostly with Captain Boleyn, and knew she would require him to monitor the plane's movements carefully in conditions like these. She'd had a navigation radio failure in instrument conditions over two years ago and had hand flown the rest of the approach flawlessly. What had earned her a commendation from the company was noticing that the device had failed in the first place. In later simulator re-creations, three of the seven participating pilots had "crashed" because they'd failed to notice the nav unit dying so completely that even the warning flags had failed to appear.

"Okay, we're on," Kurtzman said.

Boleyn engaged the approach autopilot and kept her hand close to the control wheel until she was sure the navigation unit was in firm command. "Stay alert now."

"Yassuh, boss."

As they approached the top of the marine layer, Kurtzman glanced at the altimeter. Seven thousand feet. Only the tops of the ridge-line peaks were visible sticking out of the top.

Boleyn keyed her mike. "Ladies and gentlemen, this is your captain. We're beginning our final approach into Los Angeles. As you can see outside, there is a cloud layer covering the entire area, and we might get a little bit of bounce on the way down, so I'm going to ask our flight attendants to please be seated at this time. We'll have you on the ground shortly, and thanks once again for flying TransGlobal."

The layer came up at them fast as they descended, the distance-induced illusion of slow flight gone as the first wisps fingered the nose of the plane. A few seconds later they entered the Dantean darkness and no longer bothered to look out at the undifferentiated gray wall.

Until they broke out, they would remain fixed on the instruments, their sole source of information about the progress of the approach. From a practical standpoint, there was no difference between flying the plane and flying the simulator, except for the 247 passengers and 8 flight attendants in the back.

"Coming up on the fix. Call it in, Roland."

"Okay. L.A. Approach, TG three one niner heavy inbound at the final fix, maintaining one niner zero knots, over."

"Roger, TG three—"

A burst of static overwhelmed the response.

"Don't tell me we got a thunderstorm to boot!" exclaimed Boleyn as she reached toward the radar screen and dialed the range down to twenty-five miles.

"Not in June," answered Kurtzman, a native of Southern California. "Not around here."

The sweep of the lighted band across the screen confirmed his observation. No clear images appeared on the screen other than those of mountaintops to the north, which were easily recognizable as solid smears of light reaching to the edge of the display. More clearly defined "blips" would have been indicative of thunderstorms that were undetectable by eye, embedded as they were in the thick layer.

The static coming through their headsets was not characteristic of a lightning stroke, which would have been sporadic and intense. The sound they heard had a random rise and fall but was constant in intensity.

"Want me to try the old frequency?" asked Kurtzman.

"Give it a go."

He switched over to their original frequency, which was used to control the overall inbound flow before the hand-off to the airport tower controlling the closer-in traffic. The tower had separate frequencies for the north and south sides of the field.

The same static sound poured in through the headphones.

Concerned, Boleyn reached over to the communications panel and dialed in the automated airport information, then south side approach control. The same sound came through on all frequencies.

"Doesn't it just figure?" she said. "On the crappiest day of the year."

"I hope they got their separations up," said Kurtzman.

"I'll bet they don't."

Standard procedure called for them to continue in on the last instructions they had been given. But they both knew that it was standard operating procedure for controllers to bend the rules on separating aircraft in order to accommodate the staggering flow of traffic. Disgruntled controllers had no need to strike for better conditions, as they had with disastrous results once before. All they needed to do to bring the system to its knees was follow the FAA's rules to the letter. The resulting backups and logjams would cause massive delays, because it was a mathematical impossibility for the system to function if the rule demanding five miles of separation between aircraft were followed at major metropolitan airports.

Los Angeles International sits at the apex of a TCA, a terminal control area. No plane could enter this protected space without permission, and constant radio contact was required. Planes could freely pass over this TCA, or under it where it didn't touch the ground, without contacting anybody.

At Los Angeles they could even go through the middle of it, via a special "corridor" that passed right over the airport, the safest place to be because landing and departing aircraft were never directly over the runways. Traffic under control in the TCA was never directed into the VFR corridor.

The TCA system was established after a tragic midair collision over San Diego, and since that time there had never been a midair collision inside of one. There had been several just *outside* of TCAs, possibly owing to some creative maneuvering to prevent "busting" of TCA boundaries, but the inside was safe haven, bathed in the protective glow of tracking radar and the largely competent guidance of each plane's movements by highly trained controllers who apprenticed for years before earning their own "sector" of the sky.

Which was why Captain Harriet Boleyn doubted that standard separations were under way that day. The people in the control tower had consummate faith in their equipment and their procedures, and they were judged not by their strict adherence to regulation, but by how efficiently they could move planes in and out.

The other problem they faced was that they had been slowed to 190 knots, probably because they were getting too close to an airplane ahead of them. Usually they would be allowed to resume their original speed after a few minutes.

"Did we get an expected on speed?" asked Kurtzman. Had the controller anticipated an increase, he would have said something like "Expect two three zero in three minutes," which would have allowed them to speed up at that time if radio contact was lost, but Kurtzman could recall no such clearance, not unusual in a busy terminal control area where there was a constant stream of radio chatter, and Boleyn didn't remember hearing one, either.

"Why?" she asked.

"Because if we got some *mook* behind us doing two thirty and he's out of contact also, he's gonna fly right up our tailpipes on the ILS." Once they were on the ILS, the instrument landing system, they would fly a highly accurate electronic beam all the way down to the runway. The beam was so precisely circumscribed that any other aircraft overtaking them would eventually try to occupy the same airspace.

Boleyn did a quick mental calculation and winced. "Let's hope he's real far back or going real slow or both."

She changed her preassigned transponder code to "7600" to let the controllers know the Airbus's radios were gone, waited a minute and then switched back to the original code so they could continue to track her flight.

She could feel the first stirrings of the familiar sensation pilots and scuba drivers called "the dreads," an enveloping, claustrophobic fear that came with darkness, cold and a sense of imminent danger. She wasn't worried that it would grow unmanageable, or that it would interfere with her normal functioning or in any way affect her judgment except to make her even more alert than usual.

It wasn't a problem. She just didn't like it.

0837 PST

Jerry Bradley stared at the screen in disbelief, one hand on the shoulder of Cort Botnick, the controller manning Downey sector, a piece of airspace east of the airport through which eighty percent of inbound planes flew.

"I don't fucking believe this is happening."

He looked back down the row of radar positions and called out, "Willa, your guy still gone?"

Willa Kabaker answered without taking her eyes from the screen before her. "I don't know how to tell you this, Jerry," she said, "but I think another one's just pooped out on us."

It had been less than two minutes since she had failed to get an acknowledgment of her last clearance from TransGlobal

319, only sixty seconds since the audible alarm had gone off, indicating that a "radios-out" transponder code had been issued from the flight, and only thirty seconds since Botnick had yelled out another blown communication.

Now yet a third aircraft was out of touch. It was an impossible situation, could never happen. Like most things that were impossible, there was no procedure designed to handle it.

Bradley turned and walked briskly to an unused backup position and dialed in a wide-area display, quickly taking in the salient details. It seemed at first glance that all the planes within range would not encounter any difficulties if they simply continued on their last assigned clearances, *if* all of those clearances called for standard approaches.

"Anybody give out any deviations?" he yelled loudly across the room, but there were only headshakes in response.

"Lost two, boss!" another controller yelled.

"Three here! And I got two pop-ups coasting!" Two aircraft not on flight plans had radioed in—popped up—for approach clearances; the controller had agreed to take them on but, not finding them on the radar yet, assigned them codes and got them into the system. They would "coast" until the radar picked them up and their codes could be associated with specific blips. Until then there was no way to provide separation clearances. "The hell is going on?"

As a test, Willa Kabaker pulled her headset plug out of its socket and inserted it into the jack at the vacant hand-off position next to her, spoke into her microphone, then looked up.

"I'm not talking to anybody, Jerry. It's all static, and I'm getting down-com squawks all over the screen."

As each flight crew realized that they were out of communication, they dialed in 7600 on their transponders, which lit up bright flashing characters on the radar screens with the letters *EM* for emergency added to the data block to warn the controllers. Procedures called for the air crew to leave 7600 on for one minute, then go back to the assigned code for fifteen minutes, and then repeat the cycle until communication was restored. There were several such emergency codes: for example, "7500" would let the controllers know the plane was being hijacked without the pilots having to risk a verbal radio transmission and tipping off the hijacker.

Bradley felt his world suddenly telescoped to a pinpoint as, one by one, his controllers reported a complete communications failure. Then he noticed that static was also coming over the ceiling speaker, the one that could be heard by everybody in the room. That speaker had several uses, such as sounding the various kinds of alarms triggered by the computerized ARTS III radar display system, signaling an incoming call from other air traffic facilities, and . . .

Bradley scrambled for his headset and plugged it into the backup station, dialing in a frequency of 121.5 megahertz. A burst of static hit his ears, and he turned slowly back toward the center of the room.

"Emergency is down?" he said out loud to himself, incredulity in his voice. The 121.5 MHZ frequency was reserved for emergency use only, and the overhead monitor was kept tuned to it so it could be heard by all when a call came in. When it did, the most appropriate person could grab it. Now, Bradley realized that the constant stream of static pouring from the ceiling was the emergency frequency suffering the same ill that seemed to have befallen the regular communications frequencies. He reached for the com panel on the workstation and pressed the buttons that would inhibit the channel, and the noise stopped.

"Emergency is out!" he yelled into the room. "I say again, emergency is gone!"

He had to act, or at least buy himself a few seconds to think. "Anybody see any problems with inbounds yet?" he called out.

As far as the controllers were able to tell, the last set of clearances should have been able to get all the incoming planes safely landed. Assuming the approach and ground frequencies at the airports were unaffected, the individual airport control towers could clear the runways and taxiways of all departing craft. Typically, the towers would take control of the incoming flights once they were within eight to ten miles of the airport. *If* everything worked according to procedure and *if* the weather conditions continued to improve.

If not, very large tubes of metal containing lots of passengers would be executing go-arounds, aborted landings, and heading for their alternates, a procedure that never anticipated everybody else also doing the same thing, with no revised clearances issuing from the ground.

Bradley called over the traffic management coordinator, Roberto Pinajera. "Berto, call Palmdale, tell them what's going on. Tell them to route everything out of here and inform the other TRACONs."

Pinajera nodded and returned to his console, sitting down in front of the "telco" panel. The panel contained eighty-six buttons representing every other air traffic facility in the area. Each button connected to a telephone land line that was permanently open, and any number of buttons could be pressed simultaneously. He hit the one labeled "CTR" and spoke without waiting. "Center, this is L.A. TRACON: Supervisor, please pick up."

In less than a second the phone was answered by the man in charge of the en route center, overall coordinator for all air traffic in Southern California. Center "owned" all the airspace and parceled it out to the five radar rooms, the TRACONs, via letters of agreement that specified sector boundaries, rules and procedures.

As Pinajera explained the situation, controllers who had been on break were drifting back into the room, in unquestioning obedience to the primary rule of their profession: in an emergency, the staff acted as a single organism, where teamwork and cooperation peaked as in few other fields of endeavor save mountain climbing or surgery. Several of them automatically went to the hand-off positions of the busiest sectors, watching the primary screens and quickly getting acquainted with the traffic situations. They tried their best to grasp both the airspace picture and the nature of the problem without asking any more questions than were absolutely necessary.

Bradley motioned one of them over. "Brenda, get on to all the towers in the area and tell them to update ATIS so everybody stays the hell away from here until we get this straightened out." Word would go out over the automated terminal information system that was routinely monitored by incoming flights before they radioed in for approach clearances.

Bradley didn't yet know that not one of the ATIS systems in the L.A. basin was working either.

0836 PST

"Seems to me I remembered something funny on a NOTAM couple days ago," said Captain Boleyn.

"Yeah, I remember that." Kurtzman tried to recall the Notice to Airmen but couldn't. He reached into his flight bag, a leather beauty that was his thirty-ninth birthday present from his wife, and pulled out the current set.

"Says we're to stay alert for problems. That it may be terrorist stuff. You don't suppose . . . ?"

Boleyn rolled her eyes up and looked over at her first officer. "No time to worry about that now. Besides, we can't call anybody up anyway, so let's just—"

"What about Ontario?"

She considered it, then said, "What the hell, give it a shot."

He looked up the frequency on his approach plates and dialed it in on Com 2, the standby radio. Hearing no static other than the normal level of background noise, he keyed the microphone button on his control stick and said, "Ontario Approach, TransGlobal three one niner heavy inbound for LAX, do you copy?"

The reply was faint but immediate. "TG three one niner, Ontario Approach, don't tell me you lost contact with L.A."

Boleyn, startled by the transmission, flipped the com selector on her own panel and said, "Ontario, that's affirmative! What's going on?"

"You're the third call we've gotten in the last two minutes." Weaker this time. "Sounds like a major com failure at L.A. We're calling them now."

"Are you painting anybody in our vicinity?" she asked, wanting to know if Ontario's radar controllers were seeing any blips indicating other airplanes near their own.

No answer.

"I say again, Ontario, is there any traffic near us?" *C'mon, dammit, give me a clue before I lose you!*

The controller's voice came back, even fainter than before but still discernible.

"Three one niner, you're close to our edge, but we show you clear on our side. You've got one heavy at four o'clock, six thousand—"

And then it was gone.

"Shit!" she hissed, slapping her hand on her thigh.

"Looks like we're okay," said Kurtzman by way of small consolation.

0837 PST

"L.A. TRACON, this is Ontario," blared the overhead speaker. "Supervisor, pick up."

Bradley reached up to one of the overhead panels spaced evenly across the ceiling, picked up the telephone handset and punched "ONT" on the telco pad. "This is Bradley. What?"

"Smoldt here. Just talked to a couple of your planes before they passed out of range. What the hell's happening?"

"Beats the shit out of me, Steve. Which flights?"

The Ontario supervisor gave him the numbers, then said, "I can only talk to inbounds if they call me. Your frequencies are too fucked up. You want me to tell 'em anything?"

"Yes! Get 'em out of the area and send them to their alternates, or drop them into your field if you can. I've gotta keep 'em the hell away from here 'til we figure out what's goin' on!"

"Not that you don't have enough trouble, but you suppose this has anything to do with the NOTAM? About sabotage, I mean?"

Oh, fuck me. "I don't know, Steve, but do me a favor. Call whoever was listed on the thing and let 'em know. I'm a little busy."

"You got it. Why don't you get one of your people to stay on this line with me."

"Stand by. Carelli!"

The controller appeared a moment later.

Bradley held out the handset to him. "Tony, keep talking

to Ontario. They manage to scoot any planes out of here, lemme know."

"No problem. By the way, the ground frequencies are all okay, at least at LAX."

"Thank God something's working around here."

0839 PST

The call had come in to the FAA headquarters switchboard in Washington and been routed immediately to the central flow control facility that monitored all air traffic throughout the nation.

Every flight plan filed across the country was entered into flow control's central computer, which continually projected whether flights awaiting takeoff would be able to actually land at their destinations, taking into account the progress of traffic already in the air, flight plans on file and weather conditions. If the computer calculated a likely delay, a gate hold advisory was flashed to the originating airport and the plane was held on the ground, engines off.

It annoyed the passengers to sit, unmoving, on the ramp, because it felt to them as though nothing were happening. In fact, flow control was a brilliant concept that saved millions in wasted fuel and virtually eliminated the traditional holding patterns that had once been the bane of airports like JFK in New York, back when it was called Idlewild and it had not been unusual to have planes stacked all the way up to eighteen thousand feet.

It was also safer, since regulations required planes to carry only enough fuel to get to their alternates plus a forty-five-minute reserve. As planes in the old stacks began to run low, they had to be given emergency priority to land, holding up other planes, which eventually cascaded into further emergencies until every approach was a crisis with no slack for aborted landings.

The call into central flow was taken by a midlevel air traffic manager, who passed it on to his shift supervisor, a former air force controller named Dennis Allison, who quickly conferenced in his four most senior desk managers.

After listening for several seconds, he broke in and said, "No offense, Smoldt, but you can't give us enough detail. We gotta talk to L.A."

The Ontario supervisor told Allison to stand by, and he punched L.A. back up and told Carelli to expect central flow's call into Bradley. At the same time, Allison told one of his managers to get the NTSB on the phone.

While that call was hitting the NTSB switchboard, Ontario supervisor Smoldt came back on the line to tell Allison that Jerry Bradley at L.A. was waiting for his call.

"Thanks, Smoldt," Allison said, and without waiting for a reply, he released the Ontario line and pressed the button marked "LA."

The NTSB switchboard operator had been briefed to stay alert for any calls that might relate to the Notice to Airmen. After listening to Allison's manager for less than five seconds, she told him to hang on and rang the special number in the O'Hare tower command post.

By that time Allison had reached Bradley and gotten a quick rundown and had flipped on the PA system in the flow control center. He put the mike to his mouth but kept the phone there as well so Bradley could hear him as his voice boomed out through the room.

"Attention, all desks. L.A. is hard down. I say again, Los Angeles is hard down. Indefinite hold on all inbounds, no further outbounds, stand by for reroutes for all inbounds already in flight."

He replaced the mike and spoke to Bradley. "You got that?"

"Yeah. I'm off, Allison. Gotta get back. Carelli's gonna stay on, so talk to him if you need to."

Allison thought fleetingly that it was just as well that the flying public didn't know that the entire air traffic control system still relied on vacuum-tube computers that had already been obsolete thirty years ago, and that the billion-dollar project to replace them was already thirty-three months behind schedule. He wondered, as he had on several previous occasions, if they were about to find out.

"Stanley here."

The FBI agent listened for a few seconds, then waved

frantically to the others and motioned to the speakerphone on the desk they were using as a conference table. Florence ran to it and clicked it on.

". . . all air-ground com is down, all freqs. The shift supervisor says inbounds already in or near the TCA should be okay, but separations are going to start coming apart, this keeps up much longer. Ontario can talk to some planes that are trying their freq, but that's only a couple here and there."

"Are they rerouting those out? And are all the nav systems operational?" Stanley asked the central flow control desk manager.

"Yes on both of those. But we were wondering if this might have anything to do with that NOTAM you asked us to issue. The one about possible terrorist activity?"

Jack glanced briefly at Amy and held up a hand to Stanley, then addressed the speakerphone himself.

"This is Webster. We have no way of knowing yet, but I want to get in contact with the sup at L.A."

"Name's Bradley, but he's busy as hell. You want a patch through here so we can listen?"

"Please. But just Allison, nobody else, and no speakerphone. And tell him I'm declaring a provisional national security emergency."

There was a slight pause. "You sure?"

Jack looked up at Preston Stanley, who said, "I'll back you. Do it."

"That's affirmative," Jack said into the speaker. "Tell him, and get me Bradley ASAP."

While they waited, Jack looked around at his team. "What do you think?"

Stanley was dialing a number on another line. Amy spoke first. "Possible. But the situation isn't necessarily critical yet. TCA clearances are pretty precise, and the inbounds shouldn't have too much trouble."

"But what if they bent the rules on separation?"

Amy shook her head. "They're probably only letting in Cat twos and threes," she said, referring to airplanes with highly sophisticated systems, "and those guys don't need anywhere near the full five miles anyway."

"Unless she's finagling with the navigation units," Florence said.

"Bradley here. Let's make it fast."

Jack spun toward the speakerphone. "Bradley, this is Webster, FBI. Quick question: Any indication of nav system problems?"

"No. LAX landed three since the com went out. I'll be back to you in a second."

"No! Bradley!" Jack yelled, but the shift supervisor had already left to attend to something obviously needing his attention more than Jack did.

"Jack, I've got one of our electronic specialists on the line," said Stanley, waving the telephone handset. "Dick Brindisi."

"Why?"

Stanley ignored Jack's question and spoke into the phone. "Dick, what're the odds of half of the L.A. radar room's air-ground frequencies going sour while Ontario is still open?" Pause. "Yeah, all in the same geographic vicinity, east of the airport."

He listened for a second, then said, "Hold it, Dick, hold it," and punched the speaker button on the base set. "Say again?"

"I said, it's damned near impossible. Which ones are they?"

"I'm back. . . ." Bradley's voice came over the main speakerphone from L.A.

"Stand by," Stanley said to Brindisi. "Bradley, Agent Stanley. What freqs are out?" He held the handset close to the speaker on the desk so Brindisi could hear.

"Approach control for all sectors to the north and east, ATIS at LAX Airport and the emergency frequency. Basically all air to ground."

"What about ground control?" Amy asked him.

"Those are working, at least at LAX that we know of."

Stanley put the handset back to his ear. "You get that, Dick?"

"Yeah, I got it," Dick's voice said through the speaker. "Ask Bradley are they out or noisy."

Amy didn't want to put words in Bradley's mouth. "What do you mean, exactly, the freqs are down?"

"Not down. Just so much static you can't communicate over them."

"Dick?" Stanley said into the mouthpiece.

"Take me off the speakerphone," said Brindisi.

Stanley hit the button. "You're off."

There was a pause while Stanley listened privately, then he looked up at Jack, nodded and said, "Somebody's jamming them, Webster."

Jack stared at the speakerphone for a second before he turned it back on and spoke to the L.A. supervisor.

"What's your first name, Bradley?"

"Jerry. Look, I'm really up to my ass here and—"

"Jerry, listen to me. My name's Jack. I don't want you to alarm your guys until it's necessary, but it's very likely somebody's tampering with your traffic."

There was a pause. "You're shitting me."

"Wish I was. I need a remote on your wide-area screen so we can see it here. We're in the tower at O'Hare and we've got a brite set up. Just patch yours through central flow and they'll get the picture to us." The "brite" was a simple television screen that would show them whatever was being displayed on the radar scope in L.A. Jack motioned for Florence to make the call to central flow. "Do it now, Jerry."

"Okay, stand by. But so far things seem to be flowing smoothly."

Jack ignored the assessment. "What I need is, you tell your controllers to stay alert for any deviations, no matter how slight, and let us know immediately."

"Got it. What're you going to do?"

Jack looked at Amy, who made a hurrying motion with her hands toward the speakerphone.

"Jerry, get on that patch right away and keep somebody on this line. We'll talk again when the brite is set up."

"What *are* we going to do?" Amy asked after they heard Bradley set the receiver down on a hard surface.

"Maybe Dalek will call us when she's got things really screwed up," said Stanley.

Amy stepped up to the table, placed her hands down and leaned forward.

"Now wouldn't that be something?"

CHAPTER 31

Bo pulled off the noise-dampening headset so he could listen to the mammoth Rolls-Royce twelve-cylinder as it powered the Mustang through the air.

Strangely, there were no other aircraft in the sky. He could try to figure out why later, but now it was time to exploit the situation.

He lowered the nose, then pulled the throttle back slightly as the aerodynamically clean plane quickly picked up speed in the dive. When the airspeed indicator read 280 knots, he hauled back on the stick and fed in more throttle at the same time. The nose came up and continued going up, above the horizon, then straight up and over until the plane was on its back. Bo looked out each side window in turn to make sure the wings were perfectly level, then eased off the throttle again and continued the graceful arc, tracing a perfect circle as he completed the loop.

His precision was rewarded when the P-51 returned to its starting point in the sky and was rocked softly by the wake turbulence it left during its previous passage through the same patch of air.

Bo was mystified by the lack of traffic. Except for a few

commercial jets from LAX passing him high overhead, he had seen only two light planes. A gorgeous morning, on a holiday weekend? Normally he'd be dodging aircraft all over the place as occasional pilots, too busy during the week to keep current in either their skills or the ever-changing regulated airspace, barreled around with insufficient regard to correct procedures. Where were they all?

He got the answer as he transited the mountains east of the Simi Valley and was able to look down at the L.A. basin. He could see the marine layer, a shaving-cream sea flooding the basin and completely obscuring it from view. There were nineteen active airports within its geological boundaries, and every one of them was trapped beneath the layer. None of the thousands of non-instrument-rated pilots who flew out of those airstrips could go flying, and even the rated ones didn't consider a climb through the muck worth a few minutes in the clear, especially if there was a chance they couldn't get back down.

So he pretty much had the skies to himself and couldn't resist a few aerobatic maneuvers. Then he checked his watch, leveled out and continued southeast toward the terminal control area, tuning in to the ATIS automated airport information system to get an idea of the traffic patterns LAX had established to deal with the fog.

He got only an annoying outpouring of static, so he tried the approach control frequency. Same thing.

He switched off the radio and let it cool down for a few seconds, so it wouldn't blow a fuse when he turned it back on. After powering back up, he found the same noise, and he switched back to the standard frequency used by pilots at the uncontrolled Santa Paula airport to talk to each other as they took off and landed.

He keyed the mike, broadcast his tail numbers and said, "Anybody copy?"

"Bo, that you?" came a response after a few seconds.

It was Cutter, who monitored the frequency back in the shop.

"Yeah, Joe, how do you copy?"

"Loud and clear. What's going on?"

"Nothing much, just can't raise L.A."

"You sound fine here." -

"Okay, thanks. Out."

Weird.

He reached into his flight bag for the portable radio, unraveled the wires and plugged them into the com panel.

CHAPTER 32

"Something doesn't feel right," Captain Harriet Boleyn said to no one in particular.

First Officer Roland Kurtzman looked up from his charts. "Say again?"

Boleyn scanned all the panel instruments, checked the gyrocompass indication against the older-technology, fluid-filled compass hanging in front of the windscreen, and cycled through the electronic display modes to see the engine condition indicators.

"It's not right."

"What's not right?" asked Kurtzman, making his own scan and finding nothing amiss.

"I don't know."

He turned and bent toward her with an exaggerated expression of sympathetic concern. "Whatsa matter, you having your period?" he drawled.

She didn't answer but subconsciously placed her hands, which she trusted more than the autopilot, on the control wheel.

She should have shot back with a smart-ass remark of her

456

own, and when she didn't, Kurtzman realized her discomfort was serious.

"We're heading two sixty to stay on the ILS," she said. "Should be closer to two four eight."

Kurtzman checked and saw this was the case. "Maybe we're bucking a north wind?"

"Sure looks like it, but in this fog . . . ?"

Kurtzman shrugged. "Everything else reads perfectly normal." He looked over and saw the mounting concern on his captain's face. "Strange weather, I guess," he said. "Hey, what the hell: it's California, right?"

"Jerry, you better come have a look at this."

L.A. radar supervisor Jerry Bradley strode quickly to the controller's station and hunched over the seat back.

As he leaned in to look at the screen, Kabaker started to say, "Look at this—"

"I see it. Jesus Christ. . . ."

"Something's wrong here. Webster, you still on?"

Jack leaped toward the speaker. "Yeah, Jerry, what is it?"

They huddled around the desk as Bradley's voice came over the speaker.

"Uh, one of our planes started drifting north about a minute ago. Look at your brite."

The remote display had been operational for less than a minute and had a slightly blurry quality because of the signal loss during retransmission from L.A. It was still clear enough to follow Bradley's directions.

"See that blip labeled TG three one niner?"

Amy spotted it first, put a finger to the screen and pointed it out to the others.

"Yeah, we got it," said Jack.

"You're looking at a TransGlobal inbound. Last clearance was the instrument approach for runway twenty-four right. You can see the altitude and groundspeed in the data block."

"How often do they get updated?" asked Florence.

"Every time the beam sweeps around the screen," Amy said.

"Hey, people, save the lessons for later, will ya?" Bradley said in annoyance. "You see the airport?"

Again, Amy put up her hand and pointed out the airport display toward the left of the screen. It was not an actual radar image but was drawn there by computer software to clearly indicate the position of the runways.

"The little sideways line on top is runway twenty-four right. Now watch . . ."

Bradley entered a command at his console. On the brite in the O'Hare tower, a line appeared that stretched from the TransGlobal blip down toward the airport.

"That's TransGlobal's projected flight path, based on its current position, orientation and speed."

"But it misses the airport," said Amy, confusion evident in her tone. "It's too far north."

"No shit," came the reply over the speaker. "And they're supposedly on an instrument landing system approach, locked on to the beam."

The team stared at the display, transfixed, and then Bradley said, "Now, somebody want to tell me what the hell is going on?"

"Bradley!"

Now what? The harried supervisor ran a hand through his thinning hair before looking up to see Cort Botnick standing up in front of his radar set, pointing stupidly to his screen with one hand and gesturing to him with the other.

"Stand by, Webster." Bradley put down the phone and started walking along the row of stations but was grabbed by Willa Kabaker before reaching Botnick.

He looked at her screen, watched as the blips changed position with each sweep of the radar beam. They all seemed to be heading in the same general direction.

The controller looked up at Bradley, no words necessary to communicate what was going on.

"I got the same thing in my sector, Jerry," Botnick said softly. "Same trend."

Consensus nods from two other radar positions. Bradley fought to keep his knees from weakening and toppling him.

The entire flow of traffic, except for four scattered planes, was drifting north of the correct course, away from L.A. International Airport.

"That's it. Fuck it. We're taking it around."

Kurtzman jerked his head to the left, as much at the uncharacteristic profanity as the surprising pronouncement. "Are you serious?"

But Captain Boleyn was already snapping off the autopilot switches.

"Goddamned right, and we're gonna do it by hand—needle, ball and airspeed," she said, referring to traditional aviation terminology for the venerable fallback technique when the more sophisticated instruments failed.

"Then let's give 'em seventy-seven hundred on the squawk to get their attention."

"Do it, ten seconds only, and then go back so they don't think we're in real trouble."

Kurtzman dialed the emergency code into the transponder, then asked in a slightly tremulous tone, "Are we?"

"'S'matter, son?" It was Boleyn's turn to smirk, her sense of humor restored by her decision to proactively attack the situation. "Having your period?"

In the O'Hare control tower, Florence pointed to the display and asked, "What's this shiny thing here?"

Amy came up behind her and saw the TransGlobal blip in high-intensity and blinking, with the characters *EM* added to the data block. They could hear a clanging sound coming over the speakerphone from L.A.

"It's an emergency!" she exclaimed. "They're in trouble!"

"Webster!" Bradley's voice blurted out over the speaker. "We got troubles!"

"We see it, Jerry," said Amy. "You know their problem?"

"How the hell can we know, we can't even talk to— Hey, now what?"

"It stopped," said Florence.

"What's going on?" Amy said toward the speakerphone.

"Hold it a second."

They watched the numbers in the TransGlobal data block began to change as the thin, green beam swept around the display. The blip was moving slightly south with each new update, and the altitude readout on line two of the data block, which had been falling steadily as the plane descended, stabilized and began rising.

"Well, I'll be damned," came Bradley's voice. "They're executing a missed." The TransGlobal was aborting its landing approach and heading back up, according to a standard procedure.

"Why?" asked Amy. "They weren't close enough yet to see if they'd break out of the clouds."

"I'm gonna guess," said Bradley, "but my bet, it's a twenty-thousand-hour pilot whose belly is smarter than the instruments. But that's only one plane, and we got a helluva lot more coming in, and they're starting to veer off course for no goddamned reason I can figure."

Jack realized that the TransGlobal maneuver was not what had prompted Bradley's initial outburst. He turned toward the speakerphone and said, "What troubles, Jerry? You started to say . . . ?"

"We've got an unauthorized circling around in the TCA. Nobody's allowed to enter without controller permission. Penetrated from the south, over Torrance."

"In the clouds?"

"Sort of. It's thinning out pretty quickly down there. Fuckin' idiot, probably lost and disoriented. Watch your brite. . . ."

As Bradley dialed in a new range setting for his radar screen, the display seemed to pull back into space, revealing a larger portion of the airspace around Los Angeles. Amy found the new blip in the bottom right portion of the screen. "Looks real small, like a single or something."

"I know," Bradley said with venom, reflecting the standard controller disdain for anything not carrying at least a hundred passengers. "What other asshole'd be that stupid? And it looks like we got another flight executing a missed."

"Jerry, listen—"

"No, *you* listen, Webster! I got all hell breaking loose here, I got twenty-seven planes on a goddamned collision course, if not with each other, then with some building or maybe something in the corridor I don't even know about yet. . . . *When the fuck are you going to fill me in!*"

Jack looked toward Stanley and received a reluctant nod of approval.

"Jerry, listen to me carefully." He took a long breath and rubbed the bridge of his nose between thumb and forefinger. "Somebody's beaming signals to the nav units in those planes, throwing them off course. She's also jamming all your voice frequencies."

There was silence at the other end, then: "She?"

Jack smiled grimly. "Isn't that something?"

"Not really," Bradley replied. "That was a 'she' just took the TransGlobal Airbus around."

"Hah!" Amy mouthed silently at Jack.

"Where's it coming from, Webster? The signals? And how come some of my planes are still on course? And how long you known about this?"

Jack wasn't about to get into the last question. "We don't know where it's coming from, but it only hits Autonav units. The aircraft with other makes are unaffected."

Bradley waited a moment, then came back on, a plaintive note creeping into his voice.

"What the hell do I do?"

Jack dropped his head and looked blankly at the phone. What *could* they do?

"What about direction-finding equipment?" asked Stanley, grasping but unwilling to stand idly by. "Couldn't we use DFs to locate at least the voice jamming? We know the frequencies. . . ."

"No good," said Bradley. "We use DF to locate aircraft when pilots get disoriented, mostly students, but our gear doesn't work below about eight hundred feet."

Stanley clenched a fist. "Shit!"

A strained silence filled the vacuum of ideas. Through the speakerphone, Jack and his people could hear chaos breaking out in the TRACON radar room as controllers yelled to each other. They were still trying to follow hand-off procedures as the radar blips passed from one sector to another.

"Holy Christ!" they could hear Willa Kabaker yell in the background. "Every goddamned one of 'em's coming my way!"

Kabaker was controller for the coast sector, northwest of LAX.

"Let's hold two ninety and a thousand feet per minute on the climb."

"Roger," Kurtzman answered in acknowledgment of Captain Boleyn's command. "What if somebody else is going around, too?"

"Then let's hope to hell they follow procedures good as we're gonna."

In the TRACON, a piercing alarm sounded from the over-head speaker. "That's mine!" Cort Botnick yelled. "I got CA CA over here!" He pronounced it "ka ka."

"What's going on, Bradley?" Jack demanded as the alarm and Botnick's cry came through at O'Hare.

"CA," Bradley explained in clipped, hurried tones. "Conflict alert. Picked up automatically when the computer thinks planes are getting too close. Usually not real. Hang on. . . ."

Jack looked toward Amy. "What's he mean, not real?"

"Just because they're heading toward each other doesn't necessarily mean anything because the controller may have issued an advanced instruction to turn at a certain point or to stop at a certain altitude. The computer doesn't know what he already told the planes to do."

But in the TRACON, Cort Botnick, having issued no such instructions before the communications went berserk, watched in helpless horror as the TransGlobal blip crept inexorably toward that of a Varig 747 also executing a go-around.

At O'Hare, all five people in the private command post followed along, new projection lines superimposing themselves on the old with no change. The altitude readout on TransGlobal was 2,400 feet, on Varig 2,900, but the 747 was gaining altitude more slowly than the Airbus, which threatened to overtake it in less than a minute.

"Where's the top of the cloud layer?" Jack asked.

"Thirty-six hundred," Bradley answered, catching Jack's hopeful drift and then killing it: "But they're gonna meet at thirty-four."

There was no fault on the parts of the pilots. Both were executing flawless missed approaches. Neither had any way of knowing how far off course they had been when they'd initiated the procedures.

They were at 3,100 feet.

"Y'know, we were a little north of course back there."

Boleyn considered Kurtzman's observation. "That's true," she murmured softly. "But who knows how much?"

3,200 feet.

Kurtzman shrugged. "Beats me. Why don't we nudge a tad south, anyway?"

3,300.

3,350.

"Okay, what the hell."

Boleyn put in the tiniest touch of left aileron, not so much moving the yoke as increasing the pressure of her left hand slightly.

A small shudder ran through the plane.

"What was that?"

3,400 feet.

"I dunno," said Kurtzman. "Felt like turbulence."

Boleyn smiled and said, "Maybe we flew through somebody's wake."

Kurtzman laughed, sharing in Captain Boleyn's relief because the murk outside was lightening as they approached the top of the marine layer. Soon they could discern wisps separating from the mass, and in another few seconds they popped up into the brilliant and welcome midmorning sun.

"Fuck!" Kurtzman yelled as he grabbed his control wheel and yanked it violently to the left.

"What the hell . . . !" Boleyn yelped, but she took her hands off her own yoke in subconscious trust of her first officer.

Kurtzman waited for less than a second as the huge Airbus tilted precariously on its side, then pulled the wheel back sharply, yanking the nose of the plane sideways and slewing it around into a sloppy but effective accelerated turn that pushed the both of them and 255 people in the back down onto their seats, hard, with a force nearly three times that of gravity.

Overhead and to the right, a bright splash of sun glinted off the shining aluminum underbelly of a 747 less than one hundred feet away.

Breaths held painfully in both the Los Angeles TRACON and O'Hare control tower were expelled in a collective rush as the large, single blip on the radar screens split once again, amoebalike, into two smaller ones that slowly began to diverge.

The momentary reprieve was quickly forgotten. Chaos reigned where order was the norm. Controllers, used to years of instant obedience from the radar images on their screens, could only sit, fidget and watch as something else guided their precious charges.

Anger, frustration and panic intermingled in their hearts and minds, and they were no longer capable of separating out their individual emotions. Over it all was the horrifying sense of helplessness polluting their ingrained sense of responsibility. Nobody said a word as, one by one, several of the milling controllers began breaking out secreted packs of cigarettes and lighting up.

The flight path projection lines on Bradley's radar screen, an advanced model like the ones in center control and the only one in the room capable of that function, continued to flash automatically, and the more experienced controllers who projected their own lines mentally noticed what Jack and the NTSB staffers couldn't: the lines were slowly, almost imperceptibly, changing orientation, starting to align themselves in a tighter pattern with each recalculation.

In the TRACON, Bradley sat down in front of the wide-area monitor, pulled the keyboard toward him and ordered up a second-order projection, an experimental function he'd never tried before. It would plot the change in direction of the lines and try to predict flight paths based on how the current paths were changing.

Ten seconds later the existing lines were erased from the display, replaced a moment later by the results of the second-order projection.

They all converged on a single point. It was inside a ridge in the Santa Monica Mountains.

Any planes serendipitously avoiding a midair collision would instead slam into a hill buried deep inside the marine layer. Without ever knowing what hit them. Or why.

It had been six minutes since the first inbound aircraft had lost communications with L.A. approach control.

CHAPTER 33

Bo Kincaid, tracking the Ventura VOR navigation beam on his antiquated Lectrorange nav unit, started a left turn that would keep him just outside the northern edge of the restricted Los Angeles terminal control area.

As he dipped his wing, he noticed a flash out of the corner of his eye, coming from the cloud bank below him. Turning his head to look down, he watched as a 747 rose elegantly from the thick layer, but his fascination with the leviathan turned suddenly to astonishment as an Airbus A310 appeared abruptly from beneath the 747's left wing.

He couldn't tell from his altitude how far apart the two planes were in vertical separation, but the Airbus was banked at an extreme angle, much more than typically allowed by airline company policies for normal flight. The resultant loss of lift dropped it briefly back down into the clouds before it righted itself and climbed back out, heading away at nearly a right angle from the larger craft.

In his astonishment, he had forgotten to fly his own plane and had overshot his turn. He leveled the wings quickly and then banked back to the right to regain his target heading, swiveling his head back and forth to look out the windows for any other errant traffic.

The rising and falling static noise coming from his radio was

465

still audible. He had left the radio on in case the interference stopped. He tried the other standard frequencies once more but found the same sound everywhere.

Bo gave up and turned off the built-in unit, then reached for the portable with the special crystal and turned up the volume.

There are few things people of action find more painful than an inability to act in the face of a crisis.

A surgeon opens a patient for a simple gall bladder operation and finds cancer so pervasive that only a fatal evisceration could eliminate it all. He sews the patient back up in silence without even bothering to touch the stricken organ.

An infantry colonel separated from his squad watches, trembling, from a mountaintop as an overwhelming enemy force surrounds an isolated platoon in the valley below.

A policeman stands by in shaking rage as a psychopath holds a shotgun wired to a hostage's head and walks, unmolested, through a crowd of law enforcement officers.

A fighter pilot watches as his best friend is shot down.

And now, a group of highly skilled, fiercely dedicated people stared at radar screens and watched as airplanes carrying thousands of passengers careened obliviously toward a fiery and violent cataclysm.

FBI special agent G. Preston Stanley noticed that Dr. Amy Goldberg had not moved a muscle in the last two minutes. She stood, arms folded across her chest, the fingers of one hand resting against her cheek, staring at the remote view screen of the wide-area display from L.A.

He noticed now also that, unlike the others, she wasn't watching the constantly recomputed projection lines gradually converging north of the airport. She was fixated on the bottom right side of the screen.

"What're you looking at, Amy?"

She didn't answer, nor did she make any acknowledgment at all that she had even heard Stanley's question.

"Doc?"

The finger at her cheek tapped several times. A second or two later she called out softly, without turning from the screen, "Jack?"

"What?" he answered idly, not even bothering to look in her direction.

Amy turned toward him. "Ask Bradley to aim the direction finder toward the guy in the clouds. The unauthorized blip."

He turned toward her now. "What are you talking about?"

Amy turned back to the screen and pointed her finger at the light plane in the TCA over Torrance. "The direction finder. This blip."

Jack looked at the screen in slowly dawning comprehension. "Sonofabitch," he said softly.

Stanley stood up slowly, his jaw going slack as he stared at the screen.

"Sonofabitch!" Jack said again, loudly this time as he grabbed for the speakerphone.

The direction-finding equipment wasn't in the L.A. TRACON radar room. It was in a flight service station several miles away.

Tony Carelli, phone dangling loosely from his hand, shot Bradley a sarcastic look as he waited for the FSS staffer at the other end, Erich Hoffaby, to power up the gear and tune it to one of the approach frequencies.

"This the best those federal geniuses could come up with?"

"Yeah, but until you get a better idea, Carelli, there's not much to lose, is there?"

The characteristic low-frequency whine emanating from the DF unit's speaker came through the phone line and indicated that it was powered and ready to go. As instructed, Hoffaby had turned the antenna so that it was pointed generally southward.

"Hit it," Carelli said.

Hoffaby flipped the switch that took the unit from standby to full sense, and immediately the indicator needle flipped across three-fourths of the meter face. "Hey! I got somethin'!" he said.

Carelli pulled his hand back as though bitten and stared at the phone. Bradley didn't have to ask.

"Botnick," he yelled, "you got that illegal over Torrance on your screen?"

"Yeah, why?"

Bradley didn't answer but took the phone from Carelli and spoke into it. "Hoffaby, lemme know when you got full deflection."

"Hell, I got it already. Pretty much where you said to point."

"What've you got for bearing?" Bradley asked, trying to keep his voice calm.

"Just about one six seven degrees. That'd make it about, uh, one six three from where you guys are. What's goin' on, Bradley?"

Ignoring the question, Bradley yelled out to Botnick again, "Where is he, Cort?"

The controller touched the blip with a light pen and hit a key on his keyboard. A thin line appeared, connecting the blip to the airport picture at the bottom of the screen. It was labeled with the compass orientation of the connecting line.

Botnick turned back toward Carelli and Bradley and called out, "Bearing one six three degrees, thirty-one hundred feet."

Preston Stanley was already on the phone to Norton Air Force Base and had the base commander on hold when Bradley came back on the line from Los Angeles.

"That's it!" he said breathlessly. "It's coming from that plane!"

"Are you sure, Jerry?" asked Jack. "Absolutely sure?"

"We tried all the frequencies, and then some others as a test. All the right ones worked, all the others were negative. There's no doubt. You think she's flying it herself?"

Jack looked at Amy.

"What difference does that make right now?" she asked.

Good point. "Nice work, Jerry. Keep tracking it and we'll be back to you."

He nodded toward Stanley, who turned back to the phone and spoke into it in controlled but urgent tones. "Commander, there is an aircraft in Los Angeles airspace transmitting jamming signals. Air traffic is being disrupted, and there is imminent danger of one or more midair collisions." Pause. "Yes, we have a good track, we know exactly where it is." Pause. "No, but probably a light plane. We're guessing a single."

Jack made an angry, hurry-up motion.

"Commander, listen to me. We need you to scramble some

fighters as fast as you possibly can. Don't waste time loading missiles, just arm the guns. Your authority is NS one zero five, and you can check it with the Pentagon, but do it *after* you get those planes in the air. There's very little time."

He listened for a few more moments, then he looked at Jack and said into the phone as clearly and calmly as he could, "We want you to shoot it down."

"Webster, it won't work. That's not enough time."

"That's the best they can do."

Bradley looked at his wide-area display and punched a few buttons on the keyboard. "We're gonna lose three for sure, maybe as many as six."

Carelli came up behind Bradley and asked, "What's going on?"

Bradley put his hand over the mouthpiece and said, "They're scrambling a squadron from Norton, but it's gonna take 'em seven minutes to get in the air and another four to get here."

Carelli looked at the wide-area and took in the details, then confirmed Bradley's assessment.

"They gonna shoot it down?"

Bradley nodded, too distraught to speak.

"Hey, something's going on with that single!" Botnick called out.

Bradley leaped from his chair and was at the controller's side immediately. He took a few moments to watch the blip, then got back on the phone.

"Webster, she's moving out!"

"We see it," Jack replied. "Where's she heading? What's out that way?"

"East, and dropping altitude—"

"I'll tell you why," Carelli said. "Can you hear me, Webster?"

"Yeah, what's she doing?"

"She can jam all the way to the mountains, but once she drops down east of us below our radar, we'll never find her in the ground clutter, and neither will those fighters. My guess, she can continue to knock us out for another twenty minutes, more if she slows down."

Webster couldn't see Carelli take a breath and look at Bradley. "She's gonna trash our planes, and then she's gonna disappear."

Bradley dropped back onto his chair and looked out over the radar room. Controllers with their ties loosened and shirtsleeves rolled up tapped their feet and drummed their fingers nervously. The chatter had begun to diminish as the futility of managing hand-offs and other procedural minutiae sank in. They watched the little green fireflies march slowly across their screens and tried hard not to think about what they represented.

The base commander at Norton had the presence of mind to initiate a massive dispatch of emergency people and equipment to the area surrounding the anticipated convergence point in the Santa Monica Mountains, calling on resources from hospitals, county EMS services, private ambulance companies and emergency rooms. In a few minutes another set of requests would reach their destinations and an entire set of civil service contingency plans would be put into place.

One of the FAA trainees in the L.A. radar room brought a cup of black coffee; Bradley sat and sipped the comforting liquid while trying not to dwell on the looming horror. The noise level in the control room had dropped to near quiet, until only the humming of the units cooling the vast array of electronic gear could be heard.

As Bradley brought the Styrofoam cup to his lips, he heard a burst of static from behind the closed door of the equipment and supply room. He lifted his eyebrows as the hot coffee touched his tongue and started to turn his head toward the sound when he heard the static sort itself out into a clear human voice.

"Yo, Omar, you out playin' sick today or what?"

Bradley gagged and unleashed a dribble of hot coffee that burned his lips. He managed to set the cup down quickly, but not without slopping some over the sides, which he ignored in his mad dash to stand up and bolt for the door.

He threw it open, and the bang as it slammed into his chair caused startled heads to turn throughout the room. He dove for the microphone standing upright on the table, squeezed the key and screamed, "Kincaid! Is that you?"

" 'Course it's me," the speaker rasped back immediately. "What'cha hollerin' for?"

In the command post in the O'Hare tower, they heard the commotion coming over the speakerphone, their attention shifting when the door hit Bradley's chair, which had then banged into the counter that held the open telephone.

Repeated shouts from their end failed to get Bradley back on the line, but Carelli picked up the phone and told them to sit tight for a second. Something, don't ask him what, was going on, and it looked to him like Bradley was about to soil himself.

Amy looked back at the screen and noticed a new blip appearing in the upper left, which was the northwest sector of the TCA. That wasn't unusual, but the blip also had an identifying box showing "P51 3DB" along with its speed and altitude.

"Hey, something funny's happening here."

"What?" Jack spat in annoyance, a combination of his inability to reengage Bradley and what sounded like another problem brewing.

"Got a new target on the scope, with an ID box."

"So?" asked Stanley.

"So," she said, slowly and thoughtfully, "how'd the controllers assign a new transponder code if they're not talking to anybody?"

Jack's answering look of shared puzzlement was interrupted by a sudden stream of shouted babbling from Bradley, directed not to them, but to his controllers. A few seconds later he came on the line.

"Webster, you ready for this? I got a P-51 directly over the TCA at eleven thousand feet and we're talking to him, plain as day!"

"A Mustang?" Mindlessly, Jack said it again. "A Mustang? You're talking to a Mustang?"

"Yeah, a Mustang, f'Chrissakes, you believe this shit? A buddy of mine! Data block ID is—"

"Yeah, we got it." Jack's tactical mind snapped into overdrive as he fought to assimilate this new piece of data and assess its possibilities. "How good does he fly it?"

"Are you kidding? One of the best! World War Two combat, Vietnam in Phantoms . . . He restored the P-51 from a pile of junk and—"

"Okay, okay, I got it." *Think, dammit!* "What's the single doing?"

Bradley didn't bother to ask him why he couldn't find out for himself on his remote display. "Still heading east, still dropping, and we're gonna go critical here in about three minutes, we don't do something."

Amy stepped forward. "Talk to him yourself, Jack. No relay nonsense."

"He's right," Stanley agreed.

"Okay, Jerry, listen: I want to talk to the Mustang myself, but I need one of your people in the link to control. Can you do that?"

"In a flash. We'll—"

"Hold it a second. Before you turn him over, head him toward the single fast as he can get there."

"Got it. Stay quiet and you can hear."

They listened as Bradley shouted an order, and then they heard Tony Carelli talking to the Mustang a few feet away from the telephone, close enough for them to make out his words.

"Turn right heading one five five and descend to four thousand feet, no delay. Do it as fast as you can. TCA speed limit is suspended, I say again, no speed limit, but stay above the cloud layer."

"Roger, turning to one five five, out of eleven for four," came the barely discernible reply as it mixed with the sounds of a noisy cockpit and then got mutilated on its passage through two radio sets and a telephone. "You wanna tell me what I do when I get there?"

They heard the phone being picked up, and then Bradley said, "You get that?"

"Yes," replied Jack. *And the pilot asked a damned good question, too.* "How fast can he move?"

"Watch your scope. You want him now?"

"Yes. What's his tail number?"

"Triple-three-delta-bravo, but forget that shit. Name's Bo Kincaid."

"Got it," Jack said as he turned to the display and wondered what indeed the Mustang was going to do when it got there.

And who the hell was "Omar"?

Carelli's emergency suspension of the standard 250-knot TCA speed limit was music to Bo's ears.

He cinched his four-point belt tight and pushed the stick forward, lowering the nose, firewalling the throttle at the same time. As the plane started its dive, he reached for the controls of the variable-pitch propeller and adjusted it for maximum power.

The giant Merlin engine responded happily to the power change with an ascending whine up the scale. Bo kept one eye on the airspeed indicator and another out the window, believing Carelli when he said there was no other traffic above the layer but taking no chances anyway.

Before too many seconds had passed, the airspeed needle began nudging the redline warning painted on its surface, but Bo held the dive anyway.

He'd known Jerry Bradley for seventeen years, and in all that time, not even once, not even when they had nearly run off a cliff on a late night drive home from fishing up near Castaic, not ever had he heard his voice rise even one note above its standard, even timbre.

So when "Omar" came across the radio as near hysterical, Bo kind of figured he was a tad upset.

Amy watched the blip move across the scope and the numbers change in the data block at the same time.

"Holy smokes, this guy is really cookin'!"

"How long 'til he reaches the single?" asked Jack.

Amy shook her head in unbridled admiration. "I'd say less than forty seconds. He needs to turn left about five degrees, though. Dalek's picking up speed."

Jack picked up the phone and said, "Kincaid, my name is Jack Webster. Come five degrees to your left."

There was no response, but the blip on the screen shifted to the correct heading with the next sweep of the beam. When it had stabilized, Bo's voice came into the room.

"Can't fly and talk to you too good. Only got a portable radio."

So that's how you managed to contact Bradley: a nonstandard frequency. "No problem. I'm gonna make this real simple because there's no time. There's a light plane sending jamming signals to incoming commercial flights. The whole system is going to hell in a hand basket, and there's a good chance we're gonna start losing planes in a few minutes."

Kincaid's voice stayed cool. "You know why?"

"Yeah, but there's no time to explain; you're gonna have to take my word for it. Somehow, we gotta stop it."

"How do we do it?"

Jack kept one eye on the display. "I don't know, but it's no holds barred. There's a squadron of F-15s on the way from Norton with orders to shoot it down, but they won't make it before the weather starts turning to scattered aluminum. You copy?"

There was a pause before Bo said softly, "Yeah, I copy. I'm not carrying ordnance, you know."

Jack smiled. "I know. Too bad." He checked the screen. "You're coming up on it, you'd better start slowing down. Can you see anything?"

A few seconds passed while Bo throttled back and lifted the nose to dampen the dive.

"Not yet. It's still pretty hazy."

"Three delta bravo," Carelli's voice cut in. "Come right four degrees, descend and maintain three thousand. Should be right off your nose at twelve o'clock low. And don't bother acknowledging anymore." No sense wasting time with needless verification of the instructions.

The two blips were now less than a half inch apart on the screen and still getting closer.

Abruptly, one of them shimmered and grew hazy, then solidified with the next sweep.

"Just dipping below our coverage, Webster," Bradley said. "She keeps dropping, we're gonna lose her."

Bo strained to see ahead, but even though the weather was clearing, the cluttered jigsaw pattern of the heavily populated land below made it difficult to spot another aircraft.

Using an old fighter pilot trick from before on-board radar had become available, Bo fixed his concentration on a single point on the ground and held it.

There. A movement that shouldn't have been. He looked at it directly.

"I got it!" he shouted into the radio as he tweaked the controls to maneuver in behind the plane. "It's a Mooney, late model. Got speed brakes on the wings, so it must be a two thirty-one."

"Can you get in close?" he heard Jack ask.

The Mooney was doing nearly 180 knots. Bo squeezed the throttle slightly forward and inched up on it.

"It's got some strange stuff hangin' off the bottom. Looks like a buncha antennas, maybe."

"That's gotta be it, Kincaid. Can you harass it?"

Bo smiled to himself. *Can I harass it*? He moved up until he was abreast of the high-performance single and about a hundred yards to its left. When he was sure he had the pilot's attention, he dipped his right wing, held left rudder with his foot and slid the Mustang sideways through the air directly toward the other plane.

It didn't flinch.

Bo broke off the high-stakes game of chicken with less than twenty feet between them, but not before he caught a glimpse of the pilot's face.

"Cripes, it's a girl!" he yelled into the radio.

"We know," he heard Jack say. "But it ain't no lady."

"I tried to shake her, but she's not buyin' it. What now?"

Jack had had some time to work up an idea. "Can you get over her and just forward, see if you can buffet her in your wake?"

"Easy. Stand by one."

"Jack, ask Bradley, do they have a free phone line there."

Jack complied with the request without asking Amy why and scribbled a number down on a piece of paper, which he handed to her.

"Thank you," she said. She went to an unused phone and dialed, asking for Bradley as soon as someone answered.

"Jerry? Amy Goldberg here."

The others could not hear Bradley's reply.

"Quickly, before you're needed again: What can you tell me about this pilot, Kincaid?"

There was a pause as she listened.

"I'm not certain. Something important. Anything we should know if—Yes? . . . Uh-huh."

She nodded her head slowly. "Ah, from the war. Please: tell me . . ."

Bo was starting to get irritated.

He had flown in front of the Mooney, and even though his backwash had rocked the little plane and disrupted its flight path, its pilot had recovered quickly and pulled away.

So he powered into a loop and came down at over three hundred miles per hour, shooting directly over the front of the plane's prop, causing it to bank sharply in the asymmetrical turbulence.

Again she recovered and held steady.

With no warning, the cacophony of jamming static stopped abruptly, like a waterfall suddenly disappearing. The monitor had been turned down to mute the annoying and useless sound, and they had pretty much forgotten about it, but its sudden cessation brought them up sharply, like a slap.

Out of the deafening silence came a single syllable, and it froze their hearts where they stood, paralyzed, unable even to speak.

"Jack."

It wrapped around them, weblike, and seemed to echo over and over without fading.

"It's her," Florence was the first to breathe.

In the new silence, a quick-minded controller at L.A. tried to get back on the air, but no sooner had he uttered his first syllables than the static came back on. After about half a minute, it went silent again, and again they heard it.

"Jack."

No upward, questioning inflection, no inquiry into his presence, it was more of a—

Another voice, a pilot this time, and again the static drowned it out.

Jack played the sound over and over in his mind, trying to decipher it, when the static dropped to silence again.

He reached for the phone and said, "Bradley, quickly: Tell everyone listening stay off the air, no exceptions."

He listened as Bradley scrambled to put out the message. They could all hear it over the monitor. Jack thought about the female voice that had spoken his name and realized that what he had heard was a command.

Amy read it the same way. "Talk to her. Right now."

Jack got Bradley back on the phone and said, "Patch me into that frequency, Jerry." He waited for an acknowledgment and then reached for the microphone, thinking for a moment and then holding it to his lips.

"What is it you want, Dalek?"

Amy nodded her approval. The answer was quick in coming.

"Fuck you, Jack."

It wasn't so much the words that hit them, but the sound of her voice, the syllables drawn out into a snarl, malevolent and full of bitterness and venom, breathless in their underlying hatred.

Jack struggled to contain his emotions, to compose a reply that would have any chance at all of ending the nightmare. He watched the lines converging on the radar screen and wanted to give her anything at all possible to make her stop.

But Amy had stepped forward and was staring at him, eyes narrowed in resolution and conviction.

"Piss her off, Jack. Piss her off big time."

Jack was startled. "But what if I—"

"What if you what? Make her mad? What the hell else could she possibly do to us unless she was carrying an atomic bomb?"

"She's right," said Stanley, straightening up to his full height. "Go ahead and get her completely pissed. Maybe she'll make a mistake, do something stupid, get rattled. There's nothing else to be done."

In the L.A. TRACON radar room, an alarm bell sounded. Everyone at O'Hare could hear it.

"What was that, Carelli?" Jack asked.

"Hang on a second, Doc," Bradley said to Amy as he set down the phone.

"More CA CA, Jerry," Kabaker was saying as Bradley got there. "Here"—she pointed to the conflict alert preview area on the screen—"and here."

Bradley rubbed his forehead, clapped Kabaker on the shoulder, then stepped back to the desk and took the phone from Carelli.

"Webster, we just got another conflict alert. Japan Airlines DC-10 inbound from Osaka and a United 737 from Phoenix. One of them doesn't change course, they're gonna meet for sure in less than four minutes."

Nothing.

"Webster, you there?"

Jack clenched his fist and pushed it into his chin as hard as he could. When he was sure he could speak without the rising acid in his throat betraying him, he said, "Yeah, I'm here. I got it."

There was a feeling of familiarity about the scene, the sinking sensation when competent professionals were at a complete loss and he, Jack Webster, mere human being, stood in command and was expected to have all the answers and the confident presence of King David to boot. He looked to see Amy, Florence, fellow FBI agent Preston Stanley, and then, suddenly, all the senior officers of the USS *Constellation* looking at him. He felt the floor rock back and forth gently as the great carrier plowed through the storm-ravaged sea. A pilot's life was at stake, and they were waiting for him to act.

He didn't like it. This wasn't his fault. Didn't they understand that? What the hell was wrong with them? Were they waiting for him to reveal the secret answer he'd had in his pocket all along but wasn't telling them?

It wasn't their fault, either. Nobody had forced him into a position of leadership. And why was he here again? He'd engineered his whole life around never being here again, never holding another man's life in his hands while a sea of faces stared at him expectantly.

He squeezed his eyes shut and made his senior officers disappear and took a breath and hoped nobody would notice as he jerked his mind off the carrier and back into the O'Hare control tower. With as much calm professionalism as he could summon up, he told Bradley to change frequencies, then keyed the mike and talked to Bo Kincaid.

Bo had felt it first at the base of his spine and angrily shoved it back down into some forgotten place where it should have stayed safely hidden. There was no time for that kind of crap now.

He thought he could rattle hell out of the little Mooney and go home a hero. That hadn't worked, and it poked up from the hiding place and reasserted itself somewhere in his chest, barely noticeable, a little pressure maybe, a stuffy sensation. It squirmed around inside of him, groping at will, threatening.

Now he listened through a growing fog as Jack Webster's voice scratched at him through the portable radio.

"Kincaid? We got two jetliners gonna crash in less than three minutes."

It expanded almost instantly, like an air bag in a head-on, and tried to suffocate him, not even pretending to be under his control but grabbing for his eyes and his brain in open revolt.

"Is there anything you can do? Tap her wings, maybe?"

Bo fought against the howling in his ears and answered. "Only if she cooperates with me, Webster."

Bo tried to imagine their desperation as they sat, impotent and blinded by rage, with him just a few feet away from the source of their seething frustration. He could see her face, placid and cold, as she controlled and guided airplanes laden with unsuspecting and innocent passengers and crews to certain and brutal deaths.

And he, Bo Kincaid, could do nothing.

It hit him then, mercilessly. It knew all his secrets, all his vulnerabilities, and it poured them into his tortured soul with ferocious intensity. Memories caromed off the walls inside his head, assaulting his mind with terrible images from decades before, images he'd dreamed about thousands of times but that now played out before him as though they were happening anew.

"Anything at all, Kincaid?"

His hand shook as it tried to keep the control stick steady, and he bent toward his sleeve to wipe the building tears from his eyes so he could see out the windscreen. He thought he might drown, and he pounded his fist on top of the instrument panel as hard as he could, hoping the pain would distract the monster attacking him from within.

But the beast only bellowed with greater cruelty.

"Jerry, I mean it, we're down to less than two minutes here! We gotta *do* something!"

Kabaker was on the point of losing it. Bradley could hear it in her voice.

"Webster, they're getting closer! What's Kincaid doing?"

"I don't know, Jerry. I don't know what he *can* do. Maybe the best we can hope for, he guides the F-15s onto her right away and we only . . ."

He didn't have to finish. Bradley understood.

We only lose a few planes instead of all of them.

It came from someplace high above him, from an extraordinary altitude, but not any higher than the top of his own head.

It was like a blanket, and it descended over Bo in layers, at first softly, like silk, and the beast tore at it angrily, but then the layers thickened, and as they fell, they overwhelmed the monster until Bo felt it dying under the smothering weight.

The fog around his brain started to dissipate, and very soon everything in his vision began to take on a crystalline edge. The sudden clarity should have been frightening, but the blanket protected him.

He had stopped pounding on the panel, and his hand on the control stick steadied. His whole body felt light and highly tuned, and he found that he knew things now. Not little, trivial things but mighty ones. Giant, important truths he had only half glimpsed before.

In his dawning comprehension of the ineffable rightness of his world, he keyed the microphone, held it to his lips and said, "Three delta bravo, out," and clipped it back onto its holder.

Then he punched the throttle forward, pulled back on the stick and drove the Mustang up toward the morning sun.

"Kincaid!"
Nothing.
"Kincaid, dammit, answer me!" Jack shouted.

"What the hell does he think he's doing!" Stanley exclaimed. He watched on the display as the blip held its position but the altitude readout showed a steep climb.

Bradley's voice, frantic, came over the speakerphone. "He's gonna lose the Mooney! Christ, Webster, we're down to less than two minutes here!"

"Well, what the fuck you want me to do about it, Bradley? The sonofabitch won't even talk to me!" He angrily threw the phone down on the desk, and it clattered to the floor.

"He's still right above her," said Florence. "He's not going anywhere but up."

Jack stopped and watched the radar screen, and he tried to put himself in the cockpit of the P-51. He tried to imagine what Bo Kincaid, a bona fide war hero in two conflicts, was feeling as he flew alongside a sociopathic madwoman who, with perfect impunity, was about to turn the picturesque Los Angeles basin into a theater of violent death and destruction.

From somewhere deep within his brain, in a place responsible for the integration of seemingly disparate pieces of information, an urgent message was dispatched to his consciousness. At the same time, he saw Amy Goldberg fixing him with a penetrating and knowing stare. He realized that the psychologist hadn't said a word since her phone conversation with Bradley had broken off.

Jack stood slowly and looked back at the display. He realized what the Mustang pilot was going to do. "No!" he said softly but with conviction, and started forward to retrieve the phone. But Amy's hand gripped his arm with surprising strength.

They looked at each other, and in that moment Jack knew that Amy understood it perfectly, all of it, understood Bo Kincaid and his place in the universe and maybe even something about Jack that he himself didn't know.

No, that wasn't right. It was something that Jack already

knew. He had told Amy himself over endless cups of strong coffee and the occasional single-malt Scotch, and now the canny psychologist was going to use it. Was going to make it impossible for Jack to do anything but make the right decision, no matter how it hurt.

"Leave it be, Jack," she said, quietly but firmly.

Jack looked back toward the radar screen. The Mustang's rate of ascent was slowing as it started to level off.

"Stanley, get me the L.A. sectional," Jack finally said.

Amy loosened her grip to let Jack pick up the phone, but he didn't speak into it yet. Instead he addressed Florence, who had quickly picked up the basics of how to read the radar screen.

"Where are they?"

"About nineteen miles east of LAX."

He wondered what Slattery must be feeling right now, alone in the inky blackness, about to eject into eternity miles from the storm-battered carrier.

It had been the right decision . . .

Maintenance Officer Andy Espinoza touched his arm gently. "Jack?" he said, but it sounded like a female voice.

. . . it always had been.

After a moment Jack turned his head and looked not at mechanic Andy Espinoza on the USS *Constellation*, but at psychologist Amy Goldberg in the O'Hare International control tower. He snapped forward through time and reached for the airway map, spreading it before him. He had sworn he'd never let himself be put in a position like this again, not ever. The realization that his life had come full circle dizzied him in its awful symmetry and, under more forgiving circumstances, might have toppled him, but he was needed again. Just like before. Same deal. He had always known he had made the right decision in sending F-14 pilot Brian Slattery to a certain death. He wasn't supposed to be here again, but he had made the right decision before. . . . *Dammit, this wasn't supposed to be the deal!*

Jack forced himself to feigned steadiness. "Where?" he asked Florence again.

"Here." She pointed to the spot on the map that corresponded with Bo's position as shown on the radar screen.

Jack studied it for a few seconds, then lifted the phone to his ear and spoke.

"Kincaid, you're over densely populated terrain. There's a lake about two miles ahead of you, just over forty seconds at her present speed."

Then he stopped and looked back at the display.

To the enormous surprise of everyone in the Los Angeles radar room and at O'Hare, Bo's voice came through the speaker.

"I got it."

And then the channel went dead forever.

"He's level at thirty-five hundred," reported Carelli from the sector station, but Bradley was watching on the wide-area and said nothing.

Controller Kabaker was trembling visibly, and she was grabbing onto the sides of her chair for fear of shaking herself to the floor as she watched the deadly ballet play out on her screen.

The conflict alert alarm was clanging urgently as the distance between the Japanese DC-10 and the United 737 continued to diminish.

"Jerry, we're gonna lose 'em!" Kabaker cried. "We're gonna fucking lose 'em, I'm telling you!"

Bradley did nothing. Just bit his fingernails and watched the display.

"He's dropping!" Florence yelled. "And he's moved out in front of the Mooney!"

The numbers on the Mustang's ID box were changing with every beam sweep, in small increments at first, then larger and larger.

Jack watched as the digits flashed before him.

"God be with you," he said quietly.

What the radar couldn't tell them was that Bo had rolled the plane over onto its back and started the dive inverted instead of just pushing over the top. He was going to pull maximum G's as he arced toward the deck and didn't want to risk losing consciousness from blood entering his head under pressure. This way, the force would be directed downward toward his legs, and he knew how to counteract that effect.

From his inverted position, he was able to keep the Mooney in sight behind him, but he had jettisoned the canopy and the rushing air swirled furiously around in the cockpit, making it more difficult to see than he had counted on.

He was in a power dive so fast that the effective closing speed between the two planes was nearly seven hundred miles per hour.

When he was less than a thousand feet above the Mooney, Bo pulled back on the stick once again, bringing up the nose until it was pointed right at her. There was no margin for error, and he had to stay perfectly oriented.

Jack had the frequency keyed back to L.A. approach control. He picked up the microphone, watched the radar screen for several more seconds, then keyed the mike and held it to his face.

"Hey, Dalek . . ."

He took a last look around the room.

"Fuck you too, lady."

When the Mustang was only two hundred feet away, Phyllis Dalek, distracted by Jack's message and not knowing that Bo's plane had been high above her for the last fifty seconds, noticed it now as it screamed toward her from above and slightly to her left, filling her windshield, blotting out the sun and sending hot jets of adrenaline into her central nervous system.

In the fraction of a second before the two of them would meet, now an inevitability owing to her brief distraction, she jerked her control wheel hard to the right, banking the plane steeply.

Bo had counted on it. He pressured his own stick straight back, but only slightly, and their left wings met, snapping off neatly at their respective roots and disintegrating in a hail of metal fragments. The remaining wings, suddenly shorn of the countervailing lift generated by their opposites, sent both craft into violent, spinning tumbles, the resultant stress further damaging the structures and initiating the breakup of the central airframes.

Fuel from both planes, suddenly freed and hanging unsupported in space, expanded almost instantly in the fearsome turbulence into a ragged ball almost four hundred feet across. Every molecule of fuel eventually found two more of oxygen in the ample ambient atmosphere. Three seconds after the midair collision, a metal fragment, superheated and liquefied by the impact, found the ball of volatile gases and catalyzed the molecular couplings. They combined instantly, unleashing an explosion so violent that it would be reported as far away as Riverside and creating a second sun in the morning sky directly over Herbert C. Legg Lake in Pomona, into which the debris of the totally demolished airplanes would continue to fall for the next five minutes.

Bradley had the microphone in his hands the instant the static from the automated terminal information system monitor ceased.

Without a moment's hesitation, he keyed it and said, "Japan two zero three immediate right turn to three three zero, no delay, United five seven six, immediate left turn to one eight zero, no delay, no acknowledge, *do it now!*"

The two blips less than a quarter inch apart on the radar screen began to diverge, but Bradley didn't wait to watch them.

"Attention all aircraft, L.A. Approach is back on frequency, stand by for revised clearances. Do not, I say again, *do not* key your microphones under any circumstances unless requested to do so."

He looked out over the room full of controllers, noticing for the first time the thick pall of illicit smoke and overflowing ashtrays, the frayed and harried expressions on his people. It had only been fifteen minutes since the crisis had begun, but the controllers looked as if they had fought a war.

"Start movin' 'em around, people."

The room filled immediately with urgent clearances. Two minutes later, when the frantic hubbub had subsided to a more normal level of frenzy, Jerry Bradley left the radar room,

walked to a window, lit a cigarette of his own and looked up
into the sky.

Jack Webster, by unspoken acclamation, presided over a
hushed and respectful silence, a decent interval of clenching
admiration before G. Preston Stanley, compelled by sworn
obligation, found it necessary to speak. He chose his words
carefully, trying to convey the gravity of their collective burden without unduly splintering the spell that pervaded the
room.

"The very saddest part," he said, looking around him to
make sure the message found its mark, "is that we can't tell
anybody what he did."

Florence whirled around to face him in flashing anger but
was intercepted gently by Jack.

"Easy, Florence. It has to be this way."

Tears welled in her eyes. "We never even met him. None
of us knows what he looks like." Her voice started to break.
"Who he was, or who he loved."

Amy took her hand in both of hers.

"You'll speak with Mr. Bradley. He'll tell you. And then
you'll understand."

CHAPTER 34

Larry Stilson and Ralph "Day-Glo" Beaumont sat on the stoop of the single-story clapboard house in South El Monte.

Not "sitting," exactly, since that would have been an inappropriately formal expression to describe the boneless slouch into which Ralph's body had poured itself over the course of the last several hours. Larry's body was in an equally formless posture, held up primarily by a fortuitous accident of structural mechanics as his backbone connected with an iron crossbar in the stair railing.

Every several minutes or thereabouts, one or the other of their respective spirits would rally itself mightily in echo of the primeval struggle that existed in all living things, command a surge of energy to the proper sequence of arm and shoulder muscles, close a hand around the neck of the latest in a long line of beer bottles and raise it up in an awesome display of disciplined self-control. Following a long and gurgling swig, an equally impressive reverse show of muscular coordination would ensue as the bottle was replaced on the concrete landing, with just enough impact to prevent the bottom from breaking but with little energy wasted in ensuring an unnecessarily delicate touchdown.

It should not be said that Larry and Day-Glo were capable

only of drinking beer, for these were stout and formidable men. Summoning an adrenaline-driven reserve of strength normally held in abeyance by his species only for running from lions or escaping a crazed enemy tribe, Larry was able to intermingle his tugs from the bottle with the rolling, lighting and smoking of some ace Hanoi gold scored by Ralph in the periods of rare lucidity necessitated by the need occasionally to take a pee, punch the time clock in his guaranteed-for-life county civil service job or call his sometime girlfriend, Twinkie, and hit her up for a loan. Larry, after years of concerted practice at ecology-oriented civic-mindedness, had reached the apotheosis of energy conservation: he was able to roll joints with one hand.

Larry's abilities in this regard were matched only by Ralph's dexterity in periodically taking over the glowing joint, the updated replay of ancient and sacred traditions celebrating the cyclic nature of the seasons. Back and forth, back and forth, they'd been at it pretty much since eleven the night before. Ralph suspected, though Larry might have disputed the point, that it looked as though they were finally going to get pretty stoned.

As befitted their individual personalities, Ralph "sat" with his face turned upward toward the morning sun. What little of its rays managed to get through the grime and stubble on his face did manage to ameliorate somewhat the characteristic pallor of the degenerate pothead.

Larry, conversely, faced his back to the east to avoid the annoying intrusion of all that light in his eyes. Consequently Larry failed to see what was so damned fascinating behind him that Ralph saw fit to pause in midtoke, allowing the ember to burn in wasteful unproductivity for the time he spent, jaw hanging open, bleary eyes turned upward, looking at something, Larry knew not what. Nor was he about to suffer the burden of turning his head to find out.

"Fuck'sa matter wi'you, dude?" Larry inquired with all the intense curiosity of a dust cover, at the same time noticing with some befogged corner of his alcohol-soaked brain a light coming over Ralph's face. Not the inner glow of some spiritual revelation, but a *real* light, as though somebody had flipped on a lamp somewhere.

Seeing no change in Ralph's jawline or his bloodshot eyes, Larry did as only a true friend could, reached for the wasting joint and took as deep a hit as his lungs, with only slightly less volumetric uptake than an Olympic speed skater's, could hold.

By the time he picked his head up to gauge what Ralph was doing now, Larry saw that the light was gone from his face, but he dared not chance a second inquiry for fear of inadvertently exhaling the acrid smoke he was trying desperately to hold while the alveoli in his bronchial passageways sought to leech from it every last measure of potency.

Ralph blinked his eyes once or twice to try to clear them, an act of consummate futility on a par with putting a Band-Aid on a compound fracture.

"Fugg me!" he finally managed to croak, reaching for the joint.

"Whuh?" said Larry, the word creeping from among the layers of expired smoke that boiled out of his mouth.

Ralph tried to speak and hold in the smoke at the same time, which resulted in a strained rasp that, to a normal ear, would have been incomprehensible, but which to Larry, trained in the art as well as any UN translator, sounded perfectly normal.

"Fuggin' light, man! I was like, oh wow. Y'dig?"

"Absolutely," Larry replied without hesitation, head nodding in complete understanding until the periodic motion caused his inner ear canals to register a protest, threatening to nauseate him further if he didn't stop.

The effort of that extended discourse having tired them both, they lapsed into their more usual forms of nonverbal communication, consisting in the main of continued passing of the joint, enlivened intermittently by the dialectically satisfying rolling of a new one. Occasionally it was necessary to open some new beers as well, but they had hours ago dispatched the desire that they be cold, thereby obviating the necessity for repeated trips indoors.

As he raised the bottle to his lips once again, Ralph once again froze in midflight, eyes once again fixed in space at some point high over Larry's head.

The latter furrowed his brow in annoyance at this second

interruption to the rhythm it had taken them all night and part of the morning to establish.

"Jeez Chris', wha' now?"

Ralph finished the swallow he had started—no sense being childish about this—and continued staring. "Like, uh, I dunno, y'know? 'S'like a angel or sumpin'. . . ."

Larry stared at the joint in his hand and the roaches in the ashtray. Those leftover bits too small to hold without getting burned, stripped and rerolled, would have been a month's supply for the more casual dope smoker in a lesser league than Ralph and Larry.

But he concluded that the sum of what they had consumed was of insufficient toxicity to warrant Ralph's state of hallucinated grace. This made it necessary for him to attempt to turn around, which he managed awkwardly by leaning one elbow on the concrete stair and sort of falling onto it in such a manner that gravity and his arm conspired to roll him around until he was facing backward.

At that point, the sun shot a lance into his completely dilated eyeballs, a stream of photons that slammed into his retinas and sent a shock of pain into the middle of his head, jolting him into an involuntary spasm that turned him back around to face Ralph again.

When he had fully recovered, he said, "I don' see no fuggin' angel, man," and resolved never in his entire life to turn around again, ever. Not for Ralph, not for anybody.

Ralph, duly concerned with the surprising lack of verification from his best friend, ol' what's-his-name, continued to stare at the falling apparition. "Got wings 'n' everythin', man. White ones."

Funny wings, though. Seemed to be above the descending angel instead of at its back.

Then it fell behind the abandoned asphalt plant across the vacant field, and Ralph promptly and completely put it out of what was left of his mind.

Later they wouldn't be able to remember very well how much time had passed, but at some point Ralph raised his arm and pointed to somewhere behind Larry. He began to cough, the surprise having caught him with some beer in his throat, and he was unable to communicate what was going on.

So Larry, having sworn off turning around, nevertheless forced himself to do so once again.

Trudging across the field was the figure of a man. He was weaving unsteadily, dragging one leg more than walking on it. In his arms he held a bunched-up pile of white fabric, but he didn't have hold of all of it, and the remainder streamed behind him, dragging heavily against the scraggly weeds, further impeding his progress.

Ralph and Larry had neither the presence of mind nor the inclination to go to the stranger's aid. As he approached, they could see that the left sleeve of his otherwise light green overall was singed black. A dark stain spread downward from his left thigh, spotting the concrete street with red as he crossed the edge of the field.

By the time he had walked up to the bottom of the staircase, Ralph had fallen away in a dead faint.

"I need an ambulance," the man said, but Larry was too wasted and far gone to react.

So the man dragged himself painfully and slowly up the stairs and into the house, pausing only to stoop down for a beer from the case at Ralph's back, went into the tiny kitchen, looked around until he found a phone, picked it up, dialed, poked around for a bottle opener while he waited for somebody to answer, spoke into the phone a few seconds later and then collapsed, unconscious, onto the cracked linoleum floor.

Epilogue

When our perils are past, shall our gratitude sleep?
No—here's to the pilot that weathered the storm.

—George Canning
    Song for the Inauguration of the Pitt Club
    May 25, 1802

CHAPTER 35

A cemetery was not a fun place for a young boy to be hanging out in, as Lamarr had discovered over the last forty-five minutes.

There was only so much joy to be derived from sliding off headstones, playing giant hopscotch on the grave outlines still visible beneath the encroaching undergrowth or switching flowers from one plot to another, then feeling guilty and putting them all back.

So he decided he'd had enough and began invoking his rights as a kid, folding his arms across his chest, plastering an angry frown on his face and stamping his foot loudly on the ground.

None of it fooled his Uncle Bo.

He'd watched his "uncle" off and on since they'd gotten here, sitting on a bench under a towering elm tree, cane resting on his knee, talking with that darned Mr. Webster who had monopolized so much of his time since he had arrived in Santa Paula just this morning.

Though he was too far away to hear the conversation, Lamarr had seen a circus of expressions cross Bo's face. Surprise, anger, some laughter even, but mostly just intense and focused concentration as Mr. Webster did most of the talking. Once in a while it looked as if Bo was asking a question, but mostly Mr. Webster was doing the talking.

Well, okay, they'd been at it long enough, so he stomped around and tried to get Bo's attention.

When Bo finally looked his way, Lamarr waved his arms in the air, spun around once or twice and made great, exaggerated waving motions, urging Bo to get the heck up and come on over.

But Bo only smiled and held up a hand, mouthing, "Just a minute! Just a minute!" which was buying him only a few minutes of peace at a time.

Now *what* could be so important as to keep him waiting!

Bo shook his head in amazement.

"Wild, isn't it?" Jack Webster said.

"Damnedest thing I ever heard."

Jack leaned his back against the bench and put his hands behind his head, pushing his elbows forward and grunting as he stretched his aching muscles. "Anyway, Bo, you understand why you can't tell anyone about this? Why the cover story about a stoned drug runner hitting you?"

Bo grunted and shifted his left leg. The doctor had said it would've hurt a lot less if he hadn't been so damned fool stubborn and walked on it broken for half a mile. "Doesn't bother me a bit, Jack. I'd just as soon it be this way."

"Really? My book, you should get the Medal of Honor."

Bo grunted. "Got enough medals."

He looked over at Lamarr, petulant at being ignored, and waved him back down for a few more minutes. Turning back to Jack, he asked, "That guy collecting cash in Florida? The programmer's cousin? I thought you had to have that particular card. The one Dalek had. So how'd he do it?"

"Nice thing about programming computers, you're the boss. He could validate any card he wanted to."

Bo stared up at the elm tree for a few seconds, then turned back to Jack. "I 'preciate your comin' to talk to me."

The investigator shrugged. "Sorry about your leg."

"I'm sorry about my plane."

He'd been able to scramble out of the open cockpit after the impact as he had hoped, but the vertical stabilizer shaken loose by the wild gyrations had caught him broadside and fractured his fibula in three places. Damned lucky it had, too, he knew. Otherwise he would have been pureed by the propeller that was coming his way before the providential tail fin interceded on his behalf.

The expanding shock wave from the explosion hadn't helped, either, although it had blown him closer to land and made his landing a whole lot more pleasant.

Jack rose and brushed off the seat of his pants, "Yeah, heard it was a real beauty. D model, was it?"

"Yep."

"Hmph. Too bad."

He walked to the government-issue Buick sitting at the curb and opened the door. "Got a call from Preston Stanley last night. One of the guys on our team?"

"Yeah?"

"Seems they busted a smuggling operation, ran up from somewhere down south. Can't tell you exactly where. Protect their informants and all that."

He got in but left the door open. "The runners used a P-51. Naturally, it was seized by Stanley's team."

Bo looked up. "Yeah?"

"It's standard policy to auction off that kind of stuff. Planes, boats, cars. The money goes back into a fund to finance more undercover work."

Using his cane, Bo struggled to his feet and hobbled toward the car. "And?"

"And, this particular plane was auctioned off by mail. Sealed bids. Secret opening."

"And?"

"And, you won."

"I did?"

"You were a hundred bucks higher than the next highest bidder."

Jack closed the door, started the engine and rolled down the window. "See you, Kincaid," he called, and started to drive off.

"Hey!" Bo yelled, a look of dread on his face. "How much did I bid?"

Jack leaned his head out the window and shouted back, "A

hundred bucks!" He waved once and disappeared down the street.

Bo stared for a second until comprehension dawned, then threw back his head and laughed, an unburdened, glorious laugh that started deep in his belly and boiled upward, unimpeded, exploding out of him and startling Lamarr, who ran up to him and jumped on his back.

"Yow! Watch it, boy, can't you see I'm a crippled old man?"

Lamarr raspberried in his ear. "You got about eight weeks to feel sorry for yourself, Uncle Bo, and then the cast comes off and we go flyin'!"

"Now, how'd you know that?"

"Aunty Lenore tol' me, what else?"

"That so," muttered Bo as he carried Lamarr awkwardly back toward the cemetery, one hand curled under the boy's right leg, the other holding the cane.

They walked up to an old grave with fresh flowers leaning against the headstone. Bo set Lamarr down and they stood, side by side, reading the inscription carved in 1945 when the body came home. Lamarr walked to the stone and ran his fingers over the name of Bo's long-gone friend, then came back and took the older man's hand.

Bo looked at the stone and said good-bye in his head, knowing he'd never need to say it again.

He looked down at Lamarr and knew, finally, that now he could teach the grandson of Judson Greaves what it meant to be a man.

Acknowledgments

(alphabetically)

Tom Alison, curator of the aeronautics department, National Air & Space Museum (Washington, D.C.).

Tony Chantre (whereabouts unknown) and Floyd "Red" Redderson (Santa Monica), who taught me to fly.

Retired naval aviator Rear Admiral Lew Chatham (Arlington, Va.), veteran of 366 combat missions in the Vietnam conflict; former commander, Battle Force Seventh Fleet, Carrier Strike Force Seventh Fleet, deputy chief of staff for operations, CINCPACFLT and a member of the Blue Angels naval flight demonstration team; also commanding officer of the USS *Kitty Hawk* and USS *Hassayampa*. Admiral Chatham's wife, Ann, is the widow of Gary Simkins, to whom this book is dedicated.

Maureen Egen (New York), who often fought, usually won and was always right.

The Ferguson Publishing Company, for permission to quote two lines from "High Flight" in chapter 5. This poem was written by John Gillespie McGee, an American who died in 1941 at the age of nineteen flying for the RCAF.

Bruce Lockwood, director of restoration and maintenance, Museum of Flying, Santa Monica, California.

Mick Collins (Los Angeles), Bernie Ferrari (Los Angeles), Irwin Goverman (Seattle) and Cherie Gruenfeld (my place) for ego-shattering but indispensable reviews of the manuscript.

Also Joan Goverman, Anne Hamilton, Mike Simpson, Jim Stein, Sona Vogel.

The Federal Aviation Administration, the National Transportation Safety Board, the Lockheed Aircraft Service Company and Jeppesen Sandersen were helpful and cooperative in providing a wealth of background information, even though none of their personnel was aware of the nature of the book except in the most general terms.

From the FAA:

David L. Miller, quality assurance specialist, Burbank TRACON, California (since promoted to supervisor of Reno tower).

Fred O'Donnell, assistant manager of public affairs, western Pacific region, Los Angeles, California.

From the NTSB:

Ted Lopatkiewicz, public affairs officer, Washington, D.C.

Monty Montgomery, chief, Engineering Services Division of the Office of Research and Engineering, Washington, D.C.

Dr. Gary Mucho, regional director, Southwest regional office, Gardena, California.

Greg Phillips and Robert Swain, aerospace engineers, Washington, D.C.

From Lockheed (Ontario, California):

John R. Dailey, director of public relations.

Rex. J. McLaughlin, new business development.

R.W. (Dick) Nance, senior program manager, flight recorders.

From Jeppesen Sandersen, Inc. (Englewood, Colorado):

Pat Wood.

Lee Gruenfeld

The author of the acclaimed
Irreparable Harm delivers a blistering
new thriller!

☐ **ALL FALL DOWN**
(A60-186, $5.99 US) ($6.99 Can)

☐ **IRREPARABLE HARM**
(A60-059-8, $5.99 US) ($6.99 Can)